BLOOD COUNT

www.**rbooks**.co.uk

BLOOD COUNT

Robert Goddard

BANTAM PRESS

LONDON • TORONTO • SYDNEY • AUCKLAND • JOHANNESBURG

TRANSWORLD PUBLISHERS
61–63 Uxbridge Road, London W5 5SA
A Random House Group Company
www.rbooks.co.uk

First published in Great Britain
in 2011 by Bantam Press
an imprint of Transworld Publishers

A CIP catalogue record for this book
is available from the British Library.

ISBNs 9780593065082 (cased)
9780593065099 (tpb)

Addresses for Random House Group Ltd companies outside the UK
can be found at: www.randomhouse.co.uk
The Random House Group Ltd Reg. No. 954009

The Random House Group Limited supports the Forest Stewardship
Council (FSC), the leading international forest-certification organization. All our
titles that are printed on Greenpeace-approved FSC-certified paper carry the FSC logo.
Our paper procurement policy can be found at
www.rbooks.co.uk/environment

Mixed Sources
Product group from well-managed
forests and other controlled sources
www.fsc.org Cert no. TT-COC-2139
© 1996 Forest Stewardship Council

Typeset in 11/14.5pt Times New Roman by
Falcon Oast Graphic Art Ltd.
Printed and bound in Great Britain by
Clays Limited, Bungay, Suffolk

8 10 9 7

BLOOD COUNT

ONE

'The holiday starts here,' Edward Hammond murmured to himself. He took a sip of sparkling mineral water and gazed idly across the club lounge, out through the wide windows at the gated and taxiing aircraft on the runway. Heathrow, on a grey February afternoon, made for an uninspiring vista, but Hammond's sights were already set on the ski slopes of Austria, where conditions, according to the newspaper, were outstanding: superb powder at Obergurgl, no less.

Peter and Julie were already in Austria, in the middle of a fortnight's break. Hammond had spoken to Julie last night and learnt for the first time that a friend called Sophie had joined them. This sounded to him suspiciously like a matchmaking ploy – not the first such effort on Julie's part to find him a wife during the thirteen years that had passed since Kate's death. Maybe something would happen between him and Sophie, maybe not, but marriage was certainly not on the horizon as far as he was concerned.

He was aware, of course, that he was more than averagely good-looking for a man of fifty-two. He went to some lengths (twenty in the pool, for starters) to keep himself so and had ample evidence of his attractiveness to women. His wealth and his status in the world qualified him as a desirable catch. But he did not wish to be caught. Marriage to Kate, and the manner of its ending, had left him wary of long-term relationships. Their daughter, Alice, now halfway through her first year at university, had often assured him she would not stand in his way. 'I only want you to be happy, Dad.' And that was what he always claimed and generally believed himself to be: happy – up to a point.

A man's state of mind, a psychiatrist friend had once told him, hinges on his ability to compromise between what is worth remembering and what is best forgotten; between what can be controlled and what cannot. It was a precept Hammond had tried to live by. One of the things besides the state of the Alpine ski resorts he had looked for in the newspaper was a name he knew he would eventually see in a headline. But the name had not been there. The proceedings he assumed were still continuing in The Hague did not currently merit the media's attention. And for that, at the outset of his much needed holiday, he was duly grateful.

But his gratitude was on a short lease. It ended, though he did not at first realize it, when someone close by said, 'Dr Hammond?'

He opened his eyes to find a tall, curvaceous, strikingly attractive young woman standing in front of him. She was olive-skinned and dark-haired, dressed clingingly in black, with glittering jewellery and generous cleavage vying for his attention. She had a drink in one hand and a carry-on bag in the other. A smile might have been expected to complete the package, whatever exactly the package was, but she was not smiling. Quite the contrary. She looked as if smiling was the last thing she intended to do.

'May I join you?' There was an accent – Spanish, he would have guessed – wrapped round the huskily spoken English.

'Certainly. Do we . . .' She sat down in the vacant chair next to his, dropping the bag at her feet. The ice clinked in her glass and the dangling hoops of her earrings chimed faintly in unison. 'Do we know each other?' If she had ever been a patient of his, he felt sure he would remember. But nothing stirred in his memory.

'I have seen you before.' She took a sip of her drink – it smelt like brandy – and clunked the glass down beside his. 'But we have never talked to each other. Until now.' She was breathing rapidly, he noticed. She was nervous, though what about he could not imagine.

2

'Where did you . . . see me before?'

'Belgrade.' She cleared her throat. 'Thirteen years ago.'

'Really?' He hoped he sounded airily unconcerned, though in truth he wished she had said anywhere else at any other time. His trip to Belgrade in the spring of 1996 was not something he welcomed any reminders of. The man he had gone there to treat was now being tried in The Hague. His crimes could in no sense be laid at Hammond's door. And yet . . . 'I don't . . . recall the occasion,' he said, smiling casually.

'My name is Ingrid Hurtado-Gazi, Dr Hammond,' she said quietly. 'I am Dragan Gazi's daughter.'

He was not often lost for words. A facility for fluent and reassuring phrase-making was one of the strengths of his consulting-room manner. But it had deserted him now. He simply did not know what to say. Though he did know that silence was not an option. 'I see. Right. Of course. Well . . .'

'When I saw you come in, I could not . . . believe my luck.'

'Your luck?'

'I have a problem. A big problem. That is, my family does. We need help. From someone . . . we can rely on.'

'Is your father ill?' It would not have surprised Hammond to learn that he was, though there had been no mention of it in the reports of his arrest last year.

'No. He is well. He is in a bad place. But . . . he is well.'

'Then, what . . .'

'Come over to the window.' She nodded towards it, then cast an eloquent glance round at the smattering of people near by. The spot she was suggesting put them at a safer distance from potential eavesdroppers. And she was clearly certain Hammond would value such safety.

'All right.'

They rose and moved to the window. Their ghostly reflections hovered between them and the blank grey sky, into which a plane was languidly rising. But there was nothing languid about Hammond's thoughts. They were racing to find a way out of an

3

encounter that was already uncomfortable and might, he sensed, become far worse than that. It had been a mistake ever to go to Belgrade. He had been extravagantly rewarded, but he could not say now where the money had gone. He always maintained that the character of a patient is irrelevant. But he did not really believe it. In Gazi's case, how could he?

'Where are you travelling to?' he asked, determined to retain an unflustered air as long as possible.

'Madrid. I have aunts and uncles there. It will be good to see them before I go home.'

'And home is?'

'Buenos Aires. Papá married my mother during his years in Argentina. Maybe he spoke to you about his time there?'

'No. He didn't.' Nor had he spoken about the persecutions, deportations, imprisonments, expropriations and exterminations that would later lead to his indictment by the International Criminal Tribunal for the former Yugoslavia. He had not spoken. And Hammond had not asked.

'Where are you planning to go, Dr Hammond?'

'Ski-ing in Austria.'

She fell silent and looked away, out through the window. Then her full attention switched back to him. 'I am sorry.'

'About what?'

'The chance of our meeting. Good for me. Not so good for you.'

'What?' He wondered if he had misheard. But he knew he had not. And he was beginning to doubt that their meeting was any kind of chance.

'I need you to do something for me. For my father. For my family.'

'I don't think I can help you.'

'I have not told you what it is yet.'

'No. But, as you see, I'm going away on holiday.'

'No, doctor. You must stay here. In England.'

'I beg your pardon?'

'I *am* sorry.'

Hammond looked her in the eye. 'I really can't help you.'

'Will you at least let me tell you what I need you to do?' She touched his arm. 'It will not take long. Just listen to me. Please.'

Her soft, pleading tone and the stirrings of curiosity within him won Hammond over. He would hear her out. And then he would turn her down. 'All right. Tell me.'

'As you know, my father is a rich man,' she said, lowering her voice and leaning towards him until she was almost whispering in his ear. 'But his money is hidden. It has to be. The Serbian government – and other people – would like to steal it from him. He wants us – his family – to have it. It is controlled by a man who used to work for him. We call him the Accountant. He lives here. In London. He can release the money to us.'

'Ask him to, then.'

'We have. But he has not replied to our messages. I do not know why.'

'Go and see him.'

'I cannot. I am followed everywhere. If they found out who the Accountant is, we would lose everything.'

'You're being *followed*?' Hammond glanced over his shoulder. No one in the lounge appeared to be paying them the slightest attention. Was the woman paranoid?

'It is true, Dr Hammond. I am safe here, in this room, but they were on my tail as far as check-in and they will have someone waiting for me in Madrid.'

'Seriously?'

'If it was not true, I would not have to ask you to contact the Accountant for me.'

So they had come to the crux of the matter. She wanted him to act as her courier in order to lay hands on her father's money, most of which he had doubtless stolen in the first place. It was worse than Hammond might have imagined. And he had no intention of complying. He shook his head. 'I'm sorry, but—'

'If you refuse, my father will say things about you at his trial that you will not want him to say.'

Her perfume was sweet, gardenia-scented. Was it only in his imagination that there was a tang of decay, of death, hovering behind it? He could not be sure. 'Your father can say whatever he likes. I've nothing to reproach myself for.'

'He has told me, Dr Hammond.' Her expression was unflinchingly serious. 'I *know*.'

'What do you know?'

'That part of your fee for treating my father was the murder of your wife.'

Hammond's initial reaction to Ingrid Hurtado-Gazi's bizarre statement was akin to an out-of-body experience, except that the dislocation was temporal rather than spatial. He could not actually remember when someone had last mentioned the nature of Kate's death to him. Murder in all its brutal reality bred a reticence that time only entrenched. But now, at Ingrid's few words, he was transported back in his mind to the early months of 1996 and all the chaos and anger and tragedy that they had contained.

The rapture of his first few years with Kate should, ironically, have warned him. Funny, infuriating, beautiful, electrifying, clever, passionate and energetic, Kate believed life could be an endless game. Marriage and motherhood were always likely to test her tolerance, devoted though she was to Alice. Her affair with Alan Kendall was in some senses a predictable response. It made her, as she freely admitted, 'feel more alive'. But she was never one for half measures, or for living a lie. She wanted a divorce. She wanted a fresh start.

Hammond moved out of their house in Wimbledon into a rented flat across the Common and embarked on a half-hearted affair of his own. The divorce negotiations became acrimonious. Haggling over money soured the discussions. His existence was miserable – and it promised to grow more miserable still.

That was when Svetozar Miljanović, a Serbian liver specialist Hammond had met at a conference some years previously, contacted him with a lucrative proposition. Dragan Gazi, a powerful figure in the Milošević regime, was in urgent need of a liver transplant. Hammond's team at St George's was one of the best by anyone's analysis. The Dayton Peace Accord had brought a lifting of international sanctions against Serbia. There were no official obstacles to them going to Belgrade to treat Gazi. And Hammond could virtually name his own fee. It was money he had every reason to think he could avoid disclosing to Kate's lawyer. He accepted.

He took an anaesthetist, a perfusionist and a theatre sister to Belgrade with him. They were there for ten days. The transplant itself went well. They were all too busy – and well-paid – to dwell on the war in Bosnia and Gazi's role in it. Hammond could not have denied finding it exhilarating to be sought out for his life-saving expertise and then to demonstrate it so successfully. There was something almost military about the efficiency and precision of what he and his team did.

A week after their return to London, Kate was murdered in a supermarket car park. A mugging gone wrong was the police's best guess, or the motiveless act of a madman. They checked Hammond's whereabouts at the time, but never seriously suggested they suspected him of involvement. He was distraught, Kate's death forcing him to realize he had never stopped loving her. He held himself together largely for Alice's sake. As the weeks and months passed, he lost hope that the police would ever find Kate's killer.

Miljanović reported periodically on Gazi's recovery. He was doing well. From Gazi himself there was no word.

Until now, indirectly, through his softly-spoken daughter, who gazed sombrely at Hammond in the pewter-grey light of the present day, awaiting his response.

'This . . . is . . . utter nonsense.' The words came stumbling out of him.

Ingrid shook her head. 'Not according to my father.'

'He had nothing to do with my wife's death. There was no . . . deal of any kind.'

'He says there was.'

'It's a lie.'

'But your wife is dead. And the killer has never been found. Why should my father admit he is responsible if he is not?'

Why indeed? That was a question to which there were only dark and disturbing answers.

'I believe my father, Dr Hammond. I think others will too. You have colleagues, friends, a family. How will they take this? You can deny it, of course. But will your denial convince them?'

God, what about Alice? Would she wonder if her father might have been capable, in the throes of a bitter divorce, of commissioning her mother's murder? Would the care and the love he had put into her upbringing be sufficient to banish her every doubt?

'Maybe there will not be enough for the police to act on. But there will be enough for suspicion. And that is all it takes to ruin a man in your position.'

That much was horribly plausible. There were always people willing to believe a lie, especially as cunning a one as this. And just how big a lie was it? Had Gazi really ordered Kate's killing, for some warped reason of his own? Had he foreseen the need to have a hold on Hammond? Had he anticipated that one day he might find it convenient to be able to force his surgeon to do his bidding?

'My father will say nothing if you help me. Contact the Accountant. Arrange for the money to be released. That is all I am asking you to do. It is a simple thing, easy for you to accomplish. You would be foolish to refuse.'

Simple? Easy? Maybe. Maybe not. Hammond felt as if quicksand was sucking at his feet. If he stood still, he would sink. But the way out led only deeper in.

'Well, Dr Hammond?'

TWO

Svetozar Miljanović was a small, animated man, built like a jockey, with a smile ever at the ready to transform his features. Only when he forgot himself did the melancholy and weariness emerge. And even then it required a trained eye to notice them.

Edward Hammond possessed such an eye. It was part of his diagnostic technique. Most diseases, according to his GP father, were apparent before a patient described a single symptom. It was all there, in the face, the hands, the posture. You only needed to be able to see.

What Hammond saw in his dinner companion at the Sheraton that late February evening in 1996 was desperation well concealed, but not concealed quite well enough. He felt sure Miljanović had been living and working in unenviable conditions over recent years. It could hardly be otherwise, given Serbia's pariah status in the world on account of its role in the bloody conflict in Bosnia, not to mention the hyper-inflation and gangsterism the country had become a byword for. Miljanović's cheery proclamation that 'Everything is better since Dayton' was undoubtedly accurate. But better did not necessarily mean good.

'I was sorry I couldn't help you place your hep C paper, Svetozar,' said Hammond, when it had become obvious Miljanović did not propose to raise the subject. The paper had been an illuminating examination of the rampant spread of hepatitis C in the former Yugoslavia arising from drug abuse and infected blood transfusions. It had clearly merited publication, but none of the journals had wanted to court controversy by carrying a piece by a Serbian author. 'You could re-submit it now sanctions have been lifted.'

'Maybe I will.' Miljanović's tone suggested he had more pressing matters to consider. 'When I have the time.'

'Busy?'

'Oh yes. Alcoholism. Drug addiction. And the hep C problem. They've all increased because of the troubles we've had. My fellow countrymen haven't been taking good care of their livers, Edward. They keep me very busy. And you? All is well?'

'Professionally, never better.'

'But personally?'

Hammond sighed. 'I've recently split up with my wife.'

Miljanović grimaced. 'Ah, I'm sorry. That's bad. You have a daughter, I think.'

'Yes. It's awful for Alice. She doesn't know whether she's coming or going.'

'How old is she?'

'Seven.'

Another grimace. 'A seven-year-old needs a mother and a father – together.'

Hammond summoned a rueful grin. 'You should tell my wife that.'

'Is there . . . someone else?'

'I'm afraid so. Kate's traded me in for a sportier model.'

Miljanović looked for a moment as if the weight of Hammond's distress was weighing on his shoulders as well. 'I feel for you, Edward. No man should suffer that. Your news . . . makes me wonder if I should . . . trouble you with my proposal.'

'I'd welcome anything that might take my mind off the mess my life is in, Svetozar. Propose ahead.'

'Very well.' Miljanović lowered his voice confidentially and leant across the table. 'I have a very important patient who needs a liver transplant. We simply do not have the expertise in Belgrade. Many of our best people have left the country. I have a good team. But I doubt they can cope with all the complications of the procedure. I thought of you. Your reputation is . . . as high as they come. You and *your* team could do it, Edward. I know that.'

'In Belgrade?'

'My patient cannot travel. He fears . . . an indictment from The Hague.'

'What has he done?'

Miljanović shrugged. 'Bad things, I guess. I'm not sure. He led some kind of volunteer force in Bosnia. And . . . he has criminal connections. He has *lots* of connections all round. I cannot tell you a lie. He is not a nice man. But he is powerful and he is sick and I have to treat him. I have, to be truthful, no choice.' Was this, Hammond wondered, the root of the desperation he had sensed? The patient was not someone whose death Miljanović could afford to be in any degree responsible for. But die he well might, however good his surgeon. 'I should also tell you he is very wealthy. He would be willing to pay . . . a quarter of a million pounds.'

The figure was higher than Hammond would have guessed. Ten days or so in Belgrade for the lion's share of a quarter of a million pounds. It was hard to say no to. He needed a break and, though this would scarcely be a holiday, at least it would take his mind off Kate, her grasping lawyer and the too-smooth-to-be-true man she claimed to be in love with. There might even be a way of ensuring that the money never came to the attention of the grasping lawyer, a possibility Miljanović seemed to have anticipated.

'It could be paid in any way that . . . you specified.'

'Could it now?'

'What do you say, Edward? It would be an honour for me to work with you.'

'I'd need to know a lot more before I could give you a decision.'

'Of course. Of course.'

'The patient – what's his name?'

'Dragan Gazi.'

11

'Well, I've certainly never heard of him.'

Miljanović smiled. 'Good.'

Edward Hammond recalled that first occasion when he had heard Gazi's name as he entered another, drabber, cheaper restaurant thirteen years later: Squisito, a lacklustre trattoria halfway between Bayswater Road and Paddington station, seemingly designed, with its hackneyed décor and drab clientele, to make Hammond think longingly of the food, wine and banter he should have been enjoying in Austria with Peter, Julie and Sophie.

If only he had rejected Miljanović's offer. He knew himself well enough to understand that he never would have, of course. His ego had been flattered by being invited to Belgrade to show the locals how it should be done. And he had never been paid so generously, before or since. But still it was impossible not to dwell on how much wiser he would have been to turn Miljanović down.

Hammond was a man of substance and significance. People deferred to him and sought his opinion. The world he moved in was ordered to his judgement and convenience. Being forced to do the bidding of strangers was an affront to his vision of himself. Resentment boiled within him, of a kind he had not felt since Kate told him their marriage was over. Now, as then, his inability to control events frustrated him almost beyond endurance. This should not be happening to him. But it was.

Ingrid's ultimatum had brooked no refusal. Gazi's allegations would wreak havoc in Hammond's life. The newspapers would descend into a feeding frenzy and however many of his friends and colleagues he could convince that Gazi was lying, there would still be some who doubted him. If that included Alice, the consequences would be unthinkable. He simply could not bear to contemplate a life in which she suspected him of arranging her mother's murder – or even being capable of arranging such a thing. And so, seething with barely controlled fury, he had been obliged to strike terms.

'I want the money transferred by close of business next Friday,' Ingrid had said, quietly and emphatically. 'To this account.' She had handed him a sheet of vellum notepaper, on which was written the name of a bank in the Cayman Islands and an account number, along with a mobile phone number. 'Sooner than Friday would be best. Call me when it is done.'

'How exactly do you expect me to accomplish this?'

'The Accountant's name is Marco Piravani. He is here, in London. I do not have his address. The only way to contact him is through an Italian restaurant called Squisito.' She had handed him a small card with an address and phone number written on it. Turning the card over, Hammond had found himself looking at the passport-size photograph of a square-jawed middle-aged man with thick dark hair and a moustache, tinted wire-framed glasses and a serious, not to say forbidding, expression. 'That was taken eight years ago. But you should be able to recognize him from it.'

'You've left messages for him at this place?'

'Of course. Many messages. But he has not responded.'

'Perhaps he didn't get them.'

'He got them.'

'Well . . .'

'Make him understand. If he does not transfer the money, if he has lost it or stolen it, my father will send someone after him.' She had shrugged. 'He must know that anyway.'

'And meanwhile you're sending me?'

'I can trust you, Dr Hammond.'

'It's not trust we're talking about. It's blackmail.'

Another shrug. 'I am sorry. I have no choice.'

'Apparently, neither do I.'

'As you say.'

'If I succeed, what guarantee do I have that your father will say nothing about me at his trial?'

'The guarantee that if he does you can tell the Serbian authorities where to look for his money.'

'A numbered account in the Cayman Islands. Some clue.'

'You can identify the Accountant. You can implicate me. You think I want that? I would do this myself if they were not following me. You are my best chance. Find the Accountant and make him transfer the money. He has it and we want it. It is ours. Persuade him to release it. I don't care how you do it. Just do it. Then you can go back to your secure and comfortable life, Dr Hammond. Maybe you can still get some ski-ing done. I don't want to stop you enjoying yourself. But this must be done first.'

This must be done first. Yes. Of course. It was the priority that would control Hammond's life for as long as it took him to prise Gazi's money from his evasive bookkeeper. It had required him to cancel his flight at a few minutes' notice, wrangle with officialdom over removing his luggage from the plane and concoct a lie to explain to Peter and Julie why he would not be joining them after all. The irony of the excuse he had devised – a donor had suddenly become available for a now-or-never transplant – was not lost on him. But irony counted for little set against the rage he felt that he should have to tell such a lie in the first place. He was not sure he should have agreed to do what Ingrid had demanded of him. But he could not take the risk of defying Gazi to do his worst. That was certain. Even if nothing else was.

THREE

He had not decided what he was going to do when he walked into Squisito that evening. Ingrid's experience suggested leaving a message for Piravani was pointless. If there was a quick and easy solution to the problem, he could not see what it was. The waiters did not look the loose-tongued sort. There was altogether a notable lack of Latin jollity. He ordered a beer and perused the uninspiring menu, but the invidiousness of his situation had shredded his concentration. He was aware that he was expending too much of his mental energy on revisiting the past to no useful effect, but he could not seem to stop himself. Regrets teemed in his mind.

And then something entirely unexpected happened, something too fortuitous for him at first to believe. Marco Piravani slouched into the restaurant, rumple-suited and round-shouldered and clearly well known to the staff. There was more grey in his hair than in the photograph Ingrid had supplied, but no other obvious difference. Hammond recognized him instantly and spent the next hour trying to decide how to approach the man.

It hardly helped that Piravani projected such a conspicuously unapproachable air. The waiters addressed him respectfully as '*dottore*' and the proprietor, an otherwise lugubrious fellow, greeted him with smiles and a shoulder squeeze, but Piravani barely raised his eyes from the pink pages of the *Gazzetta dello Sport* he had brought with him. He looked what in a sense Hammond knew him to be: an unsociable number-cruncher. His alcohol intake was something of a surprise, though. Rapid demolition of a bottle of house red during his meal, followed by a grappa, suggested either a drink problem or an attempt to drown a lot of anxiety.

Hammond's decision was rendered more delicate still by the possibility that he might have only one crack at Piravani. The fellow was among friends at Squisito, however coolly he treated them. Hammond was not. It was hardly the ideal environment for the kind of full and frank discussion they needed to have. And it would be better by far if Piravani was sober when they had it. Much as Hammond would have liked to sort it out there and then, he eventually abandoned the idea. He would have to be patient.

With Piravani awaiting an espresso that would surely round off his meal, Hammond laid enough cash on the table to cover his bill, exchanged a farewell nod with one of the waiters and headed out.

He went no further than the unlit doorway of a greengrocer's shop on the other side of the road, from where he had a good view of the interior of the restaurant. Ten chilly minutes passed before Piravani stumbled out into the night. There were no taxis about, so no immediate danger of his hailing one. He pulled up the collar of his coat, lit a cigarette and started off in the direction of Paddington station. Hammond darted across the road and fell in behind. Even if there had not been plenty of other pedestrians, he doubted Piravani would have noticed him. Head down and unsteady of tread, the Italian seemed to be progressing on autopilot.

They reached Praed Street and when Piravani stopped at the pelican crossing it more or less clinched the station as his destination. It was one he shared with numerous late travellers, many of whom looked to have spent the greater part of their Friday evening in a pub. Ordinarily, Hammond would have reflected on the damage all these people were doing to their precious livers, but he had no space in his mind for such thoughts now.

He followed Piravani across the road when the lights changed

16

and down the ramp into the station. The Italian paused for a last drag on his cigarette before flicking it away, then entered the crowded concourse. He steered right, heading for the platforms for commuter trains to the west. Hammond whipped out his Oyster card and went through the barrier after him. As far as he could gather from the screens, a stopper to Reading was the next service.

The train was standing at the platform when they arrived. Piravani boarded, oblivious to the fellow diner from Squisito dogging his footsteps, and was already asleep in his seat when it pulled out a few minutes later. This freed Hammond to study the man in some detail as they trundled off into the London night, but the study told him nothing he would not have guessed. Piravani had a poor diet, drank too much and exercised too little. He probably did not sleep enough either, his current stupor hardly qualifying as restful slumber.

Piravani's *Gazzetta dello Sport* was lying on the seat beside him. Hammond noticed that it was folded open not at one of the football pages but at the classified ads. One of the ads had been ringed and asterisked. He moved to the seat behind the Italian and craned over his shoulder to see what the ad was.

But at that moment the train began slowing for its first stop. The change in the engine note instantly roused Piravani, who sat up and looked around. He also noticed his newspaper, which he rolled up and slid inside his coat.

The train pulled into Acton Main Line. A glimpse of the station name seemed to reassure Piravani, who relapsed into unconsciousness. Hammond sighed and pondered what he should do when the Italian got off. 'Keep following him,' he silently concluded. It was the sensible thing to do. If he could establish where Piravani lived, he would not have to bank everything on getting what he wanted from their first encounter.

A few minutes later, as they approached Ealing Broadway, Piravani rose and moved to the doors, along with a dozen or so others. The house red was doing nothing for his speed or nimbleness. Hammond did not so much have to hurry to keep up as hang

17

back to avoid overtaking as they left the train and plodded along the platform.

A lumbering ascent of the stairs and a fumbled passage through the ticket barrier took Piravani to the exit, where he paused to light another cigarette. Most of the other passengers were long gone by now, leaving Hammond to pay rapt attention to a poster detailing weekend engineering works until Piravani got under way again.

He turned right out of the station and, before long, right again. Hammond followed him along a street of red-brick Victorian houses running parallel to the railway line. The first few houses looked to have seen better days. Detached family residences gone to seed and multiple occupancy. It was into the fenceless and paved-over front garden of one of these that Piravani turned, jingling keys in his hand as he went. There were ruptured rubbish sacks beside the spindly boundary hedge and the bass notes of some amplified rock music pounding from an upper room. The curtains at the windows were thin and tawdry. In one case, they had been replaced by a sheet. If Marco Piravani had embezzled Gazi's cash, he had obviously not blown it on luxury accommodation.

Hammond had achieved his initial objective. He knew where the man lived. Now came the demanding part. He still had no clear idea what he was going to say, but the time had come to say it. As Piravani slid his key into the door lock, Hammond closed in.

But it was Piravani who spoke first. He turned as Hammond approached and looked straight at him, smiling faintly and suddenly sober. '*Dobro veče.*'

'G-Good evening,' said Hammond, wondering just how long the fellow had been aware of his presence.

'You prefer English?'

'I *am* English.'

'So you are. And no killer, obviously.' The smile broadened. He looked more surprised than relieved. 'Negotiations are still open, then.'

'You know why I'm here?'

'Who sent you?'

18

'Ingrid.'

'Then I know.'

'Can we talk?'

'Yes. We can talk. What is your name?'

'Hammond.'

'Hammond?' Piravani's gaze narrowed. 'Wait. Are you . . . Dr Hammond? You are, aren't you?'

It was tempting to deny it, but clearly futile. 'Yes.'

'I hope you will be charging as large a fee as you did last time you came to Gazi's rescue.'

'You said we could talk.'

'I did, yes. So, come in.' He turned the key in the lock and pushed the door open. 'Come in and we will talk.'

FOUR

The hall smelt of stale food and cigarette smoke, with a dash of marijuana. Through an open doorway at the far end was a kitchen, where a thin, spiky-haired young man dressed in grungy jeans and T-shirt was sitting at a food-littered table, eating cornflakes. He looked up and made a V-for-victory sign at Piravani, but did not speak.

The Italian responded with a vague gesture of his own. 'One of the other residents,' he murmured to Hammond. 'An anthropologist would love it here.'

'Can't you do better for yourself?'

Piravani smiled lopsidedly. 'Maybe I don't want to. But come. We'll go to my room.'

They climbed the stairs, the music growing louder as they went. Piravani unlocked the door leading to his flat: a lounge, bedroom and bathroom squeezed into what had once been a single large room, with a high, delicately corniced ceiling. The furniture was plain, the colour scheme drab and there were few personal possessions to be seen. Altogether, it looked more like a down-market dentist's waiting room than anyone's home.

Piravani tossed his coat over a chair and carried his rolled copy of *La Gazzetta dello Sport* into the bedroom, returning a few seconds later without it. Hammond was sorely tempted to ask what he had spotted in the classified ads, but did not quite have the nerve. Piravani stubbed out his cigarette in a well-filled ashtray and waved him to a seat.

'Why haven't you responded to Ingrid's messages?' Hammond asked, determined to seize back the initiative if he could.

'Because I don't want to speak to her.' Piravani turned on the gas heater that occupied the fireplace with a dextrous toe-flick and smiled across at Hammond. 'You want a drink?'

'No, thanks.'

The answer did not deter Piravani from fetching a bottle and a couple of glasses from a cabinet in the corner of the room. He plonked them on the coffee table in front of Hammond, explaining the second glass with a mumbled, 'In case you change your mind,' before pouring himself a generous slug and slumping down in an armchair. 'Plum brandy. A Serbian delicacy. They say Milošević made most of his mistakes because of this. *Salute!*' He promptly swallowed a good third of what he had just poured. 'Just think. Those five years in The Hague before he died: not a single drink. Poor bastard.'

'It probably did him some good.'

'Not enough to keep him alive.'

Hammond sighed. He had had a basinful of Piravani already. 'You were – are – Gazi's accountant?'

'Yes. I kept the score for him. Ten years I did that.'

'Ingrid seems to think you're still doing it.'

'Well, I guess she's right. I have the keys to the treasure chest.'

'She wants you to open it.'

'Of course. She wants his money. They all want his money. It's no use to him now, is it? He'll die in prison. So, why shouldn't they have it?'

'You tell me.'

Piravani gave a derisive snort and sipped some more brandy, then lit another cigarette. 'How much is she paying you, doctor?'

Hammond had no intention of admitting why he was acting as Ingrid's messenger. It was preferable to let Piravani assume the worst. 'It's the family's money, Marco. Why don't—'

'Hah! *Their* money? You're joking. It's thousands of dead men's money, that's what it is. Dead men *and* women. I should know. I know where it all came from as well as where it all is.'

'Nobody forced you to work for Gazi.'

'You're right. Nobody did.' Some of the bluster went out of him at the thought. 'I did it for the same reason as you,' he went on glumly. 'The money was good. But the money is the cheese in the mousetrap. Ingrid isn't paying you, is she? She's blackmailing you.'

'What makes you think that?'

'I paid all Gazi's bills, doctor. Including the one for your wife's murder.'

It was early April, 1996, a few days before Easter. He took the call in his consulting room at St George's. At first he could not believe what they were telling him. It was impossible. Yet it was also, he was eventually forced to accept, true. Kate had been loading her shopping into her car at the Colliers Wood superstore. It was lunchtime. The car park was busy. There were numerous witnesses. But none of them seemed to see or understand exactly what happened. A car pulled up beside Kate. A man got out. Then he got back in and drove away. And soon afterwards Kate was found lying on the ground by her half-empty shopping trolley, with a bullet in her brain. If there was an altercation, no one heard it. No one even heard the gunshot. The sun was shining brightly after heavy rain. There was a lot of glare and reflection, shadow and noise. And a woman had been shot.

They brought her to A & E, but she was dead on arrival – dead long before arrival, to tell the truth. By the time Hammond saw her, she was in the hospital mortuary. All that energy, all that force of personality, all that *life*, gone. Gone, gone, gone. The incomprehension and numbness he had observed in many a dead patient's relatives were his. And he was no better equipped to cope with them than they had been.

Her handbag had been stolen, encouraging the police to believe theft was the motive. But her credit cards were never used. As thefts went, it made little sense. From the outset the police were baffled, disoriented by a crime so lacking in the normal points of reference.

One memory of the day stood now in sharp focus. Hammond had encountered Alan Kendall, Kate's lover and aspiring husband, in a corridor at St George's shortly after leaving the mortuary. Kendall was angry as well as shocked and grief-stricken. Something snapped in him when he saw Hammond. His handsome face twisted into a snarl of rage. 'You're behind this, aren't you, you bastard? You had her killed because she chose me over you.' It was fortunate there was a policeman on hand to hold Kendall off. He seemed intent on doing Hammond serious harm. The absurdity of his allegation made Hammond pity the man. It never occurred to him that there might come a day when the allegation would not seem so absurd after all.

Hammond's reaction to Piravani's remark was so instinctive that he was out of his chair and grasping the Italian by the lapels of his jacket before he had consciously formed any such intention.

'What the hell are you talking about?' he shouted. 'Gazi had nothing to do with my wife's death.'

'Let go of me,' Piravani demanded.

'Not until you tell me the truth.'

'That is the truth.'

'You're lying.'

'Why should I?'

There was alarm in his eyes but no fear. It was suddenly clear to Hammond that Piravani was prepared to suffer the consequences of ignoring Ingrid's message. He had decided to take some kind of a stand. And he was almost certainly speaking the absolute truth.

'You do a deal with Gazi, he delivers. What's wrong, doctor? Do you regret it now? Do you wish she was still alive?'

Hammond released him and stepped back. The room swam around him, as if he was drunk. For a second, he seriously wondered if he *had* done a deal with Gazi to have Kate killed. It was a fleeting taste of what others would certainly believe. He drew a deep breath. The room stilled. 'You're saying you paid someone to murder my wife?'

'I made the payment. It was just a line in the accounts to me. There were a lot of lines like that.'

'I never asked Gazi to have her killed. This is . . . insane.'

Piravani raised his eyebrows. 'You never did?'

'Of course not. I loved her. She was the mother of my child. If only for Alice's sake, I'd never have—' Hammond broke off. He was staring into a pit. The bottom, if there was one, was a long way down.

'Sit down, doctor. You look as if you've had a shock.'

Hammond retreated to his chair. He sat on the edge of the cushion, rested his elbows on his knees and began trying to massage some sense into his head. But sense was hard to find in what he now knew.

'Gazi is a strange man,' said Piravani. 'You think you understand him. But you never do.'

'I can't believe this.'

'The truth is the truth whether you believe it or not.'

'Who killed her? Who did you pay?'

'I can't remember. There were many people Gazi used for that kind of thing. It could have been any one of them. Even if I could remember, what difference would it make? It was nothing personal to him. Gazi gave the order.'

'How much did you pay him?'

'In 1996? The rate would have been . . . five thousand US dollars plus expenses.'

'Five thousand dollars?' Small beer compared with Hammond's fee for Gazi's liver transplant. Saving a life apparently cost a lot more than taking one. 'Is that . . . all?'

'Supply and demand, doctor. It's the rule in every business.'

'But . . . why did Gazi do it? He knew nothing about my wife. He knew nothing about *me*.'

'It seems he knew more than you thought. A lot of people have learnt that about him. Usually too late.'

'It makes no sense.'

'Maybe you should go to The Hague and ask him to explain it to you.'

Hammond sat back and sighed. 'If this gets out . . . I'm finished.'

Piravani shrugged. 'I guess so.'

'But it won't get out if you transfer Gazi's money to this account.' Hammond laid on the table the piece of paper Ingrid had given him.

Piravani looked at it and smiled. 'Ah. Cayman Islands. Of course.'

'How long would it take you to do that?'

'Twenty-four hours. Twenty-four banking hours, I mean. Gazi always insisted everything had to be liquid. So by Tuesday it could be there. But it won't be. I'm not going to do it.'

'Why not?'

'Too much blood, doctor. In the end, you can't ignore it. Gazi went into hiding early in 2000. He'd already been indicted by the International Tribunal and when another indictee, Arkan, was murdered, Gazi reckoned Milošević was trying to cover his tracks for when he had to answer his own indictment. So, he disappeared, straight after telling me to do the same. I've been in hiding ever since. London's the best city in the world if you want to be invisible. But invisibility isn't good for your social life. So, I've had a lot of time to think. And to read. More than a hundred thousand people were killed in three years of war in Bosnia, more than seven thousand in one day at Srebrenica. I didn't kill anyone. But I didn't stop anyone being killed either. I did nothing. If Gazi was here, in this room, I'd do what he told me to do. That's his power. But he isn't here. He's in prison. And he'll never get out. He said he'd look after me. I actually believed him. I trusted him. And he trusted me. Well, that was a mistake for both of us. Ingrid isn't going to get a cent of his money. That's *my* power. That's the only thing I can do to make up for what I *didn't* do in Serbia.'

'Listen to me, Marco. I understand what you're saying. Gazi is a monster. But he hasn't got away with his crimes. He's going to answer for them. What does it matter if his family have his money to spend. What does it *really* matter?'

'I wire it all to the Cayman Islands and forget I ever had a choice. Is that your idea?'

'My daughter lost her mother because of Gazi. Do you want her to lose her father as well? That's what it could come to if I can't convince her I had nothing to do with Kate's death. I never actually told her about my trip to Belgrade. How will that look now? How will she be able to believe me?' Hammond fumbled for his wallet and showed Piravani the photograph of Alice he always carried: sparkling-eyed, sunlight shining in her hair, holding her head just as Kate used to, smiling at her father lovingly and trustingly through the camera lens. 'This is Alice. I love her. She loves me. But all that could change, couldn't it? That could change overnight. She went through hell when her mother died. Do you want to put her through hell all over again?'

'I'm sorry, doctor. She's a lovely girl, but some things must be. You've given her everything she needs, I'm sure. A nice home. A good education. A lot of young women in Bosnia would be happy to change places with her. They'd say she was lucky. They'd say she has no idea what hell really means. Because they *do* know.'

'Do you have children, Marco?'

'Not any more.'

'What do you mean?'

'I thought I had a son. I learnt later . . . someone else was his father.' The shadow of that discovery fell across Piravani's face. He sighed. 'I was betrayed.'

'I'm sorry to hear that.' How sorry was a moot point. Hammond wanted only one thing: Piravani's agreement to transfer the money. And he was prepared to use any argument to extract it. 'Look, Marco, we've both been guilty of turning a blind eye to Gazi's crimes. I certainly didn't want to know about them. I admit that. But Alice isn't guilty of anything. She's already had to grow up without a mother because, I now discover, of my involvement with

26

Gazi. Don't you think that's punishment enough? Do you really want her to lose all faith in her father as well?'

'When NATO bombed Belgrade in 1999, doctor, they were trying to save victims of ethnic cleansing in Kosovo. It worked. But those bombs killed innocent people in Belgrade, some of them children. There's a memorial in Tasmajdan Park with a question inscribed on it. *Zašto*? Why? There's no answer. There can't be. It's what they call collateral damage. Neat phrase. Messy reality.'

'I'm pleading with you, Marco. Don't do this to my daughter.'

Piravani studied Hammond carefully as he stubbed out his cigarette. Then he took a sip of brandy and said, 'The best advice Gazi ever gave me was, "Only take decisions when you're sober". So, I hear what you say, doctor. I understand. And this is what I'll do. I'll think about it. There's nothing I could do over the weekend anyway. I'll meet you Sunday afternoon in Hyde Park. I'll be on the Serpentine bridge at three o'clock. You bring your piece of paper to me there.' He stretched forward and pushed the sheet with the Cayman Islands account number on it back to Hammond's side of the table. 'And I'll tell you what I've decided to do.'

FIVE

A sick man is not himself. In Edward Hammond's experience, that was more than a mere turn of phrase. Illness drains individuality. There is no way to tell whether a sick person when fully fit is likely to be sullen or genial, mean or generous, arrogant or humble. So it certainly was with Dragan Gazi, whose liver disease was well advanced when Hammond first met him in his private room at the Voćnjak Clinic in Belgrade. He was confused and heavily sedated, his personality crushed by his body's struggle for survival.

Only forty-eight hours had passed since Miljanović's call to report the availability of a donor and Hammond proposed to operate first thing in the morning. He and his team had flown in earlier that day. There was no time to be lost.

A week later, with the gravest danger of post-operative complications past, Gazi was recovering well. He had begun to converse with Hammond on non-medical matters. He enjoyed practising his English, he said. He was gruffly humorous and complimentary about Hammond's surgical skills as well as grateful for them. He was a thoughtful, inquisitive man. The male *and* female members of Hammond's team were charmed by him. His rugged good looks – square jaw, grey wiry hair, keen blue eyes – added to his aura. Even his liver problems were due more to hepatitis-infected blood received in a transfusion after what he called a 'wound in battle' than to heavy drinking. It was hard to dislike him.

Only during conversations in Serbian with some of his visitors did a different side to his character show itself. He spoke more harshly. He smiled less. He used a chopping gesture of the hand for emphasis. Hammond noted this but made little of it. The exact nature of Gazi's activities during the years since Yugoslavia's disintegration was something he remained studiously uninquisitive about.

The closest they came to discussing the Bosnian conflict that had been resolved only a few months previously was, as it turned out, their last exchange before Hammond and his team returned home. The prognosis, he explained to his patient, was good.

'You'll soon be able to resume a normal life.'

Gazi smiled. 'That will be good. I look forward to it.'

'And your country is at peace, so there's no reason why—'

'Peace?' Gazi laughed, as if genuinely amused. 'We are a long way from that.'

'But I thought—'

'A truce, doctor. That is all we have. That is all we ever have. War is in our soul.'

'Every war has to end some time.'

'Not in the Balkans.'

'It can't be as bad as that, surely.'

'It can be as good as that.' Gazi flashed Hammond a meaningful look. 'Lives should not always be saved.' Then he grinned, as if mightily pleased with himself. 'But I'm glad you saved mine.'

Hammond's thoughts were plucked back from Belgrade thirteen years in the past by the chirruping of his phone. It was a text from Alice. *'How was flight? Is there lots of snow?'* He looked out of the train window at the neon-spattered night and his own sallow reflection, wondering how he should reply. The truth was out of the question, of course. The lie he had told Peter and Julie would have to be recycled for Alice's benefit. He did not like it. But he had no choice. He could only hope the need to lie would soon end.

*

29

Paddington was colder and emptier than when he had left it. He felt tired now his anger had faded. He tried to tell himself Piravani would reflect on the situation and see reason. His safety was at stake along with Hammond's reputation. But he was not convinced. Piravani was looking for redemption. And safeguarding the peace of mind of a young Englishwoman he had never met was hardly going to supply it. Hammond had to devise an added incentive for Piravani to cooperate. And he had until Sunday afternoon to do it.

He had parked his car at Lancaster Gate. On his way there from the station, he stopped at a small newsagent-cum-general store to buy a pint of milk. There would be none at home, since he had not expected to *be* home that night. While he was queuing to pay, his eye was taken by a splash of pink in the newspaper rack: *La Gazzetta dello Sport*. Remembering the ad Piravani had circled, he grabbed a copy, hoping he might be able to deduce which one it was. But there was no chance of that. There were no classified ads. The explanation came to him while he was in the middle of complaining to the helpful but baffled Asian proprietor. It was the export edition. Only the Italian domestic edition included classifieds. But how had Piravani come by that? It must have been sent to him from Italy, in which case it was probably several days old at least. Whatever the ad was, Hammond was not going to get a look at it.

The house in Wimbledon would have been perfect for a family of four or five. As it was, for the past thirteen years it had been a home for two. And now, since Alice's departure to Newcastle University, just one. Walking through the front door into the cold, dark hall that night, he wished he had moved on, started afresh somewhere else. But he knew the sentiment was only camouflage for a more intense regret. If the day had taught him anything, it was that no one is ever free of their past.

*

To his surprise, he slept well, waking with a mind cleansed by forgetfulness. Then, with awful swiftness, the events of the previous eighteen hours reassembled themselves in his mind. Alice had texted again to sympathize over his suspended holiday. '*Poor u.*'

He went to the club and had a swim, shopped in a daze and returned home. It was tempting to try to take his mind off the invidiousness of his situation by contacting a friend and suggesting a drink or dinner. But that would require him to explain why he was not in Austria – or preparing for a fictitious transplant. The weekend had to be a solitary one whether he liked it or not.

But solitude can be a merciless companion. Driven back more and more to memories of his trip to Belgrade in 1996, he could not help wondering just how evil a man his former patient was. He knew the answer could easily be found. A few computer mouse-clicks later, he was surveying results *1–10 of about 385,000 for* **Dragan Gazi**. He could have read about the man and his blood-soaked career any time he pleased in the past thirteen years. But he never had. Until now.

> **Dragan Gazi** (Serbian: Драган Гази; born 30 March 1943 in Kruševac, Serbia, Yugoslavia) is a former Serbian para-military leader, currently held in the UN Detention Unit at Scheveningen, The Hague, the Netherlands, during his trial for war crimes committed in Bosnia between 1992 and 1995 and Kosovo in 1998/99.
>
> Gazi's father, Vlajko, was a member of the Chetniks, who had fought for the exiled King of Yugoslavia against German and Italian occupation during World War II. Vlajko was imprisoned by Tito's Communist regime for most of his son's childhood. In 1963, aged 20, Gazi left Yugoslavia illegally and disappeared into the European criminal underworld, emerging in South America in the early 1970s as a mercenary attached to various right-wing governments. It is widely alleged that he operated a hit squad for the Pinochet regime in Chile and later for the military junta in Argentina. While in Argentina, he

married Isabel Nieto, an actress, by whom he had a daughter, Ingrid (born 1978), and a son, Nikola (born 1980, killed in a motorcycle accident, 1993).

Gazi returned to Yugoslavia in 1982, leaving his wife and children in Argentina. He established himself as a business-man in the cement industry, but it is commonly alleged that this was a front for a range of criminal activities and that he was employed by the State Security Service to carry out assas-sinations both in and outside the country, for which purpose he supposedly recruited a band of trained hit men.

When the Yugoslav Federation began to fall apart in 1991, Gazi founded a paramilitary group called the Serb Patriot Militia, later nicknamed the Wolves, who operated as an un-official wing of the Serbian Army in the Vukovar region of Croatia and from 1992 in Bosnia, where they acquired a reputation for ruthlessness and brutality, particularly in the ethnic-cleansing campaigns against Bosnian Muslims.

The Wolves ceased operations but never completely dis-banded after the Dayton Peace Accord of November 1995. Gazi was widely reported to be ill by this time and it is believed he underwent a liver transplant early in 1996. He is alleged to have used his paramilitaries to extend his criminal network in the post-Dayton period, but they returned to their former role in 1998 when, allegedly at President Milošević's personal request, they played a part in Serbia's attempt to crush the Kosovo Liberation Army.

A few days after NATO began bombing Serbia to force its withdrawal from Kosovo, in March 1999, it was revealed that the International Criminal Tribunal for the former Yugoslavia (ICTY) had issued an indictment against Gazi for genocide, murder, rape, crimes against humanity and grave breaches of the Geneva Convention, charging him with responsibility for all such acts carried out by forces under his command in Croatia, Bosnia and Kosovo.

As the Belgrade regime began to totter in the wake of the

NATO bombings and Milošević's own indictment by ICTY, rumours spread that those whose testimonies might damage Milošević were targets for elimination. The assassination in January 2000 of Željko Ražnatović (aka Arkan), another prominent paramilitary leader who had also been indicted, seemed to confirm this. Gazi dropped out of sight. His whereabouts remained unknown for the next eight years.

He was arrested in Budva, a resort town on the Montenegrin coast, on 22 April 2008, where he had apparently been living for several years, posing as a Spanish businessman who had retired to the Adriatic to paint. He was extradited to the Netherlands and is currently in ICTY custody in The Hague. His trial opened on 8 December 2008, but has been subject to numerous adjournments and he has not yet testified.

The arrest in Belgrade in July 2008 of the even more notorious ICTY fugitive, Radovan Karadžić, sparked rumours that Gazi might have revealed where Karadžić was hiding as part of a deal with prosecutors, but his consistent refusal to cooperate with the tribunal (he has said he does not recognize it as a valid court and has declined to enter a plea) suggests otherwise.

Wikipedia's summary of the shadowy life and criminal career of Dragan Gazi should have prepared Hammond for the gruesome details of his Wolf paramilitaries' actions to be found on other sites. But those details held the force of specificity: the dates, times and locations of the torturings and ethnic rapes and mass executions; the lorryloads of bodies; the pits dug in fields; the records of the dead and the recollections of the living.

The text of Gazi's ICTY indictment ran to many pages. The list of atrocities was horribly repetitious: the same things done in different places to people whose lives were either ended or marked for ever. If Gazi personally shot or raped anyone, it was not stated. Everything was on his orders and under his command. There he was, in a photograph taken somewhere in Bosnia in 1992, dressed in battle fatigues, holding an automatic pistol in one hand and a fluffy toy wolf cub in the other, with a gathering of his human wolves around him: unsmiling, unabashed, uncompromising; the warlord in his element.

But war was not Gazi's only concern. Other sites referred to his reputation as an underworld figure: assassinations, smuggling rackets, diversions of government funds. There was apparently nothing in the stew of corruption that was Serbia under Milošević he had not played some part in. And this was the source of the money Hammond was now trying to secure for his family. The thought of it was sickening.

When the telephone rang, Hammond was grateful for the interruption. But his gratitude lasted only as long as it took him to recognize the caller's voice.

At first he believed he must be mistaken, having only the one word 'Edward?' to work on. 'Who's calling?' he asked, hoping desperately to be proved wrong.

'Alan Kendall.' So. He was not wrong. 'Planning to contact me, were you?'

'Why would I be?' They had not spoken since Kate's funeral. The idea that they had anything to say to each other now, thirteen years later, should have been preposterous. But Hammond's encounter with Ingrid Hurtado-Gazi had turned his world upside down. And here, back in it, was the man Kate had wanted to marry in his place – and would have, had she lived.

'I wondered how easy it'd be to track you down,' said Kendall. 'I thought you might have moved somewhere smaller.'

'What is this about, Alan?'

'Don't you know?'

'No.'

'That's funny.'

'Why?'

'Tell you what. I'm in your area. Let's meet. The Hand in Hand in, say, half an hour?'

'Why don't you just explain right away?'

'I'd rather talk face to face. I could come to the house if you prefer.'

No. Hammond definitely did not prefer. He sighed. 'All right. The Hand in Hand. I'll see you there.'

The house would probably have been Kendall's home if Kate had lived long enough to marry him, or even to change her will. As it was, Hammond had inherited her share and Kendall's hopes for a life with her had come to nothing.

Kate had met him at the estate agency they both worked for. He was younger than Hammond, younger than Kate too, come to that. What attracted him to her was obvious, what attracted her to him a mystery, at least to Hammond, until Kate eventually explained it to him. 'He listens. He cares. He notices.' Ah. So that was it.

The Hand in Hand, on the edge of Wimbledon Common, was only a ten-minute walk from the house. It held its own bitter place in Hammond's memories of his break-up with Kate, since it was at a table outside the pub that he had first seen her with Kendall, chatting and laughing in the sunshine as Hammond drove past, on his way home unexpectedly early, one late-summer afternoon in 1995. And hand in hand is just what they had been.

It was too cold for anyone to be sitting outside on a winter's afternoon in 2009. Inside, a selection of middle-class manhood had gathered to watch Six Nations rugby on the pub's television, leaving a corner of the bar close to the door thinly populated. Kendall was waiting for him there, cradling a pint of lager and kitted out in standard issue weekend casuals. He had put on weight and lost some hair since their last encounter. The observation gave Hammond some small satisfaction to offset his foreboding.

'Buy you a drink?' Kendall offered unsmilingly.

'OK. Thanks. I'll have a pint of bitter.' Ordinarily, Hammond would have opted for something soft, but he felt he needed to preserve a blokish equilibrium, at least to start with.

The pint came and they moved to a table by the window, a long and discreet way from the rugby mob. Studying Kendall's flushed and puffy face, his youthful good looks easily forgotten, Hammond wondered whether Kate would still have been with him had she lived. Perhaps she would have moved on to someone else, or even back to the man who still loved her. 'How have you been, Alan?' he forced himself to ask.

'If you read the papers, you'll know estate agency isn't the business to be in right now.'

'I meant . . . personally.'

'I got married . . . three years after Kate. And divorced after another three. There's a kid who costs me an arm and a leg. Otherwise . . .' He gulped some lager. 'I never found anyone like Kate. You?'

'No.' God damn it, they would soon be remarking on how much they had in common. Hammond preferred detesting the man, he really did. 'So, what's this all about?'

'You tell me.'

'Sorry?'

'Well? Don't you have something to tell me?'

'No. I don't.' Hammond looked straight at Kendall, communicating incomprehension and exasperation. 'This was your idea. Remember?'

'You're sure there's nothing you think I ought to know?'

'About what?'

'Not what. *Who.*'

'OK then. Who?' He knew the answer, of course. It was the only possible answer.

'Kate.'

Hammond took a swallow of beer. He knew he had to draw whatever it was out of Kendall without hinting at the turmoil his life was currently in. He knew he had to appear baffled but unconcerned, even though he was actually neither. 'You're going to have to explain, Alan. I've no idea what you're talking about.'

'I had a phone call at the office this morning.'

'I imagine you had several.'

'Not about houses. This was from a woman, foreign-sounding, Spanish maybe. She wouldn't give her name. She just wanted me to know.'

'Know *what*?'

'She said I should expect to hear from you. About Kate.'

'She said that?'

'Yeah. Then she put the phone down. I tried calling her back, but—'

'Number withheld?'

'Exactly.'

Hammond shrugged. 'Well, I'm afraid I've nothing to tell you about Kate. It was obviously some kind of crank call.'

'After thirteen years? What kind of crank would know about Kate and me and wait all this time to do something about it?'

'I really don't know. It's odd, I admit.'

'It's a lot more than odd, Edward. Listen.' Kendall craned across the table towards him. 'I know I said some pretty . . . extreme . . . things about you back then. Virtually accused you of . . .' He waved his hand semi-apologetically. 'I was upset. And suspicious. But the police made it crystal clear to me there were no grounds to . . . think you had anything to do with Kate's murder. OK? I under-stand. I accept it.'

'Good.'

'So, if you're holding out on me because of that, if there really has been some kind of breakthrough in the case . . .'

'There's been no breakthrough.' Kendall still loved her, more than a decade on, despite marriage to another woman in the interim. He still loved Kate. It was a disarming discovery. But Hammond was determined not to be wrongfooted by it. 'Nothing's happened. OK?'

'You're sure?'

'Of course I'm sure. It's not the kind of thing you can be vague about, is it? I don't know who phoned you, or why, but I can assure you I don't know anything about Kate's murder that you don't know.'

37

The lie had to be told. But, as the words came out of his mouth, Hammond wondered if he would soon come to regret them.

Kendall looked confused, as well he might. But he also looked convinced. 'That's weird.'

'It certainly is.'

'She didn't sound like a nutter.' He sat back and glared glumly into his lager. 'It must mean something.'

'Not necessarily.'

'No.' Kendall waggled a forefinger at him. 'It must. And I'm going to find out what it is.'

'How will you do that?'

'Maybe she'll call again. Then maybe I'll work out who she is and what the hell she's after. If I do, you'll be the first to know, don't worry.'

But worried was exactly what Hammond was.

Kendall was most of the way through a second pint when Hammond left him to it. A chill dusk was falling as he headed home, the coldness of the air doing a little to calm his thoughts.

As soon as he was out of sight of the pub, he stopped, took out his phone and rang Ingrid Hurtado-Gazi's number. But there was no answer. And he did not leave a message.

He carried on to the house, an evening of anxiety and uncertainty stretching ahead of him. As he reached the door, his phone rang. It was Ingrid.

'You have something for me, Dr Hammond?'

'A warning to lay off is what I have for you. What the hell do you mean by contacting Alan Kendall?'

'Who?'

'You know damn well who he is.' He opened the door and strode in, slamming it behind him.

'You sound upset.'

'Of course I'm bloody upset. We had a deal.'

'We still do. Arrange the release of the money and all your problems will go away.'

'I stand a better chance of doing that without you setting Kendall on me.'

'Have you spoken to the Accountant?'

'Yes. And I will again soon. I'm confident he'll cooperate.' Confident? He was a long way from that. But it had to be said. 'I just need a little time.'

'You have it.'

'What I don't need is you pulling stunts like this.'

'Get us the money, doctor. Then there will be no more stunts. I promise.'

'That's not—' But he was talking to himself. Ingrid had rung off.

SIX

Edward Hammond was ten in 1967, the year of the first ever heart transplant. He remembered his father's excitement at the news. 'This, my boy, will change the medical world.' And so it did.

Hammond did not know then that he would become a surgeon when he grew up. In what was to be his specialism, the liver, the first transplants had actually been carried out two years previously. They were still very rare when he became a medical student in the late 1970s, but had become much commoner and more successful since, until they were quite literally an everyday event.

The first he presided over remained unique, of course. A framed photograph of the patient hung on his consulting-room wall at St George's. She was sitting up in bed, smiling with the characteristic radiance of someone who had been given a new lease of life – a whole new life, indeed. She was still alive and well fifteen years later. She sent him a card every Christmas.

The saving of life, as she would have been the first to agree, is a wonderful thing. And the wonder of it is not conditional on the virtue of the beneficiary. At least, it is not supposed to be. Hammond felt affronted that one operation among all the others he had conducted in his career should now have become an albatross round his neck. No one would condemn the lawyers who were defending Gazi in The Hague. They would sit there in their robes day after day, clocking up their fees and expenses as the process ground on, and no one would utter a word of complaint. Why should he be singled out? Why should he be made to feel guilty for pursuing his professional calling?

He knew the answer, of course, which made it only harder to bear. He had been set up. He had played a double role without knowing it. In saving Gazi's life, he had pawned his own.

Such were the thoughts that swirled in Hammond's mind as he hurried across Hyde Park on a bleak, grey Sunday afternoon. His hopes of a swift resolution to his problems were pinned on his meeting with Marco Piravani and he was disappointed not to see the Italian waiting for him as he turned on to the Serpentine bridge. Hammond was punctual to a fault, but he guessed he should have expected Piravani not to be.

To his surprise, however, he recognized someone else on the bridge. The young man in a hoodie leaning against the railings and sucking on a roll-up was surely the same young man he had seen in the kitchen of the house in Ealing. The coincidence immediately aroused his suspicion. What was *he* doing here?

The young man looked up as Hammond approached and grinned. 'Hi,' he said, taking a last drag on his roll-up before flicking the butt into the Serpentine. 'Dr Hammond, right? I'm Ryan. Marco sent me.'

'Why isn't he here? We agreed to meet.'

'Yeah. So he said.'

'Well?'

'Thing is, doc, Marco's had to take off.'

'Take off?'

'Go. Leave. Hit the road.'

'He's gone away?'

'Yesterday. In kind of a hurry.'

'Damn it all.' Hammond turned and added several silent curses as he gazed out across the park. He should have foreseen this. He really should. 'Where's he gone?' he asked fatalistically.

'Haven't a clue. I don't think he's planning to come back soon, though.'

'No. I don't suppose he is.'

'Bit of a bummer, is it, Marco doing a runner?'

'You could say so.'

'Nice bloke. But you're never sure what's going on inside his head. Know what I mean?'

'Yes. I do.'

'Like, Livingstone Road's basically a student house. We're all at Thames Valley Uni. All except Marco. A middle-aged Italian accountant? I bet he could've afforded to live somewhere a lot classier.'

'No doubt.'

'And I bet you know why he didn't.'

Hammond turned back to face Ryan. 'Did Marco have a lot of luggage with him when he left?'

'No. But he wasn't exactly big on possessions. He didn't leave much behind, I can tell you that.'

'How do you know?'

'Well, I . . . took a look in his flat, didn't I? He left me his keys, y'see. To pass on to the landlord. That's actually why I'm here.'

'What do you mean?'

'Marco reckoned you'd be willing to, er, slip me a few quid for the use of them.' Ryan shrugged. 'Student loans, hey? What can I tell you? I'm on the breadline.'

'How much do you want?'

Ryan fashioned what he presumably believed to be a winning smile. 'How about fifty quid? You look as if you could spare it. Oh, and if you're driving, a lift back to Ealing. Can't say fairer than that, can I?'

Hammond could not summon the energy to argue. 'OK. Let's go.' Had Piravani left something for him at the flat? If not, why send Ryan to meet him? Maybe, just maybe, the situation was not as bad as he had first feared.

'What about the money?'

'When the key turns in the lock, Ryan. C.o.d.'

'You're a hard man, doc.'

'Come on. The sooner we're there the sooner you'll be paid.'

Hammond started walking. Ryan fell in beside him, scuffing his heels as they went. 'I almost forgot,' he said breathlessly. 'Marco wanted me to . . . give you a message. He said . . .'

'Yes? What did he say?'

'That he was . . . sorry.'

'*Sorry?*'

'That was it. And you know what? He kind of looked it too.'

Hammond pumped Ryan for information about Piravani during the drive out to Ealing, but learnt little. Piravani was already living in the house when Ryan moved in back in the autumn. Quiet, affable but unforthcoming, tolerant of the excesses of his co-tenants and always good for a loan: that was the man Ryan knew. 'He kept his head down, know what I mean? He kept it down so low you had to figure he was hiding from something – or someone.' Yes. You had to figure that.

They reached Livingstone Road and went straight up to Piravani's flat. The key fitted. But Hammond kept Ryan waiting for his reward a little longer.

'Notice anything that's missing?'

'No. But, like I told you, he didn't have much to start with.'

That was as Hammond remembered too. Piravani appeared to have managed his life with the possibility of a departure at short notice constantly in mind. Hammond stepped into the bedroom and opened the wardrobe, followed by the drawers of the bedside cabinet: all empty. And there was no sign of *La Gazzetta dello Sport*.

'How about that fifty now, doc?'

'In a minute. Tell me, did Marco get a lot of post?'

'No. Most days none at all.'

'Any kind of package or large envelope recently?'

'How large?'

'Not very, necessarily. Big enough to contain a newspaper, say.'

'A newspaper? Well, yeah, could be. A few days ago. I was here when it was delivered. Left it downstairs for when he got back. Kind of . . . squidgy, as I recall. Might have been a paper.'

'Italian stamp?'

'Maybe. I'm not sure.'

'And he'll have taken it with him, so it makes no odds. Did Marco have a computer, Ryan?'

'He carried a laptop sometimes.'

'Of course.' Hammond led the way back into the lounge. 'Everything had to be portable.'

'The dosh, doc,' Ryan pressed. 'We had a deal. Remember?'

'I haven't got much for my money, have I?' Hammond jingled the keys in his hand. 'Marco must have—' He stopped and stared down at them. There were three on the ring. 'One for the front door. One for the flat. What's the third for, Ryan?'

'What?'

'The third key. Where's the lock this one fits?'

'Dunno.'

'Fifty quid for the *use* of the keys. That's what we agreed. So, I want to use them all. Otherwise, you haven't earned your money.'

Ryan grimaced. 'Come off it, doc. How should I know?'

'That's your problem.'

'Fuck me.' Ryan squinted at the key as Hammond held it up for inspection. 'I haven't got one like that. There's nothing in the house it would—' He broke off. His squint grew pensive. 'Ah. That could be it, I guess. The lock-up.'

'What lock-up?'

Ryan smiled innocently. 'Didn't I mention he had one?'

Leaving the closest pub to the Ealing campus of Thames Valley University one afternoon, Ryan had been surprised to see Piravani crossing the road ahead of him and heading down a residential side-street. Drunk enough to give way to idle curiosity, he had followed. The trail had led to a block of lock-up garages, the same block to which he was now leading Hammond.

'He opened one of them up and went in, bringing the door down behind him, so there was no chance of seeing what was inside. But I never saw him at the wheel of a car, so I'm guessing not a vintage Lamborghini.'

'Did you ever ask him?'

''Course not. He'd have known I'd followed him then, wouldn't he?'

'Oh, I think he knew anyway, Ryan. That's how he could count on you bringing me here.'

The garage was one of a dozen in a weed-pocked yard separating the back gardens of two parallel rows of houses. There was no one around. Their only company, in the chill, gathering dusk, was a large black cat. And he seemed to find their activities singularly uninteresting.

Several of the garages were in a ramshackle state. But Piravani's was reasonably well-maintained, with the newest and stoutest door of the lot. Hammond slid the key into the lock, turned it and swung the door up.

The interior was shrouded in gloom. Spotting a switch just inside, Hammond pushed it down. A pair of bright fluorescent lights flickered into life.

As predicted, there was no vintage Lamborghini; instead, a metal table and a swivel-chair that looked as if they belonged in an office last furnished in the 1970s, a stack of several dozen cardboard boxes, four filing cabinets lined up against the end wall, and, standing on the table, a shredding machine, its function made clear by a neat row of at least twenty transparent plastic sacks crammed with shredded paper.

'Whoa,' said Ryan. 'What's all this?'

'What *was* all this, you mean.' Hammond toed one of the sacks. 'This is what Marco wanted me to see: the accountant's version of scorched earth.' He moved to the filing cabinets and opened a drawer at random. The cradles inside were empty.

He checked the other drawers and cabinets, as well as the cardboard boxes. There was nothing in any of them, except empty folders and stray paper clips. This was Piravani's answer: destroy all records and documents, then vanish. He was gone. And Hammond felt queasily certain he meant to make sure he could not be found again.

'What now, doc?'

'I give you your money, Ryan. Then we lock up and go our separate ways.'

Hammond had only one clue left to follow and little hope to vest in it. Squisito was limbering up for a slow Sunday evening when he arrived. The waiter's command of English deteriorated markedly when he flashed Piravani's photograph. Eventually, the proprietor emerged from the rear to take charge of the exchange.

'Signor Piravani is a regular customer, sir. But we know nothing about him. Of course, we will be happy to tell him you are trying to contact him. Please. Write down your phone number. We will ask him to call you next time he comes in.'

But there was not going to be a next time. The proprietor probably did not know that. But Hammond did.

He drove slowly home. Piravani had disappeared and along with him any realistic chance of complying with Ingrid's ultimatum. Hammond had another five days left to find a way of doing so, but it was impossible to imagine how they could make any difference. He was out of ideas, if not yet out of time.

He went through the motions of preparing a meal, knowing he really should eat something, even though he had no appetite. While it was in the oven, he checked his e-mail and answerphone. There was one message. Bill Dowler, Kate's elder brother, had phoned earlier. Though he kept in touch with Alice, his niece, his contact with Hammond was minimal, making his call a worrying rarity.

'Edward, this is Bill. How are you? Well, I trust. Look, I've had that creep Alan Kendall on to me. What Kate ever saw in him I'll never know. Thing is, he seems to think there's been some . . . development . . . in the case. Kate's . . . death, I mean. And he also seems to think . . . you know about it. All this because of an anonymous phone call, apparently. He sounded half cut to me and not entirely . . . rational, but, well, if anything has happened, obviously I'd . . . like to know. So, could you . . . get back to me . . . as soon as you can? Thanks. I . . . Well, I'll . . . hope to hear from you. 'Bye for now.'

In the silence that followed the end of the message, Hammond heard his own voice, reassuring Bill that Kendall was talking nonsense. Nothing had happened, certainly nothing he knew about. It would have been easy to do: one short phone call to put his brother-in-law's mind at rest. But it would also add another lie to those he had already told. And in a week, or two, or three, when Gazi decided the time had come, those lies were sure to catch up with him.

The last conversation Hammond ever had with Kate, a few days before her death, had ended with one of those lies. It was a Saturday morning and he was collecting Alice for the weekend. When he took her back the following afternoon, Kendall was on hand and he did not even get out of the car. Kate gave him a cool, acknowledging nod from the doorway as Alice ran up the path, but no actual words were exchanged. He had the distinct impression Kate did not want to speak to him.

But it had been a different story the day before. In Kendall's absence, she felt no need to bridle her tongue. She was angry with what she saw as Hammond's prevarication over supplying financial information to her lawyer. She suspected, correctly, that he was hiding something.

'You've been very elusive these past few weeks, Edward. I wouldn't mind, but Alice started to think you'd forgotten her.' Alice was upstairs at the time and unable either to confirm or contradict this, though Hammond felt guilty enough to believe it.

'I've had a lot of work on,' he responded lamely, though accurately.

'We're all busy people. Ignoring things won't make them go away.'

'I'll speak to my lawyer.'

'You do that.'

'What are your plans for Easter, Kate?' he asked, eager to change the subject.

'I'll let you know,' she replied coolly, tossing back her fringe in that characteristic way he had to remind himself he was not supposed still to find attractive. 'Have you been out of the country, by the way?'

'What makes you ask?'

'The way Fiona spoke about you. As if you weren't . . . close by.' Fiona, his PA, had reported several calls from Kate during his trip to Belgrade. Her discretion was legendary, but evidently not quite foolproof.

'You're imagining things.'

'So, you haven't been out of the country?'

'No. I haven't.' He heard pattering footfalls on the stairs. 'Ready, Alice?' he called.

'Ready, Daddy.'

And Kate said nothing, though the tightness of her gaze suggested that, for whatever reason, she did not believe him.

Hammond deleted Bill's message, poured himself a large Scotch and sat down in the kitchen, waiting for the oven timer to ping. In front of him on the wall hung a calendar, with the word *HOLIDAY* optimistically scrawled across the week he had planned to spend ski-ing in Austria. There was no one he could turn to and there was nowhere he could hide. He had never felt more alone, or less confident. He was staring disaster in the face. And he could not look away.

SEVEN

Edward Hammond had last been to The Hague to attend a conference held at the Kurhaus, a vast and ornate nineteenth-century beachfront hotel in the city's seaside suburb of Scheveningen. Its conference business was evidently slack at present. A room had been readily available and his uncertainty over how long he would be staying seemed to pose no problem.

His reasons for going to The Hague were hard to articulate, even to himself. He had to go somewhere. Remaining penned in the house in Wimbledon while Ingrid's deadline edged ever closer was simply intolerable. Movement and action, however futile or ineffectual, were preferable, if not essential. And Gazi, the source of his troubles, was in The Hague. So to The Hague he would go.

He was on the mid-morning Eurostar to Brussels before he had given serious consideration to what he would actually do when he arrived. Perhaps he should try to visit Gazi in order to reason with him. Already it sounded like a bad idea. He had no bargaining power and would only make himself look guilty in other people's eyes if they learnt of the visit. Better ideas were in short supply, however. He was on a long leash. But it was firmly staked.

Thanks to delays on the line from Brussels, Hammond did not reach his hotel until early evening. He could hear the waves crashing on the beach, but he could see them only as a pale and ghostly

49

ribbon in the darkness beyond the promenade lights. He sat in his lavishly appointed room and, later, in the frescoed restaurant, wondering just how aptly his journey could be called a fool's errand.

A run along the promenade next morning, with a razor-edged wind keening in off the North Sea, sharpened his resolution. He did not need to go to Scheveningen Prison to see Gazi. The International Criminal Tribunal for the former Yugoslavia required the man's presence in court most weekdays. And this weekday Hammond proposed to be in the audience.

Halfway along its route into the city centre, the tram from Scheveningen passed close by the anonymous building housing ICTY. But for the UN flag flapping and furling in the wind outside, Hammond might have doubted it really was his destination. The airport-class security barrier at the entrance confirmed, however, that justice of a politically sensitive nature was being pursued behind its grey walls and blank windows.

The foyer was eerily quiet. A media presence, which Hammond had somehow expected, was noticeably lacking. Leaflets in several languages were on display, detailing the charges against the defendants in the cases being heard, adorned with their photographs. He picked up the one pertaining to Dragan Gazi, who looked whiter-haired and gaunter than he remembered – and sterner, glowering unapologetically at the camera.

There was a second security barrier at the foot of the stairs that led up to the courtrooms. The guard asked him brightly which case he was interested in and directed him to courtroom number three for Dragan Gazi. Hammond went up, disconcerted by the simplicity and orderliness of the setting. It somehow seemed too bland to be true.

The courtroom itself was no less bland: an oval, yellow-walled, grey-carpeted space separated from the public viewing area by thick, very possibly bullet-proof, floor-to-ceiling glass. Proceedings had already commenced for the day, presided over by three red-robed judges. Clerks, interpreters and black-robed lawyers sat before them at their desks. One lawyer was on her feet, questioning a witness, who sat with his back to the public, but who was pictured face-on on the TV screen suspended in front of the glass. Away to the left, flanked by blue-shirted guards, sat the accused.

All this Hammond absorbed in the minute or so it took him to choose a seat, several rows back from the front. He could have sat anywhere, given that only one other member of the public was present, a slim, dark-haired woman dressed in a smart but simple black trouser-suit, who appeared to be paying Gazi close attention.

An English translation of the questioning was relayed to the public area through a loudspeaker. To hear the witness in his own language, presumably Serbo-Croat, earphones were necessary. The woman was wearing a set. She had Slavic looks – sallow skin, high cheekbones, chestnut-brown eyes. Hammond would have put her age at forty or so, one of a generation enduringly affected by the events the court was investigating.

Gazi was leaning back in his chair, heavy-lidded and seemingly bored, unaware, so it appeared, of Hammond's arrival. He had looped his earphones round his neck, requiring no translation of what the witness was saying. In his grey suit and dark tie, he looked the very image of the retired businessman he had pretended to be during his years in hiding. There was nothing threatening about him, unless it lay in his resemblance to an elderly lion, dozing in his enclosure at the zoo, whose claws were retracted, but might still be sharp.

The witness, a bulky, middle-aged man with a dashing moustache but a hesitant manner, was explaining, in tortuous detail, the administrative arrangements for the award of medals and pensions to deserving members of Gazi's paramilitary force. Only the position of the examining counsel, on the opposite side of the court from Gazi, indicated she was with the prosecution. The care he had lavished on his men, not to mention the provision he had made for their widows, sounded exemplary.

51

As Hammond slowly relaxed, satisfied that Gazi was unlikely to notice him, even if he did rouse himself from his torpor, the significance of the testimony he was hearing gradually emerged. To recognize the bravery of specific acts was to admit knowledge and imply approval of other acts. The medals and the pensions were in that sense part of a programme of incitement for the perpetration of crimes against humanity.

The translator's voice was expressionless. Hammond could only imagine what tonal subtleties might be escaping him. Nothing in the manner or posture of the woman sitting ahead of him in the public area telegraphed what she made of the witness's answers. Her gaze – and her concentration – seemed fixed on Gazi, as if she was studying him, perhaps, for signs of guilt or remorse or anger: any reaction at all, in fact, to what was being said.

But there was no reaction. Gazi was not disposed to give anyone the satisfaction of seeing him flinch or squirm. He had summoned all his lordly indifference and laid it before the court.

One thing that struck Hammond was how well Gazi looked. He was a horribly good advertisement for the long-term benefits of transplant surgery. Hammond should have felt some pride in the visible evidence of his own excellence. Instead, he reflected wistfully on the mistakes he could easily have made that would have led to his patient's death and the peace of mind he would be enjoying now as a result.

The desire to walk into the courtroom, drag Gazi to his feet and remind him how grateful he should be was suddenly so sharp that he uttered some oath he was hardly aware of and stood up so abruptly that his chair slid back and clattered into the one behind it. The woman looked round with a start of surprise, as if she had previously been unaware of his presence. She frowned at him more in curiosity than censure and he raised a hand in apology, both to her and the guard who loomed into view. Then she looked away and he sat down again. The guard retreated.

No one in the court heard anything. Most of them had their backs to the public area anyway. Gazi continued to dwell in his private world. The examination painstakingly proceeded.

Hammond continued to watch Gazi through the glass; and nothing changed. His dilemma remained. And the certainty that he would glean no answers, however long he stayed there, seeped slowly into him. But what was he to do instead? How could he escape the trap Gazi had set for him?

While he was distracted by such thoughts, the examination of the witness came to an anticlimactic close and the court adjourned for an early lunch.

Gazi was led away through a door behind him. He cast one fleeting glance towards the public area as he went. But it was directed at the woman. Hammond was out of his line of sight. Then he was gone.

The woman rose and walked past Hammond. He followed her out and down the stairs. She moved ahead of him across the empty foyer and out into the open air. The guardhouse controlling the entrance gate was to their right, but she did not turn towards it. Instead, she paused on the steps of the court, took a pack of cigarettes out of her handbag and lit one.

'Staying on for the resumption?' he asked impulsively.

She looked at him warily. 'Maybe. You?' The intonation of her voice tended to confirm she was from some part of the former Yugoslavia.

He smiled. 'I'm not sure.'

'Are you . . . a tourist?'

'No. I'm . . . not a tourist.'

'You have an interest in the case?'

'Sort of.'

'But you are British. How can it concern you?'

'Your English is excellent,' he said, in a stab at combining flattery with deflection.

'I was an English teacher . . . before the war.'

'Not since?'

'No. Not since.' She nodded, as if agreeing with herself on something. 'There is a lot of "not since" in Serbia.'

'Which is where you're from?'

'Yes. I am from Serbia.'

'Did you come here . . . for this case?'

Her wariness was suddenly magnified. 'If you're not a tourist, what are you?'

'I'm a doctor.'

'Really?'

'Really.'

'Well, there are no patients for you here, doctor.' She took a last draw on her cigarette and stepped past him to crush the butt into an ash-box next to the door. 'Excuse me.'

'Before you go back in . . .'

'Yes?' She frowned at him. Her gaze, he observed, was somehow older than the rest of her, as if she had seen much in her life that she would prefer to forget, but could not.

'Have you ever heard of Marco Piravani?'

She did not reply. She did not need to. It was immediately and surprisingly obvious to him that she had.

Her name was Zineta Perović. That was as much as she was initially willing to disclose. She was as suspicious as she was cautious. But it was clear they both wanted to learn how the other came to know Piravani. Hammond suggested they discuss their mutual interest in the Italian over lunch. Zineta agreed, on condition she chose the venue. 'We'll go into the city centre,' she declared, adding, 'We'll talk there,' in a tone that suggested she wanted to put some distance between them and ICTY before saying any more.

An attempt at small talk while they waited for the tram got Hammond nowhere. Zineta asked to see his passport and quizzed him about his occupation. He had the distinct impression she was frightened of being set up in some way and would have given him the brush-off but for his mention of Piravani.

'What do you do for a living now?' he asked when they had boarded the tram.

'I clean offices. Six till midnight.'

'How long have you done that?'

'Since I came to The Hague.'

'And when was that?'

'December.'

'When Gazi's trial began.'

'Yes. When his trial began.'

'You know him?'

'Oh yes.' She nodded grimly. 'I know him very well.'

She chose a busy little brasserie just off The Hague's main shopping street, where a babble of lunchtime chatter ensured no one would overhear them. She ordered bread and soup and added a main course only when Hammond volunteered to pay.

'I'm sorry,' she said. 'I have very little money.'

'There's no need to apologize. Would you like some wine?'

'No. No wine.'

'Do you go to the court every day?'

'Every day I can.'

'What takes you there?'

'What took *you* there? You're a busy man, I'm sure. How can you spare the time, doctor?'

'Call me Edward.'

'No. That would be like saying we're going to get to know each other. And I'm not sure we are.'

'OK. Well, officially, I'm on holiday.'

'But you're not here as a tourist.'

'No. I'm not.'

'Why, then?'

'Let's talk about Piravani.'

'OK. Tell me how you know Gazi. If I believe you, I'll tell you how I know him.'

'And if you don't believe me?'

'I'll leave you to enjoy your lunch – alone.'

'Are you always so . . . demanding?'

'I'm sorry,' she said, looking as if she meant it. 'My life hasn't

55

been what I hoped – what I expected. Yours, on the other hand, I'd guess has been . . . smooth progress all the way. I have a cousin who is a doctor. *Used* to be a doctor. He is a taxi driver now. More money, you understand. *Enough* money, to keep his family. The war is over. But Serbia isn't like it was before. It isn't the country I grew up in. They called that Yugoslavia. And the inhabitants didn't know they hated one another. No one had told them.' Her gaze lost its focus for a wistful moment. Then she was back with him. 'The truth, doctor. We will trade it. How do you know Gazi?'

Hammond sighed. Strangely, he did not doubt her ability to recognize a lie if he proffered one. They had to trust each other. But that was easier said than done. 'Thirteen years ago, he had a liver transplant. I was the surgeon.'

'Ah, yes.' She thought for a moment. 'The transplant. I remember.' She nodded. 'You saved his life.'

'You could say that.'

'Many would. Including those who would like to kill him.'

'Would you like to kill him, Zineta?'

'Sometimes, yes.'

'And how do you know him?'

She looked Hammond in the eye. There was no hint of evasiveness in her voice as she said, 'I was his mistress.'

EIGHT

Zineta ate her meal with the relish of someone who normally lunched more frugally – if she lunched at all. She had admitted her connection with Gazi, but remained guarded and reticent where Piravani was concerned. Now they were debating with themselves what to say, how much to reveal, how big a risk they should take.

'Why did you ask me about Marco, doctor?' Zineta said, breaking a thoughtful silence.

The significance of her use of Piravani's Christian name did not escape Hammond. The hint of a blush suggested it did not escape her either. They were both walking on eggshells. 'I need to find him. Urgently.'

She looked across at him. 'So do I.'

'Why?'

'You first.'

'It's . . . difficult to explain.'

'I'm sure it is. But we may be able to help each other. We can only do that if . . .'

'We're honest.'

'Yes.'

'You could be an undercover journalist for all I know.'

'If I was, would you have much to fear?'

Hammond grimaced. 'Yes, I would.'

She nodded. 'So would I. If you were.'

'You've seen my passport. You know who I am. You can phone the hospital I work at if you want to. My PA thinks I'm ski-ing in Austria. Everything I've said will check out. Do you want to do that?' He offered her his phone. 'I don't mind, Zineta. Truly I don't. I've—' He broke off.

'What is it?'

'I was about to say "I've nothing to hide". But that isn't exactly true.'

'Put your phone away, doctor. I believe you.'

'You really could call me Edward, you know.'

'All right, Edward. I believe you are who you say you are.'

'Good.'

She glanced at her watch. 'The court will soon be resuming. Gazi will wonder where I am.'

'He didn't give much sign of noticing you.'

'He doesn't give much sign of anything.'

'But he knows why you're there?'

'Of course.'

'And the reason is?'

She smiled faintly. 'Tell me why you're looking for Marco, Edward. Please. I need to know.'

'All right. But not here.' He looked around. The people at nearby tables all seemed absorbed in their own conversations, yet he did not feel entirely secure. He needed time to think. 'Let's go somewhere we can be . . . alone.'

'That's not a problem in this city. I've never felt as alone as I do here.'

'Have you travelled a lot?'

'Not recently. It's difficult when you haven't much money, or the money you have is worth nothing in any other currency. I was in London for a year in the late eighties, learning English. And I spent eight months in Paris in the mid-nineties. I was looking after my mother. She had cancer and we had to go to France to get her proper chemotherapy. That's when I stopped teaching, although the pay was so bad by then I wasn't giving up much.'

58

'What happened . . . to your mother?'

'She died.'

'I'm sorry.'

'It's OK. It's a long time ago now. Twelve years.'

'What did you do . . . after she died?'

'I went home.'

'To what?'

'A different kind of life. I'd had enough of being poor. Enough of having principles, I suppose.'

Hammond imagined her twelve years younger, wearing designer clothes and more make-up. She would, he suddenly realized, have been quite startlingly attractive. He had some idea then of what she might have done back home after months spent nursing her dying mother. 'Is that when you met Gazi?' he ventured.

'Yes.' She looked away. 'But first I met Marco.'

They said no more about Piravani, or Gazi, until they had left the brasserie and crossed the city centre to the Hofvijver. The wind had dropped and the turrets and gables of the Binnenhof were hazily reflected in the lake's placid surface. But the air was cold enough to ensure no one was sitting on any of the benches flanking the lake-side path. They walked slowly along it beneath the leafless trees.

'Are you going to tell me now why you're looking for Marco?'

'Yes,' Hammond replied. 'I am.' And so he was. But he had decided he could not trust a former mistress of Gazi with the whole truth. There was too much at stake. The money Piravani controlled was the obvious reason why Zineta should want to find him. Maybe she reckoned Gazi owed her a decent pay-off. And maybe she was right. But Hammond had to ensure the money went else-where. 'Gazi's daughter, Ingrid, approached me a few days ago. Marco hasn't responded to her messages, apparently. She needed someone to track him down and put him in touch with her. She couldn't go after him herself because she's being followed, so she claims, by Serbian government agents or . . . hoodlums of Gazi's acquaintance . . . or both. She chose me because . . . I was the only reliable person she could think of who had no obvious current connection with her father.'

'And you agreed?'

'I had to.' He took out his wallet and showed her the photograph of Alice. 'My daughter. She's in her first year at university. Ingrid threatened to . . . harm her . . . if I didn't cooperate. And her father's record made me believe it wasn't an idle threat.'

'I am sorry, Edward.' Zineta held the photograph for a moment, then passed it back to him with a sigh. 'It seems Ingrid has inherited her father's ruthlessness.'

'I'm afraid so.'

'So, why have you come to The Hague?'

'Ingrid told me to keep watch at an Italian restaurant in London where Marco was a regular customer. He turned up and when he left I followed him home.'

'Marco's living in London?'

'He *was*. But after I told him what I wanted him to do, he said he needed time to think. He said he had . . . scruples . . . about helping Gazi's family. When the time was up, I went to see him again. He'd gone. Vanished without a trace.'

'He's good at that.'

'So it seems. I came here because . . . I thought there was an outside chance . . .'

Zineta shook her head. 'This is the last place Marco would come.'

'You're probably right. But . . .'

'How long did Ingrid give you?'

'A week.'

'Does Alice's mother know what you're doing?'

'She died . . . some years ago.'

'Ah. I'm sorry.'

A silence fell between them. They sat down on one of the benches. Zineta lit a cigarette. Hammond gazed out across the lake and waited for her to give up some of her secrets, wondering if they would be any more faithfully represented than his had been.

'You know Marco was Gazi's banker, don't you, Edward?'

'Yes.'

'Ingrid wants her father's money. And there's a lot of it to want.'

'So I gather.'

'Maybe you think I'm after a cut too.'

'I wouldn't blame you if you were.'

'No? Well, I'm not, though there was a time I would have been. It was impossible for a woman on her own to make any kind of a decent living in Belgrade in the late nineties. Milošević had corrupted everything. The law didn't mean much any more. Things happened to me . . . I don't want to remember. I realized I needed protection. The mobsters all had what were called "sponsor girls". For the girls, it was . . . a way to survive. There were bars you could go to show yourself off . . . to put yourself on the market. It was shameful, but I did it. I was older than most of the girls, of course. Maybe that's why I was still . . . available . . . when Marco picked me up. I was lucky. He has a gentle nature. But, like you've found out, he has scruples, though not about money – not then, anyway. He loved making it and he loved spending it. I was happy for him to spend some of it on me. Champagne, fine food, beautiful clothes, expensive perfume, chauffeured limousines: they were good to have. Oh yes, Marco was kind to me. Actually, he was in love with me. When I told him . . . I was pregnant . . . it never crossed his mind that he might not be the father. But it crossed mine. And Gazi's.'

'Gazi was the father?'

'I couldn't say no to him, Edward. It was about survival, like I said. He had the power of life and death. He only wanted me because Marco loved me. Forcing me to betray Marco would have been enough for him. Even the pregnancy wouldn't have mattered if I'd had a daughter. But the baby was a boy. And Gazi's only son had died in Argentina, in a motorbike crash when he was . . . crazily young. So, Gazi insisted on a DNA test. I knew it was going to prove the boy was his. It was . . . fate, I suppose. I carry my son's picture like you carry your daughter's. See?'

She opened her handbag and took out a small leather photograph holder. The picture it contained was of a very young, still babyish little boy, dressed in shorts and T-shirt, sitting barefooted on a sun-dappled lawn and beaming amiably at the camera.

'That is Monir when he was just over a year old,' Zineta explained. 'He's nearly eleven now.'

'You don't have a more recent picture?'

'No. He was taken from me before he was two.'

'Taken?'

'I lived with him at Gazi's villa after he was born. The first year . . . I was happy just to be raising my child in luxury. But when Gazi was indicted by ICTY and NATO bombed Belgrade, things changed. It got so I was a virtual prisoner. Gazi was afraid Milošević would have him killed. He saw threats everywhere. Maybe he was right to. He had Marco working on a plan for them to disappear. Marco hated Gazi for stealing me from him, but still he went on taking the money Gazi paid him. He didn't have the courage to quit. And maybe he knew Gazi wouldn't let him quit anyway. Besides, the plan he came up with punished me for betraying him. That must have given him some satisfaction. In March 2000, Gazi sent me off on holiday to Cyprus. He said I looked as if I needed some sun. I couldn't understand it. Until then he'd always kept me close. I didn't want to go, because he wouldn't let me take Monir with me, but I didn't have any choice really. What he said . . . I had to do. I phoned every day from the hotel, of course, but from the fourth day on no one picked up. I didn't know what to think. I called Marco, but only got his answering machine. He didn't respond to my messages. In the end, I contacted a woman I used to teach with and begged her to find out what was happening at the villa. She phoned back later and said the place was empty: shuttered, closed up. I took the next flight home. She was right. Gazi had gone, taking Monir with him. I tracked down some of the staff. They said they'd all been paid up to the end of the month and told not to come in. Gazi had driven away with Monir, a woman they'd never seen before and one of his bodyguards. No one knew where they'd gone. I went to Marco's flat. He wasn't there. A neighbour said he hadn't seen him for days. I knew what that meant. I remember sitting at the top of the stairs outside the flat, weeping uncontrollably. After that I don't remember much for quite a while. The despair was . . . physical. It just . . . emptied me out.'

'Have you seen your son since?'

'No. I've no idea where he is. Gazi put him somewhere out of my reach – out of everyone's reach. Ingrid may know, of course. It could be that's partly what the money's needed for: to look after him. That could also be why Marco's refusing to cooperate, because once, ever so briefly, he thought Monir was his son.'

'But you think he knows where the boy is?'

'He must do. He set it all up for Gazi in the first place, so . . . there's a chance, if I can persuade him to . . .' She put a hand to her forehead. 'When I heard they'd caught Gazi, I thought I might be able to . . . get through to him. But he refuses to see me.' She sighed. 'He can't avoid seeing me in court, of course. Sitting there, day after day, looking at him, is the only way I can appeal to his conscience.'

'Does he have a conscience?'

'Probably not.' Her head fell. 'No. Of course he doesn't. I'm fooling myself.' She shivered. 'And I'm cold. Can we move, please?'

They left the bench and walked on. Hammond felt immensely sorry for this sad and lonely woman. She knew her stubborn vigil in the court was almost certainly in vain. But what else could she do to win back the child Gazi had stolen from her?

'I expect it's occurred to you, Edward, that Monir was too young when we were parted for him to remember me now.'

'That wouldn't stop him wanting to know you.'

'Perhaps not. But first I would have to convince him I am his mother. Whatever Gazi has told him, or instructed others to tell him, it wouldn't have been the truth. I have accepted that. I know it will be hard . . . for both of us. But still . . . I have to try. It took me more than a year to . . . function again . . . after I lost Monir. By then Milošević had been sent here to stand trial and there was a democratic government in Serbia. I tried to . . . adjust to life without my son. I was ashamed of many of the things I'd done during the bad times. There were people who knew I'd been Gazi's mistress. They'd look at me in the street, or maybe I just imagined them looking . . . I decided I had to leave Belgrade – leave Serbia. I applied to work for the Bosniak Commission on Missing Persons. They took me on because of my proficiency in English. So, I moved to Sarajevo. I never told anyone I was Serbian. They all thought I was from Slovenia. It was only in Sarajevo that I began to learn just how much . . . pure evil . . . the war had involved. So many killings . . . and other things . . . you wouldn't believe. And so many missing. Dead, of course, most of them, piled up, one on top of the other, in caves and pits and holes dug in fields. But their relatives were still looking for them, looking for a body to bury, looking for the truth about what had happened to them: where and when and how they'd died. Not why, though. That bit they understood. The war turned neighbours into enemies. It tore everything apart. They weren't trying to put it back together the way it was, you see. That's impossible. They just wanted to *know*. In the end, that's better than not knowing. That's why finding Monir, even if he . . . rejects me . . . would be better than never finding him at all.'

'And Marco's your best chance of doing that?'

'Right now, yes. Do you have *any* idea where he's gone?'

'Not really. Except . . . well, a few days before he disappeared, he received a package in the post from Italy.' Hammond went on to recount the story of the classified ad in *La Gazzetta dello Sport*. 'Whoever sent it obviously knew where he was living, so . . .'

'He may know where he's gone.'

'Yes. But I haven't a clue who the sender was. Did Marco talk much about his friends or family back home?'

'Never. I was at his flat a few times when his mother phoned. She'd do most of the talking, I remember. When I asked him about her, he clammed up. "The less you know about me," he'd say, "the safer you are." I think now he meant the safer *he* was.'

'Which part of Italy is he from?'

'I don't know. The north, I think. But that's more of a . . . feeling

. . . than anything else. Because of his . . . coolness. He was always very self-controlled.' She smiled faintly. 'Except when he watched football.'

'He went to matches?'

'No. I mean *watched*. On television – some Italian satellite channel. He'd drink beer and shout at the referee. I used to laugh at him when he did that.'

'Did he have a favourite team?'

'Probably. But they were all the same to me. He used to wear a special football shirt when he watched, I remember. Black with red stripes.'

'That might mean something to me if I knew anything about football.'

'But you don't?'

'No. On the other hand . . .' A hopeful thought came to Hammond. 'I know someone who does.'

He took out his phone and switched it on, confronting as he did so the unwelcome fact that he had several messages waiting. He ignored them and dialled Peter and Julie's number.

They were lunching with Sophie somewhere near a ski run Peter described as 'sumptuous'. Hammond slogged through some conversational heavy weather concerning his regrettable absence before coming to the point. To resolve an argument for a colleague, could Peter the walking (and ski-ing) encyclopaedia on all matters football-related tell him which Italian team played in black-and-red-striped shirts?

'AC Milan, Edward. Doesn't everyone know that? Now, does this sudden thirst for trivia mean you're free to join us after all?'

No. It did not mean that. After running repairs to his cover story and with profuse expressions of gratitude, Hammond rang off. 'It looks like Marco's from Milan,' he announced. 'A northerner, like you said, although—'

He stopped. Zineta seemed barely to have heard him. She had walked on a little way and was staring into space, her brow furrowed pensively.

65

'*Zineta?*'

She started and looked round at him. 'I'm sorry, Edward,' she said, smiling apologetically. 'I was . . . remembering.'

'What were you remembering?'

'Something I'd forgotten . . . until now. After watching his football matches, Marco often used to phone a friend in Italy called Guido and joke with him about the result. He could be the man who sent him the newspaper.'

'Yes. He could. Unfortunately, there are a lot of Guidos in Milan.'

'Milan?'

'Where the black-and-red-shirts play.'

'Ah.' She nodded. 'So, we need to find a man called Guido in an Italian city of more, I guess, than a million people.' She shook her head dolefully. '*Nemoguć.*' It was the first word of Serbian he had heard her speak. And he did not need her to supply a translation.

They retreated to a café in the ornate Passage Arcade. There Hammond explained what he saw as their only recourse. It meant admitting to Ingrid that he had let Piravani slip through his fingers. But he would have to admit that sooner or later anyway. And there was surely a good chance Gazi would have passed on to her whatever information he had about Piravani's background.

'You won't mention me to her, will you, Edward?' Zineta grabbed his arm for emphasis and was clearly deeply disturbed by the possibility. 'I don't want her to know I'm helping you.'

'Don't worry. I'll claim to have got this far on my own.'

He stepped out into the arcade and rang Ingrid's number. He was obliged, as before, to leave a message. Then he checked his own messages, beginning with a text from Alice sent the day before. '*Unc Bill trying 2 contact u. Wots he got nickers in twist about?*' He texted back. '*Will speak 2 Bill. Nothing 2 worry about.*' There were a couple of voicemails, one of which he assumed was from Bill, perhaps explaining why he had been bothering Alice. But they would have to wait. Ingrid was calling back.

'Where have you been and what have you been doing, doctor? You have only three days left.'

Hammond had drawn some meagre consolation from the calculation that technically he had more like six days, since Gazi could say nothing against him in court until after the weekend, but he did not propose to point that out to Ingrid. 'I've run into some problems.'

'I don't want to hear about problems. I want to hear about the money.'

'I'm going to have to deal with the Accountant through an intermediary: a friend of his in Milan.'

'What friend?'

'I'm hoping you can tell me who he is.'

'You don't know?'

'Listen to me, Ingrid. Your best chance of getting the money is to help me. What did Pira—'

'*Don't say his name.*'

'OK, OK. The Accountant. What did he do before your father hired him?'

'Same thing. For more people.'

'On his own?'

'No. He had a partner. But my father wanted . . . an exclusive service. So, they split.'

'Name of the partner?'

'I don't know. Maybe my father knows. I would have to ask him.'

'Well, ask him, then. I need to know.'

'I cannot speak to him until this evening. Right now, he will be in court.'

'Make it as soon as you can.'

'You told me you had met with the Accountant.'

'I have.'

'So, why the question about his ex-partner?'

'Because the Accountant's gone to ground again.'

'You've lost him, haven't you?' she snapped. 'How could you be so . . . *estúpido*?'

'Do you want me to go on with this, Ingrid?' He nerved himself to call her bluff. 'Or would you rather do it yourself?'

There was a pause. When Ingrid spoke again, he knew at once from the deeper, more restrained tone of her voice that he had won the skirmish. But a skirmish was all it was. There was still a battle to be fought. 'I will call you as soon as I have the information.'

'Thank you.'

'But, doctor . . .'

'Yes?'

'Make no more mistakes. For your own sake.'

NINE

Bill Dowler was six years older than his sister Kate, but to Edward Hammond the difference had always seemed greater, more like ten or twelve. There was a slight facial resemblance, slighter than ever since Bill had grown a beard, but their personalities could hardly have been more different: he calm and stoical, she vibrant and demonstrative. After thirty years in the Army, Bill had moved to a cottage in the New Forest, where he pursued a solitary life as a jobbing gardener and required, so he declared, nothing of the outside world, its failure to operate on military principles of order and discipline an abiding disappointment to him.

There was a simplistic, visceral side to Bill which Hammond sometimes found amusing, sometimes objectionable and sometimes refreshingly direct. He had taken seriously his role of elder brother to a sister who, in his opinion, seldom knew what was best for her, to the extent that Hammond was never quite sure Kate had been joking when she said, prior to his first meeting with Bill, 'If he doesn't approve of you, I expect they'll find your body in a ditch.'

That first meeting had featured an argument about the merits of the Falklands War, a conflict in which Bill had seen hand-to-hand action, so Hammond might reasonably have supposed their relationship had started badly. But not so. Kate later told him Bill had liked and respected him from the first. 'Apparently, he thinks you're just the stabilizing influence I need.'

If Hammond had truly been a stabilizing influence, of course, Kate would not have thrown their marriage into the mincer after twelve years and taken up with Alan Kendall. Bill's faith in him turned out to be sadly misplaced. To his credit, Bill never even hinted that he blamed Hammond for the break-up. But at the funeral he made his feelings very clear on one subject. 'If I ever find out who killed her, I swear I'll make sure he doesn't live to see the inside of a courtroom, far less a cell with all mod cons in some bloody holiday-camp prison.'

It was pure Bill. And he meant it. The knowledge lurked darkly at the back of Hammond's thoughts as he sat in his room at the Kurhaus Hotel that evening, receiver to his ear, listening as the telephone rang at the other end of the line in a New Forest cottage. He rather hoped Bill was not in. It would be easier to lie to an answerphone. But in the very instant the machine cut in, Bill picked up.

'Hello?'

'Hi, Bill. It's Edward.'

'At last. I was about to send out a search party.'

'Sorry I didn't respond to your message right away. I've been busy.'

'So Alice said. Ski-ing cancelled, apparently.'

'Yes. I was surprised you'd been on to her, actually.'

'I didn't have your mobile number. And since you never seemed to be home . . .'

'You didn't tell her why you were anxious to contact me, did you?'

'Of course not. What do you take me for?'

'I just don't want her to get the idea something's going on when in fact nothing is.'

'Point taken. And that's right, is it? Nothing's going on?'

'Don't you think I'd tell you if there was?'

'I'm not absolutely sure, Edward. Would you?'

'Of course.'

'I spoke to your PA yesterday. She's very good. Any politician

70

would envy her ability to avoid answering a direct question like
"Where is Dr Hammond?"'

'Well, sometimes she . . . overdoes the stonewalling.'

'I got the distinct impression she didn't exactly know, you see.
Where you are, I mean.'

Hammond swore silently. 'Why did you phone her, Bill?'

'Because you didn't get back to me. So, how about it? Where are
you?'

The truth, on that point at least, seemed the safest option. 'The
Hague.'

'What's taken you there?'

'I can't go into it. I'm bound by . . . doctor–patient con-
fidentiality.' It was a miserable excuse, but he did not have a better
one to offer. 'I can assure you, though, this trip has nothing to do
with Kate. Kendall's fantasizing. Don't let him get to you.'

'I can deal with Kendall. That's not—'

'Hold on.' Hammond's mobile was chirruping. Glancing at the
display, he saw the caller was Ingrid. 'I'm sorry, Bill. I'm going to
have to cut you off. Something's cropped up this end.'

'Just a—'

'Sorry.' He put the phone down and grabbed his mobile. 'Hello?'

'I have the information you requested, doctor.' Ingrid sounded
cooler and more collected than earlier in the day. Perhaps Gazi had
reminded her of their priorities.

'Good.'

'Are you close to a land line?'

'Yes. Why?'

'Call the number I'm about to give you on that. It's a land line
also. We need to take precautions.'

'If you say so.'

'I do.'

What worried Hammond during the switch of phones was that
such precautions might actually be necessary. He did not know the
sort of people who were on Ingrid's tail, but he was sure he did not
want them on his.

Ingrid picked up the phone after the first ring. 'Doctor?'

'Yes. What have you got for me?'

'My father says the Accountant's partner was Guido Felltrini.'

'*Guido* Felltrini?'

'Yes.'

'Excellent. He's the man I'm looking for.'

'I have their business address in Milano from 1992. You understand Felltrini could have moved offices since then?'

'Of course.' But probably only to another city-centre location. It should be possible to find this man, it really should. 'Go ahead.'

'Via Ragno seventeen, second floor.'

'Got it.'

'Are you going there?'

'I am.'

'Be careful.'

'Worried about me, Ingrid?'

'Yes, doctor. I am worried you will fail.'

That afternoon, he had promised to take Zineta with him to Milan. Her motive for finding Piravani troubled him. At some point, it could easily conflict with his own. Yet a promise was a promise. He had little that was creditable to show for his involvement with Gazi. Helping Zineta discover what had become of her son might at least make him feel better about himself. He picked up the phone and dialled the mobile number she had given him.

'*Zdravo.*'

'Zineta, this is Edward Hammond.'

'Ah. You actually called. I thought . . . you might not.'

'What made you think that?'

'Being let down too many times.'

'Well, I have an address for Guido. And I reckon our best chance of getting what we want is to speak to him face to face. I'll book us on the first flight from Schiphol to Milan tomorrow morning if you say you're willing to leave at crack of dawn – or before.'

'I'm willing.'

'Will entering Italy be a problem for you, as a Serbian citizen?'

'No. I have a Schengen visa. Since the start of last year, we Serbs have been allowed to leave our box, at least for ninety days. Italy is fine.'

'OK. I'll call you back when I know the time of the flight.'

'Thank you, Edward. This is . . . so good of you. I'm not used . . . to people being kind to me. I am very grateful.'

'Don't mention it.'

He would, in fact, have vastly preferred her not to mention it. He was only too well aware that somewhere down the road he might have to join the swollen ranks of those who had let her down.

After a call to KLM and another to Zineta, Hammond ordered a room-service meal, then stepped out on to his balcony and contemplated the night-blanked horizon in the still, bone-chilling air. There was a raggedness to his nerves and a jangled weariness to his thoughts he could not deny to himself. He had told too many lies for comfort and was taking ever greater risks in pursuit of an unworthy goal. Gazi's money, in the hands of his grasping and undeserving family, would buy restoration of Hammond's peace of mind. So went the theory, at any rate. But would it? Would it really? Last Friday afternoon, the first crack had appeared in the previously solid wall between his world and that of the likes of Zineta Perović. More cracks had appeared since. It was crumbling, piece by piece, faster and faster. And perhaps it could never be rebuilt.

It was still firmly in place the day in March 1996 when agreement was reached that Dragan Gazi's further recuperation could be managed by the Voćnjak Clinic's own staff, freeing Edward Hammond's team to leave Belgrade. Svetozar Miljanović proposed a farewell party, a popular idea considering the hard work and long hours they had put in. It was a staid little gathering at first, but livened up after transferring to a traditional Serbian restaurant and stepped up another gear when Miljanović led them off to a disco housed in the catacombs under Kalemegdan Fortress. Hammond put in no more than a token gyration on the dance floor before taking his leave, reckoning the younger element would feel more relaxed without him. Miljanović followed his example and they parted over a nightcap in the bar back at Hammond's hotel.

'*Živeli,*' said Miljanović, clinking his brandy glass against Hammond's. 'It has been an honour and an education to work with you, Edward.'

'A successful outcome, Svetozar, that's the main thing. We've been lucky there were so few complications.'

'It's true. And the main one actually pleased our man.' Miljanović was referring to the dramatic swelling of Gazi's testicles a few days after the operation. 'He told me it made him feel like a young bull.'

'Well, as long as he doesn't behave like one too soon, hey?'

Miljanović laughed. '*Da.* He should leave that to his doctors.'

'Chance would be a fine thing.'

'The night is full of chances in Belgrade, my friend.'

'Not for me. After this, I'm off to bed.'

The knowingness of Miljanović's smile recurred to Hammond less than an hour later, after he had seen the Serb off in a taxi and gone up to his room. The only other passenger in the lift was a dark-haired young woman in high heels and a figure-hugging black dress. The dress featured a thigh-high split, providing a glimpse of stocking-top, which Hammond gave an appreciative glance but little thought, until he reached his door and suddenly realized she was close behind him.

'Dr Hammond?' she asked in a thick Slavic accent.

'Yes.'

'General Gazi sent me. I am your . . . *poklon.*'

'My what?'

'I am for you.' She undid one of the buttons fastening the front of her dress, revealing the lacy fringe of something black and skimpy beneath. 'For anything you want.' Her skin was pale, almost transparent, her eyes large and spikily lashed, her parted lips glossy. The pleasure she was offering was headily apparent. For several seconds they looked at each other. Then he shook his head.

'I'm sorry,' he said. 'There's been a mistake. I'm not interested.'

As he left the balcony and returned to the warmth of his room in The Hague, Hammond remembered the girl and the weary little shrug of indifference with which she had received his rejection. He had not seen her then as someone with a life and a past and a future of her own. Nor had he wondered how long or hard she might have struggled to avoid becoming a prettily wrapped gift for a man like Gazi to send to a man like him. But that had changed now. He was beginning to see himself as she must have seen him that night. And he did not like what he saw.

TEN

Zineta asked Hammond several times during the journey to Milan how he meant to persuade Felltrini to tell them where Piravani was. His replies were vague, not because he had failed to think the matter through, but because he suspected she would be happier not knowing. He had hardened himself to do whatever he needed to do and had no wish to spell it out. She would realize what it amounted to soon enough.

Zineta's other recurring theme was gratitude. She seemed overwhelmed by his generosity, especially when she discovered that to secure their flight at such short notice he had had to buy business-class tickets. Her delight at being offered champagne by the stewardess was almost childlike and touched Hammond more than he was prepared for.

'This is how you live, Edward?' she gasped.

It was not, of course. But it was how he could live if he chose to. For Zineta, such luxuries had only ever been available as part of a deal in which she herself was a commodity. The difference yawned between then. And he wondered if it would ever be possible to bridge it. She was smiling, slightly drunk from champagne on an empty stomach. But the sadness in her eyes remained, deep and unassuagable.

It took Zineta far longer to pass through immigration at Malpensa than Hammond, but eventually she rejoined him and they headed straight for the shuttle train into the city. They were both travelling light and from the station took a taxi directly to the address Ingrid had supplied.

It was a chill, damp Wednesday in Milan, the city a noisy, congested contrast to the placidity of The Hague. Hammond had paused just long enough at the airport to buy a copy of *La Gazzetta dello Sport*, complete in this case with the classified ads, a quick scan of which had failed to yield the name Piravani amid the predictable sales pitches (as far as Hammond could interpret them) for used cars, flat shares, massage services and lonely hearts.

'Did you think the advertisement would still be running?' Zineta asked as the taxi lurched and surged through the tailgating traffic.

'It was a remote possibility. But actually this is more use as a prop. I want Felltrini to understand we're on to him.'

Making Felltrini understand anything depended first on tracking him down. Via Ragno 17 was an unremarkable mid-rise sixties office block north-east of the city centre. The businesses based there were listed at the entrance. And they did not include a G. Felltrini. The second floor was occupied by an architectural practice. They went up anyway to try their luck.

And their luck was in. Felltrini had moved on years before, according to the anglophone member of staff fielded to speak to them. But the practice used his firm as their accountants, so a current address was no problem.

It was back the way they had come, closer to the historic centre: the top floor of a handsome neoclassical building on the fringes of the fashion district. The air of gleaming affluence imparted by the jewellery store at street level was not quite matched by the decor of Felltrini's offices, but they were elegantly furnished and staffed with smartly dressed juniors, suggesting he had prospered despite Piravani's withdrawal from the business, as did a prominently displayed photograph of a slick-haired, sleek-featured, bespoke-suited

77

businessman, shaking hands with Silvio Berlusconi at some gathering of the great and good.

'Signor Felltrini?' Hammond enquired of the carmine-lipsticked receptionist.

This she managed to confirm, but Felltrini's PA, an older woman with more restrained taste in make-up and greater fluency in English, had to be summoned when Hammond pressed their case for meeting the man.

'It's an urgent and personal matter,' he explained. 'Concerning Signor Felltrini's former partner, Marco Piravani.'

The PA was unmoved by this. Signor Felltrini had left for a luncheon engagement and was fully booked for the afternoon. A meeting was quite impossible. Hammond persisted, asserting her boss would most certainly wish to speak to them. Eventually, she offered to phone him. Hammond settled for this on condition she mention in the call that they had come to see him partly because of a recent advert in *La Gazzetta dello Sport*. She agreed, while clearly implying she considered it all to be a waste of her valuable time.

'I guess now we find out if he really sent Marco that paper,' Zineta whispered to him as they waited.

'I guess we do.'

And they soon did. When the PA returned, she looked ever so slightly chastened. 'Signor Felltrini will see you at two thirty,' she announced, adding, as if to recover some lost ground, 'He is a very busy man. You should not be late.'

There was, though Hammond did not say so, absolutely no danger of that.

They did not stray far, lunching in a nearby café as the time ticked slowly down to their appointment. They were both anxious about the encounter, knowing how much was riding on it, but Zineta suffered from the additional uncertainty of not knowing how Hammond proposed to talk Felltrini into giving them what they wanted.

'Trust me, it can be done,' he assured her.

'How?'

'By betting that Felltrini's loyalty to his friend is outweighed by his concern for his own reputation.'

'What if it isn't?'

'Then we'll move on to the small matter of his personal safety. And that of his family, if he has one.'

'We will threaten him?'

'No. Gazi will do that for us.'

The bustling atmosphere that had greeted them at Felltrini's offices earlier was entirely lacking when they returned. It occurred to Hammond that he had chosen a time when he could be sure most of his staff would be absent, enjoying the traditional long Italian lunch. There was a receptionist on duty, though not the one they had been greeted by earlier. She had been told to send them straight through to Felltrini's personal office.

There was no sign of the PA, whose unattended desk they passed on their way. Felltrini was standing by the window of a spacious room furnished in varnished wood, brushed steel and blood-red leather, smoking a cigarette and gazing out across the cloud-capped rooftops of the city. He did not look quite as smooth as his photographic likeness. There was an apprehensive, slightly bowed look to him. Hammond wondered if he had been expecting something like this to happen. Perhaps he had always understood that friendship with Marco Piravani was not without its hazards, though Hammond doubted if he appreciated just *how* hazardous it might turn out to be.

'*Buon giorno, signore,*' said Felltrini, looking round at them warily as they entered. 'You are English, I'm told.'

'I'm English,' said Hammond.

'Your name?'

'Dr Edward Hammond.'

'A medical man?'

'Yes. But I'm not here on a medical matter.'

'No. Of course not. Your charming friend?' He nodded to Zineta.

'Zineta Perović,' she replied.

He gave a slight but perceptible start of surprise and drew on his cigarette to win himself a fragment of thinking time. It was quite apparent that he recognized the name. 'Where are you from, *signora*?'

'Serbia.'

'*Veramente?* And what can I do for the English doctor and the Serbian . . . ?' He extended his hand in a gesture that suggested contempt as well as uncertainty.

Sensing an attempt to gain the upper hand in their exchanges, Hammond stepped forward and slapped his copy of *La Gazzetta dello Sport* down on the wide and empty desk that dominated the room. 'What was the ad for, Guido?'

'The ad?' Felltrini gave a synthetic frown of incomprehension.

'You sent it to Marco. To warn him, maybe? I don't know. What I do know is that it proves you're in touch with him.'

'My partnership with Marco Piravani ended seventeen years ago, Dr Hammond. I agreed to see you in order only to—'

'Find out how much we have on you. That's why you agreed to see us. And the answer is: enough. What kind of a season are AC Milan having, by the way? They're the team you follow, aren't they?'

'Marco used to phone you after watching their matches,' said Zineta.

'You have come here to discuss football with me?' Felltrini responded, with just a little too much incredulity.

'No,' said Hammond. 'We've come to discuss what we want Marco to do for us.'

'But I am not Marco. And, as I explained, our—'

'You know where he is. You're old friends as well as former partners. We want you to send him a message.'

'I cannot help you.'

'You can. And you will. Unless you want it to become common knowledge that you're a close associate of the man who helped Dragan Gazi salt away his ill-gotten wealth.'

'Gazi? Should I . . . know this person?'

'Most of your clients will have heard of him and will think twice about continuing to use your services if their attention is drawn to your connection with him. A Serbian war criminal and his stolen money isn't a good story for a reputable accountant to be tied into.'

'But I am not . . . tied into it.'

'I'm afraid you are. And it's not just a question of the effect on your business. There's your family to consider.'

'*Prego?*'

'We're the nice guys, you see, the polite may-we-have-a-quiet-word type. There are quite a few other very-far-from-nice guys trying to lay their hands on the money Marco controls. If we can track you down, so can they. Especially if we tell them who you are and where you are. They'll do whatever it takes to get you to lead them to Marco. I wouldn't want to be you, or a member of your family, in those circumstances.'

'Marco must have told you,' said Zineta. 'These people are not just killers. They are butchers.'

The last word, perhaps because it came from a Serb, had a greater effect on Felltrini than anything Hammond had said. He visibly crumpled. 'I have built this firm,' he spluttered, 'from . . . from two rooms and one secretar . . . into . . .' Then the irrelevance of his commercial record impinged upon him. He took a last, shaky draw on his cigarette and crushed it out in an ashtray standing on the windowsill. 'I should not be put in such a . . .' He raised his fisted hands in protest. '*Merda!* I should have ignored the advertisement when I saw it.'

'What did it say?' asked Hammond, softening his tone sympathetically.

'It offered a reward – up to ten thousand euros – for information on Marco. There was no way to tell who placed it. Just a cellphone number. I thought . . . Marco ought to know.'

'That was kind of you,' said Zineta.

'But not clever. No, not clever at all.' Felltrini sighed heavily.

'Where is Marco now?' Hammond tried to make the question sound neutral, as if telling them was the next logical step.

'I do not know. He has left London. But . . . where he is now . . .' Felltrini gave a vast and helpless shrug. 'For him too . . . there is just a cellphone number.'

'Write it down.'

Felltrini moved at a forlorn shuffle to the desk, opened a drawer and pulled out a sheet of headed notepaper. He took an ornate fountain pen from his pocket and wrote out the number. 'He will not answer if he does not recognize the caller,' he said, sliding the sheet towards Hammond. 'And perhaps not even then.'

'But he'll answer if you ring.'

'Of course.'

'That's what I thought. And that's why you'll be ringing him. On our behalf.'

'I will?'

'I want you to explain to him the difficulty of your position: the danger – the extreme danger – he's put you in. I want you to appeal to him, as your friend, to do what he needs to do to secure your safety.'

'And what is that?'

Hammond took a piece of paper from his pocket, on which he had earlier recorded the details of the Cayman Islands bank account along with his own mobile number, and swapped it for the sheet of paper bearing Piravani's number. 'Marco is to transfer all of Gazi's funds to this account by close of business tomorrow.'

'It may take longer than that.'

'Marco himself said it could be done within twenty-four hours.'

Felltrini gave a resigned nod. 'In that case . . . I will tell him.'

'We also want to know the current whereabouts of Monir Gazi. By which I mean a precise address.'

'Who is . . . Monir Gazi?'

'Marco knows who he is,' said Zineta.

Felltrini looked round at her. 'Which are you more interested in, Signora Perović? The money . . . or Monir?'

'It's a package deal, Guido,' said Hammond. 'Just make sure you clinch it. I'll expect to hear from you by the end of the day. Or from Marco. Whichever suits.'

'What does the deal give Marco and me, Dr Hammond?'

'A peaceful life. Once the money reaches that account, it'll be in the possession of Gazi's family and there'll be no point anyone else harassing or threatening you. It'll be . . . out of your hands.'

Felltrini spread his palms. 'It was never in them.'

'Nor in mine. We're only after what I've just offered you, Guido.'

'*La vita pacifica.* Of course. We all want that.' Felltrini picked up the piece of paper. 'Marco is much smarter with numbers than I am. But he lacks what my mother would call *il buon senso.* I suppose that is why I have a good business and a beautiful home and he has only . . . a suitcase.' He smiled. 'He owes me many favours.'

'Time to call one in, then.'

'*Si.*' Felltrini gave a pragmatic little nod. 'It will be done.'

It had gone as well as it could and much better than it might have done. Hammond nevertheless felt more relieved than exhilarated when they left Felltrini's offices. Securing Gazi's money for his family was nothing to be proud of. And pressurizing Piravani through an old friend left a nasty taste in the mouth. But he was hopeful Piravani would throw in the towel after this. He had no way of knowing the threat Hammond had used to intimidate Felltrini was an empty one. The funds would surely soon be transferred.

What they would learn from him about Monir was less clear-cut. It was possible Piravani would be genuinely unable to help them even if he was willing to. And since neither he nor Felltrini had anything to fear once the money had reached Ingrid and her clan, there was ultimately no way of extracting information about the boy.

Hammond assumed Zineta's awareness of this explained her subdued mood. He booked them into a hotel and suggested, absurd though it was to find himself saying it, that they do some sightseeing to pass the time until they received an answer to their message. Zineta agreed with little apparent enthusiasm. A tour of the cathedral followed, during which she seemed lost in thought and largely unaware of her surroundings.

'This isn't working, is it?' Hammond asked as they emerged into the wide grey expanse of the Piazza del Duomo.

'I'm sorry, Edward,' she said, gazing back at the cathedral's majestic west front. 'I can't seem to . . . concentrate on anything except . . .'

'Are you nervous about how Marco will react?'

'Very.'

'Well, let's go and have a coffee. Or maybe something stronger.'

She nodded. 'Maybe.'

They set off through the thickening drizzle towards the cavernous entrance to the Galleria Vittorio Emanuele II. They were barely halfway there when Hammond's phone rang. His first thought was that the wait for Piravani's response was over. But he soon realized the call was a much less welcome one.

'Hello, Bill.'

'Edward. I was expecting you to call me back last night.'

'Gosh, I'm sorry. I've been rushed off my feet.'

'Yes, yes. You're a busy man. I understand that. Though busy with *what* I have no idea and neither, of course, does your PA.'

'I thought I explained. It's something I can't discuss.'

'If that's what you call an explanation, I must beg to differ. But never mind. I simply want to know when you're coming home. I'd like us to meet.'

'I should be back by the weekend.'

'Fine. Some time then?'

'By all means. But, er . . . I can't be definite about a return date just yet. I'll have to get back to you.'

'Of course.' Hammond thought he heard Bill follow that with a sigh.

'I'll speak to you soon, Bill, OK? 'Bye for now.'

Home by the weekend? On the face of it, there was no reason he should not be. Hammond willed himself to believe it.

The Caffè Zucca was crowded with shoppers and tourists taking refuge from the bleak weather. They sat at a table out in the galleria. Hammond ordered two coffees and one large brandy. Zineta lit a cigarette and drew on it anxiously.

'Who was that on the phone?' she asked.

'My late wife's brother.'

'Does he know about the threat to your daughter?'

The threat to Alice. Of course. How the lies multiplied. Like a colony of rats. 'No, he doesn't.'

'You have taken a lot on yourself.'

'I had no choice.'

'Do you really think the threat is serious?'

That, though Zineta did not know it, was a leading question. 'I have to assume it is.'

'Ingrid's probably bluffing, you know.' Their drinks arrived. She took a sip of brandy. He had the impression she was trying to talk down the seriousness of the situation, for both their sakes. 'If she lost the money, my guess is she would see no sense paying someone to go after your daughter.'

'So, you think I'm being conned into helping Gazi?'

'No one should help him if they can avoid it, Edward. He is an evil man.'

'I know.'

'Do you? I didn't understand *how* evil he is until I went to Bosnia. When you hear things . . . from the people they happened to . . . it's different. Very different.'

'You heard things about Gazi?'

'His paramilitaries – the Wolves – had a brutal reputation. They killed thousands. Not just in battle. They killed them . . . wherever they found them. I met a woman in Mostar who was still looking for her three children ten years after they were taken from her by the Wolves. She was looking for their bones, of course. There was no doubt they were all dead. A two-year-old, a three-year-old and a five-year-old. The soldiers kept her alive because she was

85

beautiful. She wasn't beautiful when I met her, though. Someone had carved a word on her forehead with a knife. You could still read the scars. *Vuki*. The Wolves.'

'Good God.'

'The soldiers took her to their camp and raped her many times. She met Gazi there.'

'Did he . . .'

'No. He didn't touch her. Except with his knife.'

'You mean . . .'

'He carved the word on her forehead.'

Hammond looked away. He felt physically sick. Around them, the well-dressed and the well-fed laughed and chatted over coffee and cakes. That such inhumanity as Zineta had described could break out in a country just the other side of the Adriatic seemed unimaginable. Yet it had. Civilization was a thin fabric, easily torn.

'Will she . . . testify against him?' he asked hesitantly.

'I don't think so. She would be too ashamed.'

'What has she to be ashamed of?'

'Much, as she sees it. She was raped because she was a Muslim. And she was marked so that it would never be forgotten. Serbs did that to her. And I am a Serb. I lied to her. I told her I was Slovenian. If she had known I was Serbian . . . she would probably have spat in my face. And I would not have blamed her.'

'You can't be held responsible for what Gazi and his men did, Zineta.'

'No. But Gazi's money should be spent rebuilding the lives of his victims, like that woman in Mostar, not keeping his family in luxury. You and I both know this.' She looked across the table at Hammond, her gaze direct and unforgiving, of him *and* herself.

ELEVEN

The marbled public spaces of the Hotel Manzoni echoed every footfall. There were not many of those, however, midweek finding it quiet to the point of somnolence. But this did nothing to soothe Zineta's nerves, or Hammond's, as they picked at their food and sipped their wine in the hotel's restaurant, where diners were out-numbered by waiters and the loudest noise was the chink of cutlery on china.

'What time is it?' asked Zineta.

'About ten minutes later than when you last asked,' Hammond replied, smiling wryly.

'He should have called by now.'

'Well, I wish he had. But he *will* call. I'm sure of that.'

'Because we frightened him?'

'Yes. I'm afraid so. It comes down to—' He broke off at the sight of one of the reception clerks bearing down on them. 'Hello, what's this?'

'*Mi scusi, signore,*' the young man said. 'There is a gentleman on the telephone who wishes to speak to you, Dr Hammond. He says it is urgent. His name is Piravani.'

So, Piravani had bypassed his friend – perhaps the friendliest thing he could have done. But why had he not used the number Hammond had given Felltrini? And how did he know which hotel they were staying in? 'Where can I take the call?'

'This way, *dottore.*'

The clerk ushered Hammond to a booth off reception. He picked up the phone and the call was transferred.

'Dr Hammond?' It *was* Piravani.

'Yes, Marco, it's me.'

'*Buona sera.*' The greeting was not delivered warmly.

'You've spoken to Guido?'

'Obviously, doctor. He is . . . alarmed. And I am angry that you have threatened my friend.'

'You left me little choice. You didn't turn up to our rendezvous in London. Ryan was no substitute.'

'You had the choice of telling Ingrid to go fuck herself.' He *was* angry. That was clear.

'Exchanging insults won't get us anywhere, Marco. You know what you have to do. Why didn't you call me on my mobile, anyway?'

'Because you've thrown your number around like the new tart in town. Traceability, doctor. You should think about it. If we're to do business, as it seems we must, you will have to start being more careful.'

'How did you know which hotel to call?'

'I didn't. I called seven others before I found you. That's what being careful involves.'

'All right, all right. You've made your point.'

'I hope so. Lose your phone, doctor. Throw it away. Buy another. I change mine like socks. You must do the same.'

'If you really think it's necessary.'

'I do. Now, tell me, how did you find Zineta?'

'We bumped into each other. In The Hague.'

'What was she doing there?'

'What do you think? She's looking for her son, Marco. As any mother would.'

'Some mother. She let Gazi make her his whore.'

'Whereas being his accountant was a laudable and reputable occupation, I suppose.'

'You're the guy who saved his life, doctor. Remember that.'

'I'm not in any danger of forgetting it.'

'But you'd like to.'

'Yes, Marco. I'd like to. I'd like to be able to forget this whole bloody business. But I can't. Until you transfer that money. So, what's it to be?'

There was a heavy pause before Piravani replied. 'I'll do it.'

'You will?'

'Yes, doctor. You win. OK? Like you told Guido, if you can find him, so can others. I can't risk Ingrid hiring someone to beat information out of him that he doesn't actually possess. He's the best friend I've ever had.' He sounded frustrated as well as angry. But those were good signs. They were to be expected of a man who had been backed into a corner.

'The money will be in the account by close of business tomorrow?'

'Yes. I will make sure it is.'

'And Monir? Where is he?'

'That is . . . more complicated.'

'In what way?'

'In the way that such things are.'

'Come on, Marco. Isn't it time to bury the hatchet? Zineta just wants her son back. She's not a bad person.'

'It's usually the bad people who get what they want, doctor, not the other way round. And the complication is that I don't know where the boy is.'

'That's difficult to believe.'

'It's true.'

'But you must know where he was taken. You arranged his disappearance.'

'Not personally. Anyway, that was nine years ago. I . . .' Piravani sighed audibly. 'There is someone who will know where he is now for certain. I will speak to him.'

'When?'

'Tomorrow. It cannot be done sooner.'

'All right. When will we hear from you?'

'When the transfer is done. By then, I may have information on the boy.'

'*May?*'

'Is the best I can do, doctor. Tell Zineta from me: it's more than I owe her.'

Hammond did not pass on Piravani's message to Zineta. If it was true, as quite probably it was, she did not need to be reminded of it. There was the prospect for her to cling to that she would soon learn where Monir was. That was enough. It had to be.

Meanwhile, there was more waiting to be done: that night and in all likelihood most of the following day. In this respect at least Zineta seemed better equipped to cope than Hammond. 'I know about waiting, Edward. I am an expert.'

He could claim little experience of it himself, and less tolerance. In the career he had followed, his demands and expectations took priority over those of his staff. The last five days had been a disagreeable taste of how life felt when other people set the rules. It was not a life he wanted to lead any longer than he had to.

Midnight found him lying on the bed in his room, watching a film on the television he knew well enough to follow the plot, even though it was dubbed in Italian. The soporific effect he hoped for had not so far been forthcoming. When the telephone rang, he thought it was probably Zineta, complaining of sleeplessness herself. It did not occur to him that Piravani would be calling back so soon. If it had, he would have guessed that events had taken an unforeseen turn. And he would have been right.

'I am sorry to disturb you, sir,' said the receptionist. 'You have an urgent call from a Signor Piravani. Will you take it?'

'Put him through.'

A second later, Piravani was on the line. 'I need you to do something for me, doctor.' There was no anger in his voice now. But there was anxiety.

90

'What's wrong?'

'I'm not sure. Maybe nothing. Maybe . . . everything.'

'What's that supposed to mean?'

'It means I can't make contact with Guido. I've called him several times since I last spoke to you, at home and the office. No answer. But when I spoke to him earlier, he was desperate for me to resolve the situation. He insisted I call him to confirm you and I had reached an agreement. He actually said he'd be by the phone. It makes no sense.'

'Have you tried his mobile?'

'Of course. There's no reply.'

'Well . . .'

'I want you to go to his office. That's where he was when we spoke. He said he'd stay there until I called back.'

'But—'

'This affects you as well as me, doctor. We need to know what's happened to him. I'd go myself if I was in Milan. But I'm not. I'm not even in Italy. You're less than a kilometre away. You have to go.'

It occurred to Hammond that Felltrini could simply have grown so exasperated waiting for Piravani to call that he had headed off in search of whatever late-night entertainment his tastes ran to. In that case, going to his office would achieve nothing. 'I'm not sure about this, Marco.'

'But I am, doctor. No funds will be transferred until I know how Guido is. So, phone me when you've checked the office. And use a land line, OK? I'll give you my number.' Piravani reeled off the number and Hammond scribbled it down on the bedside notepad. 'You have that?'

'Yes.'

'I'll expect to hear from you soon.'

Hammond headed straight out into the night. He did not tell Zineta he was leaving, fearing she would insist on accompanying him. As it was, he kept reasoning to himself that Felltrini was on his way home, or drowning his sorrows somewhere. There really was no cause for concern.

The drizzle of earlier in the day had turned to sleet, slicking the pavements with a layer of half-frozen mush. The streets were quiet, eerily so in the vicinity of Felltrini's office. Hammond's confidence that Piravani was making a fuss about nothing ebbed as he neared his destination.

The jewellery store was closed and securely shuttered. There was no light in the foyer leading to the lift and stairs accessing the floors above. But a light was shining, brightly, in the top-floor room where he and Zineta had been received by Felltrini. Could he still be up there? If so, why had he not answered the phone?

Hammond pressed the intercom buzzer marked *Felltrini e Soci*. There was no response, first, second or third time. He walked off along the street, considering his options, such as they were. Then he noticed a cobbled alley leading to a courtyard behind the building. He headed down it, wondering if he would see a car parked there that might belong to Felltrini. And he did. Standing forlornly in one corner of the courtyard was an Audi saloon that pretty much fitted the bill.

He whirled round suddenly, momentarily convinced that someone was watching him. But there was no one there. No one in their right mind would be there, so late on a sleety night. He knew that. He silently cursed Piravani and wondered if setting off the Audi's alarm might bring Felltrini running. What the hell could the man be playing at?

Some eddying of the slack, shifting wind was answered by a creak and a movement in the shadows at the edge of the courtyard. Hammond's heart was in his mouth. Then he realized it was a door, swinging open on its hinges. It clunked back against the jamb as he watched, but something prevented it from closing.

He walked across for a closer look. It was a fireproof door with a locking bar on the inside, the kind that stays open once used. Within, dimly lit by a green lamp above the lintel, was a flight of stairs – the plain concrete treads of a fire escape.

Something was wrong. It was no longer possible to pretend otherwise. Hammond was frightened, both for Felltrini and himself. He looked back at the car and the mouth of the alley. As far as he could tell, he was alone in the courtyard. But how far was that? The walls and doorways around him cast deep enough shadows to conceal more than one invisible observer. Suddenly, the inside of the building felt safer to him than the outside. He stepped in through the door and pulled it firmly shut.

There was nothing for it now but to climb to the top of the fire escape and establish what, if anything, had happened at Felltrini e Soci that evening. He took the stairs two at a time, reckoning hesitation would only erode his resolution.

He reached Felltrini's floor a few minutes later, breathless and sweating from more than just the ascent. A final flight of stairs led on up to the roof, but he opened the door labelled *ULTIMO PIANO* and entered the accountancy's brightly lit reception area. He was to the rear of the now unstaffed front desk, with the glass doors by which he and Zineta had arrived the previous afternoon to his right. Most of the adjoining offices were in darkness, but the route to Felltrini's was not.

'Guido,' Hammond called. 'Are you in there?'

There was no answer. He rounded the reception desk and strode along the short passage that led to Felltrini's office and, before that, his PA's. He turned in through the open doorway. And there he stopped.

The sight was difficult to take in at a glance. But as Hammond stared at what lay before him, its reality revealed a catalogue of horrors. Felltrini was spread-eagled on the floor, one of his eyes gazing sightlessly at the ceiling, while through the other his ornate fountain pen had been driven nib-first. His mouth was enlarged by a massive burn, caused by the bare-wired end of a cable coiled beside him. It had been wrenched out of the back of the nearby photocopier and was still plugged in and switched on. His shirt and trousers were gaping open. Scorch marks were visible on his chest and stomach. Hammond did not doubt that there were more scorch marks elsewhere. When death had finally arrived, courtesy of a bullet through the brain, Felltrini had probably been grateful. There were fragments of brain tissue and skull in the halo of blood around his head. Execution had followed torture. Whatever he had revealed, it had won him no reprieve.

There were no signs of lividity, so he could have been dead only a few hours at most. Hammond had seen many corpses in his career, but none like this one. He felt sick – and very, very frightened. His heart was palpitating, his whole body trembling. Who could have done such ghastly things to another human being? The murderer must have been intent on extracting information from his victim before killing him. The extent of the torture suggested it had not been easy to do so. Or perhaps Felltrini had simply not possessed the information demanded. He had known Hammond's name, though, and Zineta's. He might well have given those up. In fact, he almost certainly had. Fortunately, he had not known where they were staying.

Piravani's whereabouts might be a different matter, though. Hammond took two steps towards the telephone on the PA's desk, thinking to warn him as soon as possible, then stopped. The police would be all over this office come morning. A record of a phone call made in the middle of the night, just a few hours after the murder, was bound to attract their attention. It was wiser by far to call Piravani from the hotel.

Hammond retreated to the doorway and looked down at Felltrini. The sight of the fountain pen protruding from his eye like some weird kind of antenna was somehow more disturbing than all the blood and burns. 'I'm sorry, Guido,' Hammond murmured. 'I never in—'

A sound had caught his ear: a mechanical whirring somewhere within the building. He turned and hurried back to the reception area. The sound was louder here. Looking through the glass doors on to the landing, he saw the cause: the numbers over the lift were illuminating in a remorseless sequence – 1, 2, 3 . . . At 5, whoever was riding the lift would reach the top floor. There was no time to lose.

As he made for the fire escape, Hammond noticed a car key with an Audi symbol on its fob lying on the reception desk. It had to be Felltrini's. Perhaps he had dropped it there earlier, after the failure of his own attempt to leave. Hammond stopped and grabbed it, some instinct telling him that with the car he would be much safer from pursuit than if he simply ran for it.

The manoeuvre cost him a few crucial seconds. He had barely reached the fire-escape door when he heard the lift bell ding. He flung the door open and plunged down the stairs. Two flights took him to the fourth floor, another two to the third, another two again to the second. Then something pinged off the handrail ahead of him. There was a simultaneous explosion of sound, followed by another roar as a bullet whined past him and took a chip out of the edge of one of the treads. But he ran on, hugging the wall, gambling that the gunman could not get a clear shot at him without descending further.

He reached the ground floor and paused for a fraction of a second, just long enough to hear racing footfalls on the stairs above. Then he rushed to the door, thrust down the bar and barged his way out into the courtyard.

As he ran across the sleet-slicked cobbles, he pointed the key at the car and began pressing the remote-control button frantically. The indicator lights flashed and the door locks released when he was about halfway there. He scrambled in behind the wheel, slammed the door, fumbled for what felt like an eternity before finding the ignition, then turned the key and thanked God when the engine burst into well-tuned life. A thrust of the gearstick into drive and he was away, prodding switches in search of the headlamps as he went.

But he was not fast enough. The fire-escape door flew open as he accelerated across the courtyard. A burly, black-clad figure ran out and turned towards him, raising his arm. At that moment, the headlamps came on in response to one of Hammond's random prods. The gunman tried to shield his eyes from the glare with his left hand as he aimed with his right. He fired. A bullet ricocheted off the wing of the car and splintered the windscreen. Hammond ducked instinctively but late, realizing as he did so that the gunman could hardly miss with his next shot, as he drove past him into the alley leading to the street. He wrenched the wheel to the right and pushed his foot down.

The impact was a solid thump, followed a split second later by a heavy jolt as the car hit the wall. He bounced back from the steering-wheel with a sharp pain in his chest and took his foot off the accelerator. The gunman was sprawled face down on the bonnet, trapped by his waist. When Hammond shifted the gear-stick into reverse and eased back, the man slid down into the gap, but the gun stayed where it was.

Hammond was breathing heavily. And each inhalation brought a stab of pain around his right lung, suggesting he had cracked a rib. But if he had paused to fasten his seatbelt, the gunman might have got more than one shot at the car and then . . . He shook his head, trying to corral his thoughts into a rational response. He opened the door and climbed gingerly out. The headlamps were trained on a stuccoed patch of wall. But the light from them spread down into the shadows beneath the bumper and reflected off a dark pool of blood. He moved cautiously round the bonnet for a clearer view.

The gunman was slumped at the foot of the wall, crumpled and motionless, his face concealed by a black balaclava. He was losing blood rapidly. His chances of survival depended on prompt attention from a paramedic, which he was unlikely to get. The shots he had fired could easily have been heard, however. The police would probably be on their way soon. Hammond's instinct as a doctor was to help him as best he could until better-equipped assistance arrived. But the man had tried to kill him. And Hammond could not risk being found on the scene. There was just too much for him to explain.

Nor could he risk being seen in the car that would tie him to its owner's death. He leant back into the car, wincing from the pain that he no longer doubted meant at least one of his ribs was broken, and turned off the engine. Then, clutching his hand to his side to stabilize the fracture, he headed along the alley to the street.

There were shadows everywhere and it required no great effort to imagine a second gunman lurking in any one of them. But if he existed he would surely have come to his accomplice's aid long since. Hammond reasoned his way into believing the coast was clear and started off down the street.

TWELVE

'*Pronto.*'

'It's me, Marco. I have bad news.'

'What's happened, doctor?'

'Guido's dead.'

'*Gesù.*'

'I found him at his office. He'd been shot.'

'Someone shot Guido?'

'Yes. I'm sorry, Marco. Truly I am.'

'I knew it. When he didn't answer the phone, I . . . This is your fault, doctor. Do you realize that? If you hadn't contacted him, he'd still be alive.'

'Maybe. I—'

'Why couldn't you leave him alone? His only crime was being my friend.'

'I *am* sorry, believe me. But I don't see how our visit—'

'Did he know where you're staying?'

'What?'

'*Did Guido know where you're staying?*'

'No. No, he didn't.'

'Then you're safe. For a while, at least. He didn't know where I am either. That was probably what they— Before they shot him, doctor, did they . . . torture him?'

'Yes. I'm afraid they did.'

'*Perdoni mio*, Guido.'

'Listen, Marco, we have to—'

'Think, doctor. That is what we have to do. I will phone you back. Tell reception to transfer my call to you whatever time it comes in. You understand?'

'Yes. But—'

Their conversation had ended there. Now, after emphasizing to the night porter that all calls should be put through whenever they came in, Hammond lay on his bed, gazing at a Modigliani print on the opposite wall and trying to put the nightmarish events of the last couple of hours into a pattern that allowed him to believe his life was not in the process of disintegrating.

The pain of his broken rib had served during his walk back to the hotel as a distraction from the severity of his situation. But he was in no pain as long as he did not move and the reality of what had happened could no longer be suppressed.

He suspected he was still in shock and should therefore distrust his instincts. They veered from returning to London on the first available flight and pretending he had never been in Milan to phoning the Italian police and telling them everything he knew. What Piravani was going to propose he could not imagine. Felltrini's murder and his own responsibility for a second death had transformed his involvement in Dragan Gazi's machinations from a squabble about money into a battle to stay alive.

How that transformation had come about he was not exactly sure. Every step he had taken since his encounter with Ingrid had seemed at the time like the only one he could take in the circumstances. But this was where those steps had led: to Felltrini screaming for mercy and being shown none; to the sound he could clearly remember of hard steel driving flesh and bone into solid stone; to blood, lots of it, pooling darkly in the night.

And he was not finished with blood. Suddenly, to his horror, he saw a crimson tide of it advancing across the floor towards the bed.

He tried to sit up, but something powerful and muffling held him down. He fought against it and broke free.

Then he was awake. And the blood had vanished. And he was alone, bathed in sweat, pain subsiding slowly from his waking jolt. And nothing had changed. Felltrini and the gunman were still dead. And he was still trapped in his hotel room, so badly strung out that the difference between being asleep and awake was beginning to elude him.

He lay back, struggling to still his mind and relax. He needed to think, but to think well he needed to rest. And rest was a long way off.

Then the telephone rang.

'I'm on a land line, doctor. Don't try calling me on the number I gave you earlier. It's discontinued. Whoever killed Guido will have it and I can't risk them locating me. There's no way you can locate me either.'

'I suppose not.'

'I should cut you loose now. With Guido dead, there's nothing you can threaten me with.'

'I'm not threatening you, Marco.'

'Not any more, no. Not since you learnt what sort of people you're messing with. You're a frightened man, with a lot to be frightened of.'

'I can't argue with that.'

'Do you know the only reason I'm talking to you? It's Guido. I went to school with him. I watched my first match at San Siro with him. I started in business with him. He was my best and oldest friend. My only real friend. Now he's dead. And he didn't die easily, did he?'

'No. He didn't.'

'I'm probably even more to blame than you are. I should hav . . . foreseen this.'

'Do you know who might be responsible?'

'I think so, yes. But tell me first exactly what happened.'

'Are you sure you want to know?'

'I'm very sure, doctor.'

And so Hammond told him, in as much detail as he felt either of them could bear, reciting the facts without dwelling on the horror of what he had found and what had occurred.

When he had finished, Piravani's initial response was to murmur some words in Italian. Then he said, 'Todorović is behind this,' as if the conclusion was quite self-evident.

'Who?'

'Branko Todorović. Gazi's general enforcer for his underworld dealings.'

'How can you be sure?'

'Because I know his methods. And I know what he's looking for.'

'The money?'

'No, doctor. He'd like to get his hands on the money, I'm sure. But that's not what he's really after.'

'Which is?'

Piravani did not answer.

'Marco?'

'Yes, doctor. I'm here. I was thinking. About the risks I have to take and the risks I *might* take. I was weighing them in my mind.'

'What does Todorović want?'

'I'll explain when we meet.'

'And when's that to be?'

'Tomorrow. I'm sure the man you killed was acting alone. Otherwise you wouldn't have escaped. He hung around outside after killing Guido because he didn't get any useful information out of him. Poor Guido didn't have the information to give. Well, if Todorović thinks he can—' Piravani checked himself. 'This is what I want you to do. Leave the hotel at six tomorrow morning. Go to Stazione Centrale and buy a ticket to Zürich on the seven ten Cisalpino. Get off at the second stop: Lugano.'

'Lugano, Switzerland?'

'Yes, doctor. Switzerland.'

'Is that where the money is?'

'It's where we'll meet. That's all you need to know. Remember: book through to Zürich, but get off at Lugano.'

'All right. We'll be there.'

'*We?*'

'I can't abandon Zineta, Marco. She might be in danger. Whatever you and—'

'You *must* abandon her. Not for my sake. For yours.'

'What do you mean?'

'How did they find Guido? Ask yourself. Who knew he was still in contact with me? Two people only. You. And Zineta. Someone tipped them off. They would never have got to him so quickly otherwise. So, who was it? You? Or Zineta?'

'You can't be serious.'

'But I am. She has betrayed you, doctor. She mustn't know where you're going. Otherwise, we're both finished. You understand? Finished . . . like Guido.'

Hammond could not fault Piravani's logic, but that did not mean he believed Zineta had tipped off Todorović. There was simply no way he could convince himself of that. Everything he had seen of her, in their admittedly short acquaintance, spoke against it, especially her revulsion at the appalling acts committed by Gazi and his associates. Maybe a member of Felltrini's staff was responsible, though quite how that could be so he struggled to understand. But not Zineta. No, Piravani had to be wrong about her.

He had agreed to behave, however, as if Piravani was right: to leave the hotel without contacting her and travel to Lugano alone. The longer he considered the matter, however, the greater the conflict in his mind between the guilt he would feel for cutting her adrift and the urge to put Piravani's assertion to the test. If she had betrayed him, he wanted to be sure of it. He *needed* to be sure. And then . . .

The phone in her room rang seven or eight times before she answered and the drowsiness in her voice was surely genuine. Could she really have been sleeping after setting Todorović's attack dogs on Felltrini? It hardly seemed possible. 'It's Edward, Zineta. We need to talk. Now.'

'Wha . . . What time is it?'

'Just gone three.'

'What's wrong?'

'I can't explain on the phone. Can I come to your room?'

'OK. Yes. Give me . . . five minutes.'

Hammond gave her just as long as it took him to walk to the lift, go up one floor and locate her room. She answered the door wrapped in an oversized bathrobe with M for Manzoni embroidered on it in gold. She was tousle-haired and still blinking away sleep, but Hammond's own appearance – drawn, dishevelled and clutching his ribs – snapped her into full alertness.

'What's happened to you, Edward?'

'Felltrini's dead. I'm lucky to be alive myself.'

The genuineness of her shock seemed unmistakable. 'When?' she gasped. 'How?'

'Before I tell you, do you have any painkillers?'

'Paracetamol?'

'Would be fine.'

'Are you . . . injured?' she asked as she fetched a foil from her handbag.

'Broken rib.' He prised out a couple of tablets.

'I'll get you some water.'

She went to the bathroom and poured him a glass. He gulped the tablets down, studying the alarm and confusion in her expression in search of some sign of falseness. There was none to be seen.

He eased himself down into the room's only armchair and began his account of the night's events. Zineta sat on the end of the bed, listening to him intently, frowning and open-mouthed. If she had tipped off Todorović, her shock and dismay were part of a superb piece of acting. Hammond felt increasingly certain she was innocent, but knew he had to be cautious. Of his planned rendezvous with Piravani in Lugano – of the whole of their latest conversation, in fact – he said nothing.

'Have you told Marco?' she asked when he had finished.

'Do you think I should?'

'Felltrini was his oldest friend. He has to be told.'

'I agree. But Marco only agreed to our terms in order to protect Felltrini.'

'You think he'll . . . back out now?'

'He might.'

'But . . . he's expecting to hear from you.'

'Yes. So, who do you reckon he'll blame for his friend's death? We're the only people who knew they were still in touch with each other.'

'Us?' Her hand was to her mouth. And her frown had suddenly acquired a dark cast of self-doubt, its meaning as yet impenetrable.

'Who did this, Zineta? That's what I'm asking myself. Serbs?'

She nodded dismally. 'I guess so.'

'Ingrid said I should watch out for a man called Todorović. Does that mean anything to you?'

Very clearly, it did. 'Todorović. No. It can't be. He couldn't have . . .' She shook her head slowly. 'This makes no sense.'

'Could he have been responsible?'

'Yes. But . . .' She raised her hands to her forehead and ran her fingers down tightly over her temples and cheeks. 'How would he have found out?' The question seemed posed more to herself than to Hammond. 'How would . . .' The repetition trailed into silence. Then she looked across at him, the ghastliness of Felltrini's fate eclipsed in her mind by something ghastlier still. 'Edward, I . . . I . . .'

'What is it?'

She closed her eyes for a moment, then said, 'This is my fault.'

'Your fault?'

'Todorović found out about Felltrini . . . through me.'

So, it was true. Zineta was the traitor. But why was she admitting it so readily? Hammond stared at her, still unsure what exactly she *was* admitting. 'You told him?'

'No. Todorović?' She shuddered. 'I would never . . . help such a man.'

Frustration won out over the paracetamol-dulled pain in his side. Hammond pushed himself out of his chair and grabbed Zineta by the shoulders. He would have the truth from her now, without further ado. 'You just said he found out through you. *How?*'

She looked up at him, her eyes full of pleading. 'I am sorry, Edward.'

'*What did you do?*'

'Before I left Serbia, I was . . . approached by an ICEFA agent.'

'Who are ICEFA?'

'The Investigating Commission of Economic and Financial Abuses. They're a government body responsible for tracing billions of dollars of public funds that went missing under the Milošević regime.'

'What did they want with you?'

'The agent offered Foreign Ministry help to locate Monir if I . . . helped them find Gazi's money. I couldn't help them. I told him that. Marco controlled the money. And I had no idea where Marco was. Neither did they. But that changed . . . when I met you.'

'So, you told them we were trying to get to Marco through Felltrini?'

She swallowed hard. 'Yes.'

'Why? Marco was going to lead you to Monir anyway.'

'I never believed he would. He's still bitter about what I did to him. The Foreign Ministry, with all their resources, were a safer bet. I phoned my contact before we left The Hague.'

'A government agent?'

'Yes.'

'So where the hell does Todorović come in?'

'There's so much corruption in Serbia, Edward. Don't you see? My contact must have passed the information on to Todorović. He betrayed me. And . . . poor Signor Felltrini paid the price.'

'What was all that you said in The Hague to me about honesty and truth?'

'They were things I badly wanted to believe.'

'*For God's sake!*' Hammond let go of her and took a stride towards the window. A stubborn prod of pain in his side doubled him up over the armchair, from where he looked back, breathing hard, at her guilty, anguished face. 'How could you be so . . . so stupid?'

She began to cry, a single tear trickling down her left cheek. 'I never . . . suspected . . . anything like this . . . might happen.'

'Well, it has, Zineta. Thanks to you.'

More tears came, flowing freely. 'God forgive me,' she sobbed. 'How will I ever . . . find Monir now?'

He felt sorry for her then, sorrier than ever, despite what she had done. She should have trusted him. But after the life she had led, had it ever been likely she would? He stood slowly upright and ferried a box of tissues from the desk behind the chair to Zineta's lap. 'Don't cry,' he said, pulling the first one out for her. 'I understand why you did it.' He sat down stiffly on the bed beside her. 'I wish to God you hadn't. But . . . I do understand.'

'I am so sorry, Edward.'

'Me too.'

'Shall we go to the police?' She mopped her eyes and turned to look at him. 'If you say we should, I will.'

He shook his head. 'We can't risk it.'

'Then what are we going to do?'

'I don't know.' He sighed. 'We'll think of something.' Then he sighed again. 'We have to.'

THIRTEEN

It was still dark when the 07.10 Cisalpino pulled out of Milano Centrale at the start of its journey to Zürich. Edward Hammond sat in a window-seat in the first-class carriage, hoping he looked the part of a businessman making an early start to a routine day. His reflection in the glass was reassuring on the point. There were no obvious signs of the stress he was under or the paracetamol-dulled pain he was in.

It was Thursday morning. Last Thursday morning at this time, he had been towelling down after a swim before setting off for St George's and a crowded but undemanding schedule of consultations and case conferences. The recollection felt absurdly and impossibly distant, like the memory of another life accessed under hypnosis – an easier, safer, surer life than the one he was now leading.

Further back in the train, Zineta would be blending in as best she could with other travellers to Switzerland, fearfully wondering, no doubt, whether Hammond was equal to the task he had set them. He was to leave the train at Lugano to meet Piravani as agreed, but she was to stay on until the next stop, Bellinzona, and return to Lugano an hour later. In the intervening period, Hammond was to persuade Piravani that they could trust her despite her indirect responsibility for Felltrini's death. And if it was hard to predict what they would do next if he succeeded, it was impossible to imagine the consequences of failure.

107

'Whatever happens, I'll meet you at the station in Lugano,' he had said. 'If I'm not there when you arrive, just wait.' There was nothing else she could do in that event, of course. They could no longer safely use their phones and there had been no opportunity to buy replacements. She was utterly reliant on him. Circumstances had forced trust upon them.

Dawn had broken by the time the train reached Como. The rain of Milan had turned to snow and the whiteness of the world beyond the window merged in Hammond's mind with the blankness of his immediate future. If Zineta was relying on him, then he was relying on Piravani: to be reasonable, to be rational, to be persuadable. But whether he would be any of those things in the wake of his best friend's death was seriously doubtful.

Lugano. The snow was heavier, falling steadily from a low, grey sky. The surrounding peaks were barely discernible, the roofs of the city thickly carpeted. Hammond stood on the platform as the other disembarking passengers left. He looked around in search of Piravani, but there was no sign of him. The train pulled out, with Zineta on board. And still Piravani did not show.

Hammond headed for the exit. He passed the queue for the funicular down into the city centre and emerged at the front of the station. Traffic ground past through the slush. On the other side of the road, taxis waited in an exhaust-clouded line. The few pedestrians to be seen did not include Piravani. 'Where are you, Marco?' Hammond muttered to himself. 'For God's sake, where are you?'

As if in answer, the front window of one of the taxis slid open and the driver's hand emerged, clutching a square of cardboard with DOTT. HAMMOD written on it in prominent felt-tipped capitals.

Hammond hurried across the road, wincing as every minor slip told on his broken rib. Shielding himself from the snow with his day-old copy of *La Gazzetta dello Sport*, he peered in at the swarthy, smiling man holding the card. 'My name's Hammond. Are you looking for me?'

'*Dottore Hammod?*'

'Hammond.'

'*Si, si.* Hammond. I am . . . to take you.'

'Take me where?'

'*Incontrare Marco. Si, si? Andiamo. Andiamo subito.*'

There seemed no point arguing. Hammond climbed into the back and they sped away, studded tyres gripping the road cleanly as they followed a zigzag route down into the city. The driver, whose younger, skinnier likeness dangled in front of him on a laminated licence card, spied the snow-blushed pink of *La Gazzetta dello Sport* and launched into what sounded like a critical assessment of last night's televised football. Hammond was required to do no more than grin and nod as the head-tosses and steering-wheel slaps proceeded.

The rush hour was in progress in Lugano and the going was slow. Hammond had no idea how long the journey to wherever Piravani was waiting would take. He supposed he should have guessed Marco would judge meeting him at the station too risky. He was a cautious man, with a lot to be cautious about.

Lake Lugano, flat, grey and cold, stretched suddenly ahead of them as the driver took a right off the main road heading east out of the city. The football-themed monologue cut off as he pulled in and pointed to a gateway leading into a lakeside park. 'Parco Ciani,' he announced. 'Where I bring you . . . for Marco. *Arrivederci, dottore.*'

The park was no doubt a pleasant spot for children, mothers, dogs and venerable citizens at most times of the year, with trees reaching to the shoreline and flower borders brightening the scene, the mountains that now loomed vaguely through the murk prettily reflected in calm blue water, with ducks dabbling and songbirds twittering.

All was very different this chill, snow-blanked morning. Hammond made his way gingerly along the main path towards the office- and apartment-blocks of downtown Lugano that loomed ahead of him further round the bay. He was tired and cold, his stomach growling from lack of breakfast. The bag he was carrying and the smooth soles of his shoes prevented him from walking fast enough to warm himself up. He felt foolish as well as desperate. He should have found a way out of this long before now, he reflected bitterly, he really should.

The park appeared to be deserted, though it would have been easy enough for Piravani to hide behind one of the numerous large trees or bushes. Not knowing whether he was meant to wait for him to show himself or not, Hammond moved on at a slow but steady pace. It was as he passed a summerhouse-styled public toilet at a confluence of several paths that he was suddenly aware of a figure falling in beside him.

'You don't look well, doctor,' said Piravani. He was dressed for the weather, in stout shoes, thick trousers, parka and woolly hat, with an umbrella to shelter him from the snow. 'You're walking like an old man.'

'I broke a rib last night.'

'You should be more careful.'

'So you keep saying.'

'Got rid of your phone yet?'

'No. But I haven't used it.'

'Give it to me.'

'Is that really necessary?'

'Oh yes. It is necessary.'

Hammond wrestled the phone out of his pocket and handed it over. They walked on in silence. As the path drew closer to the edge of the lake, Piravani stopped and hurled the phone far out into the water. 'I'll buy you a new one later,' he said, smiling grimly.

'I am sorry about Guido, Marco,' said Hammond, aware how lame the sentiment must sound. 'Truly.'

'I believe you.'

110

'I had no idea—'

'You have an idea now, though, yes? The same one Guido probably had when he realized he was going to die.'

'Why did you agree to meet me?'

'I didn't. Your memory's failing, doctor. *You* agreed to meet *me*.'

'If you say so.'

'You really don't look well.'

'Neither would you if you'd had the kind of night I had.'

'But you look better than Guido, right?'

'Yes.' Hammond nodded dismally. 'Right.'

'I guess we should find you a coffee somewhere warm. Got any Swiss francs on you?'

'No.'

'I'll pay, then. On the way there, I'll tell you about Todorović.'

The walk from the park along the promenade into the old city was not a long one, though it seemed so to Hammond, especially when he had to negotiate the snow-caked steps of an underpass below the lakeside highway. He had neither the energy nor the inclination to interrupt Piravani's potted biography of Branko Todorović, small-time crook turned big-time villain.

According to Piravani, Todorović was just the sort of closet sadist and aspiring racketeer who would have stayed safely locked in the Pandora's Box that was Tito's Yugoslavia if only Milošević and his kind had not insisted on opening it. Todorović was cleverer, crueller and, crucially, more realistic than most. He was content to work for others and thrive on the commission they paid him. He began as little more than an errand-boy for Gazi, but had become, by the time Piravani arrived on the scene, a vital middleman between Gazi and criminal elements at home and abroad. He was also an enthusiastic dispenser of rough justice to those who talked too much or failed to pay their debts. He managed Gazi's smuggling operations while the boss was busy butchering Muslims in Bosnia or Kosovo. Since Gazi's disappearance, however, he had moved into semi-respectable business on his own account, his name

111

linked with office and hotel developments in the new, disinfected, post-Milošević Serbia. He had survived and he had adapted. But he was still at heart the same merciless and murderous Branko Todorović, as Felltrini's fate amply demonstrated.

The obvious question, which Hammond did not actually pose, was how Piravani could be sure Todorović was responsible for Felltrini's death. The answer was delayed until they had reached a large Viennese-style café near the foot of the funicular station and ordered breakfast.

'Todorović used to have a nickname, doctor. They called him "Torto", short for *Tortura*: torturer. You see? It always was his . . . speciality. His and the people he used when he rose above doing it himself. I follow Serbian news on the *Politika* website. It's the main national paper. That's how I know about his business ventures. A shopping mall in New Belgrade; a ski-chalet complex in Kopaonik; a boutique hotel just round the corner from Belgrade cathedral: the guy's trying to buy himself some class. Gazi's arrest must have scared the shit out of him. What would the old man say? More importantly, what could he prove? Todorović was never directly involved in the Wolves' military activities, but he ran their armaments supply chain and there are dozens of murders he could be tried for if there was the evidence to tie him to them. Which there is. As he knows.

'Gazi turned a little paranoid after Dayton. Well, it was a paranoid time, so I guess it made sense. Anyhow, he started recording selected meetings and telephone calls at the villa in Dedinje. Insurance, he called it, against betrayal. "If anyone takes me down," he said, "they go down with me." There was a lot of dirty stuff on those tapes. Pay-offs for politicians. Gangland hits. Drug deals. Arms shipments. Everything he was into. Todorović was a frequent visitor, to report on jobs he'd done for Gazi, to take instructions. The tapes would destroy him if they got out. In Belgrade *or* The Hague. He must have been afraid they'd be found with Gazi. But Gazi didn't have them. They were too hot for him to hold on to. They damned him as well as the other people on them. That's why Todorović is looking for me, doctor. He thinks I have them.'

'But you don't?'

'No. When Gazi went into hiding, he left the tapes at the villa. They were too dangerous to carry and too valuable to destroy. So, he put them in a wall safe, bricked and plastered over so you'd never find it unless you demolished the whole building . . . or you knew where to look.'

'Which you do?'

'Of course. I actually helped him brick the safe in. He trusted me, you see. Because I wasn't Serbian. Because I wasn't one of them. And also because the tapes incriminate me as well. But that doesn't matter. The Serbs are welcome to lock me up if they ever catch me as long as Todorović gets what he deserves. Guido was my friend. It is a bond that cannot be broken. Todorović is responsible for his death. I'm going to make him pay for that. I'm going to make sure he spends the rest of his life in prison. And you're going to help me do it.'

'*Me?*'

'Yes, doctor. You. There are too many people in Belgrade, Todorović included, who would recognize me. I need someone they *wouldn't* recognize to check out the villa so we can decide what we need to do to retrieve the tapes.'

A croissant and a cup of strong coffee had begun to revitalize Hammond. The realization had just dawned on him that Piravani wanted to recruit him for a particularly hazardous burglary. 'That's crazy. How the hell do you propose to get inside, knock down half a wall and make off with the safe without anyone noticing?'

Piravani scowled. 'I don't know,' he said levelly. 'I'll work it out when we get there.'

'You keep saying *we*. What makes you think I'm going to let you drag me into this?'

'Two reasons, doctor. One, Guido would still be alive if you hadn't led Zineta to him. This is your chance to make up for that. Two, with Guido dead, you can't force me to transfer Gazi's money to Ingrid's account in the Cayman Islands. But I'll do it, *if* you help me nail Todorović.'

'Which probably involves getting myself arrested by the Serbian police for breaking and entering.'

Piravani shrugged. 'There'll be risks, naturally.'

'Too many risks.'

'Not for someone Gazi's threatening to accuse of complicity in his own wife's murder. Think, the tapes might actually exonerate you. I don't know. But it's possible. Anyhow, I'm going too fast. This is the deal. The money's here, in Lugano. In one of the banks the locals run so discreetly and efficiently. I used to own a small apartment in Campione d'Italia, on the other side of the lake. As an Italian citizen, I was free to travel there from Belgrade during the sanctions period. That was crucial to managing Gazi's finances. It meant we could get his money out of Serbia and keep it safe here in Switzerland. It's still waiting for him. Or for Ingrid. A simple signature or telephone call from me and the whole lot flies across the Atlantic to Grand Cayman. That's what you want, isn't it? That's *all* you want. Well, you can have it. *If* you help me.'

'Look, Marco, why don't you—'

'I'll make it easy for you, doctor. If the new owner of the villa's turned it into a fortress and there's obviously no way of getting to the tapes, I'll give the idea up.' Hammond did not believe that for a moment. Piravani would not abandon his quest for vengeance whatever obstacles were in his path. 'You risk nothing by going to Belgrade. You can pull out at any stage.'

That much was true. And there was no other way to persuade Piravani to transfer the money. Certainty on the point camped itself glumly at the centre of Hammond's thoughts. Maybe the trip to Belgrade would be the last hoop he had to jump through. *Maybe.* 'Someone may already have found the safe and emptied it, Marco. Has that occurred to you?'

'I doubt it. No one else knows it's there. If Todorović had got hold of the contents, he wouldn't be looking for me. If someone else had, quite a few people, including Todorović, would be in prison. No. It's still there. I'm sure of it. So, are you going to help me or not?'

The question could no longer be dodged. And there was, as Piravani must have foreseen, only one answer Hammond could give. 'All right. I'll go to Belgrade with you.'

'Excellent.' Piravani extended his hand across the table. It was a formality that took Hammond aback. But there was a solemnity to the gesture that was somehow more worrying. And it reminded him that he had still not mentioned Zineta. He shook Piravani's hand cautiously.

'I'll expect you to honour our earlier bargain, Marco. The whereabouts of Monir Gazi as well as the transfer of his father's money.'

Piravani frowned. 'Why should you care about the boy?'

'Because Zineta didn't betray us. At least, not in the way you think.'

'What do you mean?'

Hammond explained as best he could. Whether Piravani was convinced or not was impossible to tell. He listened in sullen silence.

'I told you to leave Milan without speaking to her,' he growled when Hammond had finished. 'You've put us both in danger. What were you thinking of?'

'We can trust her now, Marco. She's learnt her lesson.'

'No, doctor. I trusted her once. Never again.'

'She's waiting for me at the station. I promised to go back for her.'

'You brought her to Lugano?'

'I'm not going to abandon her.'

'Why not? Fancy her, do you?' Piravani's face was flushed with anger. 'Or has it already gone beyond that? It wouldn't surprise me.'

'She just wants her son, Marco. That's all.'

'You're suddenly the expert on what she wants, are you?'

'No. But I gave her my word I'd stand by her.' So he had. And,

115

to his surprise, the fact was all-important to him. He did not like the things he was being forced to do to protect his good name. There had to be some line he would not cross. And this was it. 'You know she never wanted to become Gazi's mistress, Marco. You're blaming her for what he did to you.'

'I thought your specialism was hepatology, not psychiatry.'

'It's unworthy of you to go on punishing her like this.'

'*Unworthy?*'

'You've both suffered enough. Why prolong it? Tell her where her son is. Or tell me. You don't even have to speak to her if you don't want to.'

Piravani stared long and hard at him, the edges of his mouth twitching faintly beneath his moustache. Then he whipped his glasses off and pressed two fingers against the bridge of his nose. His biggest problem, Hammond now grasped, was that he no longer believed what he badly wanted to: that Zineta had deliberately betrayed them. 'Why did you have to be such a good surgeon? If Gazi had died on the operating table . . . all our lives would have been so much . . . happier.'

The same thought had occurred to Hammond many times of late. He shrugged helplessly. 'Sorry.'

'I need some air. Finish your breakfast and pay the bill with this.' Piravani tossed a fifty-franc note on to the table. 'Meet me in the piazza we crossed on the way here in ten minutes.'

'Why? What's going to change in ten minutes?'

'Maybe my mind.' Piravani shrugged. 'Or maybe not.'

The Piazza della Riforma stood open to the palm-flanked highway and beyond it the lake, across which the snow drifted like a curtain draped from the low, yellow-grey sky. Piravani was waiting for Hammond in the shelter of the porticoed entrance to one of the city's numerous banks, smoking a cigarette and gazing out grimly at the swirling flakes.

'You want a drink?' he asked, proffering his hip-flask.

Hammond realized that, yes, he very much did want a drink. He took a swig. The liquor was smooth and warming.

'*Prepečinica*,' said Piravani. 'Double distilled.' He retrieved the flask and took a swig himself. 'Best thing to come out of Serbia.'

'Is this the bank?' Hammond nodded to the thick smoked-glass doors behind them.

Piravani smiled. 'No. Gazi's money isn't in there. But it's not far away.'

'Neither is Zineta.'

'Thank you for reminding me, doctor. Unnecessary, but . . . kind of you.'

'What are you going to do?'

'Confess, as every good Catholic should.' He drew on his cigarette. 'I don't know where Monir is. And I have no way of finding out for sure.'

'But you said—'

'There was a man who could tell me. I know what I said. I reasoned you'd settle for the money if I could string you along about the boy for a while. It wasn't me who arranged his disappearance. Gazi must have been afraid Zineta might be able to charm the truth out of me, so he didn't trust me with that job.'

'You must have had some idea what was going on.'

'Of course. But not the particulars. Gazi said he had something arranged and I needn't concern myself with it.'

'So . . .'

'There's nothing I could tell Zineta even if I wanted to. Exactly.'

'She's pinning all her hopes on you, Marco.'

'Then she's making a big mistake. Not for the first time.'

'What am I going to say to her?'

'I suggest you say I've insisted you accompany me to Belgrade, for reasons I've refused to give. In return, I've agreed to transfer the money and tell you all I know about Monir, but only after we've been to Belgrade.'

'You just admitted you don't know *anything* about him.'

'True. But the answer may well be on those tapes, doctor.'

Piravani gave Hammond a disarming half-smile. 'You see? You really will be doing your best for her.'

'In the unlikely event that we succeed in spiriting the tapes out of the villa.'

'As you say.' Piravani took a long, final draw on his cigarette and ground the butt into the Swissly sleek stubber mounted on the pillar beside him. 'Zineta can't come with us, doctor. Send her back to The Hague. Tell her to wait for you there. She can listen to the tapes before I deliver them to the War Crimes Tribunal. Most of the conversations will be in Serbian anyway, so they'll make more sense to her than to me. If they lead her to Monir, well . . .' He shrugged. 'I won't stand between a mother and her son. You're right. It would be . . . unworthy. And Guido wouldn't want me to be that.'

FOURTEEN

The snow had eased by the time the 10.55 to Basel was announced at Lugano station, but the temperature was, if anything, lower. Passengers began emerging with their bags from the fuggy interior of the waiting room, shivering and grimacing in the chill. Hammond was already on the platform with Zineta. But only one of them was planning to board the train.

It had been easier than Hammond had expected to persuade Zineta to return to The Hague. Felltrini's death, and her share of the blame for bringing it about, had left her half-disabled by guilt, which Piravani's refusal to meet her had only compounded. Hammond knew he was exploiting her emotional fragility, but he told himself it would be in her best interests in the end. Self-serving though Piravani's argument was that Gazi's tapes might reveal where he had sent his son, it was undeniably plausible. Zineta did not know about the tapes yet, of course. If they turned out to be completely inaccessible, she never would. For the moment, all she knew was that the price of Piravani's cooperation was Hammond's presence in Belgrade – and her absence.

'It's hard to believe he's just a few minutes away,' she said, turning to gaze down at the rooftops of the old town. She shook her head sadly. 'So near, yet so very, very far.'

'Maybe you'll see him soon in happier circumstances,' said Hammond, silently doubting it.

'He's going after Todorović, isn't he?' She looked at him, her eyes full of concern. 'You know that, don't you, Edward?'

Hammond shrugged. 'I certainly can't think of any other reason why he wants to go back to Belgrade.'

'You should be careful. The war's been over ten years. But it's still a dangerous city if you ask the wrong questions in the wrong places.'

'Oh, I'll be careful all right. You can be sure of that.'

'You really have no idea why he wants you to go with him?'

'He's afraid he might be recognized. I'll be able to move around more freely than he will.'

'But to move around doing what?'

The rumble of the arriving train gave Hammond the excuse he needed to dodge the question. 'Don't worry about me, Zineta. I can handle the situation.'

'But I have no way of contacting you.'

'*I'll* contact *you*.' She had supplied him with the number of the office-cleaning agency she worked for in The Hague, where she would leave her new mobile number as soon as she had one. 'If all else fails, call my PA. But only if all else really does fail.' She nodded her understanding.

The train came to a halt. Most of the other passengers were bunched near the waiting room. No one else was boarding at the door Zineta headed for. She pressed the button and it cranked slowly open. 'What time will you reach The Hague?' he asked as she stepped into the carriage.

'About eleven o'clock tonight,' she replied through a brittle smile. 'Later, maybe, in this weather. You'll be in Belgrade by then.'

'I hope it's not too grim a journey for you.'

'As a Serb, I'm used to grim journeys. Oh, I have something for you.' She pressed a folded piece of paper into his hand. 'My brother Goran's address and phone number. If you run into any trouble, he might be able to help you. I'll call him tomorrow and ask him to do anything he can if he hears from you.'

'I don't expect he will. But thanks.'

'He's always been a good brother to me.'

Boarding was complete. A whistle blew. Zineta leant forward and kissed Hammond on the cheek. 'Take care,' she said softly.

'You too.'

A bleeping heralded the closing of the doors. Hammond stepped back as they clunked shut and exchanged a wave with Zineta through the glass. Then the train started moving.

He took the next funicular down into the town and went straight to the café where he had breakfasted earlier. Piravani was waiting for him, frowningly perusing Hammond's day-old copy of *La Gazzetta dello Sport*.

'She's gone?' the Italian growled.

'Yes. She's gone.'

'Good.' Piravani tossed down the paper and sighed heavily. 'Guido was even crazier about football than I am, you know. Just think. If he hadn't regularly bought this pink rag, he wouldn't have seen that advertisement. Then you'd probably never have tracked him down. And then . . .'

'He'd still be alive.'

'Yes.' Piravani nodded thoughtfully. 'Still alive.'

'We can't turn back the clock, Marco. I'd like to, every bit as much as you would. But we're stuck with the present.'

'Present? Yes, doctor, you're right. Actually, that's what I have for you. A present.' He took a brand-new mobile phone out of his pocket and handed it to Hammond. 'I put a hundred francs on it for you.'

'Thanks.'

'Now, I was planning to fly from the local airport, but the snow's caused a lot of delays, so we'll take the train to Zürich instead. We've plenty of time. The Zagreb flight's not until six o'clock.'

'Zagreb? I thought we were going to Belgrade.'

'We are. But I don't want any record of our arrival in Serbia, so we'll take the overnight train to Belgrade from Zagreb. That means there'll be no computer logging of our names and passport numbers.'

'Tomorrow's Friday.'

'So?'

'Ingrid's expecting to have the money by the end of the day.'

'No chance. You'll have to stall her.' Piravani smiled faintly. 'I'm sure you'll think of something to tell her, doctor. Just don't mention where you're going. Or that you and I are working together. The less she knows – the less anyone knows – the better it'll be for us.'

A woman he did not know answered the land-line number Ingrid had given him. He had established by now that it was in Madrid. But that was all he had established. The woman spoke just enough English to assure him Ingrid would call back. By the time she did, he and Piravani were standing on the platform at Lugano station, awaiting the next train to Zürich. Piravani paced up and down near by, puffing at a cigarette, throughout the conversation that ensued.

'You have changed phones, doctor,' said Ingrid, sounding almost impressed. 'You are learning, I see.'

'Oh yes. I'm learning a lot.'

'Where are you now?'

'Switzerland.'

'That sounds promising.'

'It is. But, even so, I'm not going to be able to get you what you want by tomorrow.'

'You must.'

'It's going to take until Monday at least.'

'My terms were clear. By close of business Friday.'

'Listen to me, Ingrid. It can be done and I'm going to do it. But your deadline's unrealistic. I can't explain why to you now. You wouldn't want me to. I simply need more time. Not a lot. Just a few days. I'm sure your father will be willing to wait that much longer.'

'Maybe. Maybe not. You are taking a big risk, doctor.'

'Nothing I can do about it, I'm afraid. Are we agreed?'

There was no reply. In the background, Hammond could hear someone gabbling in Spanish: quite possibly the woman he had spoken to earlier. Then Ingrid said snappishly, '*Silencio!*' and the gabbling stopped.

'Ingrid?'

'Nothing is agreed. I will think about what you have said. That is all.'

'You got your extra time?' Piravani asked as Hammond slipped the phone back into his pocket.

'She said she'd think about it.'

'Then you got it.' Piravani smiled. 'And with luck you won't need to go to a penalty shoot-out.'

The next call Hammond had to make was in its own way equally critical. He needed to assure Alice there was no reason to worry about him without actually telling her where he was going or why. As usual, her phone went straight to voicemail. He fondly supposed she might be in a lecture or seminar. The message he left was well-rehearsed, his words carefully chosen, his tone deliberately light.

'Hello, darling. How are you? Just to let you know, I've had to fly to Zürich to deal with an emergency. I'll be away until after the weekend. To complicate matters, I've lost my phone, hence the change of number. If you hear from Uncle Bill, tell him I'll be in touch as soon as I've stopped chasing my tail. Keep safe. Lots of love. 'Bye for now.'

Fortunately, like all well-adjusted twenty-year-olds, Alice had absolutely no interest in what her father was doing. She texted back casually at some point in the afternoon: '*Ok, dad. No probs. Time u got rid of old fone anyway. More features on new ones. A xx.*' She made no mention of Bill and she sounded monumentally unconcerned. That was exactly how he wanted her to be. And how he wanted her to remain.

Normality still ruled in Alice's world, though Hammond could easily remember a time when that had seemed inconceivable. The

123

weeks after Kate's murder had been an ordeal for him, but for Alice they had been the purest torture, her childhood paralysed by grief and disbelief and incomprehension. It was bad enough that her mother was dead, worse still that some strange man, for reasons nobody could even guess at, had killed her one fine day in a super-market car park.

Hammond had consoled himself that at least Alice had not witnessed the murder, as she might have done had Kate been running late and decided to go shopping after collecting her from school rather than before. Of course, that would have altered the time of Kate's arrival, so the apparently motiveless gunman would presumably already have killed some other shopper. Hammond's reasoning made no sense, unless the gunman was not motiveless, a possibility he had never quite been able to put out of his mind.

Perhaps he went too far in his efforts to shelter Alice from the reality of what had happened to her mother, although at the time it seemed to him impossible to go far enough. Her uncle Bill took a more robust view and did something Hammond would have recoiled from. He took Alice out one day during her half-term holiday, six weeks or so after the murder. On the way back from a visit to Chessington Zoo, they stopped off at the Colliers Wood superstore. 'Because,' he explained to Hammond later, 'she asked me to.'

She had never asked her father to take her there. Perhaps she had feared he would refuse, or, ironically, had worried how he would cope with going. Uncle Bill was to her the safer option. She wanted to see where her mother had died. It was as simple as that. Six weeks after the event, of course, nothing distinguished that one bay-marked stretch of car park from any other, except in her mind. But she wanted to stand on the spot and look around her. She wanted to be able to remember it.

Hammond did not discuss the experience with her until Bill had left. Alice seemed anxious to put his mind at rest at once. 'Don't worry, Daddy,' she said, cuddling up to him. 'There's nothing there to be frightened of.'

124

Her words reassured him, as they were meant to. They were a sign that she was strong enough to survive. And Hammond had believed her. There was nothing to be frightened of.

But there was. He knew that now.

Ingrid's deadline was not the only thing due to expire on Friday. Hammond's leave, which he had looked forward to spending with Peter and Julie on the Austrian ski slopes, would also come to an end. But there was no realistic prospect of him returning to St George's, ready to tackle his normal caseload, on Monday morning. From the departure lounge at Zürich airport, he phoned his PA and told her to ask – beg, if necessary – Roy Williamson to cover for him the following week. Numerous consultations would have to be rescheduled, even so. A lot of people were going to be inconvenienced. 'Apologize to one and all for me, will you, Fiona? An emergency's cropped up in my private life I have to deal with.' Well, that was true enough. An emergency it certainly was.

'When I left Belgrade nine years ago, I thought I would never return,' Piravani declared as the plane to Zagreb reached cruising altitude. 'But I guarantee this will be my last visit.'

'When was your first?' asked Hammond.

'May 1992. I'd handled the accounts for an air freight company Gazi had a stake in. He'd been impressed by some of the . . . tax efficiencies . . . I'd introduced. The UN was all set to impose sanctions on Serbia and the war in Bosnia had just begun. Gazi saw sanctions as a problem *and* an opportunity. There was big money to be made from sanctions-busting, but he had to export the cash in US dollars and Swiss francs to protect it from his enemies and the hyperinflation of the Serbian currency. That's where I came in.'

'Why did you take the job?'

'Because I wasn't cut out to be a by-the-book accountant. I wanted to be rich and I knew that's what Gazi would make me. It was actually fun at first. The first year or so was really exciting. The financial tricks. The fringe benefits. The whole buzz of it. It was only when I began to find out what Gazi's business really amounted to and what his paramilitaries were doing in Bosnia that I realized I'd sold my services to a gangster and a murderer. And by then . . .'

'It was too late to pull out.'

'I knew too much for him to let me go, doctor. I could be rich. But I couldn't be free. Until Gazi was dragged down with the rest of Milošević's cronies, anyway. And even then . . .'

'The memory of all those fees you'd paid on his behalf to politicians and smugglers and hit men wouldn't go away.'

'No.' Piravani sighed. 'It wouldn't.'

'And one of the fees you paid was mine.'

'It was, yes.'

'I thought it was easy money at the time.'

'There's no such thing, doctor.' Piravani shook his head, incredulous, it seemed, at the folly of what he had done in the pursuit of wealth. 'I learnt that lesson from Gazi. And now you're learning it too.'

FIFTEEN

Hammond would have been hard-pressed to imagine a more dispiriting arrival at any destination than his and Piravani's in Belgrade in the frozen darkness of Friday morning. Back in 1996, he and his team had been met at the airport by a pair of chauffeur-driven limousines and whisked off to the city's smartest and newest hotel, where Miljanović and the director of the Voćnjak Clinic had been waiting to greet them. Thirteen years later, everything was very different, notably Hammond's state of mind, not to mention the state of his body. Piravani had failed to secure sleeper berths for them on the train from Zagreb and the ride had been anything but smooth. Six hours in a poorly sprung seat had proved more than a match for a maximum dose of paracetamol, ensuring Hammond had been jolted painfully awake every time he had succeeded in dozing off.

They emerged from the chill cavern of the railway station into a pre-dawn gloom through which sharp needles of icy sleet were slashing. The road that ran past the station was already busy with traffic: vans, buses and cars rumbling past in an eye-stinging miasma of exhaust fumes. 'How could we have stayed away so long, hey?' quipped Piravani.

He led Hammond past a hopeful swarm of taxis to the bus station next door and into a dismal café. Most of the customers looked as if they had spent the night there, or on one of the

127

benches outside. Piravani left Hammond at a table and went up to the counter to buy coffee and bread rolls, a process which involved a lengthy debate about something with the sullen man behind it.

'Congratulations, doctor,' said Piravani when he rejoined Hammond. 'You look so bad you almost blend in.'

'There's nothing wrong with me that a bath, a shave, a hearty breakfast and a good hotel wouldn't put right.'

'Sorry. No can do any of those. I'll have to fix us private accommodation to avoid our passports being registered with the police. The standard might not be what you're used to. Drink some coffee. That should help. Do you want a cigarette? At least the Serbs don't bother where you smoke.'

'I'll pass, thanks.' Hammond took a sip of coffee as Piravani lit up. It did help – slightly. 'What was the commotion up at the counter?'

'My Serbian currency's still got Yugoslavia printed on it. Our friend wasn't keen on taking it. I'll get some up-to-date notes when the exchange office opens.'

'What then?'

'I find us somewhere to stay and something to get around in. While you take a look at the Villa Ruža. Here . . .' Piravani whipped out a street map of Belgrade and opened it up. 'This is where we are now.' He tapped with his finger at the bus and train symbols located at the city-centre end of one of the bridges across the Sava, where the river began to curve west towards its junction with the Danube. Then his finger slid south to the neighbourhood of Dedinje. 'See the x? That's the villa.' At some point, he had marked the location with a small red x. 'Take a taxi to the Tito Mausoleum and walk from there. It's not far. Find out what's going on. Gazi never actually sold the place, but the government will have seized the property and sold it on. We need to know who owns it now, whether they live there all the time and what sort of security they have. You follow?'

'This is an exclusive area, right?'

'The most exclusive in Belgrade. Milošević lived in Dedinje.'

'Then I'd guess the neighbours aren't likely to be eager for a chat with a stranger, assuming any of them ever show their faces on the street.'

'Just look around. See if any nearby properties are for sale. If they are, make a note of the agent's name and number. They might be a useful contact.'

'Well, I . . .'

'You agreed to help me, doctor.'

'Yes, but—'

'So help, OK?'

'Yes, Marco. OK.' Hammond swallowed some more coffee. 'I'll do the best I can.'

'Take a bus back into the centre when you've finished. Meet me in Trg Republike at midday.' Piravani's finger slid back up the map. 'Here. The city's main square. Wait by the horse.'

'The what?'

'The statue of Prince Mihailo Obrenović on horseback, in front of the National Museum.' Piravani looked suddenly thoughtful. 'It's what Zineta often used to say to me. "*Kod konja.*" "Meet you at the horse."' He gazed past Hammond into the unplumbable depths of his past. 'But she'll never say it to me again.'

Hammond was too tired to summon any words of consolation. He tore his bread roll in half, smeared the yellow grease from the small carton labelled *ПУTEP* on one of the halves and took a bite. 'Some jam would have been nice,' he said, more as a statement of fact rather than a complaint.

Piravani smiled grimly. 'Maybe tomorrow, doctor.'

The taxi driver was a voluble Tito nostalgist. All the way to the last resting place of Yugoslavia's great leader he sustained a panegyric on the late lamented president. Hammond would have found it difficult to concentrate on this even if he had not been distracted by jolts of pain from his ribs – the journey progressing as it did in a series of violent accelerations and emergency brakings, often accompanied by brief skids as the unstudded tyres lost their grip on hard-packed patches of ice – since he had no interest in the unifying genius of Marshal Tito and no intention of visiting his grave.

In point of fact, he had visited it once before. Back in 1996, Miljanović had insisted on taking him to the House of Flowers one afternoon when he could be spared from ministering to Gazi's post-operative needs. The grave itself he remembered as plain, not to say austere, the adjoining museum of Tito-related artefacts less than riveting. Miljanović, however, like the taxi driver, recalled Tito's era as a golden age of pan-Slavic harmony. 'Everything has gone wrong since he died, Edward. He would weep if he could see what we have done to his country.'

Hammond did not doubt that. He was close to weeping himself as he waited for the taxi to pull away from the foot of the slope that led up to the mausoleum, though his tears were induced by the knife-edged wind rather than the ravages of history. The city stretched away before him, a pewter sky slung over it like a cowl. Behind him were the villas of Dedinje, widely spaced and screened by conifers. After checking where he was in relation to the red x on his map, he set off.

A steady climb past snow-carpeted parkland took him to a long, quiet road of high-walled residences. There was no possibility of striking up an illuminating conversation with a garrulous local. The only people he could see were bored-looking security men in gatehouses at the fronts of several properties.

The scene was in fact vaguely familiar. En route to or from the House of Flowers, Miljanović had driven Hammond past a similar stretch of Dedinje's real estate, commenting unfavourably on some of the kitsch extravagances the nouveau riche of Milošević's Serbia had encouraged their architects to indulge in. Several of the villas Hammond glimpsed over their boundary walls as he made his geriatrically slow way along the road had indeed been tastelessly extended, although some of the extensions were already showing signs of dilapidation. All that new money had been spread thinly.

The Villa Ruža was a triumph of elegance by comparison, a salmon-pink neoclassical mansion replete with pillars and balconies standing four-square at the end of a lawn-flanked drive. The walls screening it from the road were a matching pink and in the centre of each of the firmly closed wrought-iron gates was a cleverly worked likeness of a wolf. Gazi had left his mark.

There was some kind of intercom attached to one of the gate pillars, but no gatehouse or any other obvious sign of security. Worryingly, from Hammond's point of view, there were no cars on the drive and the windows of the villa were all shuttered. The property gave every appearance of being unoccupied, though immaculately maintained. He would be unable to argue that covert entry was impossible. And that was likely to be all the encouragement Piravani needed.

A Range Rover with reflective windows cruised slowly past as Hammond walked on, heightening his sense of being observed even as he was observing. The whole area had a quality of nervous stillness about it, though he was aware that his own apprehensiveness might well be the root of it. More powerfully than ever, he felt he should not have allowed his life to be pulled so far off course that he found himself in Belgrade with Piravani, plotting a burglary. But how he could have avoided it remained obscure. A man who is not in control of events is at the mercy of them. And he was assuredly such a man.

Descending towards the Crvena Zvezda football stadium, where it was safe to suppose he could catch a bus, he suddenly recognized the curve of a road as it passed a low-rise apartment block, and realized the road led to the Voćnjak Clinic. It was only about a quarter of a mile away. He stood gazing in the direction he would have to take to reach it, depressed by the contrast between the circumstances of his two visits to Belgrade. There were others to blame for that contrast beside himself. But he bore his share. And that thought only deepened his depression.

*

131

A ride on a Belgrade bus was an experience his VIP treatment had spared him in 1996. Now, after a lengthy wait outside the football stadium, he clambered aboard one, swiftly abandoned the idea of buying a ticket in the crush of passengers and braced himself against a handrail as best he could. The destination, shown in Cyrillic lettering, had meant nothing to him, but the bus was going in the right direction as far as he could tell.

The ride ended some way short of Trg Republike, but Hammond had time in hand and took reviving refuge in a coffee shop before trudging on to his destination, pausing en route to buy a badly needed hat – a fur-lined cap with earflaps.

He had been to Trg Republike before, he realized when he arrived, although there was nothing particularly memorable to his eye about the square, with snow-patched greenery, frozen fountains, surging traffic and buildings locked in a stand-off between nineteenth-century grandeur and twentieth-century brutalism. Piravani was nowhere to be seen and it was cold enough to ensure no one else was waiting by the large equestrian statue outside the National Museum. Hammond pulled down the flaps on his hat and started walking round the base of the statue, hoping he would not be kept waiting long.

He was halfway through a fourth circuit when several sharp toots on a horn drew his attention to a rust-pocked white van that had pulled up on the pavement on the north side of the square. Piravani was gesticulating at him from the driver's seat.

Hammond hurried over and climbed in. He had barely closed the door behind him when Piravani took off. 'I almost didn't recognize you in that hat,' he complained. 'What have you got for me?'

'The villa's closed up,' Hammond replied, pulling off his hat. 'In good repair and recently painted, but shutters over the windows.'

'Excellent. Security?'

'Nothing. No gatehouse. No guard. But I'd guess there's an alarm, at least.'

'So would I. I'll take a look myself after dark. Learn anything else?'

'There were no gabby neighbours, Marco. No estate agents' signs. No builders in anywhere. The area's deathly quiet. One car drove along the road the whole time I was there.'

'Quiet is good.'

'I'm glad you think so. Where are we going now?'

'Your new home away from home, doctor. Trust me: you won't like it.'

They crossed the bridge over the muddy brown Sava into New Belgrade, leaving the old city behind and entering a remorseless sprawl of drab, grey, post-war apartment blocks. Sleet was sweeping horizontally across their façades: there was no shelter here from the wind.

The weather was, in fact, much as it had been when Hammond arrived with his team in March 1996, but then it and the cheerlessness of their surroundings had made little impact on him. Thirteen years later, his cushion of professional indifference was gone. He was out in the world, exposed and fallible. Looking down at the shanty dwellings on the riverside below the bridge, he felt suddenly and dismayingly close to those whose lives contained neither comfort nor security of any kind.

Whatever its visual shortcomings, however, New Belgrade contained two modern upmarket hotels: the Inter-Continental and the Hyatt Regency. It was in the latter that Hammond and his team had stayed. He recognized its prow-like frontage as they drove past, his recollection of its de-luxe facilities sharpened by the certainty that he would not be sampling them.

'Sorry, doctor,' said Piravani, reading his mind. 'You have to rough it this time.'

The block they parked outside was a dismal clone of all the others that surrounded it – geometrically arranged buttes in an architectural desert. A grim graffiti-spattered entrance led to a still grimmer concrete stairway where the air seemed even colder than outside. They started climbing, Piravani having to wait on each landing for Hammond to catch up. Their destination was the third floor. Piravani produced a key and led the way into a small two-bedroomed flat. It was actually more brightly decorated and better furnished than Hammond had feared, though the view through the door that led on to a tiny balcony, where a clothes rack had been left to rot, was dominated by the soaring grey flank of an adjacent block.

On the dusty worktop in the kitchen Piravani dumped the bulging plastic bag he had carried from the van. 'Beer, coffee, orange juice, milk, butter, bread, cheese, ham,' he announced. 'Enough to keep us going.'

'For how long?'

'A few days. That's all we'll need. Win or lose.'

'I still don't understand how you hope to get the tapes, Marco.'

'I have to work on a plan, OK?' Piravani lit a cigarette and flapped it at Hammond as if shooing away a fly. 'But it can be done. First we eat. Then we sleep.' He yawned. 'I'm too old to think with a tired brain.'

Hammond was not about to argue with that. Piravani activated the heating, which turned out to be surprisingly efficient, and cut some sandwiches. A couple of those, washed down with a bottle of Serbian beer, converted Hammond's fatigue into heavy drowsiness. The bed he chose needed a new mattress, but he was too tired to care. The thin curtains reduced the grey afternoon light to a soothing subfusc. Closing his eyes was like flicking a switch from on to off.

SIXTEEN

It was dark when he woke. In the kitchen an orange light was beating like a pulse. Stumbling into the room, he confronted a giant neon-lit sign in the middle distance, blinking out some message in Serbian that was lost on him. Between them, traffic roared past on the highway feeding the city: a blur of white, red and amber into which snow fell from an invisible sky.

He switched on some lights and registered the time: nearly seven o'clock. He had slept for the best part of five hours. Piravani had evidently been less weary. In a note scrawled on a scrap of paper wedged prominently under an empty beer bottle, he explained: *'Gone to Dedinje. Could be late when I get back. Take it easy.'*

A shower and a shave in the no-frills bathroom restored a measure of normality to Hammond's sense of himself, though everything took him far longer than usual thanks to the lengths he had to go to avoid jarring his ribs. He treated himself to a couple more paracetamols afterwards and a cup of coffee, opening a window to clear the smell of Piravani's cigarettes while he drank it.

By now, taking it easy no longer appealed. Piravani's note implied it might be many hours before he returned. The prospect of spending those hours in the hutch-like flat with nothing to distract him from the direness of his situation was intolerable. He needed to remind himself of the ease and order that had previously obtained

135

in his life. Then he remembered that he was not far from the Hyatt Regency, which boasted a good restaurant as well as an atmosphere of cosmopolitan sophistication. The walk there would hardly be a pleasure – it was still snowing – but the effort would be well worth it.

Entering the Hyatt Regency was a deeply healing experience for Hammond, a lesson in how reliant he had become on the insulation only money can buy from the harsher realities of the world. Marble and pale wood predominated in the spacious lobby, where neatly uniformed staff attended to the needs of well-dressed guests in an atmosphere of calm efficiency. Water tinkled soothingly in the sunken atrium's goldfish pond. Subdued swishes and pings announced the comings and goings of the lifts. He could have been in any top-end hotel in any one of several dozen capital cities around the globe. And thus it was possible for him to pretend, for a while at least, that he was not in Belgrade at all.

He sauntered into the Metropolitan Grill, procured a table for one and concentrated as far as he was able on the menu and the wine list. It proved surprisingly easy. Smoked salmon, fillet steak and a good claret were for the present the limit of his needs. With every mouthful he felt more like his old self.

It was an illusion, of course, a surrender by his better judgement to alcohol and haute cuisine. When he left the restaurant at the end of his meal, he was seriously contemplating a cigar as well as a brandy in the bar. But such indulgences were soon to be banished from his thoughts.

A group of people was spilling out of the function suite on the other side of the atrium as he emerged into the lobby. They were almost all male, lounge-suited and Slav-featured. Their flushed faces, loud laughter and back-slapping good cheer suggested a good deal of drinking had already been done. But this did not deter most of them from heading for the bar.

Who saw and recognized who first Hammond could not afterwards have said. All he knew was that he was suddenly looking straight into the smiling eyes of Svetozar Miljanović.

'Edward! Is it really you?'

'Good God. Svetozar.' Hammond forced a grin. 'Great to see you.'

Miljanović said something in Serbian to his two companions, who ambled on into the bar. Then he clasped Hammond by the shoulder and pumped his hand. 'What are you doing in Belgrade, Edward? And why didn't you tell me you were coming?'

Valid questions both, to which Hammond had no ready answers. 'It's just a . . . overnight stop. I've been at a . . . conference . . . in Athens.' (Athens? Why had he said that? If Miljanović asked what the conference was about and who was hosting it, he would be sunk.) 'I thought I'd . . . take the opportunity to . . . revisit Belgrade.'

'You *should* have told me.' Miljanović seemed delighted to see him – and reassuringly unsuspicious. 'How are you, my friend?' He frowned faintly, as if Hammond's appearance gave him cause for concern.

'Oh, a little tired. Otherwise fine. What about you?'

'Fine also.' And Miljanović did look well: greyer and marginally more lined than when last they had met, but as lean and sprightly as ever. 'Are you staying here?'

'No. The, er . . . Inter-Continental.' It was the only other hotel he could name and he felt sure claiming to be a guest at the Hyatt Regency would be a mistake. 'What have you' – he gestured towards the function suite – 'just been to?'

'Ah. *Sledeći Novi Beograd*: the Next New Belgrade. It is a consortium that has plans to develop some land around the proposed Metro route to the airport. This evening they have been showing an invited group of businessmen the advantages of reserving space out there – for a big fee, naturally. Lots of CGI and statistics and champagne. The director of the Voćnjak sent me to represent him. The party is just breaking up.'

'Well, I'd better . . . leave you to join your friends.'

'Oh, they are not my friends, though they are so drunk they

137

think they are. I have done my duty. Why don't you and I go on somewhere? Maybe the bar of your hotel.'

'I don't know, Svetozar. The thing is—'

'You're right. It'll be like here – full of businessmen getting smashed. I know a better place. Come. I'll drive. My car's outside.'

'No. I'd fall asleep on you. I really think—'

'It's been thirteen years, Edward. One brandy for old time's sake?'

Resistance, it had become clear, was futile. 'All right. One drink.'

They fetched their coats and headed for the exit, only to encounter a thick knot of potential tenants of *Sledeći Novi Beograd* tangled around a tall, bulky, clarion-voiced man wearing a spectacularly well-cut suit made of some shimmering and doubtless very expensive material. He had a mane of jet-black hair that his craggy features suggested could hardly be its natural colour, the impression of vanity this created reinforced by his expression and bearing. The fawning behaviour of those around him suggested they at least believed he had plenty to be vain about.

'Our principal host this evening,' Miljanović whispered. 'Branko Todorović.'

Hammond was glad Miljanović was not looking at him at that moment. He could hardly have failed to notice his flinch of shock and dismay. He fell back half a pace, shielding himself from Todorović's line of sight.

'I should thank him. The director would expect it. Excuse me.'

'Sure. I'll, er, wait outside.'

Hammond risked a backward glance as he closed fast on the revolving door leading out of the hotel. Miljanović was shaking Todorović's hand, grinning and nodding as he did so. Todorović responded with a shoulder squeeze and an appreciative smile. Then he looked away. And for a fraction of a second his and Hammond's eyes met.

'Are you well, Edward?' Miljanović asked as he joined him on the other side of the revolving door. 'You look . . . I don't know, not . . . yourself.'

'I broke a rib recently, that's all. You know how doctors are with pain.'

'Ah yes. Hypochondriacs every one of us. Still, you should go gently. This way.' Miljanović guided him solicitously towards the car park.

'A wealthy man, is he, Todorović?'

'Evidently. He and his backers are throwing money around in the middle of a recession, so . . . they must have plenty of it. But no one wants to ask them where they got it, believe me. Corruption didn't end with the war. And a lot of those who got rich under Milošević stayed rich.'

'Such as Todorović?'

'Exactly. Once he smuggled petrol. Now he sells the future. Which I must live in. Be grateful you do not need to have anything to do with him.'

'I have thought of you often over the years, Edward,' Miljanović said as he steered his modest Škoda out of the car park. 'Have you . . . married again?'

'No. I haven't.'

'I am sorry to hear that. A loving wife is the best thing a man can possess.'

'Have you acquired one yourself?'

'No. I only tell you what my mother says. My father was the luckiest man in Yugoslavia, according to her. He even managed to die before the country fell apart.'

'But things are stable here now, aren't they?'

'Stable? Oh yes. At least, I guess so. But they're not how they were when I was young.'

'You sound like the taxi driver who took me out to the House of Flowers.'

'Didn't *I* take you there?'

'Yes. You did.' Damn. A single thoughtless remark was a step into a minefield. 'I, er . . . wanted to see it again.'

'Really?'

'Is that so strange?'

'To be honest, Edward, you being here at all is strange. Though I have a theory about why you've come.'

'Like I told you, I—'

'Enough.' Miljanović patted his arm. 'When you have a glass of *šljivovica* in your hand, I will tell you my theory. *Then* you can deny it. If you dare.'

'Dragan Gazi.'

Miljanović smiled wryly as he pronounced the name of their former patient. He had waited until after they had drunk a toast to happier things before unveiling his explanation for Hammond's presence in Belgrade. They were seated at a corner table in one of the floating nightclubs on the Danube riverside. The choice at this time of the year was limited, but the *African Queen* was quiet and comfortable, plushly furnished and adorned with black-and-white photographs of bygone Hollywood stars, one of whom, Errol Flynn in the guise of Captain Blood, was freeze-framed in mid-sword-flourish above Miljanović's head.

'Before you tell me I am talking nonsense, Edward, let me . . . elaborate. Gazi is on trial in The Hague. You will have given his trial more attention than most people, because you and I have a . . . personal interest . . . in his case. His crimes are terrible, more terrible than I imagined thirteen years ago when I agreed to approach you for help treating him. And we saved his life, did we not, you and I? So, you ask yourself, as I have asked myself: how many people died because we gave Gazi a new liver? He is charged with the murder of several hundred Kosovar Albanians between autumn 1998 and spring 1999, so I guess the answer is . . . a lot too many. Is that our fault? Are those deaths *our* responsibility? No. Of course not. We are doctors. We treat the sick even if they are murderers. But, but, but. It troubles you. It troubles me. Maybe if he had not paid us so well, it would be easier. But he did. And we both took his money. Now it . . . eats at you. Me too. And that is why you have come to Belgrade. There is no logical reason. Gazi is not here. And his victims never were. But your memory of him – your link with his crimes – is here. And so . . . you have come. Is that not the truth, Edward?'

No. It was not. And yet, as Hammond pondered the point, he realized that in a sense it was. Circumstances had brought him where his conscience might eventually have led. Miljanović's reasoning was sound, even if misplaced. But revealing why it was misplaced was simply not an option. 'Yes. You're right, Svetozar. I suppose that is . . . what it comes down to.'

'Well then, my friend, consider this. If Gazi had not killed those Kosovar Albanians, someone else would have. Arkan's Tigers, maybe. We helped bring Gazi to justice by saving his life. Arkan was gunned down in the lobby of the hotel you are staying in and buried with military honours. He will never be tried. His former followers depict him as a fallen hero. But it will be different with Gazi. When all his crimes have been catalogued and examined, there will be no way for people to call him anything except a mass murderer who deserves to spend the rest of his life in prison. Console yourself with that thought.'

'Is it consolation enough, Svetozar?'

'It is for me. It should be for you. Of course, I have the advantage, if that is what it is, of being a Serb. I know from experience that nothing can be perfect. We cannot punish every evil. Peace relies on pragmatism. When we got rid of Milošević, I believed, like a lot of other Serbs, that everything he stood for was finished. But what happened? We elected a prime minister who tried to end the crime and corruption and two years later he was assassinated. Since Đinđić was shot, we've all had to be more . . . realistic. There are rumours that Todorović used to work for Gazi. It's probably true. But that didn't stop all those businessmen drinking his champagne and shaking his hand this evening. It didn't stop *me*. Do you see, Edward? There are more war criminals in Belgrade than there are in The Hague. But here there are no trials. Only deals and compromises. We cannot run before we can walk. We cannot walk before we can stand up. And we are only just beginning to find our feet.'

'So, that makes Todorović fireproof, does it?'

'Yes. It probably does.'

'I suppose there's always a chance the International Court will turn up something to use against him.'

'After all these years?' Miljanović smiled at Hammond indulgently and shook his head. 'That, my friend, is too much to hope for.'

'Are you really leaving tomorrow, Edward?' Miljanović asked as they emerged from the *African Queen* an hour later into the cold shock of the wintry night. 'It is such a short visit.'

'I have to be at work Monday morning,' Hammond explained, regretting that he had to go on deceiving Miljanović. 'And I'll need Sunday to sort myself out.'

'There is plenty of work I can offer you here if you want it, though none of the patients pay as well as Gazi. I have lots of liver cases. Far more than thirteen years ago.'

'Drink-related?'

'Many, of course. But the big increase I see is in cancer.'

'Really? Why would that be?'

'Blame it on the war, Edward. Like everything else. NATO used shells containing depleted uranium in its bombing campaign and their attacks on oil refineries and petrochemical plants released a lot of other toxins into the atmosphere. Factory fires raged for days. The rain turned black. We're still treating the results of NATO's "humanitarian" intervention.'

'I never heard anything about this.'

'Why would you? We were the bad guys.' Miljanović laughed.

'What's funny?'

'I was just thinking. All that pollution can't have done Gazi's liver any good.'

'No. But ironically he looked very well when I—'

They stopped. Miljanović peered at him in the darkness, the furrows on his brow dimly lit by the lanterns of a nearby barge. 'You have seen him?'

'Well, I . . . Yes. I went to The Hague, Svetozar. I sat in on his trial for a while. He didn't speak. He didn't move much, in fact, and he didn't see me. It was all rather . . . anticlimactic.'

Miljanović signified his understanding with a nod. 'I have thought of going myself. Not just to see Gazi. But to . . . remind myself what they all did. I sometimes feel I need to. So that I can understand why we really were the bad guys.'

'*You* weren't, Svetozar.'

'Are you sure? I didn't stop any of it happening, did I?'

'How could you?'

'That's what we Serbs always say to excuse ourselves. How could we have made a difference? But I sometimes think it's the wrong question. I sometimes think we should ask: how *couldn't* we?'

Miljanović naturally offered to drive him to the Inter-Continental, but Hammond insisted he would prefer to walk. 'I need to clear my head, Svetozar.'

'In this temperature, Edward, you will freeze it while you are clearing it.'

'I have my hat.'

'OK. Walk then. But remember: you are ignoring a doctor's advice.' He gave Hammond a hearty handshake and a rib-jarring hug. 'Ah, forgive me,' he said, as Hammond winced. 'I forgot your injury. And I also forgot to ask how it happened.'

'It's a long story.'

'Was sex involved?'

'Sadly, no.'

'OK. You tell me next time.'

'That's a promise.'

'Take care, my friend.'

'You too.'

Trudging through the snow, which had stopped falling but lay thickly on the pavements and in treacherous slush-filled drifts over the kerbs, Hammond was beset by more guilt than he would have expected to feel for concealing the truth from Miljanović. If only he really had come to Belgrade to salve his conscience. Instead, he was there to shore up his reputation. Good might come of it, in the form of evidence against Todorović that would stand up in court, but his willingness to see Gazi's ill-gotten wealth bestowed on his undeserving family remained. He wondered whether Alice was the reason for that or just the excuse for it. Was he trying to protect her – or himself? Neither seemed a good enough answer any more.

He had been away from the apartment much longer than he had anticipated. The likelihood was that Piravani would have returned by now. Hammond prepared himself for a prickly reception.

It came before he even made it into the block, a horn sounding several sharp beeps as he crossed the car park. Then a pair of head-lamps flashed at him and he recognized the van.

Piravani lowered the window and scowled out as he approached. 'Where the fuck have you been, doctor?' He did not sound pleased. 'You locked me out.'

'I assumed you'd have a key.'

'I told you to stay in the apartment.'

'I don't remember you saying that.'

'*Where have you been?*'

'I had dinner at the Inter-Continental.' The lie came auto-matically.

'Not the Hyatt Regency?'

'No. Why?'

'That's something, I guess. Let's go in. I'm freezing to death out here.'

Piravani said no more until they were inside the flat. He opened a bottle of beer, took a couple of swigs, then slammed a Serbian newspaper down on the kitchen table. It was printed in Cyrillic script, rendering it doubly unintelligible to Hammond.

'Today's *Politika*,' Piravani growled. 'I've had plenty of time to take a thorough look through it.'

'Sorry. I just couldn't stay cooped up here.'

'A pity. But at least you chose the Inter-Continental. According to the paper, our friend Todorović was hosting a reception at the Hyatt Regency this evening to launch a property-development project.'

'So what?' Hammond's discomfiture was growing by the second. 'He wouldn't have noticed me even if I had gone there. Besides, he doesn't know what I look like.'

'How can you be sure of that?'

'Well, I just . . . assume he . . .'

'You've done a lot of assuming tonight, doctor. Do me a favour. Cut it out.'

Hammond sighed. 'All right. You're the boss. What did you learn from your visit to Dedinje?'

'That it looks like the villa's still got the alarm system Gazi had fitted. Which gives us a way in.'

'How?'

'I'll explain later. There's something else in the paper you should know about first.' Piravani folded it open at an inside page and pointed to a head-and-shoulder photograph of a shaven-headed, bull-necked man with close-set eyes and a sullen jut to his chin. 'Recognize him?'

'No. Should I?'

'Not really. It was dark when you drove into him.'

'You mean . . . this was the man I . . .'

'Yes. Guido's killer. Identified by the Milan police as Branislav Jeličić. It turns out he's been wanted by the Serbian police for the past two years as a possible co-conspirator of the people who organized the assassination in 2003 of Zoran Đinđić.'

'Đinđić? The Prime Minister?'

'That's right, doctor. Todorović only hires the best.' Piravani glanced down at the photograph. 'You were lucky to get the better of him.'

'Does the article mention Guido?'

'Yes. The police think Jeličić killed him before he was killed himself. Beyond that . . . they're in the dark. Or so they say. Ever had your fingerprints taken?'

'No.'

'Good. In that case there'll be no match on their database for the prints they'll have found in the car. But that's not our only problem. They'll begin making connections soon, if they haven't already, between Guido and me and Gazi and possibly Todorović as well. We need to move fast.' Piravani smiled drily at Hammond. 'You'd better get some sleep, doctor. It'll be an early start in the morning.'

SEVENTEEN

The rising sun cast low-angled darts through the swirling clouds as Hammond crossed Kalemegdan Park, his shoes crunching on patches of ice-crusted snow, his breath misting in the still, cold air. Following the route Piravani had prescribed for him, he veered to the left round the ramparts of the fortress and descended a long flight of steps in cautious fashion, then climbed equally cautiously towards the Pobednik Monument.

The paved plateau round the monument was deserted. The Messenger of Victory atop his column had no audience as he gazed across the Sava towards the tower blocks of New Belgrade. Hammond was carrying his trusty prop – the by now tattered copy of *La Gazzetta dello Sport*. He walked across to the railings at the edge of the plateau and leant against them. He unfurled the paper as if genuinely interested in out-of-date team news from Serie A and glanced down at a barge making slow but steady progress along the Sava towards its confluence with the Danube.

Piravani's plan for entering the Villa Ruža undetected hinged on his knowledge of its alarm system. As back-up in case of power cuts, there was a heavy-duty rechargeable battery. Piravani knew where it was housed and reckoned he could disconnect it within minutes of breaking in. If the electricity supply had failed in the locality, no attention would be drawn by a brief activation of the alarm. All they needed to ensure was that the supply had indeed failed. Removal of the battery would then kill the system. And it was to meet the man who could arrange such a failure that Hammond had come to Kalemegdan.

On one level he regarded participating in the break-in as an act of lunacy. But the lure of a swift resolution of all his problems – almost surgical in its directness, now he came to think about it – was irresistible.

A noise caught his ear as he contemplated the barge far below him: the paying out of a ratcheted line. He turned and saw that he had been joined on the plateau by a man with a small terrier on a retractable lead. The terrier was sniffing round the base of the monument, oblivious to Hammond. But his owner was looking straight at him.

Feeding his dog a little more slack, the man walked across to join Hammond by the railings. He was stocky, grey-haired and sixtyish, muffled up in quilted coat, scarf and cap. A trimmed moustache and thick-framed glasses gave him a mild, bureaucratic look. He matched to a T Piravani's description of Radomir Plessl, the senior manager at Elektrodistribucija Beograd, who had arranged for Gazi to be spared the inconvenience of the power cuts that had been so frequent under Milošević in return for generous supplements to his meagre salary. Piravani had been in touch with him and confirmed he was still eminently corruptible. The only real difference was that this time he would be cutting off the power to the Villa Ruža, not keeping it on, an irony which might have explained the smile playing at the edges of his lips.

'*Dobar dan*,' said Plessl. '*Hladno je, ne?*' His smile broadened at the sight of Hammond's blank look. 'I said it's cold, isn't it?'

'Yes. Yes, it is.'

'But Trinko, he has to have his walk, so here we are.'

'Mr Plessl?'

'*Da*. I am Plessl.'

'This is for you.' Hammond handed him a thickly filled brown envelope, partly concealed by *La Gazzetta dello Sport*.

Plessl took off a glove, prised the envelope open and fanned through the wad of notes inside, then, seeming satisfied, slipped it into an inside pocket of his coat. 'Say thanks to Marco for me,' he said.

'I will.'

'What time does he want the outage?'

'One o'clock tomorrow morning. For two hours.'

'OK. I'll make it a few minutes before one. It'll look more . . . natural.'

'I'll tell him.'

Plessl's arm was jerked as Trinko reached the limit of his lead. He glanced towards the dog, then back at Hammond. 'I have to go. It's clear, what we have arranged?'

'Yes.'

'I don't know what Marco is planning to do, but . . . good luck.'

'Thanks.'

'*Doviđenja*.' Plessl touched his cap, then plodded off after Trinko.

Hammond watched Plessl wander away further into the fortress, then folded his paper and headed back the way he had come.

It was hardly to be expected that he and Plessl would be the only visitors to the park, early and bone-numbingly cold though it was, so there was nothing inherently suspicious about the figure who appeared away to Hammond's left as he neared the exit on to Pariska: a tall, broad-shouldered man in a black overcoat, bare-headed despite the chill, walking fast. Yet Hammond was suspicious – and afraid.

His fear notched upwards when he saw a more or less identically dressed man of similar bearing loitering on the pavement just beyond the exit. He stopped, then stepped to one side, flourishing his newspaper and wondering if the man approaching from behind him would simply walk on by and the threat dissolve into misplaced anxiety.

But it did not dissolve. Glancing round, he saw the two men closing in on him. It was too late to make a run for it and he sensed his best bet was to bluff it out. They looked like plain-clothes police and, in the circumstances, he could only hope that was exactly what they were.

His hunch was swiftly confirmed when one of the men produced a badge from inside his coat and held it out for Hammond to see. '*Policija*,' he said gruffly, adding a good deal more in Serbian to which Hammond was not equipped to respond.

'I'm sorry,' he said. 'I don't understand you.'

'*Engleski?*'

'Yes. I'm English. I'm a British citizen.'

'Passport?'

Reluctantly, he produced it. The man with the badge took it from him and glanced at the last page. Then he said, 'With us, please,' pointing towards the road. He made no move to return the passport.

'What's this about?'

'*With us, please.*'

'What do you want?'

At that the other man grabbed him firmly by the elbow and said something in Serbian that sounded both uncompromising and insistent.

'I recommend cooperation,' said his colleague. And something told Hammond that it was good advice.

He was shepherded out of the park. A large grey salt- and snow-grimed Mercedes was drawn up at the side of the road. A rear door was pushed open as they approached and a heavy hand on the shoulder impelled Hammond towards it.

'Get in.'

He obeyed, queasily aware that it was likely to be more than just a car he was getting into. This was the moment, it seemed clear to him, when his life left the tracks he had followed so long and so complacently. This was the moment he had told himself would never come. And now it had arrived.

The rear seat was a broad expanse of worn leather, but a tight squeeze once he had been bundled in between the English-speaking policeman and the waiting passenger – similarly overcoated, but an altogether slighter figure, younger and better-looking, with dark, short-cropped hair and a boyish face. He said something to the driver, who did not so much as glance round at Hammond. They started away with a jolt and a skid. The non-English-speaking policeman was sitting beside the driver. He did not look round either. To them this was purely routine; to Hammond, the start of a nightmare. It all depended, he reflected, on your point of view.

The English-speaking policeman stretched across Hammond to deliver his passport to the younger man, who began leafing carefully through it, page by page.

'What's going on?' Hammond demanded, though to his own ear the demand fell pitifully flat.

'One moment.' The perusal of the passport continued.

'I have a right to—'

'You have a right to nothing, Mr Hammond.' The younger man smiled fleetingly at him. 'Trust me. I know our laws better than you do.'

'It's Dr Hammond, actually.' As soon as the words were out of his mouth, he regretted the attempt to assert his status.

'Really?' The younger man plucked a badge from his pocket and showed it to Hammond. There was a lot of Cyrillic script, an insignia of some kind and a laminated mugshot. 'My name is Uželać. Radmilo Uželać. These gentlemen are police officers, assisting me with my investigations.'

'Aren't you a police officer?'

'No. I am with ICEFA, a specially appointed government commission. Perhaps you have heard of us.'

'I don't think so.' But Hammond had heard of them, of course. It was someone at ICEFA – for all he knew, Uželać himself – who had fed Zineta's tip-off to Todorović. He wondered if fear of just such an intervention was the reason Piravani had insisted he should be the one to deliver the bribe to Plessl.

'We are responsible for tracing the estimated thirty billion

151

dollars stolen from the state by Milošević and the criminals who thrived under his regime.'

'Well, I wish you luck.'

'Your good wishes will not take us far, Dr Hammond.'

'They're all I can offer you, I'm afraid.'

'I don't think so.'

'Where are you taking me?'

'Nowhere. We shall cruise the streets while you and I discuss what you can do to help ICEFA.'

'You've got the wrong man, Mr . . .'

'Uželać.'

'I know nothing about funds siphoned off under Milošević. I'm just a British tourist.'

'Really? Well, you seem to be touring the wrong country. According to your passport, you're in Croatia, not Serbia.'

'Oh, I came on here by train. No one stamped my passport, that's all.'

'What attracts you to Belgrade in February? Our famously mild winter weather, maybe?'

'I don't know. I just . . . wanted to see the city.'

Uželać sighed and lit a cigarette, which acted as a trigger for the two policemen to light up as well. Hammond considered and rejected the idea of asking for a window to be opened. 'I'd offer you one, doctor,' Uželać said between puffs, 'but I'm sure you're too sensible to accept. Bad for the health. Very bad. Though not quite as bad as getting yourself mixed up with people like Dragan Gazi and Branko Todorović.'

'Who?'

'Please don't ask stupid questions. We have film of you handing an envelope containing five thousand dinars to a senior employee of the municipal electricity company. You weren't hiring him as a tour guide. He has in fact already told us what the money was for. You are therefore guilty of attempted bribery *and* sabotage.'

'Sabotage?'

'Of the electricity supply to part of the city. Serious charges, Dr

152

Hammond. If convicted, you could be sentenced to many years' imprisonment.'

As Uželać said it, the prospect sounded hideously plausible. Hammond's throat tightened. 'It was . . . the repayment of a debt. There was no bribe.'

'Plessl says otherwise. And Plessl will be believed. We will make sure of that. If we have to. But maybe we won't have to. I'll give you a chance to come clean.' Uželać looked round at Hammond, studying him closely. 'Do you know why we're not doing this at my office – or in an interrogation room at Police HQ?'

'You want to keep our discussion off the record.'

'Yes. But *why*?'

Hammond shrugged helplessly. 'I don't know.'

'Then I'll tell you. We have a mole at ICEFA, Dr Hammond. One of our agents – as yet unidentified – is supplying information to one of our principal targets, Branko Todorović, former associate of the notorious Dragan Gazi, currently on trial for war crimes in The Hague. As a result, a recent operation to apprehend Gazi's accountant, Marco Piravani, was fatally interfered with. Piravani's ex-partner, Guido Felltrini, was murdered at his office in Milan on Wednesday night to prevent him revealing to us Piravani's where-abouts. Actually, thanks to Plessl, we believe we know where Piravani is: here, in Belgrade. He contacted Plessl yesterday and they agreed this morning's meeting. That makes you Piravani's messenger *and* co-conspirator.'

'I know nothing about any conspiracy.'

'Please, doctor, please. Let's be reasonable. You came to Belgrade with Piravani to help him carry out a criminal act. Why you're help-ing him I don't need to know at this time. He has something on you. Todorović has something on you. Gazi has something on you. Whichever. It doesn't matter. What matters is the criminal act – and its consequences. That is what you're going to tell me about.'

'I'm not a criminal. I'm a—'

'Tourist. Yes. I know. Repeating the line doesn't make it any more convincing.'

153

Uželać said something to the driver in Serbian and he took an abrupt turn off the road. Hammond had no idea which direction they had been going in since leaving Kalemegdan. And the rubbish-strewn expanse of concrete they were now crossing beneath a motorway flyover gave him no clues. The car pulled in behind one of the huge pillars supporting the flyover and stopped. There was a rumble of traffic above them, but nothing moved in Hammond's field of vision except a flattened cardboard box, sliding and flopping in the wind.

'Here's the situation, doctor. You paid Plessl five thousand dinars to cut the electricity supply to the Villa Ruža tonight. The Villa Ruža used to belong to Dragan Gazi. My guess is you and Piravani plan to break into the villa. Or maybe you've hired some men to do it for you. Whichever. The power cut is necessary to disable the alarm. The current owner is abroad and has no known connections with Gazi. So, what are you after?'

Hammond said nothing. He truly did not know what to say.

'My guess,' Uželać continued, 'is that Piravani has decided to respond to Felltrini's murder with a direct move against Todorović. To make that move he needs something he hid in the villa during the time Gazi lived there. Documents. Records. Incriminating material. Something only he knows about. And you, of course – his accomplice. Whatever it is, we'd like to see it. We'd like to be the ones to use it against Todorović – and whoever else it implicates. So, why don't you tell me, doctor? What exactly is it you're looking for?'

'I can assure you, Mr Uželać, I don't—'

'Please don't assure me of anything, doctor. It's pointless and . . . too late. I don't have time to be patient with you. Tell me. Or my two friends here will take you over there' – he pointed towards the next pillar – 'and beat the shit out of you. You *will* tell me. I can promise you that. The only question is how many teeth you have left when you do it. Oh, what sort of doctor are you, by the way?'

'I'm a liver specialist.'

'Uhuh. Do you operate on people?'

154

'Yes. I perform surgery.'

'Well, never again, or at least not for a very long time, after these two have finished stamping on your fingers. *Pravi, Franko?*'

Franko, the English-speaking policeman, responded to the question by grasping Hammond's left hand in a crushing grip. Hammond winced as his knuckles ground together. 'Let go of me,' he gasped. But Franko did not let go.

'*Dosta*,' said Uželać. Then, and only then, Franko relaxed his hold.

'I'm a British citizen,' Hammond said hoarsely. 'You can't treat me like this.'

'We will if we have to. We can't let Todorović go on spitting in our faces. He has to be stopped. Now, here's the good news. We can work with you, doctor. You see, we can't break into the Villa Ruža and search for whatever Piravani hid there. That would be illegal. But you and Piravani can. And if you can convince me the material you plan to retrieve will destroy Todorović, we'll let you. We'll be waiting outside to take the material from you, of course. But there'll be no charges against you. We'll put you on a plane to London, or wherever you want to go, and that'll be the end of the matter. The same goes for Piravani. Once he's released Gazi's money to the Ministry of Finance. A clean break for both of you.' Uželać smiled. 'What do you say?'

EIGHTEEN

Hammond trudged doggedly across the bridge over the Sava through the exhaust fumes of the slow-moving Saturday traffic. The tower blocks of New Belgrade loomed ahead and, in one of them, Marco Piravani was awaiting his return. What precisely Hammond was going to say to him he had still not finally decided. The deal he had struck with Uželać was justified to his satisfaction by sheer necessity. What alternative had there been, after all? He would have gained nothing by obliging them to beat the truth out of him. They had already guessed most of it anyway and needed only to stake out the Villa Ruža to prevent Piravani going through with the planned break-in, whatever happened.

That rationalization only carried him so far, however. The deal ensured Gazi's money would never reach his family. All Hammond had left to cling to was the hope that the tapes would prove he had not been complicit in Gazi's decision to order Kate's murder. Uželać had agreed to supply a lawyer of Hammond's choosing with a transcript of the tapes in due course, which was something, though not much. There was also the chance Gazi would conclude, once his money had been seized by the Serbian authorities, that carrying out his threat against Hammond was pointless. Maybe the wily old Wolf was just bluffing. Maybe.

But Uželać was not bluffing. He had Hammond and Piravani exactly where he wanted them. As yet, however, Piravani did not know that. And Hammond was still wrestling with the problem of whether he should tell him or not. It was easy to imagine the Italian insisting Uželać could not be trusted, calling off the break-in and fleeing the country. He had adjusted to the life of a fugitive long since. But Hammond had not and did not intend to start. To restore the order and normality his existence had until recently hinged on, he needed to deliver the tapes to Uželać. And only Piravani knew where they were hidden. In the final analysis, telling him was surely too risky.

'Are you always truthful with your patients, Edward?' Kate had once asked him.

'I certainly don't lie to them,' he had replied.

'But you might keep certain things back?'

'If I thought it was in their best interests.'

'So, it's all down to your judgement?'

'Yes. I suppose it is.'

'What took you so long?' was Piravani's greeting when Hammond reached the apartment. 'I was starting to worry.'

'I got a little lost between Kalemegdan and the bridge,' Hammond answered, slumping down in one of the utilitarian armchairs.

'No detours to the Inter-Continental or the Hyatt Regency?'

'None.'

'Glad to hear it. So, how did the meeting go?'

'According to plan. Plessl will cut the power just before one a.m.'

'Good.'

'Did you buy everything we need?'

'Oh yes. We're fully equipped. Don't worry.'

'Hard not to.'

'True. But . . .' Piravani held a copy of that morning's *Politika*. 'You'll be pleased to know there's still no mention of you in connection with Guido's murder and the death of Branislav Jeličić.'

'I'm hoping it'll stay that way.'

'No reason why it shouldn't, doctor. If everything turns out well tonight, the question of who killed Jeličić will soon slip to the bottom of their agenda. We'll stop in Lugano on our way to The Hague and I'll transfer Gazi's money to Ingrid's account. Then you'll be in the clear.'

'You make it sound very simple.'

Piravani smiled. 'That's because it will be.'

They spent the rest of the daylight hours penned in the apartment. Piravani had bought plenty to eat and drink, along with a couple of DVDs for them to watch. Steven Seagal and Sylvester Stallone wreaking assorted mayhem did not constitute entertainment as far as Hammond was concerned, but Piravani, fuelled by numerous bottles of beer, found them uproariously amusing. He slept for several hours after the film show and Hammond tried to do the same, without success. The break-in was no longer quite the fool-hardy enterprise it had originally promised to be. In a sense, it was now officially sanctioned. But he was dreading the moment when Piravani realized what was really going on. One way or another, the night was bound to end badly.

Piravani surfaced from his siesta to a mug of strong coffee and several cigarettes, then announced he was going out – alone – for an hour or so.

'There's something I have to check,' he explained, thereby explaining nothing at all. 'Stay here, OK? I'll be back long before we have to leave.'

He was back, in fact, well within the hour. Hammond's gentle enquiries about what he had been doing were just as gently deflected. He was surprisingly relaxed as the evening advanced, checking through the tools and other kit he had bought with calm meticulousness.

They headed out, wearing identical black boilersuits and gloves, just after midnight. A fast drive along the expressway took them across the Gazelle Bridge and into Dedinje. By 12.45, they were in

158

position in a side-road near the Villa Ruža. Whatever surveillance Uželać had arranged was discreet to the point of invisibility. If he had not known better, Hammond might have thought they had a chance of pulling off the break-in and getting clean away afterwards. But appearances, as he knew, could be deceptive. One of the numerous parked cars or vans they had passed presumably contained a police team ready to pounce when the time came.

'I'm impressed, doctor,' said Piravani, as he smoked a cigarette while they waited for the nearest streetlamp to go out. 'I never thought you'd go through with this.'
    'Neither did I. But you left me no choice.'
    'True. But if you lose your nerve . . . you lose it.'
    'You convinced me the risk was worth taking.'
    'We've been lucky. If the villa was occupied . . .'
    'But it isn't.'
    'No. So, maybe we really can get what we want.'
    'I believe it, Marco. Don't you?'
    Piravani gave a low chuckle. 'Sure, I believe it.'

A disused service alley, colonized by weeds, some as big as bushes, made larger still by encrustations of snow, led off the side-road between the rear boundary walls of adjacent villas. The first few yards of it were illuminated by the feeble sodium gleam of the widely spaced streetlamps. When they faded and died a few minutes before one, darkness descended like a cloak. And Piravani murmured decisively, 'We go.'

The night was marginally milder than the day had been. The wind had dropped and sundry drippings and tricklings hinted at a thaw. Piravani shouldered the rucksack in which he had stowed the gear and led the way along the alley. The snow was knee-deep in places and the footing uneven. Haste was out of the question. But such moonlight as there was, heavily filtered by cloud, was reflected off the snow, revealing their surroundings in dim gradations of black and white.

After five minutes or so, Piravani called a halt. They had reached the rear wall of the Villa Ruža. It was partly concealed by the tangled shoots of a rampant thorn bush. Piravani used wirecutters to clear a path, then rigged a rope ladder to climb to the top of the wall, where there were three strands of barbed wire to be severed. He managed the whole thing with greater athleticism than Hammond would have judged him capable of.

Hammond's own ascent was slow and painful. But at length they were over the wall and wading through a snowdrift to reach the shrub-fringed edge of a lawn. Beyond it, on a terrace of higher ground, was the house. Piravani steered a direct path towards it across the lawn, hardly seeming to care about the footprints they were leaving in the snow. If not in a hurry, he was certainly a man with a mission. An alarm tripped by the power cut was wailing somewhere in the middle distance, which Hammond caught himself reckoning was better for their purposes than silence. It had set a dog barking as well, adding more useful noise to disguise any they made. But their stealth, as he well knew, was in vain. They were not going to get away with anything.

They reached the terrace and Piravani veered to the left, where a single-storey wing could just be made out in the shadow of the main house. He paused for a moment to orientate himself, then proceeded cautiously across snow-covered gravel to a door, next to which stood two dustbins beneath an uncurtained sash window. He shone his torch into the interior and muttered 'OK, OK' to himself in evident satisfaction.

'Everything as you remember it?' Hammond whispered.

'Looks to be, yes. Break the glass and we're in. I'm not sure where the nearest movement sensor is, but I'll trigger the alarm before I reach the control box for certain. You wait here until it's dead. Clear?'

'Clear.'

'Good.' Piravani took off the rucksack and reached into it for a hammer. He rolled the closer of the two dustbins on to its side and positioned it beneath the window. Then he knocked a hole in one of the panes of glass, stretched in to raise the latch and pushed the window up. 'Easy, hey, doctor?'

'Just be careful.'

'OK. Hold on to the bin.' Hammond held it in place as Piravani hopped up and clambered through the window, then vanished into the darkened interior. A moment later the alarm started beeping. According to Piravani's own estimate, that gave him thirty seconds to disable it before it went off.

He did not set about his task hesitantly. Hammond saw flashes of the torchbeam inside, then heard a door being wrenched open, followed by a jumble of indecipherable clunks and rattles. Next came several loud hammer blows and the sound of wood or plastic splintering.

The alarm cut in with an ear-splitting yowl, but was almost immediately cut off again. The house was quiet once more. Piravani reappeared at the window. 'Come on in, doctor,' he said. 'We've got the place to ourselves.'

Hammond passed the rucksack through, then scrambled in after it, holding his breath to minimize the pain in his ribs. They were in a scullery, the squat shapes of a dishwasher and a couple of washing machines dimly visible among the shadows.

'Follow me,' said Piravani. Keeping his torch trained on the floor ahead, he piloted them along a passage running past a couple of similar rooms and the kitchen before emerging into a corner of the main hall. They moved towards the big front door, weak moonlight glimmering milkily through the extravagantly curlicued fanlight above it, then turned at the foot of the broad marble-balustraded staircase and headed up it.

Piravani chose which room to enter off the landing without hesitation. They stepped into a large, square room with windows looking out to the rear of the house. Various items of furniture were shrouded in dust-sheets, one of which had slipped off, laying bare a huge widescreen television. A few murky oil paintings adorned the walls.

'Close the curtains,' said Piravani, setting down the rucksack and unzipping it. Hammond pulled the curtains across and turned to find his companion shining a torch at one of the paintings. It showed a stag being torn to pieces by hounds on some heavily impastoed mountainside. 'Already I dislike the owner,' Piravani growled. 'It'll be a pleasure to run up a big redecorating bill for him.'

He unhooked the painting and tossed it into the dust-sheeted lap of an armchair, then pulled a pick out of the rucksack and started at the wall with a will. The plaster cracked and fell away in ever larger fragments as he struck it, the blows echoing like thunder in the empty house. Soon a stretch of brickwork beneath was laid bare.

'Shine the torch on the bricks,' he panted.

Hammond did as he was told. Piravani stepped back and squinted at the wall as the torchbeam ran slowly along the exposed courses.

'There,' he said suddenly.

'What?'

'The newer mortar. It's a lighter colour.' Peering closer, Hammond saw that over an area about two feet square there was indeed paler mortar between the bricks than elsewhere. 'That's where the safe is.'

They took a hammer and chisel each and began gouging out the mortar. It was a slow, laborious exercise. There was nothing slipshod about Gazi's bricklaying. Nearly ten minutes passed before they dislodged the first brick. But they were rewarded by the sight beneath of the dimpled metal of the safe.

With one brick removed, it was possible to use a crowbar to loosen those around it. They fell away, one by one, and there, in front of them, was the door of the safe. Hammond had expected something bigger. But it had obviously been big enough for Gazi's purposes.

'I bet he's lain awake a few nights at Scheveningen worrying about whether anyone would ever find this,' said Piravani. 'Well, he can stop worrying now. About that, anyway.'

'You do know the combination, don't you, Marco?'

'Oh yes. His son Nikola's date of birth. Twenty-two eleven eighty. Shine the torch on the dial.'

Hammond watched as Piravani rotated the dial to register the numbers. At the last turn, there was a decisive click. He pulled the handle down and eased the door open.

A shoe box filled the interior of the safe, with hardly any room to spare. Piravani lifted it out, flicked a dust-sheet off a nearby coffee table and set it down. As he removed the lid, Hammond trained his torch on the contents: stacks of audio cassettes, held together with rubber bands. Piravani lifted one stack out and took off his glasses to study the tiny pencilled note on the label of the topmost cassette, then did the same with another stack and another after that.

'The labels show the dates covered by each cassette,' he explained. 'They run from December ninety-five to March two thousand. Every conversation Gazi had here in that period that he wanted a secret record of. This is the complete set.' He replaced the lid and stowed the box in the rucksack. 'We have what we came for, doctor.' The torchlight gleamed on his teeth and spectacle lenses as he smiled. 'Good work, hey?'

'We can congratulate each other later, Marco. Shall we get going?'

'Sure. But . . . there's a small change of plan.'

'What do you mean?'

'Doctor, doctor. Do you think I'm a fool?' Piravani clicked his tongue reprovingly. 'You were picked up by the police when you left Kalemegdan. Plessl told me all about it. He didn't actually want to double-cross me, you see. The police forced him to. They had their eye on him as a former Gazi stooge long before I contacted him. Now, the only reason you could have for not mentioning your run-in with the *policija* is that you did some kind of deal with them. I don't blame you. They probably didn't leave you much room for negotiation. But you should have told me. You really should. Because they'll be waiting for us back at the van, won't they? Waiting – to relieve us of the tapes. Well, I've no intention of letting that happen. Which is why we aren't going back to the van.'

'Listen to me, Marco. I only—'

'Don't bother, doctor.' The voice that cut in was not Piravani's. It came from the landing. Instinctively, they both turned towards it. 'He's quite right. You're not going back to the van.' Then recognition struck Hammond like a fist. The voice belonged to Radmilo Uželać.

A torch more powerful than either of theirs suddenly flooded the part of the room they were standing in with light of a dazzling intensity. Of Uželać all they had caught was a glimpse – a dark shape silhouetted in the doorway. Now even that was gone.

'I have a gun and I'll shoot if either of you moves towards me. Is that clear?'

'It's clear,' hissed Piravani, shielding his eyes as best he could.

'You never said anything about coming into the house,' Hammond protested, ashamed by his stupidity in trusting the man. 'In fact, you said . . . ICEFA weren't allowed to take such action.'

'What I said isn't important. What I'm saying *now* is. I want the tapes.'

'*I* not *we*,' growled Piravani. 'Don't you see, doctor? This isn't a police or ICEFA operation. This guy works for Todorović.'

'I work for myself.'

'OK. You plan to sell the tapes to Todorović. Like you sold him the information that got Guido killed. It makes no difference in the end.'

'Just give me the tapes.'

'Why don't you come and get them?'

'Because I don't have to. Take the box out of the rucksack and slide it across to me. If you don't, I'll shoot you both. *Then* I'll come and get them.'

'You're going to shoot us both anyway. Otherwise we'll blab to your bosses that you've sold out.'

As Piravani said it, Hammond realized he was undoubtedly right. This was where the deal he had struck had always been heading. The two policemen and the driver of the car were all in on a cut of whatever Uželać could extract from Todorović. ICEFA had never known about the break-in. And they would never know about the tapes either.

'The only reason you haven't shot us already,' Piravani went on, 'is that you haven't actually seen the tapes with your own eyes. You want to be sure, don't you? Just in case I'm playing some kind of trick. You want to be completely certain.'

'Give me the box.'

'You do it, doctor,' sighed Piravani. 'I couldn't bear to do it myself.' He urged Hammond forward with a gentle push in the back, as if admitting the game was up.

Hammond stepped slowly across to the rucksack and bent over it. He opened wide the half-closed zip and lifted out the shoe box containing the tapes.

And then the first shot was fired.

NINETEEN

Hammond dived for the floor as noise exploded in the room. One shot, then another, then a third, fourth, fifth – in rapid succession. Uželać's torchbeam swivelled crazily across the walls and ceiling, then something heavy thumped down close to Hammond, the boards bouncing beneath him. A moan came from behind him. Rolling round, he saw Piravani kneeling by the coffee table, his hands braced on the rim. All light was at floor level now, casting gigantic, swollen shadows.

Hammond pointed his torch at Uželać. The Serb lay on his side, legs drawn up, clutching a wound with one hand as with the other he reached for his gun a few feet away.

'Finish him,' gasped Piravani. 'Quick.'

Self-preservation is a potent instinct. It cleansed Hammond's mind of panic and doubt and left only kill-or-be-killed ruthlessness in their place. He grabbed the hammer, jumped up and took two stooping strides across the room.

Uželać was beneath him, still stretching for the gun. Hammond kicked it out of his reach and only then noticed the pool of blood he was standing in. It was spreading fast, and blood was bubbling from the Serb's mouth as well, his breath coming in desperate heaves of his lungs. Hammond was startled by the realization that he would have used the hammer if he had needed to. That was clear to him. But he did not need to. Uželać was dying in front of him.

'Don't worry,' he said, turning back to Piravani. 'He's—' But the Italian was no longer propped up against the table. He had slumped to the floor. Hammond rushed across to him. 'Marco?'

'I don't feel good, doctor,' said Piravani through gritted teeth. 'He caught me with a shot.'

'Where? I can't see any blood.' Hammond scanned Piravani with the torch, anxiously but in vain. There was no sign of a wound, though his dark clothing and the confusing interplay of shadows made it hard to be sure.

'Somewhere in my gut. *Gesù*, it hurts.'

If he was bleeding internally, there was nothing Hammond could do for him without getting him to a hospital. He pulled out his phone. 'I'll call for an ambulance. What's the emergency number?'

'It's lucky for me you don't know.'

'Don't be stupid, Marco. What's the number?'

'We call no one, doctor. The police will be close behind any ambulance. Ask yourself how many others are on Todorović's payroll. We have to get those tapes to The Hague.'

'You'll never make it without proper medical attention. What about the Voćnjak Clinic? I could contact Miljanović.'

'You think we can trust him?'

'I think we have to.'

Piravani pondered the dilemma for a moment. Then a phone started beeping – in Uželać's pocket. 'That'll be his back-up boys. They heard the shots and want to know he's OK. We've got to get out of here before they come looking for him. Maybe we can contact Miljanović once we're clear of the house.'

'Can you walk?'

'I'll have to.' Piravani levered himself back on to his knees. Hammond knelt beside him, supporting him beneath his arms. The torchbeam caught drops of blood on the floor. He was bleeding, though not copiously. Any exertion might change that. But it seemed that was a risk they were going to have to take. 'Get the gun. It's behind me.'

'I didn't even know you had a gun,' said Hammond, fumbling in search of it with one hand as he continued to hold Piravani up with the other.

'Bought it last night. A gun is a wise precaution in this city, doctor. As you've discovered.'

'Were you the first to fire?'

'Oh yes. I reckoned he'd be watching you, not me. Nailing him then was the only chance we had.'

Hammond found the gun and picked it up carefully. It was smaller than Uželać's, a snub-nosed revolver that Piravani must have found easy to conceal in his boilersuit. 'Got it.'

'Good. Put it in your pocket.' At that moment the phone stopped beeping. 'They'll wonder why he hasn't answered. They'll probably wait five minutes at least to see if he comes out, but we don't have much longer than that. How many are there?'

'There were three of them with Uželać at Kalemegdan.'

'OK. Let's say three. One will stay by the van. Another will follow Uželać's route in – he must have tracked us through the snow to the open window downstairs. The third will guard the front gate. They'll reckon they have us surrounded.'

'And won't they?'

'No. Because Gazi's a paranoid son-of-a-bitch, like I told you. Milošević was a prisoner in his own house by the end. Gazi saw the danger of that happening to him and constructed—' Piravani winced and broke off, then took a slow, soothing breath. 'He constructed a tunnel. It runs from the cellar to a sewer access shaft in the next side-street. I loosened the manhole cover when I went out this evening. It's how I was planning to leave. There's a second van, doctor. Parked near by. We just have to hope . . . the new owner of this place . . . hasn't blocked the tunnel.'

'You're in no condition to scramble along a tunnel, Marco.'

'I'm in a condition to *try*. Help me up.'

Getting Piravani on to his feet was a struggle, but Hammond managed it, ignoring as far as he was able the jabs of pain from his ribs. The Italian was obviously in much greater pain and seemed to be functioning on willpower alone. They staggered past Uželać's motionless body through the sticky pool of his blood to the door, where Hammond left Piravani propped against the wall for a moment while he retrieved the rucksack, with the box of tapes zipped away inside. Then they lurched across the landing and started down the stairs, Piravani leaning heavily on the balustrade as he negotiated each step. To Hammond's relief, there was no apparent increase in his bleeding. But the relief was highly conditional. The likelihood was that his abdomen was slowly filling with blood. Willpower would only carry him so far.

The entrance to the cellar was beneath the staircase in the hall: a door opening on to steeper, narrower steps that led down into a gulf of darkness. Hammond was supporting most of Piravani's weight by now. The Italian had to stop to recover his breath and gather some strength before they proceeded.

They descended into tomb-like chill and musty air that caught in the throat. Casting the torchbeam ahead of them, Hammond saw a large, concrete-floored chamber, mostly given over to the storage of unwanted furniture. A wine rack covered one wall, no more than a quarter full with bottles, empty metal shelving another.

'I either sit down or fall down,' gasped Piravani, resting against the upturned legs of a stack of dining chairs. 'Put one of these near the shelves.'

Hammond lifted a chair out of the stack and set it down, then led Piravani across to it. The Italian gave a sigh of relief as he flopped on to it that sounded like air escaping from a punctured tyre. He held his head back as if only by doing so could he prevent himself toppling forward.

'How do you feel, Marco?' Hammond asked, unable to tell in the dust-moted torchlight how pale he actually was.

'Weak. That's how, doctor. But we don't have time for—'

There was a noise above them: a creaking board from the direction of the kitchen. Instantly, Hammond switched off the torch. Total darkness enveloped them. Neither man spoke or moved. Piravani's shallow, faltering breaths were the only sound in the cellar.

As his ears strained to catch any further noise upstairs, Hammond hoped, more fervently with every passing second, that the creak had just been some random expansion or contraction of the woodwork. He would not allow himself to believe that one of Uželać's accomplices was already in the house.

But they were. Because there came in the next second the distant, muffled beeping of Uželać's phone. And the hurrying, undisguised footfalls of someone hunting the sound.

Piravani grasped Hammond's shoulder and pulled him close enough to whisper in his ear. 'Be quick. There's a gap at one end of the shelving that you can reach into to pull it away from the wall. It's hinged at the other end. The door to the tunnel is behind it.'

'He'll hear me for sure, Marco.'

'I know. Give me the gun. I'll hold him up here while you get away.'

'I'm not leaving you.'

'You have to. I can't go any further. The tunnel's about a hundred metres long. It leads to a hatch into the sewer access shaft. There's a ladder from there to the manhole.'

'*I'm not leaving you, Marco.*'

'Only one of us is thinking straight, doctor. If you stay with me, the tapes will end up with Todorović. You have to deliver them to The Hague. Otherwise all this has been for nothing. Don't try to leave the country by train or plane. Here's the key to the apartment. And the key to the other van.' He wrestled them out of one of his pockets and pressed them into Hammond's hand. 'There's a recorder you can play the tapes on in my bag. Take that and my money belt in case you need to bribe your way out, then drive to the Romanian border. The E70 will get you there in—'

Uželać's phone had stopped beeping. There was total silence in the house. Then they heard another floorboard creak.

'He's found the body,' Piravani continued, calmly but urgently. 'He'll start searching the rest of the house soon. It could take him a while to get down here, but I won't have the strength to push the

170

shelving back into place after you for much longer, so we have to move now.'

Hammond tried to force his brain to decide what he should do, but it simply would not obey. Either he abandoned Piravani or he gave up trying to escape. The chances of them both surviving were vanishingly slim. He was frightened, but he was also angry. He did not deserve to face this stark choice. But here it was, before him.

'Promise me you'll get the tapes to The Hague, doctor. It's all I ask.'

'Marco, I—'

'Just promise me.'

And there, in that instant, the choice was made. It formed as something hard and sharp in Hammond's mind. He squeezed Piravani's hand. 'I'll do everything I can.'

'Give me the gun.'

'Here.' Hammond folded Piravani's fingers round the handle of the revolver.

'Don't worry about me. I'll phone for an ambulance as soon as I've dealt with our friend upstairs.'

'You do that.'

'Thanks for not mentioning the money.'

'What money?'

'Gazi's, of course. It's what got you into this, remember.'

Hammond had genuinely forgotten. The money. How pitiful his attempt to buy Gazi's silence seemed now. How pitiful – and how pointless. 'I don't care about that any more, Marco.'

'I'm glad to hear you say that, doctor.'

'It's true.'

'Good. Go now.'

'Are you sure?'

'Oh yes. I'm sure.'

'I'll see you, Marco.'

'I hope I'll see you too, doctor. *Buon viaggio.*'

Hammond switched the torch on, waited a second for his eyes to adjust to the brightness of the beam, then moved to the end of the

171

shelving unit and reached into the gap between it and the side wall. He was able to squeeze his fingers behind the unit. Setting the torch down, he grasped it with both hands and started pulling.

At first, it would not budge. He filled his lungs, disregarding the pain from his ribs, and tried again. This time the unit moved, scraping loudly across the floor and pivoting out from the concealed hinges at the other end. He shone the torch into the space behind and saw the door of the tunnel: thick steel, fastened with two large bolts.

He glanced back at Piravani, who urged him on with several flaps of his arm. Hammond raised a hand in acknowledgement – and farewell. Then he dodged behind the unit and made his way to the door.

He slipped the bolts, pulled the door open and shone the torch along the tunnel. It was about four feet wide and six feet high, running dead straight into total darkness. The walls, floor and roof were rough cement, festooned in cobwebs. A man would have to be desperate indeed to use it as an escape route.

He stepped into the tunnel, pulled the door shut behind him and tapped it three times as a signal to Piravani. Then he started walking.

He had to stoop slightly to clear the roof, and judging distance when he was carrying the only source of light was more or less impossible. He hurried forward, struggling to prevent his mind dwelling on the possibility that his exit might somehow be blocked. He had never suffered from claustrophobia. He knew the fear he felt to be entirely rational. A muffled thud behind him was surely the shelving unit sliding back against the door. Whatever choice he had vanished with the sound.

Eventually, his torchbeam picked out a gleam of steel ahead. He quickened his pace and saw what it was: a circular hatch, about two feet in diameter, set in the wall at the end of the tunnel.

The lever on the hatch was even stiffer than the bolts had been. He was sweating in the sub-zero chill by the time he had shifted it and the pain from his ribs seemed to have invaded every part of his body. He had to give himself a moment to recover before he could open the hatch. And then all he saw, at the end of a short crawl-way, was a second hatch.

The pain did not matter now. He wanted out of this. He wanted to see night sky above his head. He clambered into the crawl-way and wedged himself against the wall. Then he grasped the lever and heaved at it. It gave.

A gust of foul, sulphurated air confirmed he had reached the sewer access shaft. The hatch opened out into it, adjacent to a metal ladder that led up twelve feet or so to the manhole cover. He could see the cover as he leant out into the shaft with the torch, grab-holes set tantalizingly around its circumference. Concerned that the beam might attract attention, he switched the torch off and thrust it inside his boilersuit, then braced himself for the ascent.

Exactly how he made it from the crawl-way to the ladder was obscured by a fog of pain. But there he was, hauling himself up, hand over hand, rung, by rung, in the choking darkness. He had counted the rungs before switching off the torch and now he counted them down as he climbed.

But somehow he had miscounted. There was one fewer than he was expecting. The faint moonlight seeping in through the grab-holes fell on his knuckles as he grasped the topmost rung. He had made it.

Whatever Piravani had done to loosen the manhole cover had been effective. It required little effort to raise it clear of its lip. Hammond peered out along a dark, deserted street. There was no van in sight. He tried the other way.

And there it was, no more than ten yards from him, a battered old Transit very similar to the one they had driven to Dedinje earlier in the night. He pushed the cover aside, then, with one final effort, hoisted himself up through the manhole.

He crouched in the road, summoning his resources. He had always considered himself a fit man, but he did not feel it now. He wondered what was happening back inside the Villa Ruža. And then he tried not to wonder. Piravani wanted him to make good his escape, not waste time agonizing.

He stood up, toed the manhole cover back into position and headed for the van, feeling in his pocket for the key. He reached the driver's door, grasped the handle and tried to slide the key into the lock. But it would not fit. He took out the torch and shone it at the lock, assuming he must somehow have missed the keyhole. But no. That was not the problem.

The problem was ice. The van had been standing there since Friday in sub-zero temperatures and the lock had frozen. Piravani's foresight had not stretched as far as bringing a can of de-icer with them. Hammond swore under his breath, took off one of his gloves and rubbed the lock, then cupped his hands and blew warm air on to it. But it made no difference. The lock was frozen solid.

So was the lock on the passenger door. He had his getaway vehicle. But it was of little use to him if he could not get into it.

There was only one thing for it. He took the hammer out of the rucksack and with several blows smashed a hole in the passenger's window, then reached in and opened the door using the internal handle.

He was actually congratulating himself for having the presence of mind to enter that side rather than showering the driver's seat in broken glass when he heard a shout from somewhere behind him. Glancing back, he saw the flash of a torchbeam.

'*Stanite!*' came a bellowed voice from the direction of the beam.

In the same instant, several lights came on in villas and gate-houses lining the road that until now had been veiled in darkness, streetlamps flickered into life and an alarm – it had to be the Villa Ruža's – began wailing loudly.

'*Stanite!*'

Hammond had no intention of waiting to find out what the word meant. He scrambled into the driving seat, with the rucksack on his back pushing him so far forward that he was bent over the steering-wheel, and began searching for the ignition. But the dashboard was a confusion of shadows and he could not find it.

Then he did see it, thanks to the torchbeam shining into the cab. The man who had shouted at him was nearing the broken window. Hammond thrust the key into the ignition and turned it. The engine spluttered and died.

'*Stanite sada!*'

He turned the key again. This time the engine spluttered and started. He shoved the gearlever into what he hoped was first and pressed his foot down on the accelerator.

Only as the van skidded forward did he realize that the windscreen was opaque with ice. Even if he had been able to find the headlamp switch, it would have been of little use to him. He wound down the window and leant out. The road ahead was clear and the tyres had begun to grip. Steering was awkward, but he dared not slow down.

The streetlamps were a help but also a hazard. They might well enable the man with the torch to catch the van's registration number. If, as Hammond suspected, he was a security guard for one of the villas, he would probably phone it into the police within minutes. The getaway had already gone wrong.

Hammond's orientation was not holding up well either. As he reached the end of the road and slewed right, he hoped rather than judged that he was turning away from the Villa Ruža, not towards it. The gentle downhill slope seemed to confirm he had made the correct choice, but he knew he could not drive much further like this. He would have to stop and clear the windscreen.

But he could not afford to stop yet. He had to put some distance between himself and the villa. He glanced at the illuminated speedometer. He was only travelling at fifty kilometres per hour, though it felt a lot faster thanks to the cold air blasting into his face. He pushed the accelerator down further.

Then the steering suddenly slackened. He was skidding on black ice as the slope steepened and a crossroads loomed ahead, with no buildings visible beyond it. He stabbed at the brake, but that only exaggerated the skid. The van took its own course, surging across the junction, mounting a kerb and careering down a grassy incline.

Hammond jerked his head back into the cab as bushes and branches began slashing at the side of the van. The wheels were juddering, the whole vehicle bouncing. Instinctively he let go of the steering-wheel and threw himself down across the seat, expecting a collision with a tree or some other large obstacle at any moment.

But no collision ever came. The van began to bog down in the snowy ground and the shrubs it was bursting through slowed it still further until eventually it ran out of momentum and shuddered to a halt.

Hammond pushed himself up and craned his head out of the window. The van was embedded in snow and mud up to its wheel arches. It was clearly going nowhere. The engine had already cut out, probably because the exhaust pipe was blocked. He swore wearily, took off one of his gloves and rubbed his face. What the hell was he supposed to do now?

He clambered out of the van and looked back the way he had come. There was no sign of pursuit. But there would be soon enough. He flashed the torch ahead of him: a shrub-pocked waste of snow led towards the streetlamps of a distant road. The river – and New Belgrade – were somewhere in that direction. He unloaded the tools into the van to lighten the rucksack, then started walking.

TWENTY

Hammond was dead on his feet by the time he reached the apartment. His mind was almost as drained as his body, which was in its way a blessing, sparing him too vivid a contemplation of what might have happened to Piravani. It was just gone four o'clock and he knew that if he lay down he would instantly fall asleep. But sleep was out of the question. Piravani's plan had him heading fast for the Romanian border, if not already over it. Instead, he was still in Belgrade, with no means of leaving the city in the near future.

He changed out of the boilersuit and immersed his face in a basinful of cold water, seeking to shock his brain into thinking clearly. He owed it to Piravani – he owed it to himself – to do whatever was most likely to get the tapes to The Hague. But how would the Italian act in these circumstances? What choices would he make?

He needed help. He needed it badly and he needed it now. Who was there he could turn to? Shoving a wad of dinars from Piravani's money belt into his wallet, he noticed the piece of paper on which Zineta had written her brother's address and phone number. '*If you run into any trouble, he might be able to help you.*' Well, he had run into trouble all right. There was no doubt about that.

He rang the number without pausing to consider all the possible ramifications. He had had a bellyful of ramifications.

The likeliest outcome, he reflected as the ring tone repeated itself

177

over and over again, was that Goran would simply not answer. It was, after all, the middle of the night.

But then the phone was picked up and a gruff, sleepy voice said, '*Da?*'

'Goran Perović?'

'*Ko je to?*'

'Am I speaking to Goran Perović?'

'*Da*. Yes.'

'I'm sorry to call you like this, but Zineta—'

'You are Zineta's English friend?'

'Yes. I'm—'

'Don't say your name. Listen good. The police are watching me since Friday. This line could be bugged.'

'I need your help, Goran.'

'*Zvinite*. Sorry. I can't help you. Too much danger. For you *and* me. Sorry.'

'But—'

'Sorry.'

The line was dead.

Panic began to set in. If Goran's phone really was being tapped, it might be possible to trace the call Hammond had just made. He had to leave the apartment without delay. The rest of his thinking could be done on the hoof. He abandoned his travelling bag, stowing his clothes and toiletries in the rucksack along with the tapes and the pocket recorder, grabbed some cheese to sustain himself and headed out. He had Piravani's passport with him as well as his own. He also had the money belt, which contained enough pounds, euros and Swiss francs to pay his way across Europe several times over.

A plan of sorts formed in his mind as he trudged east from the apartment block towards the city centre. Piravani had presumably warned him off trains and planes because the railway station and the airport were easy to stake out and there would be no services

178

until morning anyway. But there was no way of knowing how many police officers had been in league with Uželać. Those who had been covering his back at the Villa Ruža were probably busy right now trying to explain to their superiors what had happened there. Only Uželać had examined Hammond's passport. None of his personal details were known to anyone else. He should be able to walk straight through the border crossing. Once in Romania, he would surely be in the clear.

He was a long way from the border of course. And he had no transport of any kind. What he did have, though, was plenty of money. At the Hyatt Regency or the Inter-Continental he should be able to find a taxi driver willing to take him where he needed to go.

He tried the Inter-Continental first. Unsurprisingly, at such an hour, there were no taxis waiting, but one pulled up after five minutes or so to disgorge a drunken quartet of dinner-suited men and party-frocked women who had evidently enjoyed a much more carefree Saturday night than he had.

The taxi driver, a foxy-faced freelancer with a vehicle well short of limousine standard, greeted Hammond's cautious approach with a mixture of opportunism and indifference.

'I need a ride out of the city.'

'Where you want to go?'

'Romania.'

'*Rumunija?* The country?'

'Yes. The country.'

'Is a long way.'

'I know. Just get me to the border.'

'Still a long way. So it cost.'

'How much?'

Looking Hammond up and down seemed as crucial to the calculation as the distance. The verdict was accompanied by a take-it-or-leave-it shrug. 'One thousand dinare.'

Hammond took it.

*

The taxi driver followed a route straight through the city centre to the bridge over the Danube. There was hardly any traffic. The streets were largely empty. It was too late by now even for the latest of revellers and too early for everyone else. They passed the statue of Prince Mihailo Obrenović in Trg Republike on their way. Hammond found it hard to believe that it was less than forty-eight hours since he had waited beside the statue for Piravani to pick him up. He had still been intent then on complying with Ingrid's demands. Now, he was intent on something altogether worthier, though its consequences for him were as yet unclear. But he had promised Piravani he would see it through to the end. And he was driven on by his determination to do just that.

The taxi driver mellowed sufficiently in the course of the journey to do Hammond a favour at the border. They stopped behind a queue of lorries waiting to cross and he cadged a lift on Hammond's behalf, securing one for him as far as Timişoara.

'Timişoara has airport,' he announced. 'You maybe fly to *Bukurest*.'

Hammond had named Bucharest as his ultimate destination for the simple reason that he could not name any other Romanian city. 'Excellent. Thanks very much.'

'Worth tip, I think.'

And Hammond was inclined to agree.

The Serbian border police paid him little attention. His passport received a cursory glance and a blurred exit stamp. It was clear no manhunt was in progress for him. Whatever the Belgrade police had found at the Villa Ruža – however it had ended for Piravani – he was not implicated.

But that would not remain the case for long. As soon as Todorović learnt of the break-in, he would guess what had been removed. And he would come looking for it. There was no doubt about that.

It was strange, therefore, how certain Hammond was that he was acting for the best. Abandoning the attempt to buy off Gazi had lifted a load from his conscience. He was doing the right thing – for the right reason. He felt a perverse sense of liberation as he sat in the cab of the lorry, the rucksack at his feet, heading north through the pre-dawn darkness. He had not hitchhiked since his student days and oddly the hazards and stresses he had recently endured had left him feeling more like the young man he had been then – status and possessions stripped away, pretensions gone, reputation disregarded, but principles in some measure restored.

He was back in the more familiar surroundings of a club lounge at Bucharest airport later that day, with several hours at his disposal before KLM's next flight to Amsterdam. He had bought a new phone and felt safe at last to make the calls he had been rehearsing in his mind since leaving Belgrade: the calls that would take him past the point of no return on the course he had set himself.

Miljanović had jotted his home number on the back of a Voćnjak Clinic card. Hammond reckoned he was unlikely to be working on a Sunday. And so it proved.

'I did not expect to hear from you so soon, Edward. Have you decided to accept my offer?'

Only then did Hammond remember Miljanović's semi-serious suggestion that he go to work in Belgrade. 'Look, Svetozar, I'm sorry, but this is very important. I need to ask you an enormous favour.'

'Are you in trouble, Edward?' Miljanović's tone had altered instantly to one of genuine concern.

'No. At least, not now. But . . . I was mixed up in things in Belgrade I couldn't tell you about. Still can't, actually. It's safer for you not to know the details.'

'Does this have something to do with Gazi?'

'Yes. And not just Gazi either. Some of those . . . war criminals who are still in Serbia. But if all goes well I'll soon be able to explain what I mean.'

'This is very—'

'I know, Svetozar, I know. But listen. Do you think you could possibly find out whether a man suffering from a gunshot wound was admitted to a Belgrade hospital last night?'

'A gunshot wound? What are you involved in, my friend?'

'I really can't explain. Not yet. Will you do it?'

'Of course. It is . . . not a problem. But—'

'Middle-aged Italian. His name may not be known. Between you and me, though, it's Marco Piravani.'

'Piravani? He was Gazi's—'

'Exactly. But he's one of the good guys now. I want him to get the best possible treatment. I'll pay.'

'I do not understand. How are you and—'

'I know you don't understand, Svetozar. But you will. And when you do I think you'll be . . . well . . . pleased to have helped.'

Miljanović thought about that in silence for a second, then said, 'You can count on me, Edward. You must know you can.'

'Thanks. I really appreciate it. And, er, you'd better . . . check the mortuaries as well.'

'You think Piravani could be dead?'

'More likely than alive, to tell the truth.'

'I will make the calls.'

'Let me know what you find out, will you?'

'Of course. You will be on this number?'

'For a while.'

'And you *will* explain everything – when you can?'

'That's a promise.'

'Hello?'

'Hi, Bill. It's Edward.'

'Good God. I thought I'd never hear from you again.'

'Sorry. Life's been . . . complicated.'

'So I gather. How is Zürich?'

'Zürich?'

'That's where you are, isn't it? So Alice seems to think, anyway.'

'No. I . . . Look, Bill, I've had to do a bit of . . . covering up lately. When I say life's been complicated, I mean it.'

'But you can't tell me why, right?'

'On the contrary. That's exactly what I want to do. Fill you in on everything that's been happening.'

'Fire away, then.'

'I can't discuss it on the phone, Bill. It's . . . sensitive stuff.'

'Was Kendall right, Edward? Have you found out something about Kate's murder?'

'Yes. I have.'

'For God's sake. Why didn't you tell me?'

'I couldn't. But I can now. Or rather I will, if you'll meet me tomorrow. In The Hague.'

'The Hague? Have you been there all this time?'

'No. But I'll be there tomorrow. I'm going to book a room at the Kurhaus Hotel, on the seafront at Scheveningen. You want me to make that two rooms?'

'All right.'

'I'll pay.'

'So you damn well should, in the circumstances. Why do I have to travel to—'

'Just be there, Bill, OK?'

'OK. But—'

'No buts. I'll see you tomorrow. 'Bye.'

Contacting Ingrid involved the by now familiar rigmarole of speaking to a barely bilingual intermediary who arranged for him to be called back. As a result he did not know where Ingrid actually was. Though, of course, she did not know where he was either. Which was just as well, given what he had to say to her.

'Another change of phone, doctor? You are becoming very cautious.'

'Even though there's nothing for me to be cautious about any more.'

'What do you mean?'

183

'Your father's money isn't going to be transferred to the Cayman Islands, Ingrid. *That's* what I mean.'

She was shocked into silence for a moment. Then she said, 'Have you lost your mind? I have warned you what will happen if you do not arrange the transfer.'

'Tell your father he can make all the accusations against me he wants. I'll take my chances. I'm not helping you get hold of his money. It's as simple as that.'

'But . . . you said you needed until Monday.' It was undeniably satisfying to hear the consternation in her voice.

'So, it's good of me not to make you wait until then to hear the bad news, isn't it?'

'Where are you?'

'That's no longer any of your business.'

'And where is the Accountant?'

'Goodbye, Ingrid.'

On the plane, he felt almost light-hearted. He drank too much complimentary champagne and gazed out blithely at the rolling clouds above Europe. It was not until he woke from a short, deep sleep that the reality of what he had done impinged on him. He had burnt his bridges. There was no way back.

And Piravani? What had he suffered to win Hammond the freedom to do the right thing at last? Miljanović had phoned during the flight. Hammond called him back as soon as he cleared customs at Schiphol.

'Piravani is alive, Edward.'

'Thank God.' Somehow, against the odds, Piravani had got out of the Villa Ruža alive – just.

'He's in intensive care, at the Central Clinic, heavily sedated. I am told . . . he has a police guard.'

'He would have.'

'He was involved in some kind of shoot-out last night at the

184

Villa Ruža, the house in Dedinje where Gazi used to live. You know what ICEFA is?'

'Yes.'

'I thought you would. Were you . . . there with him, Edward?'

'Do you really want to know?'

'I'm not sure.'

'Then just tell me what his chances are.'

'No better than fifty-fifty.'

'Do they know who he is yet?'

'No.'

'I'd like it to stay that way as long as possible.'

'I shall say nothing, Edward. Not a word.'

'Thanks.'

'You're welcome. But remember: if Piravani does pull through, he will have to answer a lot of questions.'

'So will I, Svetozar. And, when the time comes, I'll be glad to.'

It was Sunday evening and Hammond had no way of contacting Zineta until the office-cleaning agency she worked for opened on Monday morning. There was nothing to be gained by going on to The Hague that night, so he booked into the Schiphol Hilton. Only then, holed up in one of its hundreds of identical rooms, did he dare listen to any of the tapes.

He understood virtually nothing that he heard in his random sample, of course. Gravelly male voices, one of which he recognized as Gazi's, conversed and debated and discussed. Milošević; Kosovo; NATO: those were individual words he thought he caught. For the rest, he did not have a clue. But to Zineta – or any other Serb – it would all make sense. He willed himself to believe the tapes would do everything Piravani had hoped – everything and more.

TWENTY-ONE

Hammond checked out of the Hilton promptly the following morning after an early breakfast and headed for The Hague. He called the office-cleaning agency from the train. As agreed, Zineta had asked them to supply him with her number.

Her first reaction, when she heard his voice, was relief that he was alive and well. 'Where are you, Edward? I've been so worried about you these past four days. Goran called me yesterday from a payphone and said he was under police surveillance, so he hadn't been able to help when you contacted him. But you wouldn't have contacted him at all if you hadn't been in trouble. Are you really all right?'

'I'm fine. I'll be in The Hague in about half an hour. I'm on the train from Schiphol.'

'Is Marco with you?'

'No. There's a lot I have to tell you, Zineta.'

'Is it good news?'

'Some of it is.'

'The apartment's only a few minutes from Hollands-Spoor station. Come straight round.'

'Give me the address and I'll be there.'

Zineta's apartment was over a cheap convenience store, whose lugubrious Asian proprietor watched with beady inquisitiveness as Hammond pressed the bell by Zineta's name-card.

He heard her running footsteps on the stairs. Then the door opened. 'Edward.' She looked weary and somehow gaunter than he remembered. But her smile was warm and genuine. She hugged him. And Hammond was aware that this too the shopkeeper would observe and note for future reference. 'Thank God you're all right.'

She led the way up three flights of stairs to the attic flat: bedsitting-room, kitchenette and bathroom that were tiny in floor area and seemed tinier still thanks to the slope of the roof. Thin grey light slanted in through the dormer windows, falling mockingly on Zineta's attempts to brighten her home from home: a rubber plant standing next to the sofa, a striped rug in front of the hissing gas fire, a colourfully embroidered cloth on the table. In this, the place where she lived, her exile from her native land was somehow magnified.

'Where's Marco?' she asked at once.

'In hospital. In Belgrade.'

'What happened?'

'He was . . . shot.'

'*Shot?* My God, Edward, what . . .' She put her hands to her head. 'How is he?'

'I'm not sure. It could be touch and go.'

'You mean . . .'

'I've asked Svetozar Miljanović to make sure he gets the best possible treatment.'

She lit a cigarette, her hand shaking as she held the lighter. 'I guess this is what I've been expecting to hear since you put me on that train in Lugano. I knew he'd . . . take whatever risks he thought he needed to take to get at Todorović.'

'You were right.' Hammond winced as he took the rucksack off and lowered it to the floor. 'Mind if I sit down?'

'No. Of course not. Please. I am forgetting my manners.' She ushered him into an armchair. 'Is there anything I can get you? Coffee, maybe?'

'Just a glass of water to wash down my next paracetamol.'

'Sure.' She fetched one from the kitchenette and watched him swallow the pill. 'You look . . . as if you've been through a lot, Edward.'

'Well, I suppose I have. Your contact at ICEFA, Zineta. Was his name Radmilo Uželać?'

'Yes.' She sat down opposite him. 'How did you know?'

'We met him in Belgrade. When I helped Marco break into the Villa Ruža.'

'You helped him do *what*?'

'Hear me out. Marco was looking for something Gazi left in a wall safe at the villa – something he could use against Todorović. Uželać was looking for it as well. But, in his case, he wanted to sell it to Todorović, just like he'd sold the information you supplied that got Felltrini killed. It was actually down to me that he knew about the break-in.' He sighed. 'I'd better explain.'

There were no evasions or omissions, no massaging of the facts. He wanted Zineta to understand exactly how and why events had followed the course they had. She pressed him to tell her what Gazi had hidden in the safe as soon as he mentioned it, but only when he had related everything else that had happened was he willing to satisfy her curiosity.

He lifted the shoe box out of the rucksack, stood it on the coffee table between them and removed the lid. Zineta peered in at the contents. 'What are they?' she asked.

'Gazi recorded every important meeting or conversation he had in his study at the villa between December 1995 and March 2000. And here they are, on these tapes: hundreds of hours' worth of evidence that Marco's confident will see Todorović join his old boss in Scheveningen Prison.'

'Does Todorović know you have these?'

'He must know by now someone has.'

'What are you going to do with them?'

'Hand them over to ICTY. They're evidence against Gazi as well as Todorović. But the point is, Zineta, they may also contain information about—'

'Monir.' She spoke her son's name as if it was some kind of talisman. There was a sudden gleam of hope in her eyes. She reached out and laid her hand on the nearest bundle of tapes. 'My God,' she murmured. 'The answer could be here.'

'That's why I brought them to you. I promised Marco I'd deliver them to ICTY. But first . . .' Hammond pulled the recorder out of the rucksack and stood it next to the shoe box. 'You should listen to them. Since everyone on them is speaking Serbian, they mean nothing to me, but there may be something there that will get me out of a lot of trouble.'

Zineta frowned at him. 'I don't understand.'

'I told you I'd agreed to help Ingrid get hold of her father's money because she'd threatened to harm Alice. That wasn't exactly true.'

'No?'

He shook his head. 'No.'

Then he told her the truth. He was surprised by how much better it made him feel. It was clear to him now that he should have done it a lot sooner. Just as he should have defied Ingrid to do her worst right from the start. The irony was that if he had, Gazi's hoard of tapes would have remained walled up in the Villa Ruža.

'I still have no idea why Gazi ordered Kate's murder,' he concluded with a sigh.

'But these tapes may tell you.'

'They may tell *you*.'

'Oh, I think I know already, Edward. Living with him for as long as I did taught me how his mind works. He hates owing anyone anything. He always has to be the man who stands alone. Owing you his life would dent his . . . self-sufficiency.'

'He paid me a handsome fee. That was all he owed me.'

'Maybe not, as he saw it. Did he know your wife had left you for another man?'

'Svetozar knew. So did every member of my team. Any one of

them might have said something about it in his presence, I suppose. People are never as careful with your confidences as you'd like them to be.'

'In Gazi's world, an unfaithful wife deserves to die. You see? He was doing you a favour.'

'A *favour*?'

'He was paying his debt to you in kind. A life for a life.'

It sounded crazy. But it also sounded horribly plausible. 'Oh God. It really was my fault she died, wasn't it?'

'No. It was Gazi's doing. You're not responsible.'

'I wonder if Kate's brother will see it that way.'

'Will you tell him?'

'Yes. Later today, as a matter of fact. I've asked him to meet me here in The Hague.'

'Shouldn't you wait until we know whether there's anything on the tapes to prove you didn't ask Gazi to have Kate killed?'

'No. Either there is or there isn't. And either Bill believes me or he doesn't. It's the truth for me now – wherever it leads.'

'That's a brave decision. If Todorović knows the tapes exist, he'll already be looking for you.'

'But he doesn't know who I am. Uželać is dead. And he can't get anything out of Marco while he's sedated. So, we have some time on our side.'

'Not much. He's bound to guess you'll deliver them to ICTY.'

'I agree. So, first thing tomorrow, we do just that.'

'I can't listen to all these tapes in one day, Edward. Like you said, it must be hundreds of hours.'

'But Gazi didn't set up Monir's removal until he'd decided to go into hiding himself. That limits your search to the last set of tapes: January to March 2000. And Kate was murdered on the third of April, 1996. That also limits the search.'

'Yes.' Zineta nodded as she contemplated the task ahead of her. 'I see.'

'It's worth trying, don't you reckon?'

She spread her arms and smiled at him. 'Of course. I never

expected . . .' Then, abruptly, she began to cry. 'I'm sorry, so sorry. It's just . . .'

He stretched across the table and clasped her hand. 'You never expected you might actually get a chance to learn where Gazi sent him?'

'No. I . . .' She swallowed hard. 'I didn't.'

'If there's something on these tapes that helps you, Zineta, it will have been worth it – whatever else they prove or don't prove.'

'Thank you for saying that, Edward.' She stood up and moved to the window, where she dried her tears with the back of her hand and lit another cigarette and gazed out at the city that stretched away from her towards the sea. 'Will Marco pull through, do you think?'

'I don't know. I hope so.'

'So do I. I'd like to . . . thank him as well.'

'You may find no mention of Monir at all. You understand that, don't you?'

'Oh yes. There are no guarantees. But the only way I'll know for certain . . .' she turned to look at him and summoned a smile, 'is to listen to the tapes.'

'And there may also be a lot of stuff you'd prefer not to have to listen to.'

'Don't worry, Edward. I know what kind of a man Dragan Gazi is. I know what I'm in for.'

'Then . . .'

'I'd better make a start, hadn't I?'

Zineta phoned the agency and cancelled her shift for that evening. They agreed Hammond would return to collect the tapes at nine o'clock, giving her close to twelve hours to glean what she could. When he left, she was already listening to the first of them through the recorder's earphones, hunched over the coffee table, frowning in concentration. They exchanged a farewell wave, then he stepped out through the door and headed down the stairs.

*

It was a cold, grey day in The Hague, though nowhere near as cold as it had been in Belgrade. Hammond walked slowly through the city, savouring the lightness of his thoughts. Everything was simple now: deliver the tapes; refute Gazi's accusation, if he ever made it; trust the people closest to him to believe him when he spoke the truth.

He stopped for a coffee in the Passage Arcade. Checking his phone, he found a text message had arrived within the last hour from Miljanović. '*Your friend stable & unconscious. No change expected soon. Prognosis uncertain.*' He uttered a silent prayer that Piravani would recover. He more than anyone deserved to see Todorović stand trial at ICTY.

Hammond texted back his thanks, finished his coffee and headed on, steering a steady course towards Scheveningen. He passed the Gothic pile of the Vredespaleis, home of the International Court of Justice, then came, on the other side of the park beyond it, to its annexe dedicated to the affairs of the former Yugoslavia.

Gazing at ICTY's unpretentious premises from the street, he imagined proceedings had already begun for the day in the trial of Dragan Gazi. He could go in, if he wanted, and sit at the front of the public gallery, and wait for his former patient to notice him. He wondered if Ingrid had told her father yet that the money was not coming after all; that Dr Hammond had refused to play ball. Probably not. But sooner or later she would have to. Because Dr Hammond was not going to change his mind.

It was mid-afternoon when Bill arrived. Hammond returned to the Kurhaus from a late lunch at a nearby restaurant to be told his brother-in-law was waiting for him in the bar.

Bill had never quite mastered the art of casual dressing since leaving the Army. There remained a military sharpness about the cut of his trousers and the creasing of his shirt fronts. And the beard he had grown was as well-trimmed as any of the lawns he was responsible for. A few seconds passed before he noticed Hammond walk into the bar and during those seconds Hammond reflected on the tenuous nature of their relationship. Their tastes, opinions and personalities were scarcely harmonious. Though they did not dislike each other, there had always been a slight mutual mistrust, detectable more in what was not said than what was. But reticence would not help them in the present case. The time had come for candour.

'Bill. Good to see you.'

Bill put down his beer and clambered off his bar stool. They shook hands, Bill's grip as crushing as ever. There was a wariness in his eyes, Hammond noticed. This might have been the expression he wore in his active service days when entering sniper country. 'Good to see you too, Edward. There have been times this past week when I thought I never would again.'

'I'm sorry if I've been elusive.'

'Not to mention evasive.'

'Room OK?'

'The room's top-notch. But I wasn't actually looking for a winter break on the North Sea coast, so I'd raise no objections if you got on with explaining why you've summoned me here.'

'It was hardly a summons.'

Bill looked askance at him. 'If you've found out something about my sister's death, I'd like to hear it.'

'*My sister.*' It sounded like an assertion of the primacy of the sibling bond as opposed to the merely marital. Hammond acknowledged he was in no position to dispute it. 'Shall we go outside? We'll have all the privacy we need on the promenade in this weather.'

'All right.' Bill squinted out at the cloud-filled sky. 'I'll fetch my coat.'

'OK. I'll see you out there.'

Hammond had five minutes or so to himself, leaning against the railings and looking down at the wind-scoured beach, while he waited for Bill to join him. The next set of railings along from where he stood was missing for some reason. Two strips of red-and-white tape had been fixed diagonally across the gap, to warn of the danger. But Hammond had no need of warnings. He knew exactly what he was doing.

'Here I am,' Bill announced, looming up behind him in a duffel coat.

'Good.' Hammond turned and smiled. 'Let's go, shall we?'

TWENTY-TWO

'This is one hell of a lot to take in,' said Bill Dowler, shaking his head thoughtfully as he looked across at Hammond.

They were sitting at a table on the canopied and heated terrace of one of the seafront cafés along Strandweg, a dearth of other customers ensuring they could speak as freely as they wished. Hammond was drinking coffee, but Bill had opted for whisky, and not just because he needed to warm himself up. He was clearly shocked by what he had been told – shocked and confused. Whatever he had feared or expected to learn, Hammond's explanation of how Kate had come to be killed was certainly not it.

'You're really saying Gazi arranged her murder as some twisted way of rewarding you for saving his life?'

'Looks like it. I can't be certain of his reasons. But I can be certain he arranged it.'

'Kate died . . . because you got mixed up with a Serbian warlord?'

'I didn't know I was getting "mixed up" with him. It was just another case to me, Bill. More lucrative than most, I grant you, but at the time I thought I'd probably need the money.'

'Because of the divorce?'

'Exactly.'

'I never even knew you'd been to Serbia.'

'Well, I didn't shout about it from the rooftops. I wasn't breaking any sanctions, but I knew it could be a sensitive subject in some quarters. What I didn't know, obviously, was that . . .'

'It would get Kate killed.'

'Look, Bill, I—'

'And how did Gazi come to know she'd left you anyway?'

'Someone in my team must have let it slip. Or Miljanović, his specialist in Belgrade.'

'You broadcast your marital problems to all and sundry, did you?'

'Of course not. But there were times I was performing . . . below par . . . because of the strain. I had to put people in the picture. And word gets around. You must know how it is.'

'No. I don't think I do. I'd have made a pretty poor soldier, I can tell you, if I'd allowed my personal affairs to interfere with my duty.'

Hammond was tempted to ask exactly what personal affairs he was referring to. Bill's life seemed to have been singularly free of anything that could be described as such. It gave him a capacity for censoriousness about the frailties of others that Hammond had quite forgotten. 'I've spent just about every hour of the past week regretting agreeing to treat Gazi. If I could go back and change my decision, I would. But I can't. And there was no way I could foresee the consequences of treating him, anyway. Most of my transplant patients are simply grateful to be given a new lease of life.'

'Well, it seems he was grateful too, Edward. He just had his own way of showing it.'

'Yes. But how was I to know that?'

'You could have read the newspapers. I was out of the front line by the time the Army deployed in Bosnia, but the stories I heard from the blokes who went made it bloody obvious the Serb commanders were a bunch of psychopaths. It wasn't exactly a secret.'

'Well, I'm afraid it wasn't so clear to me, Bill.'

'Because you didn't want it to be. How much did he pay you?'

'A lot.'

'*How much?*'

Hammond sighed. The truth was a harder road to tread than he might have imagined. 'Two hundred and fifty thousand pounds.'

'A quarter of a million?'

'Yes. A quarter of a million.'

Bill snorted his disapproval. 'Nice work if you can get it.'

'That's what I thought – at the time.'

'When Kendall accused you of hiring someone to kill Kate, I reckoned he was mad. But what you're telling me is that he wasn't actually that wide of the mark.'

'I didn't ask Gazi to have her killed, Bill. You have my solemn word. I'm a doctor. I try to save lives, not take them. I was angry and distressed when she left me. But I never hated her. If I'd wanted to kill anyone, it would have been Kendall, not Kate.'

Bill sat back and frowned at Hammond, searching his face for some sign that he was lying, which only Hammond could be absolutely sure he was not. 'All right, Edward. I believe you. But Kendall won't. You can be sure of that.'

'I'll deal with him when the time comes – if it comes.'

'What do you mean, *if*?'

'It's an open question whether Gazi will carry out his threat, that's all.'

'And if he doesn't, you'll just . . . let sleeping dogs lie?'

'I don't know. It depends whether there's anything about Kate on the tapes.'

'If Gazi ordered my sister's murder, I want him to stand trial for it.'

'So do I. But if there's no evidence . . .' Hammond shrugged. 'He's going to spend the rest of his life in prison whatever happens.'

'That's not good enough.'

'It may have to be.'

Bill shifted uneasily in his chair. The possibility that he might know who had murdered Kate without being able to prove it offended his sense of the natural order of things. 'I'm sorry,

Edward, but I'm not prepared to let Gazi decide whether this comes into the open or not.'

'You must do what you think best. But I'd be grateful if you left it to me to tell Alice.'

'When will you do that?'

'As soon as I get home.'

'And when will that be?'

'Within a few days. After I've delivered the tapes to ICTY.'

'All right. I'll take no immediate action. But about these tapes. Would Gazi really have been so stupid as to record material that incriminates him?'

'Piravani reckons he planned to use them to blackmail his way out of trouble after the fall of Milošević, but had to get out in a hurry and banked on them never being found.'

Bill nodded sombrely, as if satisfied on the point. 'You have told me everything, haven't you?'

'Everything.'

'Then I'll back you up.' Bill extended his hand across the table in a gesture that surprised Hammond. They had an understanding, it seemed. And it required a handshake to seal it.

'Thanks.'

'But I'd like to ask the Perović woman a few questions before you surrender the tapes.'

'*The Perović woman.*' Hammond bridled inwardly. A Serbian warlord's former mistress was a low form of life in Bill Dowler's vision of the world and no doubt that of many others as well. She was going to receive a lot of unwelcome and unflattering attention in the weeks ahead. They would have that in common.

'When can I see her?'

'This evening. I said I'd call for the tapes at nine.'

'You're sure you can trust her?'

'She's as much a victim in this as anyone else.'

'Mmm.' Bill sounded unconvinced. 'I'll see what I make of her.' He pushed back his chair. 'Listen, Edward, I . . . think I'll take a walk. On my own. You understand? I need to . . . take stock of everything you've told me.'

'Of course.'

Bill stood up and began struggling into his duffel coat. Hammond jumped up to help him, wincing at a jab of pain from his ribs. 'It's all right,' said Bill, looking at him oddly. 'I can cope. Probably better than you can.'

Hammond forced out a smile. 'You could be right.' He subsided back into his chair. 'I'll see you later.'

After Bill had gone, Hammond sat on at the table alone, wondering exactly what was going on in his brother-in-law's mind. Bill kept so much bottled up inside him it was hard to gauge his reaction. He evidently believed what Hammond had said, yet nevertheless blamed him in some measure for Kate's death.

Greed and poor judgement seemed to be the principal crimes laid at Hammond's door and he was not well placed to deny either of them. All he could do was try to atone for them. Telling Bill the truth – and later, still more painfully, telling Alice – amounted only to a start. Where the process would end he could not tell.

He did not see Bill again until they set off to meet Zineta that evening. They travelled by taxi to Hollands-Spoor station, Hammond surprising himself by how instinctively he took the precaution of not going directly to her apartment. An increasingly tense silence prevailed during their journey through the still, quiet city. Neither was willing to make the effort to engage in small talk and the only subject they really wanted to discuss was off limits in the presence of the driver. Bill's permanently furrowed brow suggested he was still thinking hard about Hammond's revelations of earlier in the day.

It became apparent, however, when they got out at the station and headed for Zineta's apartment on foot, that he had done rather more than just think about them.

'I went to the court this afternoon, Edward,' he suddenly declared. 'I wanted to see Gazi in the flesh.'

It should have occurred to Hammond that Bill might want to sit in on the trial. 'You saw him?'

'Yes. And a nasty piece of work he is too. Cold. Arrogant. Brutal.'

'You could tell that?'

'It's in his eyes. I've seen the look before. Some of the Provos had it in Northern Ireland. Killing people for the sake of it sucks something out of your soul. It's the lack of whatever that is – humanity, I suppose – that you can see in their gaze.'

'Well, he's certainly responsible for a lot of killing for the sake of it. And he's going to pay for it.'

'I read the summary indictment. Not pretty.'

'I know.'

'Really? You know all about the murders he's accused of in Kosovo, do you? They happened after you saved his life. Several hundred, all told. How do you feel about that?'

'I thought the war was over when I treated him. I had no idea it was going to flare up again.' To Hammond's relief, they were within sight of the apartment now. 'Zineta lives just along here.'

'Not good enough.'

'Sorry?'

'Your excuse, Edward.' Bill stopped, forcing Hammond to look at him. 'Just not good enough.'

Hammond had neither the time nor the inclination to mount a defence of his questionable record. They reached the brightly lit premises of Prawiro en Zoon. Trade was slack, freeing the lugubrious proprietor to cast them an appraising glance as Hammond rang Zineta's bell.

It was around the time of his second prod at the bell that a queasy sense of foreboding crept into him. After the third, he stepped to the edge of the kerb and peered up at the attic windows. There was no light showing.

'I thought this was a definite appointment,' said Bill, joining him at the kerbside.

'It was.'

'Which floor is she on?'

'Top.'

'She's not there, is she?'

'She must be.'

'But she isn't.'

'Damn it.' Hammond strode back to the door and tried the bell again. There was still no response.

'You said you could trust her.'

'I could. I do.'

'So, where is she?'

'I don't know.' He whipped out his phone and dialled her number. No reply. Then he checked for messages. Nothing. The queasiness was turning by now to a cold dread.

'Edward.'

'Wait a minute.'

'*Edward.*'

'*What?*'

'The shopkeeper's waving at us.'

Hammond looked round and saw that Prawiro, as he took the man to be, was indeed beckoning to them. He walked into the shop, with Bill at his shoulder.

At closer quarters, Prawiro's lugubriousness seemed more like studied world-weariness. He was a short, bald-headed man of indeterminate age, slightly built but pot-bellied, installed behind a counter crammed with confectionery, magazines and electrical accessories. He gazed at them with a mixture of obsequiousness and contempt.

'You are looking for Mejuffrouw Perović?'

'Yes.'

'What is your name?'

'Hammond.'

'*Doctor* Hammond?'

'Yes. That's me.'

'Here.' Prawiro produced an envelope from beneath the counter. 'For you. From Mejuffrouw Perović.'

Hammond took the envelope – his name was written on it in large, slightly uncertain capitals – and tore it open. Inside was a single sheet of paper. He had no way of verifying that the writing on it belonged to Zineta, but he did not seriously doubt it.

Edward – I am sorry. I cannot let you have the tapes back. They are my only chance. I am very sorry. Z.

TWENTY-THREE

'What's going on?' Bill demanded, peering over Hammond's shoulder.

'I don't know. I don't understand.'

'Let me have a look at that.' He snatched the note and read it aloud.

'I know what it says,' Hammond murmured bleakly.

'She's gone – taking the tapes with her?'

'Apparently.'

'Gone where?'

'I've no idea.'

'You.' Bill glared at Prawiro. 'Where's Miss Perović gone?'

Prawiro smiled feebly. 'I do not know, sir.'

'But she gave you this letter for us?'

'For Dr Hammond, yes.'

'When?'

'About . . . three hours ago.'

'What did she say?'

'She said . . . she would be away for a while. And she asked me . . . to keep the letter for Dr Hammond. That is all.'

Hammond took out his phone and tried Zineta's number again, with the same result. But this time he left a message. 'This is Edward, Zineta. I've got your note. Please contact me. I need to know what's happened. Whatever it is, we can sort it out. Please call as soon as you get this.'

'You think she'll respond?' Bill asked sceptically when he had finished.

'I hope so.'

'You *hope*?'

'What else can I do?'

'Come outside.'

Bill marched decisively back out on to the pavement and walked on a few yards beyond the door leading to the flats. Then he stopped and turned to face Hammond. He looked angry as well as confused.

'Why has she taken the tapes, Edward?'

'I don't know. It may have something to do with her son.' As Hammond said it, he realized there could in fact be no other explanation. 'There must have been something on the tapes that held a clue to Monir's whereabouts, although why she didn't feel able to share that information with me I can't imagine.'

'Monir? Her son by Gazi?'

'Yes.'

'Doesn't putting your faith in the man's former mistress – the mother of his son – seem foolhardy to you?'

'Obviously not, Bill. Since that's what I've done.'

'Yes. You have.'

'She must have panicked. As soon as she's had a chance to think it over, she'll—'

'Save it, Edward. I'll tell you what I think, shall I? Either she really has played you for a sucker . . . or you're trying to play me for one.'

'*What?*'

'The tapes might have supported your version of events rather than the version Gazi's threatening to give to the court. But now they've gone missing. So, very conveniently, we'll never know what they'd reveal. If anything.'

'There's nothing convenient about it. I'm as frustrated as you are.'

'I doubt that. Because you know, whereas I don't, whether the tapes really exist at all.'

'Of course they *exist*.'

'I only have your word for that, which at present looks highly questionable. Gazi's planning to spill the beans about Kate's murder. Maybe all this is just a ruse to persuade me you played no part in his decision to have her killed.'

'A *ruse*?'

'I'm simply not sure, you see, one way or the other. And I'm afraid this isn't a situation in which I can afford to give you the benefit of the doubt. We're talking about my sister; my own flesh and blood. I owe it to her to bring those responsible for her death to justice.'

'It was Gazi's doing, Bill. I've told you that.'

'I know. You've told me lots of things.'

'Are you saying you don't believe me?'

'I'm saying I don't know what to believe. Zineta Perović and the famous tapes might have convinced me. As it is, they've both vanished.'

'I didn't set this up, Bill. Everything I've told you is true.'

'Maybe. Maybe not.'

'You can't seriously think I asked Gazi to have Kate killed. Come on. You know me too well for that.'

'Do I?' Bill was breathing heavily now, struggling with suspicions too grave to be stifled. 'I think the time's come to call in the professionals on this, Edward. I'm going home first thing in the morning. I'll give you forty-eight hours after that to go home yourself and tell Alice the truth – whatever the truth is. Then I'll contact the police and demand they reopen their inquiry into Kate's murder.'

'For God's sake, Bill, we can—'

'No. I'm done with talking. And I'm done with you for the present, Edward. I'm sorry, but there it is. I'll take a taxi from the station back to the hotel. There's nothing more for us to discuss. Goodnight.'

With that, Bill thrust his hands into the pockets of his duffel coat and strode off in the direction of Hollands-Spoor station.

Hammond thought of going after him, but something in Bill's stride and the set of his shoulders warned him off. He watched his brother-in-law reach the next corner and disappear round it without a backward glance. Then he was alone. And helpless. With Zineta's note crumpled in his hand.

He did not know where to go or what to do. He crossed the road and stared up at the windows of the attic flat, to no purpose whatsoever, since they were still unlit and her message had been clear enough: she had gone, taking the tapes with her.

There was a shabby bar a few doors along. He drifted into it, ordered a *jenever* and sipped it slowly, gazing out through the uncurtained top half of the window at the door to the flats. The bar had only a few customers and the street was quiet. Few vehicles passed and even fewer pedestrians.

A sense of folly as well as dismay began to seep into Hammond. Why had Zineta done this to him? Why, for that matter, had he not anticipated she might? The tapes must hold the answer. But for some reason associated with Monir, she had determined he could not be told what it was.

As he began to think his way unavailingly through the baffling turn of events for the third or fourth time, a figure drifted into view on the pavement opposite and stopped by the door to the flats. He was a short, shaven-headed, compactly built man of forty or so, dressed in a leather jacket, jeans and roll-neck sweater. As Hammond watched, he pressed one of the bells – Zineta's?

Flicking a five-euro note on to the bar to cover the *jenever*, Hammond hurried out and crossed the road, to find him stepping back to see if there were any lights on in the attic flat.

'Looking for Zineta?'

'What?' The man whirled round and frowned at Hammond. He was wearing glasses and their gold frames glinted in the lamplight, along with a silver earring.

'So am I, as it happens.'

'Who are you?' The accent was neither Dutch nor English. It sounded, based on Hammond's recent visit to Belgrade, distinctly Serbian, with a thin slice of American.

'A friend of Zineta's.'

'Me too. You're English, aren't you?'

'Yes.'

'Are you Edward?'

'Er . . . yes.'

'She mentioned you. Do you know if she's all right? I hoped she'd be at home but . . . you're looking for her as well, you said?'

It was Hammond's recollection that Zineta had claimed to know no one, or at any rate to have made no friends, in The Hague. He struggled to balance caution and curiosity. 'I did, yes.'

'I'm a bit . . . worried about her, that's all.'

'Why?'

'I'm Stevan Vidor. I met her at ICTY. I work there as a translator.' He extended a hand – and a smile. 'Zineta never mentioned your last name, but she said you were a friend. And I guess you're maybe a little worried about her, like I am.'

'What makes you think that?'

'Well . . .' Vidor shrugged. 'You look it.'

'I'd arranged to call on her this evening. I was . . . disappointed not to find her in.'

'Do you know about a tape she had?'

'A tape?'

'Yeah. She played it to me. I speak French as well as English, you see.'

'French?'

'There was a conversation in French on the tape. She needed it translating.'

'What was the conversation about?'

'Well, I don't know if I can . . .' Vidor drew back a pace. 'I guess it's her private business.'

It was a fair point. Hammond had to give something if he was to receive anything in return. 'Sorry. I should have introduced myself. Edward Hammond. I am worried about Zineta. We have that in common. I was in the bar over there, trying to decide how to contact her, since she isn't answering her phone. Why don't you let me buy you a drink? We might be able to help each other out.'

Vidor thought the invitation over for a moment, then nodded. 'OK.'

Re-entering the bar, Hammond tried to look and sound more relaxed than he felt. Vidor seemed a pleasant fellow, but it was probably unwise to let him see how crucial the information he possessed might be.

'What'll you have?'

'A Pils would be great.'

Hammond ordered two and they sat down at a table by the window, where a fat red candle was burning low. The shadows it cast made Vidor's expression hard to read, though that, Hammond supposed, cut both ways. 'Are you Serbian, Stevan?'

'Yes. But I got out in ninety-one, before the war started. I could see what was coming and I didn't want to get caught up in it. Although I guess you could say I *am* caught up in it, working at ICTY.'

'How did you meet Zineta?'

'She came to the court so often it was hard not to notice her. But always it was for the Gazi trial. It made me wonder what he'd done to her. We got talking one day by the coffee machine during an adjournment and I asked her for a date. I had to ask twice more before she said yes. We went out the Saturday before last. I had a nice time. I'm not so sure about her.'

'Did she tell you how she knew Gazi?'

'Yes. I think she thought it would put me off.'

'But it didn't?'

'It's not for me to judge how people survived under Milošević. I wasn't there.'

'That's very broadminded of you.'

'Translating testimonies at ICTY every day makes you broad-minded. But I reckoned I hadn't convinced Zineta of that, because she never replied to any of my texts and she stopped coming to the court. Then her phone stopped working altogether. I thought I must have blown it big time.'

'Actually, none of that was anything to do with you.'

'So she said when she called me today. She asked if we could meet during my lunch break. That's when she played me the tape. She told me she'd got it from . . .' Vidor pointed his Pils bottle at Hammond. 'Well, from you.'

'It's true. I lent it to her. The plan was for me to retrieve it this evening.'

'Are you saying . . .'

'What was on the tape, Stevan?'

'A telephone conversation, in French, between two men. One of them was Dragan Gazi.'

'You recognized his voice?'

'I did once the other guy had called him "*Monsieur Gazi*". It was a surprise. I didn't even know Gazi spoke French. But there are a lot of missing years in his past. I guess he must have spent some of them in France.'

'Who was the other guy?'

'A lawyer. Name of Delmotte.'

'What were they discussing?'

'The adoption of a child.'

A child. Of course. Monir. It was all about Monir. 'Did they name the child?'

'No. But it was a boy. They called him *le gamin*. And Gazi was obviously his father. He was making arrangements for his son to be supplied with papers identifying him as an orphan so he could be adopted by one of Delmotte's clients. Gazi was concerned about what would happen to the boy while he was . . . *souterrain*, as he put it – underground. This was shortly before he disappeared in March 2000. A date for the boy to meet his adoptive parents had been fixed, but Gazi wanted to bring it forward and was pressuring

Delmotte to come up with the paperwork. He said an associate of his called Todorović—'

'*Todorović?*'

'Yes. You know him?'

Hammond hesitated. 'I've heard of him.'

'Me too. He's quite well known in Belgrade. Anyway, Gazi said Todorović was ready to deliver the boy as soon as Delmotte gave the go-ahead.'

'Deliver him where?'

'I don't know. It wasn't mentioned.'

But Todorović knew. That was clear. As it must have been to Zineta. *He knew.* And she had something he badly wanted: the tapes. Suddenly it was all too obvious why she could not let Hammond have them back. She was planning to trade them for her son. 'You told Zineta all this?'

'Sure. Of course.'

'How did she react?'

'She was wound up pretty tight. And doing a lot of thinking. You could see that on her face. She didn't actually say much. She thanked me and . . . then she took the tape and left.'

'You didn't try to stop her?'

'No. Though maybe I should have. It sounded like information ICTY would be interested in. It's an open secret Branko Todorović is on the Prosecutor's grey list – people likely to be indicted if serious evidence against them turns up. I suppose I was . . . too taken up with Zineta's side of things. I mean, she's the boy's mother, isn't she?'

'Yes. His name's Monir.'

'*Was.* It probably isn't now.'

'I suppose not.'

'I got the impression there was more than just the one tape.'

'There are . . . quite a few more.'

'And what's on them?'

'I don't know. The only parts I listened to were in Serbian. But they probably constitute the sort of evidence you're talking about.'

'That's what I thought. How did you get hold of them?'

More hesitation. Hammond had only just met this man. He seemed trustworthy, but seeming and being were not the same. 'Have you got any identification, Stevan?'

'Sure.' Vidor took out his wallet and produced a laminated card adorned with his photograph, the UN symbol and ICTY's logo of a globe cradled in the scales of justice: *Stevan Vidor, translator/ traducteur*. There was no doubt of its authenticity.

'Well, I was actually planning to hand the tapes over to ICTY once Zineta had listened to them.'

'Any idea where she's gone?'

'None.'

'I might be able to help you with that.'

'How?'

Vidor leant across the table and lowered his voice. 'We need to come to an understanding, you and I. I want to help Zineta. I like her – a lot. Plus it'll look bad for me if it comes out I'm involved with a member of Gazi's family, which I guess the mother of his son kind of is, and didn't stop her suppressing vital evidence against him.'

'The last thing she'd do is suppress evidence against Gazi.'

'Unless she felt she had to, in order to get her son back.'

It was true. And it was the only possible explanation for what she had done. 'What do you want from me, Stevan?'

'I'm suggesting we collaborate, Edward. We both want to find Zineta and deliver the tapes to ICTY. And we both know things the other doesn't. For instance, Delmotte. I'm good at my job. I have an ear for accents. It's why I came to see Zineta this evening. There was something in Delmotte's voice that wasn't pure French. It only came to me later. He isn't French. French-speaking, but not actually French.'

'What, then?'

'He's a Luxembourger. I tracked him down through the Luxembourg lawyers' association website. I have his office address. That's what I was planning to tell Zineta.' Vidor sighed. 'I thought it would impress her. I thought . . .' He shrugged. 'I guess I thought it would make her accept my help.'

Doing right by his employer apparently counted for less than winning Zineta's attention any way he could. Hammond suddenly understood. Vidor was more than merely attracted to Zineta. He was in love with her. And that might be to Hammond's advantage. In the circumstances, indeed, it was likely to be the only advantage he had.

'I can't even phone her now to tell her what I've found out,' Vidor continued, shaking his head miserably.

'No,' said Hammond. 'But I can.'

TWENTY-FOUR

'*This is Edward again, Zineta. Listen to what I have to say. I know what you're doing. I understand. I really do. But there's no need to involve Todorović. I have the information you need. Stevan Vidor's with me. We've found out where Delmotte is. We can use the evidence you have of his dealings with Gazi to force Monir's new name and address out of him. You see? We can get what you want without giving Todorović what he wants. Think about it. It's the best way. It means Marco won't have risked his life for nothing. Think about it and call me. Soon.*'

'Maybe you shouldn't have mentioned me,' Vidor said as Hammond rang off. There was self-mockery as well as self-pity in his tone. 'She probably doesn't trust my motives.'

'I doubt she trusts her own motives. She probably panicked when she saw the chance the tape gave her. I'm hoping she's already had second thoughts. With any luck, she won't have contacted Todorović yet.'

'But if she has?'

'We can move faster than him.'

'And if she doesn't call?'

'She'll call. We just need to give her time to think the situation through. Meanwhile . . .'

'We should head for Luxembourg.'

'We should certainly make sure we're there when Delmotte

arrives at his office tomorrow morning. With or without Zineta.'

The obvious way to travel was in Vidor's car. He estimated the journey would take three to four hours, so it was agreed he would collect Hammond from the Kurhaus at five o'clock the following morning.

Hammond paid his bill in advance when he returned to the hotel, then went straight up to his room. There had still been no response from Zineta, but even if there had he would not have told Bill what he and Vidor were going to do. Bill had taken his stand and Hammond doubted any argument he advanced would shift him from it. The forty-eight-hour deadline meant he had until Thursday to redeem himself in his brother-in-law's eyes. It was not long. But if all went well it would be long enough.

He called Zineta again and left another message. Sooner or later, she would see reason. She had to. If not . . .

Sleep arrived, tardily and shallowly, courtesy of late-night Dutch television. The knowledge that the world was proceeding on its trivial and unintelligible way, heedless of his doubts and fears, acted as a kind of sedative. He had stopped asking himself what he had done to deserve his recent misfortunes. All that mattered now was what he had to do to end them.

Vidor was waiting outside in his car, engine idling, when Hammond emerged from the hotel just before five o'clock. It was cold and a fine drizzle was falling from the night-shrouded sky. Dawn felt a long way off.

The Peugeot was small and more than a decade old, with defective heating. But progress was swift, even if it was un-comfortable. Little was said, neither having the taste or energy for idle conversation. They were allies of necessity and the weight of that necessity rested heavily between them.

The going slowed as it grew light, commuter and commercial traffic rumbling in ever greater numbers on to the motorways of Belgium. Even so, they made good enough time for Vidor to

214

propose a breakfast break at the last service area before Luxembourg City. As they sat hunched over their coffee, orange juice and croissants, Hammond's phone rang, raising the hope that Zineta was at last responding to his repeated messages. But all he found was a text from Miljanović. '*Looked in on your friend this morning. No change. Getting best attention.*' He shook his head dismally at Vidor. 'It's not from her.'

'Still confident she'll call, Edward?'

'Yes. I am.'

'Well, I guess you know her better than I do.'

'I'm not sure about that.'

'Do you regret getting involved in all this?'

'No. Strangely enough, I don't.'

'How did you, anyway? Get involved, I mean.'

'It's a long story. I'll make a full statement of the circumstances when I deliver the tapes to ICTY. Talking of which, shouldn't you be phoning in to say you'll be absent today?'

'Neat change of subject. I left a message, saying I wouldn't be in, before I picked you up. Now we've dealt with that, why don't you tell me where you got the tapes?'

'Belgrade.'

'It's a big city.'

'Your home town?'

Vidor chuckled at Hammond's shameless evasiveness. 'No. I'm from Subotica, up near the Hungarian border. Vidor's a Hungarian name. Maybe you've heard of the Hollywood director King Vidor? My father claims we're related to him.'

'Your parents are still in Serbia?'

'Yes. Parents. Plus brothers and sisters. They all stayed. I'm the only one who got out.'

'Do you see much of them?'

Vidor grimaced. 'Going back isn't easy. For me or for them.'

'How did you end up in The Hague?'

'Serbo-Croatian translators aren't in much demand anywhere else.'

'Do you enjoy the work?'

'Enjoy? That's not exactly the—'

The chirruping of Hammond's phone silenced them instantly. Hammond looked down at the caller display. 'It's her,' he said quietly. 'At last.'

He was already on the move when he answered, heading for the relative privacy of the open air after an explanatory signal to Vidor, designed to imply it was the eavesdropping of the other people in the cafeteria he was concerned about, although in truth he was grateful for the excuse to talk to Zineta alone.

'I'm sorry, Edward,' were literally her first words, uttered with a hoarseness he sensed had nothing to do with the quality of the connection.

'There's no need to apologize. I meant what I said in my messages. I understand why you did it. You should have waited and talked it over with me, but in your shoes I might have done the same.'

'I saw a chance to find Monir and I felt I had to take it.'

'Where are you now?'

'Schiphol. It must sound crazy, but I wanted to be ready . . . to go wherever he is . . . as soon as I heard.'

'Have you contacted Todorović?'

She did not immediately reply. There was only static and guesswork to fill the void as he emerged into the drizzle-blurred morning.

'Zineta?'

'Yes.' Her voice had sunk so low it was hard to catch her words. 'I contacted him.'

'You spoke to him?'

'Yes. I left a message with an . . . assistant. Then Todorović phoned back. In person. He wants the tapes badly. I had his complete attention.'

'What did you agree with him?'

'He said he would call me again some time today with arrangements for me to see Monir. When I saw him . . . when I was sure he was my son . . . I'd . . .'

216

'Hand over the tapes?'

'Yes. There's enough on them to destroy Todorović, Edward. And he no longer owes Gazi anything. He doesn't care about me or Monir. It's just a . . . business transaction to him.'

'Are you sure about that? You can't trust a man like him. Doesn't he deserve to be destroyed anyway? Marco certainly thinks so.'

'Do you know . . . how Marco is?'

'Stable. But it could still go either way.'

'Poor Marco. Poor you.' She shook her head. 'What have I done?'

'You took what you thought was your only chance. But now we have another chance. A better one. Thanks to Stevan Vidor.'

'I never meant to involve him. I couldn't think of any other way to find out what Gazi and Delmotte were discussing. Stevan is sweet, but . . . this isn't his problem.'

'Maybe not. But he's a part of the solution. He's worked out where Delmotte is. We plan to confront him this morning. Why don't you come too?'

'Where?'

'Luxembourg. There must be plenty of flights from Schiphol.'

'But . . . what do I do about Todorović?'

'Nothing. If we get what we want out of Delmotte, you can leave Todorović dangling.'

'He knows I have the tapes, Edward. He'll come after me.'

'Not if he's under arrest. Which he will be as soon as we deliver the tapes to ICTY.'

She fell silent once more. Hammond paced up and down an empty parking bay, telling himself to give her the time she needed. It was not easy and he had nearly exhausted his patience when she said, 'All right. I'll come.'

Vidor's spirits lifted when he heard Zineta had agreed. They headed towards Luxembourg City, hitting heavy rush-hour traffic as soon as they left the motorway. By the time they had found a space in an underground car park off Boulevard Royal, their plan to be waiting for Delmotte when he arrived at his office was in serious disarray.

The compactness of the Old Town told in their favour, however. With Vidor navigating expertly from an internet map, they reached Delmotte's offices – the ground floor of an elegant old house hear the Grand-Ducal Palace – before assorted church clocks had finished striking nine.

A demure young receptionist was conveying a cup of coffee into one of the rooms overlooking the street when they entered. When she returned, Vidor explained, in his most fluent and flattering French, what they wanted: an immediate audience with Delmotte. As far as Hammond could gather, this was met with well-trained resistance. Vidor dropped the name Gazi, which clearly meant nothing to the secretary, and mentioned '*une adoption*'. She eventually consented to convey their message to Maître Delmotte.

As they waited for his response, Hammond's phone rang. There was a text from Zineta. '*Arr lux 1045. Can u meet me at airport?*' He was still maladroitly thumbing his reply – '*May b late but will b there*' – *on* when the secretary returned, looking mildly surprised. Delmotte had granted them an audience.

'She's on her way,' Hammond whispered as they went in.

'So are we,' said Vidor.

Delmotte's office was a stylish graft of twenty-first-century work space onto eighteenth-century salon, yew panelling and old-master reproductions blending with Italian furniture and state-of-the-art desktop technology. The law was evidently a lucrative profession in Luxembourg, though Hammond reminded himself that Marcel Delmotte might have strayed beyond the letter of the law more than once in pursuit of a fat fee if his dealings with Gazi were anything to judge by.

Delmotte himself appeared, at first sight, to be the very embodiment of solicitorial self-effacement: middle-aged and soberly suited, thin, delicately bespectacled, blandly courteous. But the fretful workings of his tight little mouth and the frownful dartings of his gaze suggested a great deal of anxious thinking was going on behind the urbane façade.

There was some introductory sparring in French, but as soon as Delmotte appreciated that one of his visitors did not speak the language, he switched to English. 'I have only a very little time that I can spare you, *messieurs*. What is it I can do for you?'

'Is adoption law a speciality of yours?' Hammond asked provocatively.

'A speciality? I would not say so.' Delmotte took a measured sip of coffee in a show of unconcern. 'I may know of another *notaire* better qualified to advise you if—'

'Do you know who Dragan Gazi is, *maître*?' Vidor cut in.

'Gazi? *Mais oui, naturellement.* The Serbian militia leader, arrested last year and . . . sent to stand trial at the International Court in The Hague.'

'Have you ever met him?'

'Certainly not.'

'Or had any dealings with him?'

Delmotte managed a smile. '*Non.*'

'We know better,' said Hammond. 'Your discussions with him in March 2000 regarding the adoption of his son were recorded. And we have the recording.'

The smile was still in place, but had become a caricature of itself. And a vein in Delmotte's temple seemed suddenly more prominent. 'You are mistaken. I have had no . . . dealings . . . with Dragan Gazi.'

'The tape tells a different story. You supplied documentation enabling Monir Gazi to be classified under a different name as an orphan. And then you arranged his adoption by a client of yours. No doubt Gazi paid you well, since what you did must have amounted to a criminal act. Whether it would get you a prison sentence I can't say. You know the Luxembourg courts better than we do. But a heavy fine and the end of your legal career would surely be the least you could expect.'

Delmotte licked his moustache nervously. He looked from one to the other of them, seeking in their faces some sign of what his choices might be. 'Any such recording . . . must be a fake.'

'It's you on the tape, *maître*,' said Vidor. 'I recognize your voice. The conversation centred on Gazi's wish to bring forward the date when "*le gamin*" could be shipped out of Serbia. Eventually, you agreed a ten per cent supplement to your fee in return for "*l'expédition de la procédure*". Remember?'

'This is . . . a lie.'

'We have the tape.'

'And therefore,' said Hammond, surprised by his own coldness, 'we have you at our mercy.'

Delmotte closed his eyes for a second, then said, 'Supposing such a tape existed, your duty would be to take it to the police.'

'We prefer not to have to do that.'

'*Vraiment?*'

Hammond smiled. 'Really.'

Delmotte reached for his coffee cup to win himself some thinking time, only to discover it was empty. With a heavy sigh he replaced it in the saucer. 'How much do you want, *messieurs?*'

'We're not here for money,' said Hammond.

'*Non?*'

He shook his head. 'No.'

'Then . . .'

'We're here on behalf of Monir Gazi's natural mother. She wishes to meet her son. She wishes to know the child she brought into this world.'

Delmotte wrung his hands. 'Are you sure you would not prefer . . . compensation for your time and trouble, *messieurs*? The . . . reunion . . . you desire would be . . . *problématique*.'

'We're confident in your ability to arrange it. And we can't be bought off. It's the boy or nothing.'

'Well, perhaps I could . . . make some enquiries. Naturally, I would require this . . . tape you speak of . . . before I—'

'You get the tape when Monir meets his mother.' The loss of one from Gazi's collection was, Hammond reckoned, a small price to pay. 'And she wants to meet him today.'

'Today? *Impossible.*'

'For your sake, it better hadn't be.'

Delmotte's brow furrowed as he engaged in an earnest assessment of just how impossible it actually was. 'I cannot . . . guarantee this. But . . . I can . . .'

'Make a few phone calls?'

'Yes. But . . . if the boy's mother thinks she can . . . take him away from his—'

'Just fix a meeting for later today, OK? How it turns out isn't our concern.' In truth, Hammond had thought no further than bringing Zineta and Monir together. That was all she had ever said she wanted: a chance to re-enter her son's life. 'Once you've got the tape, there's no proof we know of that you were ever involved in the matter.'

'How can I be sure . . . there are no other copies of the tape?'

'You have to trust us.'

Delmotte stared at Hammond as if he had just made a tasteless joke. '*Trust you?*'

'What choice do you have, *maître*?' Vidor asked. 'This is your only way out of a heap of serious trouble.'

That much was undeniable, as Delmotte seemed to concede with a doleful bob of the head. 'I will . . . make some calls,' he murmured.

'We'll give you the rest of the morning,' said Hammond, pressing their advantage. 'You have until noon to set something up. Is that clear?'

'*Oui, oui. Très clair.*'

'Good. We'll see you then.'

'I would prefer to meet somewhere else, *messieurs*. It would be best for all of us, I think. I suggest . . . la place de la Constitution. It is not far.'

'OK. We'll be there. At noon. Make sure you are too.'

'Oh, I will be. As you say, what choice do I have?'

*

'What do you think?' Vidor asked as they walked away from the lawyer's office a few minutes later.

'I think Monir's in Luxembourg,' Hammond replied. 'Otherwise a meeting today really would have been impossible. As it is, I think Delmotte's going to do whatever he feels he has to do to get the tape. And that amounts to exactly what we want him to do. Thanks to you, Stevan, I think Zineta is going to be reunited with her son.'

And at that Vidor beamed.

TWENTY-FIVE

It was a quiet morning at Luxembourg airport. Most of the passengers off the flight from Amsterdam were business travellers, for whom various limo drivers were waiting, the names of the parties they were due to chauffeur away prominently displayed on large squares of card. Edward Hammond was, in fact, the only person waiting at the arrivals gate without such a card. Stevan Vidor had insisted on staying with the car, claiming he did not want to 'crowd' Zineta. Hammond had not devoted much effort to wondering what exactly that meant. His priorities lay elsewhere.

Zineta was one of the last passengers to emerge and, as soon as he saw her, Hammond realized that betraying him had taken a heavy toll. She was red-eyed and pale, trembling slightly as she walked towards him. As he advanced to meet her, she raised one of the two holdalls she was carrying and offered it to him.

'The tapes are inside,' she said hollowly. 'I never should have taken them. Please take them back.'

'You haven't seen Monir yet,' he said, keeping his hands by his side.

'Whether I see him or not, the tapes should go to ICTY. It was wrong of me to try and use them as bargaining chips. I knew it was wrong, of course. But still I did it. Now I . . .' She shook her head in acknowledgement of her own folly. 'Please take them.'

He accepted the bag. And after a moment's hesitation he hugged

223

her. 'It's all right, Zineta. I don't blame you for what you did.'

'You should do,' she said, her voice muffled by his shoulder.

'We can put everything right. That's all that matters.'

'Can we?' She broke away and looked at him. 'Can we really?'

'Has Todorović been in touch since we spoke?'

'No.'

'Then we still have time on our side. Delmotte's agreed to arrange for you to meet Monir.' He took her other bag as well, which she hardly seemed to notice, and ushered her towards the escalator that led up to the exit.

'How soon can I meet him, Edward?'

'Later today, if Delmotte does his stuff. The fact we have a recording of his conversation with Gazi means he has a powerful incentive to make it happen.'

'But . . . where is Monir?'

'Somewhere in Luxembourg, is my guess. The city, or near by.'

'He's been brought up here?'

'Looks like it.'

'So, Luxembourg is all he's known?'

'I suppose so.'

They reached the foot of the escalator. But Zineta stepped smartly to one side, forcing Hammond to jump back off.

'What's the matter?'

'I was stupid to take the tapes and contact Todorović.' She put her hand to her forehead. 'Maybe I'm still being stupid.'

'How?'

'Monir doesn't remember me. He probably doesn't even know he's been adopted. Maybe it's better if he never does.'

'He'll find out eventually. They always do.'

'You think I should see him if I can?'

Here was Hammond's chance to talk her out of meeting her son. He had the tapes back, after all. There was nothing to be lost by calling Delmotte off and a good deal to be gained. But, oddly, he could not bring himself to attempt it. He should have been angry at Zineta for what she had done. But all he saw before him was a lonely, frightened woman who no longer trusted her emotions. 'I think you'll regret it if you don't see him, Zineta. I truly do.'

She thought about that for a moment, then nodded solemnly. 'Yes. Of course.' She looked at him, with some of her determination restored to her gaze. 'Let's go.'

They saw Vidor as soon as they entered the short-stay car park. He was pacing up and down beside the Peugeot, smoking a cigarette with nervous intensity. Zineta grabbed Hammond's elbow and drew him to one side, so that they were screened from him by the flank of a van.

'I feel so sorry for Stevan,' she said. 'I've caused him so much trouble.'

'I think he welcomes it.'

'What do you mean?'

'You do realize he's in love with you, don't you?'

Zineta's wide-eyed reaction suggested she had realized no such thing. 'That's crazy.'

Hammond shrugged. 'Sometimes love is.'

Hammond hung back while Zineta spoke to Vidor. As far as he could see through the windows of the van, their physical contact was confined at first to a brisk triple cheek-kiss. He could hear them speaking in Serbian, too softly for him to catch individual words, though Zineta's tone suggested she was asking to be forgiven. That amounted to pushing at an open door where Vidor was concerned, who conquered his diffidence sufficiently to put an arm on her shoulder, but never managed the hug he obviously wanted to give her. Hammond felt sorry for both of them. They were clearly not at ease with each other. Whether they would ever be – whether they would ever have the chance to be – he did not know.

An hour later, they were waiting for Delmotte in Constitution Square, laid out atop one of the bastions of the city's seventeenth-century fortifications. Below them, at the foot of the rocky crag on which the Old Town perched, were the winding paths and greenery of the Pétrusse valley, with the southern suburbs stretching away beyond. Luxembourg, even in grey, wintry weather, looked an affluent, orderly, civilized place. Hammond could see the thought running through Zineta's mind as she tugged fretfully at a cigarette and gazed up at the slender spires of the nearby cathedral: if Gazi, for whatever reason, had given their son the comfort and security of an upbringing here, should she do anything to endanger it?

They had walked to the square from the car park on Boulevard Royal, unaware that there was parking to be had in the square itself. It was into one of these spaces that a vintage Citroën saloon made a smart turn off Boulevard Roosevelt as midday approached, with Marcel Delmotte at the wheel.

He somehow looked smaller than he had in his office, perhaps due to the outsized overcoat in which he was enveloped, or else the hunch-shouldered apprehensiveness he projected. He glanced suspiciously around him as he emerged from the car, as if concerned that there might be more people waiting for him than he had been led to expect.

'It's just us, *maître*,' said Vidor.

Delmotte cleared his throat and drew the collar of his coat tight about his neck. He looked at Zineta. 'Is this . . . the mother?'

'My name is Zineta Perović,' she said, nettled by his tone. 'Monir Gazi is my son.'

'Legally, that is—' He broke off with a sigh. '*N'importe.*'

'Have you done as we asked?' put in Hammond.

'Yes, *monsieur*. I have . . . made arrangements.'

'When does Zineta get to meet Monir?'

'I can take you to him now.' He allowed himself a small smile at Zineta's gasp of surprise. After nine years of searching it was suddenly too swift and simple for her to believe. 'But consider, *madame*. He has had a happy childhood. He has no idea that the people who have raised him are not his parents. Are you sure you want to see him?'

'I'm quite sure, thank you,' she said, mastering herself.

'The tape?'

'Here.' Hammond held it up. 'You want to hear it?'

'There is a tape player in my car. I will listen to it as we go.'

'And where are we going?'

'You will find out when we arrive. Your terms, *monsieur*, not mine. The tape, when . . . Madame Perović . . . meets her son. Are we agreed?'

Hammond looked at Zineta. Her responding glance told him she was as ready as she would ever be. He nodded. 'Yes.'

'Shall we go, then?'

Vidor and Zineta got into the back of the car, with Hammond riding in the front. Delmotte crossed the Pétrusse valley, then took the airport road, which also led to a motorway junction. After a few minutes, he pressed a button low on the dashboard, activating the tape player. '*S'il vous plaît*,' he said, glancing at Hammond.

Zineta had wound the tape back to the beginning of Delmotte's conversation with Gazi. The Serb's guttural French sprang from the loudspeakers as soon as the cassette engaged. '*Maître Delmotte? C'est Dragan Gazi.*' Then came Delmotte's courteous response. '*Bonjour, Monsieur Gazi. Comment allez-vous?*' He sounded pleased to take the call. Nine years later, he looked far from pleased to be reliving it.

And he did not relive it for long. Just after the first use of the word '*l'adoption*', he pressed the eject button. '*Ça suffit*,' he said flatly.

'As you please.' Hammond retrieved the cassette.

'Who made this recording, *monsieur*?'

'Gazi. He recorded all important telephone conversations. For his own protection, as he thought.'

At that Delmotte gave a bitter little laugh. 'I should never have . . .' But he could not bring himself to finish the sentence. He merely shook his head.

'How much did he pay you?' Hammond asked.

'Too much to say no to. So I believed. It was a bad time for me. There was a divorce. I—'

'A *divorce*?'

'Yes. That amuses you?'

No. It did not. But Delmotte could hardly appreciate the irony that they had both succumbed to Gazi for the same reason.

'You should know it was a bad time for me also,' said Zineta. 'I lost my son because of what you did for Gazi.'

'If I had refused, he would have found someone else.'

'Is that your excuse?'

'He said nothing about you, *madame*. I assumed the boy had no mother and what I did, though technically illegal, gave him a better life than he would have had in Serbia. Are you rich? Are you married? Do you have a career?'

'No,' she answered simply.

'Then you should be pleased by the upbringing he has had.'

'He would have had a fine upbringing if he had stayed with his mother,' declared Vidor.

'*Peut-être*,' Delmotte said with a sigh. And he said no more.

They joined the motorway heading north, but left at the very next junction and drove back into the outskirts of the city. Here, on the Kirchberg plateau, were massed the soaring office blocks of the European Union's Luxembourg operations: a mountain range of gleaming steel and tinted glass, with yet more summits under construction.

'The boy's parents both work for the EU,' said Delmotte as they cruised past the vast, anonymous structures. 'They have senior positions, with high salaries and excellent conditions. They wanted a child to share their lives with, but could not have one of their own. I assisted them with a solution to their problem. They believed they were adopting an orphan of the war in Kosovo. They did not know – they still do not know – that he is Gazi's son. Will you tell them?'

A glance at Zineta confirmed to Hammond that she had no clear idea what she would say to these people she had never met, who had become the parents of her child. 'What have you told them so far?' he asked, in part to mask her indecision.

'I contacted the mother this morning and said a woman claiming to be the boy's real mother might be planning to abduct him.'

'*Abduct him?*' gasped Zineta.

'You take a great deal on yourself, *maître*,' said Vidor tightly.

'I said what was necessary to achieve the meeting at short notice that you demanded. The mother collected the boy from his school and took him home. She is waiting for me there. Waiting for *us*, though she does not know it.'

'What about her husband?' Hammond asked.

'He is attending a meeting in Brussels.'

'What are their names?' Vidor demanded. 'You may as well tell us now.'

'Bartol. He is French. She is Irish. Émile and Mary. They have changed the boy's name to Patrick.'

'Patrick Bartol,' said Zineta numbly.

'He is eleven years old, *madame*. He has no memory of you or of Serbia. He speaks French, English and German. But not Serbian. Not a word. If he is anything, he is a Luxembourger. He has lived here for as long as he can remember.'

'Leave him in peace? Is that what you think I should do?' Delmotte offered no reply. In the end, Zineta answered the question herself. 'Well, maybe I should. And maybe I will. But even so . . . I must see him.'

They drove on, heading north through ever greener and more scattered suburbs until they left the city behind. Then, turning off the main road, they reached a wooded, hilly district, where large, modern villas set deep in their own grounds were strung out along a gently zigzagging road.

'This is Forêt Pré,' said Delmotte. 'It is considered a very desirable development.'

'And Monir lives here?' Zineta asked, gazing through the car window at the terracotta roofs and the manicured lawns and the carefully composed stands of conifers.

'The Bartols live here, yes,' said Delmotte. 'We are very close now. You should decide what you will say to Madame Bartol.'

'So should you, *maître*,' said Vidor. 'After all, you're the one who's lied to her.'

Delmotte ignored the gibe. 'This is their house, on the next bend,' he said simply, slowing as they approached a pillared entrance. 'She has left the gate open for me.' He slowed still further and came to a halt twenty yards or so short of the turn-off. 'Are you sure . . . you want to do this?'

Zineta nodded. 'Drive on.'

TWENTY-SIX

The drive described a wide loop between a belt of trees and a shrub-edged lawn en route to a flagstoned courtyard partly enclosed by a large, low-roofed, L-shaped house that would not have looked out of place in Spain or California, but sat oddly in the dank and sunless Luxembourg countryside.

The stillness of the weather, the quietness of the neighbourhood and the tension of the moment met in a vacuum of uncertainty as they got out of the car. A tiny pebble scraping on a stone beneath Hammond's foot was loud to his ear. And the careful closings of the car doors were like muffled gunshots.

Then, all at once, he was aware of an additional presence. A figure had appeared round the corner of the house, from the direction of the front door: a boy of about eleven, dark-haired and narrow-faced, thin, but healthily so, with sparkling brown eyes and a complexion of telltale Slavic sallowness. He was dressed in school uniform minus the blazer and tie: monogrammed sweater, white shirt and grey trousers. He smiled at them cautiously.

'*Bonjour.*'

'*Bonjour, Patrick,*' said Delmotte. '*Est-ce que ta mère est à la maison?*'

Hammond glanced at Zineta. She was staring at Patrick, transfixed, trembling as if she had seen a ghost, as in a sense she had.

Patrick had opened his mouth to answer Delmotte's question

when a woman strode round the corner and grasped him protectively by the shoulders. She was short and slim, with brown, bobbed hair and a round face. Her black trouser-suit and white blouse suggested that she, like her son, had not found time to change since arriving home. Her complexion, unsurprisingly, was wholly different from his: pale, almost white, though flushed about the cheeks. She frowned anxiously at them.

'Who are these people, Maître Delmotte?' she asked. 'I thought you'd be alone.'

'I am sorry, *madame*. The situation is not quite . . . as I described it.'

'Go inside, Patrick,' she said to the boy, lapsing into French when he made no immediate move. '*Vite, vite.*'

Patrick, perhaps sensing his mother's alarm, scurried off obediently. Mary Bartol took a few hesitant steps towards them, glancing first at Delmotte, then at Zineta. Already, Hammond suspected, she had guessed who this woman was.

'What is going on, *maître*?'

'There's no danger to your son, Madame Bartol,' said Hammond in an effort to ease the tension. 'My name is—'

'You're English?'

'Yes. My name is Edward Hammond. My friends here are Stevan Vidor and Zineta Perović.'

'We are Serbian, *madame*,' said Vidor.

'Serbian?' She turned on Delmotte. 'Will you kindly explain, *maître*?'

'Perhaps . . . we should go inside,' he suggested lamely.

'Not until I—'

'I'm his mother,' Zineta said suddenly and forcefully. 'You must see it. He has my eyes.'

Mary Bartol stared at her in slowly mounting consternation. Yes. She had seen the resemblance. And yes. She knew what it meant. But bringing herself to admit it was quite another matter. 'His natural mother is dead,' she insisted. 'Patrick is an orphan . . . from Kosovo.'

'I regret, *madame*,' said Delmotte, 'that is not true. I . . . mis-informed you.'

'You *misinformed* us?'

'I *am* his mother,' said Zineta. 'His father is also living. He is not an orphan. And he is not Kosovar.'

'Nonsense. We have his birth certificate. He was born in Mitrovica.'

'He was born in Belgrade.'

'Why don't we talk about this indoors?' Hammond put in. 'No one here has any intention of abducting Patrick, *madame*, whatever Maître Delmotte may have told you.'

'What are your intentions?'

'Zineta has spent nine years looking for her son. And now she's found him. It's as simple as that. We have no intentions.' To his dismay, he realized that was literally true. What happened next was for no one to dictate.

'Even if what you say is correct—'

'It's correct, I assure you.'

'Even if it is,' Mary Bartol persisted, 'you have no right to come here like this.'

'Call the police, then. You might be able to get us arrested. But at the end of that process you'd lose Patrick. The adoption was fraudulent and therefore illegal. They'd take him away from you. Don't you see? We have to talk about it.'

She turned towards Delmotte. 'Was it fraudulent?'

He nodded feebly. '*Oui, madame.*'

'*What?*' The crumbling of a confident, unquestioned assumption was written on her face. 'How could—'

She broke off at the sound of another vehicle on the drive. Turning, Hammond saw a plain grey van speeding towards them. He and everyone else was too surprised at first to react. It clipped the edge of the lawn and skidded to a halt beside the Citroën. Two men jumped out, dressed in brown overalls. They were stern-faced and powerfully built. And they were both holding guns.

'Oh my God,' shrieked Mary Bartol. 'What's—'

'*No speak*,' shouted one of the men. His gaze and the aim of his gun swivelled between them.

A third man emerged more slowly from the van, also armed and overalled, though older than the other two, with short grey hair, sunken eyes and a long scar that distorted one side of his mouth. 'Where's the boy?' he growled.

No one answered. Delmotte looked simply incapable of it. Zineta was trembling so violently Vidor had to grasp her arm to steady her. Mary Bartol was gaping at the intruders, open-mouthed with terror. For his part, Hammond felt eerily calm, as if his experiences in Belgrade had somehow inured him to such events.

The man with the scarred face barked something in Serbian at one of the other two, including his name, Obrad. He strode over to Mary Bartol, grabbed her by the wrist and half dragged, half led, her towards the front door of the house. 'Call him to come to you,' Hammond heard him say.

'Where are the tapes?' Scarface demanded.

When no immediate answer was forthcoming, he stepped across to Zineta and held the gun to her head. She closed her eyes and murmured a few words to herself. Hammond saw Vidor begin to raise his arm to protect her. Then he stopped. There was no protection in this situation.

'They're in the boot of the car,' said Hammond.

'*Gepek*,' Vidor translated promptly, fearful of the slightest misunderstanding.

Scarface removed the gun from Zineta's head and pointed it at Hammond. 'Get them.'

Hammond moved slowly to the boot. The other gunman hovered at his shoulder. He was unshaven and greasy-haired, with a flattened and probably sometime broken nose that made his breathing threateningly audible, like a beast preparing to pounce.

Hammond opened the boot and raised the lid. He lifted out the holdall containing the box of tapes and showed it to Scarface.

'Put it on the ground. Open it.'

Hammond knelt down, unzipped the bag and exposed the tapes.

'*Dobro. Torba,* Miloš.'

Miloš, the man with the broken nose, waved Hammond aside, then picked up the bag. At that point there was a shout from the house.

Scarface shouted back, 'OK.' He took a few steps towards the van, covering their route to the front door. 'Walk into the house,' he barked. 'Slowly.'

They started moving, with Delmotte in the lead and Vidor bringing up the rear. They had gone only a few yards when Vidor stumbled, then quickly recovered himself. For a fraction of a second, his head was low by Hammond's shoulder, shielded from Scarface. And in that fraction of a second he whispered, 'Trust me.'

Hammond did not dare react in any way. What Vidor meant he could not imagine. But it was a warning of some kind – a warning and a promise.

They rounded the corner of the house and approached the front door. It was wide open. Obrad was standing in the hallway behind Mary and Patrick Bartol, holding his gun at Mary's head. Patrick was clutching his mother's hand. He looked on the verge of tears. Obrad's expression was blank, his narrow-set eyes heavy-lidded, as if this was all in a day's work.

He pulled Mary and Patrick back as the others filed into the hall, kicked a door to his left fully open and gestured for them to go through.

They entered the dining room. 'To wall,' Obrad ordered. Hammond heard Miloš's breathing again. He was close behind them. They followed Delmotte round the dining table to the wall facing them, where an oil painting of an idyllically tranquil pastoral scene hung, and lined up against it. 'You also,' Obrad said to Mary. She led Patrick meekly across to join them, casting a glance at Hammond that mixed fear and accusation. What horror had they brought to her door?

Scarface stepped into the room, where Miloš was already standing guard, leaving Obrad in the hall. He stood the bag on the table and looked at each of his captives in turn, unhurriedly and

235

analytically, as if assessing their powers of resistance. 'Hands on heads,' he said. They obeyed. Then he pulled a phone out from his overalls and dialled a number.

The call was answered promptly. And the person who answered proceeded to do most of the talking. Scarface was reporting to his boss. And he was being told what to do.

The call ended. 'We wait,' he announced. 'The chief will be here soon.'

'Who is . . . the chief?' Delmotte asked hesitantly.

'Branko Todorović,' said Vidor, in a fatalistic tone.

'*Da*,' said Scarface. 'That is right.' He barked an order at Miloš, who handed him his gun then walked over to where Hammond and the others were standing. He began frisking them one by one, starting with Delmotte.

'I have had dealings with Monsieur Todorović,' the lawyer protested, some of his pomposity slowly reflating itself. 'There is no need . . . for any of this.'

'You are the lawyer Delmotte?'

'*Mais oui.* I mean, yes. I am Delmotte.'

'I have a message for you from the chief.'

'What is it?'

'Wait and I will tell you.'

Miloš moved on to Zineta, grinning at her as he took the chance to fondle her breasts and touch her between her legs. She did not react. She stared straight through him. She was no longer trembling, Hammond noticed. She was slowly regaining her self-control. Miloš bypassed Patrick and gave Mary more of the same. She whimpered and bit her lip, struggling to control her emotions for her son's sake. Then it was Hammond's turn. Miloš dropped the smirk and checked him over cursorily, so cursorily, in fact, that he failed to detect the tape Hammond had pocketed after playing it to Delmotte in the car. Miloš was looking for only one thing – a weapon. And he was evidently capable of looking for only one thing at a time. He gave Vidor the once-over, then went back to collect his gun. '*Ništa*,' he reported.

'The message for me?' Delmotte prompted.

'*Da*. The message.' Scarface smiled, though thanks to his scar it was more like a scowl. 'He said you could leave.'

'*Leave?*'

'Drive away. Go home. *Bilo šta*. You are free. Provided . . . you do not contact the police.'

It struck Hammond at once that this condition, if the offer of freedom was genuine, was unenforceable. Once he was out of their clutches, Delmotte could do anything he liked. There was something wrong. But not, apparently, in Delmotte's opinion. 'I will not tell anyone what has happened here.'

Mary looked round at him in disgust. 'What in God's name are you saying? Have you gone mad, *maître?*'

'It sounds like he's already done a deal,' said Vidor matter-of-factly.

'*Shut up*,' bellowed Scarface. 'All of you. You will speak only when I say you can. Do you understand?' He nodded, evidently satisfied that he had got the point across. '*Dobra*. So . . .' He looked at Delmotte. 'You want to leave?'

'Yes. I want to leave.'

Though his companions dared not speak, their disgust at his treachery must have been obvious to Delmotte. Hammond could only suppose Vidor was right. The lawyer had struck some kind of deal with Todorović following their visit to his office. That explained how Scarface and his crew had known where they were going when they left Luxembourg City.

'Go, then,' said Scarface. Delmotte lowered his hands from his head and started across the room. He did not look back, in apology or farewell. It was horribly clear he meant to tell no one of their plight. They were on their own.

Delmotte reached the doorway and Scarface gestured for Obrad to escort him to his car. The pair moved off down the hall. The note of their footfalls changed when they stepped out on to the flagstoned path that led to the courtyard. Hammond bitterly imagined the eagerness with which Delmotte was looking forward to driving away. He was probably congratulating himself on how adroitly he had extricated himself from a perilous situation.

'Lawyers,' Scarface sneered. 'I hate them.'

At that moment there was a loud crack of a gunshot at the front of the house.

Scarface gave a dry little chuckle. 'One less to hate now.'

TWENTY-SEVEN

The shock of Delmotte's execution and the knowledge that any one of them might be next filled the room with an atmosphere of disabling dread. They could neither move nor speak, but their brains were free to race and scramble over a near future governed by the nonchalant callousness of their captors.

Scarface sat straddling one of the dining chairs, chewing gum and exchanging occasional remarks with Miloš, who stood by the door. Hammond had no idea what they were talking about, although their tone was casual. But there was nothing casual about the firm hold they kept on their guns. Obrad did not return for five minutes or so. When he reappeared, there was no hint in his manner of what he had done, although Hammond had little doubt the dark specks on his overalls were sprayed droplets of Delmotte's blood.

The ordeal was grim enough for the adults, but for Patrick it was close to unendurable. Mary did her best to hold him still and calm him, by smoothing his hair with slow, repeated strokes. But he was clearly aware of what had happened to Delmotte and no amount of maternal reassurance could dispel the fear that gripped him.

Scarface had allowed Hammond, Vidor and Zineta to take their hands off their heads, but they were required to keep their arms folded. Since they could not look directly at each other, Hammond had few clues to the others' state of mind. Zineta made not a sound. And Vidor was simply an immobile presence, his plea to trust him as baffling as when he had uttered it.

In the event, they did not have long to wait before they heard the low, powerful note of a car engine. Todorović had arrived. A resolution of some kind could not be far off.

Hammond was surprised by how philosophically he contemplated the possibility of death. Why this did not frighten him more he could not have explained. He actually felt greater agitation when he recalled the missteps that had led him and his companions into their current plight. He should have known he could not out-manoeuvre Todorović. And he should not have taken Delmotte at his word in the smallest matter.

Such regrets were futile now, though. Obrad went to open the front door and a few moments later Branko Todorović strode into the room.

His physical bulk was magnified by the voluminous fur coat he was wearing and the booming baritone of his voice. Scarface was reduced to sudden servility during what Hammond assumed was his report of progress so far. He had hastily removed the gum he was chewing and stood almost to attention. Todorović listened to him impassively, as if the adequacy of his crew's performance was in some doubt. Then, doubtless to Scarface's considerable relief, he cracked a smile and clapped him approvingly on the shoulder, addressing him genially as Slavko. '*Dobro rad, Slavko. Dobro rad.*'

The smile was fleeting, however. He spent several minutes examining the tapes, then walked across to Zineta and loosed what sounded like a mixture of accusations and insults at her, to which she replied in cool, measured tones. Hammond admired her self-possession. She was not going to be intimidated.

'Where is your husband, *madame*?' Todorović demanded, switching to English as he turned his attention to Mary Bartol.

'He is . . . travelling back from Brussels,' she answered hesitantly.

'When do you expect him?'

'I'm . . . I'm not sure.'

'If you cooperate with us, he will find you and your son alive and well.' Todorović chuckled derisively. 'Perhaps you can spend a quiet evening together, watching television.'

'Just tell me . . . what you want.'

'Maybe I already have it.'

He moved past her and stood in front of Hammond, staring into his eyes.

'We have met before, haven't we?'

'I . . . don't think so,' said Hammond.

'I never forget a face. What is your name?'

'Edward Hammond.'

Todorović frowned, struggling to recall where he had heard the name before. Perhaps fortunately, the struggle appeared to be unavailing. But he was in little doubt of the role Hammond had recently played. 'You were with Piravani in Belgrade. You are the Englishman who helped him steal the tapes, aren't you?'

Denial would only have diverted suspicions elsewhere. 'Yes,' Hammond admitted.

'And you?' Todorović looked towards Vidor.

'I'm Stevan Vidor. I work for the International Criminal Court in The Hague.'

'*Odakle ste?*'

'I am Serbian.'

Without the slightest warning Todorović struck him in the mouth with a swinging blow of his hand. Vidor gasped and staggered back against the wall. Hammond saw blood trickling from his lower lip. '*Pacov,*' snarled Todorović. He turned smartly away and leered down at Patrick Bartol. 'Traitors are the worst kind of people, boy. And Serbian traitors are the worst of the worst. Remember that.'

'Yes, sir,' mumbled Patrick.

'You're a Serb too. Not a Luxembourger. You're part of a proud nation. And you must never betray it. Otherwise you're no better than him.' He pointed at Vidor. 'Understand?'

'Yes, sir.'

'Make sure he does understand when he is older, *madame*,' Todorović said to Mary. 'You owe it to him.'

Without waiting for her response, he spun on his heel and stalked back to the other end of the table, where the tapes were still sitting in their box. He took them out, batch by batch, and stacked them next to the box. Hammond could clearly see that one of the batches was a tape short. He wondered if Todorović would notice. He did not have to wonder for long.

'The last tape is missing.' Todorović held up the offending batch. 'Who has it?'

There was no sense in forcing him to order a search. Hammond raised his hand cautiously. 'Me.'

Todorović said nothing, but beckoned for Hammond to surrender it. He took the cassette out of his pocket, stepped forward and placed it on the table. When Todorović went on beckoning, he slid it towards him. It glided smoothly over the polished wood and ran out of momentum only a foot or so short of its target. 'Thank you,' said Todorović, picking it up and slipping it neatly under the rubber band that held the others in the batch. He smiled. 'Piravani is a fool. And you, Hammond, are a fool for helping him. Fools don't get the better of Branko Todorović.'

Talking about himself in the third person was a symptom of megalomania Hammond did his level best to ignore. It was important to believe this was no more to Todorović than Zineta had claimed: a business transaction, now approaching its conclusion.

'Those tapes . . . are what you came for?' asked Mary Bartol.

'Yes, *madame*.' Todorović was still smiling.

'Then, please, take them and go. I know nothing about them. Your dealings with these people' – she nodded in Hammond's direction – 'are no concern of mine.'

'No concern? You think that?'

'I assure you they aren't.'

'And I assure you they are. These tapes prove who the boy's real father is. Dragan Gazi. Heard of him?'

'The war criminal?' The words were out of her mouth before she had weighed their effect.

'*War criminal?*' Todorović roared, causing Mary and Patrick to flinch. 'You sit here in your big house in a country that has no character or culture of its own and you judge us Serbs for what we have done to preserve ours?'

'I . . . I'm not judging anyone.'

'No. You let those fuckers in The Hague do that.'

'Please. Please.' She began to sob. Patrick looked up at her and began to cry too. 'I don't know . . . who Maître Delmotte . . . I mean, I don't know . . . what he arranged . . . or who for. He . . . lied to my husband and me. But if the tapes are all you want, then . . . then . . .'

'We should leave you in peace, yes, *madame*? We should leave you to go on with your comfortable life?'

'Yes,' she murmured. It was more of a plea than an answer.

Zineta said something in Serbian then, something that sounded pointed and practical. It was clear she had no intention of pleading.

Todorović replied curtly, without looking at her. Yet Hammond had the impression, based more on the man's posture than his tone, that he reluctantly acknowledged the sense of what Zineta had said. He sighed and patted the pile of tapes. 'OK, OK. Gazi and his son are nothing to me. The war is over. I have moved on. We have all moved on.' Another, heavier sigh. 'What I require now is certainty. Did you make copies of these tapes?'

'No,' said Hammond.

'Is that the truth?'

'We didn't have time. There are no copies.'

'So you say. But how can I believe you?'

'*There are no copies.*'

Todorović gestured to Slavko, who passed him his gun. He flexed his fingers and thumb around it, then strode across the room to where Zineta was standing and clapped the weapon to her temple. Hammond saw her swallow hard and moisten her lips. But she did not react in any other way. Perhaps she had been preparing herself for such an event ever since the gunmen had burst out of the van.

'Are there any copies?'

'No,' said Hammond. 'There are none.'

'Shooting Gazi's whore would be no problem to me. It would actually be a pleasure. You are giving me the excuse I need, Hammond. Where are the copies?'

'There aren't any.'

'I think there are. And I want to know where you've hidden them.'

'*For God's sake, there aren't any.*' Hammond looked into Todorović's eyes and saw only the certainty that he was not bluffing. He was willing, if not eager, to kill Zineta.

'I'll count to three. Then—'

'There are copies,' said Vidor suddenly. Hammond swung round and stared at him in amazement. What was he saying? What was he thinking of?

'Aha,' said Todorović. 'So, now there are some. When did you make them?'

'He made them.' Vidor pointed at Hammond. 'Before he arrived in The Hague. One tape from each batch: a random sample.'

Vidor's expression gave nothing away, but Hammond knew he had to trust him. He must have foreseen Todorović would assume copies existed, even though they did not. How he meant to sustain the pretence, and to what purpose, Hammond could only wait to find out.

'Why didn't you tell me this, Hammond?' Todorović demanded.

Hammond turned to face him. 'I . . . thought . . . I thought we could . . .'

'Send me away with the originals, but still have some dirt to serve up to those bastards in The Hague? Is that what you mean?'

'I . . .'

'Maybe you're the one I should shoot.' Todorović whipped the gun away from Zineta's temple and pointed it at him.

'Shoot him and you'll never get the copies,' said Vidor bluntly.

With a visible effort, Todorović stifled his anger. 'Where are they?'

'In a left-luggage locker at Luxembourg central train station. We dropped them off there before we collected Zineta from the airport.'

'And the key?'

'In my pocket.'

'Show me.'

Hammond could read the astonishment in Zineta's gaze as she watched Vidor produce the key and hold it out for Todorović to take. It was hardly less than the astonishment he felt himself. Not only had they made no copies of the tapes, but Vidor had been nowhere near the railway station. Surely the key could not be authentic, though it certainly looked as if it fitted a locker somewhere.

'The number?'

'Ah, the number,' said Vidor. 'I'm not sure I can remember.'

'*Šta?*'

'It's twenty-six.' Vidor's memory seemed suddenly to have been restored. But then— 'Or is it? Maybe I'm holding back the real number in case you start shooting my friends, Branko.' Something had altered in his voice. He was shedding a disguise. The real Stevan Vidor was only now making himself known. 'Hammond doesn't know it, you see. He waited outside in the car, while I went in to find a locker. So, it's twenty-six. Unless or until I say otherwise.'

Todorović took several deep breaths as he glared at Vidor. His face was red with barely suppressed fury. His dearest wish appeared to be to punch his tormentor in the face before putting a bullet through his brain. But he could not. If there were copies of the tapes out there somewhere, he had to have them. And to do that he had to keep Vidor alive.

'Why don't you and I go and get them, Branko? Then you'll have everything you need to safeguard your position in the Serbian business world. You can go back to making money and we can forget this ever happened. I'm sure your men can dispose of Delmotte's body and clean up the mess. Madame Bartol isn't going to involve the police with all those irregularities in her son's adoption to worry about, are you, *madame*?'

'No,' said Mary Bartol. 'Absolutely not.'

'You see? It's a good deal. And I know you like a good deal. Give and take on either side. And a healthy profit for you.'

Todorović was grinding his teeth so fiercely he was in danger of cracking a molar. But his breathing was slowing. He was beginning to see reason. He did not like the look of it, but he recognized it all the same. 'OK.' His acceptance came in a reluctant growl. 'We will go to the station, Vidor. And you will give me the copies. One of my men will go with us. The other two will stay here, with Hammond, the women and the boy. If I am satisfied by what you give me, I will call my men and tell them to leave. If I am not satisfied, I will also call and tell them to leave. But they will kill the hostages first. You understand? All four. Their lives depend on you now, Vidor. That is the only deal there is going to be. I hope you like it.'

TWENTY-EIGHT

Zineta's pained, questioning gaze was waiting whenever Hammond looked towards her. She believed Vidor, of course, and was wondering why Hammond had not told her he had copied some of the tapes. Letting her think he had deceived her was a small price to pay for surviving their brush with Todorović, but how Vidor's ploy was designed to achieve that he did not know. He could only do as Vidor had asked: trust him.

Todorović had taken Obrad along when he set off with Vidor. The drive to the railway station in Luxembourg would take half an hour, maybe more. That left the hostages, as Todorović had all too accurately termed them, with an anxious wait for news. Though he could not afford to show it, Hammond had cause to be the most anxious of them all, tortured as he was by the question of what exactly Vidor planned to do. Zineta and Mary Bartol thought there really were copied tapes waiting in a left-luggage locker at the station. But he knew better. Or worse.

The key to the locker was surely the key to the puzzle. Either it fitted a locker in a different station – The Hague, maybe – or Vidor had an accomplice, who had delivered the key to him at the airport while Hammond was waiting for Zineta in the arrivals hall. Whichever the case, Vidor could hardly be the lovesick translator he had presented himself as. He was playing an altogether deeper game.

Slavko and Miloš knew nothing of this. To them the interlude was merely a tiresome extension of the job in hand. They chatted idly, chewed gum and kept a close eye on their captives. Slavko was old enough to have fought in Bosnia or Kosovo, quite possibly with Gazi's Wolves. He knew how to kill with an untroubled conscience. Obrad had dispatched Delmotte like a surplus kitten in a litter. There was no reason to suppose Miloš would behave any differently. Man, woman or child: it made no difference to them.

A quarter of an hour or so slowly passed, leadenly timed by the ticking of a longcase clock in the hall. By then little Patrick Bartol's nerves had been stretched too far for his bladder to bear. His squirmings were becoming so desperate that Slavko demanded to know what was the matter with him.

His mother explained and asked if Patrick could use the toilet. Slavko refused. 'Piss in your pants or hold it, kid.' Patrick looked so aggrieved that Slavko laughed. Miloš joined in. And Patrick began to cry.

Then the telephone rang. Not Slavko's mobile, which they were waiting for, but the Bartols' land line. Receivers in other parts of the house began burbling in unison. Mary Bartol took an instinctive step forward, but Slavko barked at her to stop. 'Let it ring,' he rasped.

And it did ring, several times, before Mary said, 'I think it's my husband. I left him a message earlier . . . asking him to contact me.'

'You can speak to him later.'

'But—'

'*Later.*'

'No.'

'*Šta?*' Slavko was on his feet now, pointing his gun at her.

'You don't understand. I told him it was urgent. That I'd had to . . . take Patrick out of school. That I'd . . . wait for his call. If I don't answer . . .'

Understanding dawned slowly on Slavko. If Émile Bartol was worried about his wife and son, he might contact the local police, or a neighbour. It was a problem Slavko did not need. But avoiding

248

it required swift action. 'Come, come. Quick.' He waved Mary forward. 'Speak to him. Tell him everything is all right. Tell him you and the boy are fine.'

Slavko grabbed Mary's arm and piloted her out into the hall. Zineta clasped Patrick by the shoulders to stop him following. Miloš stepped into the doorway. Behind him, Hammond saw Slavko barge his way into the study on the opposite side of the hall. He dragged Mary with him. The answering machine had already cut in when he snatched up the phone on the desk and pressed it to her ear. She took it from him, pushed a button to override the machine and started speaking – in French.

'*Émile? . . . Hi, chéri . . . Non, non, pas de problème. Je vais très bien, Patrick aussi. Je me suis fait une erreur. Je . . .*'

The angry, baffled expression on Slavko's face warned Hammond of the danger a fraction of a second before the Serb shouted, 'English. Speak English.' Then he froze. So did Mary. So did they all. The silence in the house was so complete they could hear Émile Bartol's voice at the other end of the line, though not what he was actually saying. Mary stared helplessly at the receiver, clutched in her hand. Then Slavko grabbed it from her and slammed it down.

He pulled her towards him. 'I'm sorry,' she gasped. 'I didn't think. But I never . . .' Her words tailed off. What she had said or not said to her husband was immaterial. Slavko knew no French. And that too was immaterial now. Émile Bartol had realized something was wrong – very wrong.

Slavko raised his gun and pointed it at Mary's forehead. She shrank away, but his grasp on her arm was too strong. He had made a decision. He was going to kill her. He was going to kill all of them. Miloš was watching him, waiting for the shot that would start the bloodshed.

Then Patrick moved, breaking free of Zineta, darting across the room and dodging past Miloš before he could react. He raced into the study and launched himself at Slavko, sinking his teeth into his right hand, which was holding the gun. Zineta started after him as

Slavko cried out in pain and surprise. Miloš made a hopelessly late swipe at Patrick that took him blundering into Zineta's path.

Hammond moved too, flinging himself round the other side of the table out of Miloš's line of sight. He heard Slavko's gun go off: a loud crack, followed by a splintering of plaster. Mary screamed. There was another shot, another splintering of plaster.

Acting on instinct rather than any kind of judgement, Hammond caught Miloš's throat in the crook of his arm and yanked him back. He saw Zineta duck into the hall, heading for the study. Throwing every ounce of strength he had into the struggle, Hammond pulled Miloš further back, his spine creaking from the strain. The Serb choked and spluttered and tried to regain his balance, but the momentum was against him. They crashed to the floor close to the table, Miloš's weight knocking most of the breath out of Hammond's lungs and jarring his ribs so badly it felt like he had been stabbed. He heard several more shots fired, in quick succession, in the study. But this time there was no splintering of plaster, only the high-pitched note of Mary screaming.

Miloš was inert, a dead weight pressing down on him. Hammond pushed against it and managed to slide clear. He scrambled to his feet. It looked as if Miloš had struck his head on the edge of the table as he fell. He lay unconscious, slack-mouthed and sightlessly staring, his fingers loose around the handle of his gun. Hammond grabbed the weapon and plunged through the doorway.

Mary was no longer screaming. She had slumped to the floor of the study, with her back against the door, jamming it wide open. Patrick was standing next to her, still and silent as a figurine, staring at Slavko, who lay propped up against one of the tubular legs of the desk. The front of his overalls was dark with blood, the patch spreading fast and liquidly. Blood was flowing from his mouth and nostrils as well. He coughed thickly and squinted at Hammond, as if everything he saw was through a blurring, thickening curtain. He raised his right hand feebly, then looked down at it, frowning in evident perplexity at the absence of his gun.

The gun was in Zineta's hand. She was kneeling back on her heels beside him, shaking like a leaf in a breeze and gaping open-mouthed at the damage those last few shots had inflicted. That it was fatal damage was in the next instant confirmed when Slavko's breathing cut off in gurgling mid-inhalation and his head fell forward.

Hammond stepped slowly into the room. Only Patrick appeared to notice his arrival. 'Miss Perović shot him,' he said, in the precise manner he might have used when answering a teacher's question in class. 'But only after I stopped him shooting *Maman*.'

Zineta turned and looked up at him. 'Are you . . . all right, Edward?' she asked bemusedly. 'Where's . . . the other man?'

'He knocked himself out. Don't worry about him.' He crouched down beside her. 'How did you get the gun off this one?'

'I didn't. He was still holding it when it went off. But I'd twisted his wrist trying to stop him firing . . . at Madame Bartol and . . . I don't know whether it was him or me . . . or both of us . . . who pulled the trigger.' She laid the gun carefully on the floor. 'He is dead, isn't he?'

'Oh yes. He's dead.'

'We ought to call the police,' said Patrick, sounding bizarrely chirpy.

'Yes,' said Hammond. 'We ought.' He stood up and seized the telephone, then hesitated.

'One one three,' said Patrick.

Hammond dialled the number. 'I'll speak to them,' said Mary Bartol, clambering unsteadily to her feet. 'I know . . . what to say.'

'OK.' Hammond passed her the phone. Her hand was shaking violently as she took it.

'Please . . . take Patrick into another room. Away from—' She broke off as the call was answered and began talking rapidly and urgently in French.

Hammond turned and helped Zineta up, then shepherded her and Patrick out into the hall. He tried to force himself to think logically and practically. When would the Luxembourg police reach

251

them? What could they best do to help Vidor in the meantime? And how long would it be before Miloš regained consciousness? 'Does your father have any rope, Patrick?' he asked, calculating that they should tie the man's wrists and ankles together to prevent him moving just in case he came to before the police arrived.

'There's some in the garage,' Patrick replied brightly. 'The quickest way is through the kitchen.'

The boy's buoyant mood was his brain's defence mechanism to ward off the reality of what had occurred, Hammond reckoned. It would not last indefinitely. But while it did he seemed unaffected by the death he had just witnessed and the danger they had all been in. 'OK, Patrick. Lead the way. I'll just—' A glance into the dining room silenced him. Miloš was no longer lying by the table.

Hammond had to step into the doorway of the room to convince himself Miloš had really gone. He had. But *where*? Out to the van was his first and most optimistic guess, since the man was welcome to flee the scene if he wanted to. They were safer without him.

Then Zineta screamed. Hammond turned and saw Patrick pull up halfway along the hall towards the kitchen. A figure staggered across the patch of light reflected from the kitchen's tiled floor. It was Miloš. He cannoned against a worktop, then righted himself and lurched out through the doorway. A bright metallic gleam was the first warning Hammond had that he was holding a knife – some sort of large chopping knife with a wide blade.

Miloš's head swayed as he focused on Patrick, then he started lumbering towards him, raising the knife to attack. The boy had time enough to turn and run away, but he did not move. Instead he stared, almost curiously, at the spectacle before him.

'Get out of the way,' Hammond shouted. But Patrick did not react. And Hammond did not trust himself to use the gun he was still holding other than at the closest of ranges. He started along the hall.

But Zineta had started sooner. She reached Patrick when Miloš was nearly on him and scooped him up, lifting him off the ground as she turned into Miloš's path, shielding the boy from his attacker.

Miloš lunged with the knife, missing his intended victim, but striking Zineta instead with a deep thrust somewhere around the waist. She cried out and fell. Patrick fell with her, but rolled clear and scrambled up, blocking Hammond's path. Hammond dodged round him as Miloš stooped over Zineta, swivelled the knife in his hand and plunged it down into her.

Hammond fired at the same instant that the second stab struck home. The gun jolted in his grasp as he pulled the trigger two or three more times. One bullet entered Miloš's neck. He gasped and pitched away from Zineta. Then another gouged a bloody cavity out of his nose, before a third pierced his skull and he dropped to the floor.

Hammond was possessed now by instincts he barely recognized as his own. He bent over Miloš and pressed the gun to his temple. He felt sure the man was already dead, but his need for certainty on the point was overriding. He fired two more shots. Bone splintered and blood sprayed. Miloš did not move.

Only then did Hammond turn and kneel beside Zineta. And only then did he realize just how much blood she was losing. It was gouting out of her. 'Call an ambulance,' he shouted at Patrick.

'One one two,' said Patrick numbly. It was clear shock had finally overtaken him. And small wonder. The pool of Zineta's blood was spreading fast towards him.

'Call for one. *Now.*'

Patrick belatedly turned and ran towards the study just as his mother stepped out if it, still holding the phone, the cable stretched out behind her. Her mouth fell open as she took in what she saw.

'*Ambulance,*' Hammond roared. '*Fast.*' Then he looked down at Zineta. She was lying doubled up on her side, her face locked in a grimace of pain. He tried to turn her on to her back, so that he could see exactly where the blood was coming from, but she wailed in agony. His guess, based on where her hands were pressing the wound, was that the knife had punctured the femoral artery. Miloš had stabbed her twice, so there had to be a second wound in the same area. But the arterial injury was the more serious – and the more life-threatening. Blood was pumping out of her with horrifying speed.

'I'm going to try and stop the bleeding, Zineta,' he said, unfastening her jeans and searching for the pressure point in her groin. 'Hold on. Just hold on.' He was a doctor. Surely he could save her. He knew what to do. With enough force applied in the correct place, he could stem the blood loss until the paramedics arrived.

But it was immediately obvious to him that the pressure point was itself the location of the tear to the artery. And it was a big tear. He could not trace the artery above it. There was another wound in the abdomen impeding him. And there was so much blood. He was kneeling in a small lake of it.

'I feel . . . cold,' Zineta moaned.

'Don't worry. That's natural. I just need to— Oh God.' As he eased her hands away, he saw how hopeless the task was. The injury was simply too severe. Nothing was going to work. He understood that very clearly. She was going to die. And he would not be able to prevent it.

'Will Miss Perović be all right?' Patrick called from the doorway of the study.

'Get some towels,' Hammond shouted back, searching ever more desperately for a viable pressure point. He glimpsed Mary Bartol in the hall, clutching Patrick by the hand.

'Fetch them from the bathroom,' she said, releasing Patrick and pushing him towards the stairs. He started up them, his feet pounding on the treads.

'Is Monir . . . unharmed?' Zineta asked weakly. She was terribly pale now, her face sheened with sweat.

'Your son is fine,' Hammond replied.

'Thank you . . . for calling him that.'

'There's an ambulance on its way.' He glanced up at Mary, who nodded in confirmation. But her expression told its own story. She knew the ambulance would arrive too late.

And so did Zineta. 'I'm sorry, Edward. I've caused you . . . much trouble.'

'You've nothing to apologize for.'

She clasped his arm. 'If you get the tapes back . . . listen to the ones for . . . March and April . . . ninety-six. They'll help you prove . . . you didn't ask Gazi . . .'

'Forget the tapes. All that matters is saving your life.'

She smiled feebly. 'I know you would . . . if you . . . could.'

Patrick came racing back down the stairs. Mary stopped him as he reached the bottom. Hammond sensed rather than knew the struggle was over – and in vain. He looked down into Zineta's eyes.

'Ask Monir . . . to hold my hand . . . Please.'

Hammond beckoned Patrick forward. Mary came with him. In her gaze there was a signal of understanding – and consent. Hammond took Patrick's hand and pressed it into Zineta's cupped palm. She curled her fingers around it.

'*Doviđenja*,' she murmured. 'Good—'

Then nothing. But a dying sigh.

TWENTY-NINE

However bad things had been during the previous eleven days, Edward Hammond had kept assuring himself that with luck, effort and honesty they would improve; that there was a way through the troubles he was caught up in, not just for him, but for others whose lives had been blighted by Dragan Gazi. Zineta Perović, he only now realized, was the acid test of those assurances. And they had been shown to be worthless. Because Zineta Perović was dead.

'Did she mean a lot to you?' Mary Bartol asked him at some point, as they waited for the police and ambulance to arrive. And his answer had framed itself almost independently of him. 'More than I ever knew.' He had thought he could rescue her from an existence crippled by her dealings with Gazi. But unfortunately what she had ultimately needed him to do was what, as a doctor, he was uniquely qualified to do: save her life. And he had failed.

His struggle to right some of the wrongs he had unwittingly contributed to by saving another life – Gazi's – was made a mockery of by her death. It seemed to him now to have been a hollow enterprise from the first: a squalid salvage operation to protect his reputation. Only thanks to Zineta and Marco Piravani had it been diverted to serve nobler ends. And what were they worth if Zineta – and quite possibly Marco as well – had to die in the pursuit of them? It was too much for too little; it was altogether too much.

His state of mind – at once detached and despairing – evoked first sympathy, then tight-lipped tetchiness, in the Luxembourg police officers who found themselves dealing with four violent deaths in the normally peaceful setting of Forêt Pré. For his part, he could not seem to impress upon them the urgent need to rescue Vidor from Todorović's clutches. In the end, he had to leave most of the explaining to Mary Bartol. And she it was who conveyed to him the bewildering news, passed on from Police HQ and officially confirmed, that three men, one of them believed to be Branko Todorović, had been arrested at the Gare Centrale in Luxembourg City, and that Stevan Vidor was alive and well.

'How?' he asked.

But she had no answer for him. She was as confused as he was.

Confusion mounted when Émile Bartol arrived. He had already been en route from Brussels at the time of his earlier phone call, in response to a message from Mary reporting a family emergency. That emergency had escalated in the course of the call and he was understandably beside himself with worry. But his relief at finding his wife and son unharmed, at any rate physically, did not prevent him bombarding Hammond with demands for a clear account of his role in events – something he was presently incapable of supplying. Even the police seemed to understand that. Émile was eventually persuaded to accompany Mary and Patrick to hospital. By then Patrick was exhibiting symptoms of profound shock.

Hammond was also in shock, but not of a kind medical attention could help him cope with. He agreed to be transported to Police HQ for questioning. As he was driven away, the first of the body bags was carried out of the house. He did not know if it contained Zineta. But he did know that the irrevocability of death had never seemed starker to him.

The police supplied him with replacement clothing. His own was saturated with blood and his overnight bag was still in Vidor's car.

He was left in a windowless waiting room with assurances that someone would be along soon to take a statement – someone who would be able to clarify the circumstances of Todorović's arrest.

'Soon' turned out to be a loose concept. More than an hour elapsed in a solitude that Hammond would have found both disturbing and exasperating if he had been in firmer control of his thoughts. As it was, time drizzled through his fingers as he stared at the blank walls and watched the events leading to Zineta's death wind, unwind, rewind and agonizingly coalesce in his fixed and horrified memory. Where shock ended and grief began he could not have said. Both were equally disabling.

He had experienced death before, of course, personally as well as professionally. But not even Kate's murder had affected him like this. He had not been with her at the time. He had not seen her blood, or heard her dying words. And he had not been the same man he was now. That truth dawned slowly on him in the bland blue Luxembourg police waiting room. The previous eleven days had changed him. He could never go back to what he was before. He had become an exile from himself.

At last the door opened. And the surprise of recognition seeped into Hammond's awareness. The 'someone' was Stevan Vidor.

They shook hands, stiffly and self-consciously, as if neither was quite able to take stock of the alterations he saw in the other. Hammond was puzzled, though it took him a moment to realize why. Vidor's demeanour was not that of a man who had just lost the woman he loved. Nor was it that of an innocent caught up in events beyond his control. Clearly, he was neither of those things. As to what he was . . .

'I'm sorry, Edward,' he said. 'I thought we'd be able to get you all out safely.'

'*We?*'

'I work for ICTY, like I told you, but not as a translator. I'm a UN special investigator, liaising with the police in The Hague *and* here.'

Hammond knew he should have been angered by the mis-representation Vidor was admitting, but the emotion was beyond him. 'Are you saying . . . the police knew what was going on all along?'

'Not exactly. But they knew I was hoping to flush Todorović out. They had a squad waiting for him at the train station. I made the arrangement at the airport, while you were in the terminal waiting for Zineta's flight. I couldn't risk the police following us from there in case Todorović spotted them.'

'So we just had to take our chances?'

'There was no certainty he'd show up.'

'But if he did . . .'

'When Zineta played me the tape, I realized we had a unique opportunity to net Todorović *and* enough evidence to convict him. It looked as if we'd blown it when she disappeared, but thanks to you we got a second chance. I couldn't let it slip. We don't know yet what we'll get from the tapes, but they could prove to be one of our biggest breakthroughs.'

'And Zineta?'

'I really am very sorry. I reckoned the men Todorović left at the house would surrender once they realized he'd been arrested and we had them surrounded. That was how it was supposed to work. But operations like this are never completely predictable.'

'You're right there.'

'I've been told she bled to death.'

Hammond sighed. 'The gash to the artery was too big. I couldn't . . .' He looked away. 'I couldn't save her.'

'I'm sure you did everything you could.'

'Everything I could, yes. But not enough.'

'I don't know, of course . . . how close you were to her.'

Hammond shook his head mournfully. 'Neither do I.'

'She died trying to save her son's life, yes?'

'Yes.'

'And she succeeded.'

'So she did.'

'It's a fine way to be remembered.'

Hammond looked Vidor in the eye. 'I'd rather she was with us now.'

'Me too.'

'You could have levelled with me.'

'Too risky, Edward. Sorry.'

'Yet you expected me to trust you at the Bartols' house.'

'That was an extreme situation.'

'Yes. It certainly was.'

'I'll make sure the police go easy on you. Minimal questioning. Fast-tracked paperwork. There'll be no . . . complications.'

'Thank you,' Hammond said flatly.

'It's not just for your sake. I'm hoping you'll agree to help us . . . with something else.'

Something else? How could there be more? Was he never to be done with Gazi? He sat down. 'You'd better tell me what it is.'

'Trapping Todorović was a bonus, Edward. I was originally interested in Zineta because she was Gazi's former mistress. We thought she might be involved in a conspiracy we've picked up rumours about. It turns out we were on the wrong track. She had nothing to do with it. But—'

'What kind of conspiracy?'

'A plan to break Gazi out of prison.'

Hammond looked up at Vidor incredulously. 'Surely not.'

'It seems incredible, I know. Security at Scheveningen is state-of-the-art. But recent intelligence that's reached us suggests there's a serious plan, involving serious people, just waiting for the green light.'

'What are you going to do about it?'

Vidor sat down slowly in the chair opposite and leant forward, hands clasped together. 'That's where you come in.'

'What's any of this got to do with me?'

'Haven't you guessed? The organizers, whoever they are, won't move until they're paid. They've been in negotiation with Gazi's daughter, Ingrid. The money she's promised them is in a

Swiss bank account, controlled by Gazi's former accountant, Marco Piravani. But no one, including Ingrid, seems to know where Piravani is.'

So, at last, the truth. Ingrid did not want the money to featherbed herself and her relatives for the rest of their lives. She wanted it to buy her father's freedom. Hammond remembered pleading with Piravani back in London to pay her and have done with it. '*What does it matter if his family have his money to spend?*' he had asked him. '*What does it* really *matter?*' And now here was the answer. It could hardly matter more.

'Ingrid realized we were keeping her under surveillance and decided she couldn't risk contacting Piravani directly. Until I met you in The Hague, we had no clue as to how she meant to communicate with him. I suppose blackmail must feature in this somewhere, because you're the same Edward Hammond – *Doctor* Edward Hammond – who gave Gazi a liver transplant in March 1996, aren't you?'

Hammond gave a dismal nod. 'Yes. That's me.'

'The details don't matter to us. But I'd guess you and Piravani both had good reason to go after the tapes and he obviously wanted you to be able to control the money if anything went wrong for him in Belgrade, as evidently it did.'

'What do you mean?'

'Don't you know?'

'I don't control the money, Stevan. I know *that*.'

'But you do. Our enquiries indicate Piravani changed the access terms for the account at the end of last week, giving you the same rights as he has.'

The reason was instantly clear to Hammond. Piravani had not known what the money was really intended for. Otherwise he would not have offered to transfer it to the Cayman Islands in return for Hammond's help in retrieving the tapes. He had decided to ensure their deal could be honoured even if only one of them made it out of Belgrade.

'The issue is this, Edward. We want the people behind the

261

break-out plan to show themselves. They've probably bribed staff members at the prison or even ICTY. If so, we need to identify them. The only way to do that is to get the plan put into practice. Whatever they try, we'll be ready for them. But they won't try anything unless they are paid.'

'And that's what you want me to do – pay them?'

'Exactly. I can arrange for us to fly to Lugano tomorrow morning. Then we go to the bank and transfer the money. They'll need to be certain you're the Edward Hammond Piravani nominated, but your passport will prove that. It's simple. But only you can do it.'

Suddenly, thanks to Piravani, Hammond was a powerful man. He did not feel it. He had, in truth, never felt less powerful. He tried to marshal his thoughts. He knew he was in a position to dictate the terms of his cooperation, but he hated himself for doing it. 'Are you sure this is the best way to catch these people?'

'In our determination, it's the only way.'

'Then I'll do it. But I need something from you in return.'

'Name it.'

'Copies of the tapes covering March and April 1996.'

'No problem.' Vidor nodded thoughtfully. 'That's the period of the liver transplant.'

'Yes.' He said no more. And Vidor did not press him to.

'Well, I can have the tapes ready for you by the morning.'

'Thank you.'

'That's settled, then?'

'Yes. But, tell me, what will happen to Todorović?'

'Extradition, in due course. A comfortable cell at Scheveningen. And a long, scrupulously fair trial at ICTY. Like Gazi.'

'Who won't escape?'

'Not a chance.'

'And Zineta?'

'The police will contact her family in Belgrade. I guess they'll want her body sent back there for burial. It could take some time to arrange.'

'She has a brother. I have a phone number for him. I'd like you to contact him and explain as much as you can of what's happened. How she died. *Why* she died.'

'OK. But . . . wouldn't you prefer to speak to him yourself?'

'No.' Hammond bowed his head. 'I don't think I could bear to.'

THIRTY

Vidor was as good as his word where the Luxembourg police were concerned. Hammond was given an easy ride by the officer who interviewed him, in correct but stilted English. The particulars of the four deaths at Forêt Pré were punctiliously recorded, though perhaps no more punctiliously than if they had happened in a road accident. Vidor's UN status seemed to confer a degree of immunity on Hammond. He would be required to return to the Grand Duchy at some point for a formal examination by the judge appointed to the case, but he was meanwhile free to leave with Vidor. Indeed, his departure was positively encouraged. 'The Todorović arrest will cause much media interest, doctor,' the officer explained. 'It would be best for everyone if you . . . were not here.'

Vidor had booked him a room in a hotel out at the airport. He was driven there in a police car at the conclusion of his interview. The morning flight to Lugano, via Geneva, was at seven. There was nothing for him to do until then but wait, eat and sleep – as best he could. He was tempted to phone Alice and tell her what had happened, but there was so much to explain it could only be done face to face. It was fairer to leave her in ignorance, at least for a little longer.

He questioned the wisdom of another call he eventually went ahead and made: to Miljanović, to check on Piravani's condition.

264

But he really did need to know whether Marco was conscious yet, and responding to any of the many questions the Belgrade police would have for him.

The answer was no. 'Still comatose, Edward,' Miljanović announced. He was home for the evening, with a Bach CD playing in the background, conjuring up for Hammond an enviable vision of domestic tranquillity. 'But there are a few encouraging signs, I'm told.'

'Have they identified him yet?'

'The police haven't. But the director of the clinic has received enquiries about him from people who seem to know who he is. I assume you could tell me who those people are.'

'I could. But it's better for you if I don't, Svetozar. Besides, I doubt the director will hear from them again.'

'Something has happened?'

'Yes. It'll be big news at your end tomorrow, I should think.'

'Something good?'

'Yes. I suppose it is.'

'But you don't sound happy about it, my friend.'

'It came at a price.'

'Was the price worth paying?'

'No,' Hammond replied with searing certainty. 'It wasn't.'

He lay awake, fretting and regretting, between interludes of un-consciousness, as the night passed. When he woke for the last time, roused by his alarm clock, he fleetingly forgot where he was or why. Then memory reasserted itself with unpitying force. He thought of Zineta and believed for a moment that his hands and arms were still covered in her blood. As he stood in the shower, he cried, uncontrollable sobs racking his chest, the pain from his ribs as nothing compared with the pain of recollection.

Vidor was waiting for Hammond in reception. He handed him a pair of CDs and a player to listen to them on. 'We transferred the tapes to disc,' he explained. No other comments were exchanged.

They found nothing to say to each other at all, in fact, until they had checked in for the flight and were sitting in the departure lounge, watching dawn break slowly over the runway.

'I spoke to Goran Perović last night,' Vidor reported, staring into the middle distance. 'He'll be arriving later today.'

'How did he take the news?'

'Like he'd been expecting it for a long time.'

'Did you tell him he has a nephew here in Luxembourg?'

'No. But he'll find out. From the Bartols, if they have any sense. It'll go better for them that way.'

'What about the press? If they learn Patrick is Gazi's son . . .'

'Let's hope they don't.'

'But they will, won't they? They always do. Somehow.'

'It's not our problem, Edward.'

'I wish I could believe that.'

Vidor sighed. 'So do I.'

A colleague of Vidor's was waiting for them at Lugano airport: a solemn, long-faced man who introduced himself to Hammond as Hans Furgler. His accent confirmed him as a German-speaker, quite possibly Swiss, though he did not say so, confining his remarks to the practical arrangements for their visit.

'I have booked us rooms at the Hotel Principessa. We can wait there for confirmation of the transfer,' he said as he drove them out of the airport. 'But we can go straight to the bank now. It will just have opened.'

'The transfer Hans is referring to is out of the Cayman Islands, not in, Edward,' Vidor explained. 'We're monitoring an account in Liechtenstein which we believe is the route Ingrid will use to pay the gang who are planning her father's escape. We want you to call her as soon as you've completed the transaction and tell her you've changed your mind and the money is on its way after all. Of course, the Caymans are six hours behind us, so it'll be mid-afternoon before she can access the funds, but we expect her to move whatever the initial payment amounts to as quickly as possible. We'll stay here, overnight if necessary, until it's clear there's been no glitch in the system. This has to be done right, you understand.'

'I understand.' It seemed, then, for reasons beyond Hammond's control, that he would probably not be back in England before Bill's deadline expired. It could not be helped. The tapes Vidor had supplied would exonerate him. 'Tell me, Stevan. When will I be able to go home?'

'Soon.' Vidor gave him a sympathetic half-smile. 'Then your life can revert to normal.'

But it would not, of course. Not for a long, long time. If ever. Hammond knew that. And so, he sensed, did Vidor.

Much of the snow that had greeted Hammond the week before was gone, though it still capped the peaks around Lugano. The sky was a clear blue, sunlight dancing and sparkling on the lake and corrugating the wooded slopes. It was easy to imagine, all too easy, that he would find Zineta waiting for him at the station if he went there. But she would not be, of course. She was not waiting for him anywhere in the real world.

The Banca Borzaghini was a small, discreet establishment, expensively appointed with dark wood, pink-veined marble and immaculately dressed staff. Vidor could be of no help to him in the stating of his business to a succession of ever more eminent functionaries. He waited in the foyer. Eventually, Hammond was shown into an office furnished in the style of a nineteenth-century gentleman's study, where he was received by a softly spoken and improbably handsome middle-aged man whose card identified him as Umberto Castelli.

'Marco called me last Friday and said you might come to see us, Dr Hammond.' Castelli's use of Piravani's first name was a surprise. The Borzaghini's services were evidently highly personalized. 'And he subsequently faxed authorization for you to act on his behalf. But I must be sure you are Dr Hammond, of course. Perhaps I may see your passport?'

Hammond handed it over. Castelli examined it with conspicuous care, then smiled.

'So, how may I help you?'

'I want to transfer the funds you're holding for him to . . . this account.' Hammond proffered the piece of paper Ingrid had given him during their fateful encounter at Heathrow.

'The Cayman Islands.' Castelli nodded. 'I see.' There came a second nod. 'All the funds?'

'Yes.'

Castelli consulted his computer screen. 'That is . . . in excess of twenty-three million francs. Around . . . fourteen million pounds.'

'The whole lot, please.'

'Very well, doctor. And when—'

'Straight away.'

'Straight away.' Castelli tapped fluently at the computer keyboard. 'Your signature on the appropriate transfer instruction' – the document began to feed out of the adjacent printer as he spoke – 'and it will be done.'

Hammond checked the balance and the number of the Cayman Islands account, then signed the form. Castelli compared the signature with the one on his passport and returned it, along with a copy of the instruction.

'You wish me to initialize the transfer, Dr Hammond?'

'Yes, please.'

'It will be instantaneous, but you appreciate it will not be possible for the Cayman Islands account holder to draw on the funds until the bank there opens and registers the deposit?'

'Of course.'

'And may I ask . . . if all is well with Marco? When I spoke to him, he sounded . . . stressed.'

Castelli seemed to regard his client as a friend. Hammond had not expected that. It made withholding the truth of Piravani's condition all the harder. 'You needn't worry about Marco.'

'I'm glad to hear it. Have you known him long?'

'Long enough.'

268

'He's never previously—'

'I'm a little pressed for time, Signor Castelli. Could we proceed with the transfer, please?'

'Certainly.' Castelli smiled tightly and looked at the computer screen. 'Twenty-three million seven hundred and twenty-nine thousand two hundred and twenty-one francs, net of our charges.' He tapped a button. 'Transferred.'

'Thank you.'

'Do you have a number where I can contact you, doctor? There'll be no problem but just in case . . . and for our records . . .'

Hammond gave Castelli the number.

'*Grazie.* And is there anything else I can do for you?'

'No. You've been most helpful. Thanks again.'

Hammond rose and Castelli ushered him to the door. 'Are you staying in Lugano, doctor? I could recommend—'

'We're at the Principessa.'

'Ah. Very nice. Very—'

'Goodbye, *signor*.' Hammond offered his hand in a conclusive gesture. And Castelli took it. Their business was at an end.

The Principessa was, as Castelli had said, very nice, in a quiet, efficient, Swiss version of niceness. Its rooms commanded a good view of the lake, though it was one block back from the front. Business appeared to be slack, but the staff were not disposed to advertise the fact, the receptionist contriving to imply that the provision of three adjacent rooms was a miracle of organizational ingenuity.

Checking in completed, Hammond made the call to Ingrid that he knew was as necessary as it would be humiliating. As before, the unknown woman in Madrid answered. But, this time, she gave him a separate number for Ingrid. It was a mobile that went straight to voicemail. Gritting his teeth, Hammond recorded a succinct and, for its recipient, a satisfying message.

'This is Edward Hammond. I've changed my mind. I've decided to do what you want. In fact, I've done it. As of less than an hour ago, the transfer took place. Check if you don't believe me. Twenty-three million plus loose change. It's all yours. Congratulations. I—'

'Ask her to phone back,' Vidor whispered.

'OK,' Hammond mimed. Then: 'I'd be grateful if you'd call me to confirm you've got this message, Ingrid. I need to know we're done. 'Bye for now.'

'Good,' said Vidor as he rang off. 'I think that'll get her attention.'

Strangely, however, it did not. First one hour, then another, then several more slowly passed without word from Ingrid. Hammond tried to put the time to good use by playing the CDs Vidor had given him. But listening to an impenetrable sequence of conversations in Serbian, awaiting the moment when his own name was mentioned, proved beyond him. Zineta had assured him the evidence he needed was there somewhere and he did not doubt it, but someone else would have to find it. He went for a walk along the lakefront as far as the park where he had met Piravani. He sat on a bench and gazed across the lake at the hummock of Monte San Salvatore. He wondered how he had reached this moment of self-reproachful misery in his life. And the worst of his wondering, the worst by far, was that he knew how. He knew exactly how.

Then his phone rang. He answered quickly, without checking who the caller was. He wanted this over. He wanted this to be in the past, not part of the present, still less the future. 'Ingrid?'

But no. It was not Ingrid. 'I'd have called you sooner if I hadn't been so angry,' said Bill. 'What are you playing at, Edward? You spin me that cock-and-bull story about tapes. Then you do a runner. I'm giving you a last chance to explain yourself.'

Hammond sighed. He was tempted to hang up. But Bill would only call back in an even fouler mood and he could not afford to turn the phone off. 'Zineta's dead,' he said quietly. 'Killed by one of Todorović's heavies. I should have saved her. But I couldn't. You think you're angry with me? Well, so am I. As for what I'm playing at, I'm clear about that at least. Todorović is going to join Gazi in

270

prison and I'm doing what I have to do to make sure they both stay there. The tapes exist. I have copies of the ones that prove I had nothing to do with Gazi's decision to have Kate killed. You can believe me or not, as you please. I'll be home within a few days and we can talk about it then. For God's sake – for Kate's sake – don't speak to Alice before then. I don't much care whether you speak to the police. It's up to you.' Then he rang off.

And Bill did not call back.

Nor, for that matter, did Ingrid.

Vidor was evidently also growing anxious. Hammond found him pacing up and down on the promenade with a cigarette on the go some way short of the Principessa.

'I was beginning to worry,' he admitted. 'Where have you been?'

'I needed some air. And, to save you asking, there's been no call.'

They went to a small bar-café near by, where they sipped their coffees in distracted silence, while the proprietress gossiped loudly with the only other customer.

'Shouldn't you let Furgler know where we are?' Hammond asked eventually. 'He might be worried too.'

'Hans worried? I doubt it. This is just another job to him.'

'Isn't that what it is to you?'

Vidor frowned. 'Of course not. I left Serbia eighteen years ago, but that doesn't make me any less of a Serb. I hate what Gazi and Todorović and the rest of their kind did to my country – what they did to my family. We have to make sure it never happens again.'

'What did they do to your family?'

'Oh . . .' Vidor looked away. 'Nothing they didn't do to lots of others. Like I told you, I got out, but my three brothers fought in Bosnia. One of them . . . didn't make it through.'

'I'm sorry to hear that.'

'He didn't die in action. He killed himself, after the war was over.'

Hammond winced. 'That's terrible.'

271

'There were lots of suicides, during and after the war. I guess . . . people couldn't see a future for themselves.'

'Can they see one now?'

'I hope so. I truly do.'

'What about the rest of your family? Are they . . . all right?'

'Not really.'

'Do you see much of them?'

'No.' Vidor shook his head. 'I don't.'

'Do they approve of the work you're doing?'

'They don't know what I'm doing. They think I don't care, you see. They think I've . . . forgotten.'

'Shouldn't you tell them you haven't?'

'Oh, I will. When the time's right.'

'When will that be?'

'As soon as this Gazi business is over.' Vidor's expression softened. 'Yes. That's when I'll tell them.'

'What do we do if Ingrid doesn't call me?' Hammond asked as they wandered back to the hotel.

'It doesn't really matter whether she calls you or not. She got your message. We'll know that for certain when a chunk of the money moves from the Cayman Islands to Liechtenstein. That's what we're really waiting for. It could be today. But it might not be until tomorrow. I'm sorry, Edward. Until it happens, we have to stay put, just in case you need to go back to the bank.'

'I hate this.'

'So do I. But it won't last long.' Vidor sighed. 'It'll just feel like it.'

THIRTY-ONE

Without asking Vidor whether he should or not, Hammond rang Ingrid several more times as the afternoon stretched uneventfully into the evening. She did not answer. Nor did she respond to the messages he left. And no news reached them of a large payment into the Liechtenstein account. All they could do was the last thing Hammond wanted to do: wait.

A text message reached him at some point from Miljanović. But there was little new in it, at least about Piravani. '*No major change. Prognosis hopeful.*' Then came: '*Heard news re Todo!*' Hammond acknowledged the message, then texted Alice. '*Will b home soon. Need to c u. Can u come down to London this w/end?*' He had decided in his own mind that he would be home by then whatever happened. And sooner or later he was going to have to face Alice with the truth, so it had better be sooner. But his daughter was oblivious to the urgency of his plea. '*No go, dad. One after?*' He summoned a weak '*OK*' in reply. The weekend after next felt to him at that moment like the middle of the next decade.

A late supper with Vidor and Furgler in the largely empty hotel restaurant did nothing to lift his spirits. 'Our best guess,' Vidor reported, 'is that they'll move the money tomorrow morning.' He sounded confident on the point. But his confidence was far from contagious.

Later, after Furgler had taken himself off to bed, Hammond and Vidor gravitated to the bar.

'I am so sorry about Zineta,' Vidor said over their second whisky, after the first had been downed in silence. 'You know that, don't you, Edward?'

'You're sorry. I'm sorry. Everyone's sorry.' Hammond stared at his whisky. 'That doesn't bring her back to life, does it?'

'Nothing can do that.'

'Then what use is sorrow?'

'I guess it depends what you do with it.'

'Well, I've got plenty. So, if you think of something, let me know.'

Vidor nodded solemnly, as if giving the problem his serious attention. 'I will.'

The whisky knocked Hammond out that night more effectively than he would have expected. He woke bemusingly late, roused by the ringing of his phone, and was still three-quarters asleep when he answered. But the voice at the other end was like a douche of cold water. He was instantly alert.

'Good morning, Dr Hammond.'

'Ingrid?'

'I got your message.'

'What, er . . . took you so long?' He rubbed his eyes and squinted at his alarm clock, which he had not bothered to set, thinking he would wake early enough without it. To his surprise, it was nearly nine o'clock.

'I thought we ought to meet to discuss the situation, doctor. So, I had to . . . make travel arrangements.'

'Meet? What do you mean?'

'I am here. In Lugano.'

'But I never—'

'Be on the nine forty-five funicular to Monte Brè. We'll talk there.' And with that she rang off.

*

274

He had not told Ingrid where he was. And by her own admission she had never known where Piravani had banked her father's money. So, how had she discovered he was in Lugano? The question swirled confusingly in his mind as he grabbed the hotel phone and dialled Vidor's room number. A second later, he heard it ringing through the wall between them. But Vidor did not pick up.

Hammond threw on some clothes and rushed into the corridor. He hammered on Vidor's door and shouted his name. There was no response. Then he tried Furgler's, with the same result.

By now, he had attracted the frowning attention of a strait-laced businessman making his way to the lift, whose frowns must have deepened when Hammond overtook him and hurried down the stairs. It was only two flights to reception, but he carried on down to the basement restaurant, where breakfast was served. There was no sign there of them, so he doubled back to reception.

'My friends, er . . . Mr Vidor and Mr Furgler,' he panted to the man on duty. 'Have you, er . . . seen them?'

'They went out, I think.' He squinted at the key-rack. '*Si.* Yes. A little while ago.'

'Together?'

'Yes. Together.'

'Did they say when they would be back?'

'Ah . . . no.'

'Did they leave a message for me?'

Another squint at the key-rack. 'No. No message.'

There was nothing else for it, then. He would have to go. And he would have to go alone. 'How do I get to the Monte Brè funicular?'

'It runs from Via Pico, at the eastern end of town. About a ten-minute ride by taxi. You want me to call one?'

'Yes.' Hammond nodded decisively. 'Right away.'

He made it in the end with time to spare. The morning was cold but clear and the two or three other passengers waiting aboard the funicular were dressed for hiking. Ingrid Hurtado-Gazi was not

275

among them. Somehow this did not surprise Hammond. He expected her to arrive at the last moment.

But she did not. At 9.45 precisely, the train clanked into motion. Hammond watched the lakeside buildings slowly recede, frustration and bafflement competing for mastery of his thoughts. What was Ingrid playing at?

An answer began to emerge at the first stop, when the passengers all disembarked and crossed the road to join another more steeply pitched funicular for the continuation of their journey to Monte Brè, whose wooded summit loomed above them.

The schedule allowed an excessive amount of time for the transit to be completed. Hammond sat alone in one of the compartments of the second train as the minutes ticked slowly by. They were due to proceed at 10.05. At 10.02 a dark blue BMW convertible pulled up outside the station. And Ingrid Hurtado-Gazi got out.

She was dressed in shades of black that varied from inky to night, an extravagantly flared, wide-collared fur coat and film-star dark glasses ensuring that no one could mistake her for a hiker. She bought a ticket and walked quickly up the stepped platform just as the beeped warning of the train's imminent departure began to sound. The door closed behind her as she slipped into Hammond's compartment and the train jerked into motion. She sat down opposite him.

Immediately, he caught a gust of her perfume. Only then did he remember its overripe, gardenia scent. Her leather trousers creaked as she crossed her legs and smiled at him with no more than a hint of triumph. 'Good morning, Dr Hammond,' she said, in the sweetest of tones.

'How did you find me?' he demanded at once.

'The Banca Borzaghini, Lugano, was the source of the transferred funds.'

'But you couldn't know I'd still be here today.'

'You were not likely to leave until you heard from me.'

That was true, but as an explanation it seemed to Hammond not quite good enough. And it begged an obvious question. 'Why did you want to meet me, anyway?'

'To express my gratitude, doctor. You have done what I asked. Late, it is true. But late is better than never.'

'No thanks are necessary, Ingrid. I simply . . . did what I had to do.'

'But only a few days ago you made it very clear you weren't willing to do it.'

'I changed my mind. I . . . faced up to the reality of the situation.'

'How very sensible of you. I must—' She broke off as her phone began ringing, muffled by her coat. 'Excuse me. I'm expecting an important call.' She took the phone out and answered it. '*Diga? . . . Si, soy yo . . . Si, entiendo . . . Gracias . . . Adiós.*' Important or not, the call was certainly brief. Her smile broadened as she tucked the phone back into her coat pocket. 'It is a good day, Dr Hammond.'

What was she talking about, he wondered – the weather? 'You got what you wanted, Ingrid. OK? If you think I need reassurance that your father won't mention me at his trial, forget it. I'm sure he'll stick to our deal. It wouldn't be in his interests – *your* interests – not to.'

'His trial? You are not worried about that, doctor. I feel sure. Neither am I.'

'Shouldn't you be? He's facing a life term.'

Bizarrely, Ingrid laughed. She craned her neck to admire the view, slowly expanding as the train climbed to take in the whole of Lugano, spread out greyly around the misty blue curve of the lake below them. Sunlight flashed on her jewelled necklace. Her eyes danced, as if she was suffused with joy. 'Switzerland is a wonderful country, don't you think? So clean. So efficient. So . . . purposeful.'

The air was cooling rapidly as they ascended. But something else was sending a chill through Hammond's blood. He knew the game he was playing. But Ingrid, it seemed, was playing one all of her own. 'I think I'll get off at the next stop and wait there for a train down,' he said. 'We have nothing more to—'

'You're going to the top, doctor,' she interrupted, turning her gaze on to him. 'We both are.'

'Now I've paid you the money, Ingrid, you don't get to tell me what to do any more.'

At that moment, the train pulled up at a small platform. The down train coasted in on a passing loop beside them. If he hurried, he could probably catch it before it left. But as he made to rise, Ingrid grasped his forearm and said, 'My father is free, doctor. That call was confirmation. The plan worked perfectly. He has escaped.'

'What?' He could not believe what she had said. And yet he did not doubt the accuracy of her words. Suddenly, the world shifted around him.

'He is free.'

'That's . . . absurd. He can't . . .' The train started moving again. Doubts and questions suddenly locked together in his mind. The money. The escape plan. The trap he had helped to bait. But who had it been baited *for*?

'A prison transport van travelling from Scheveningen to ICTY was hijacked one hour ago, doctor. The guards were disabled with CS gas and their six prisoners were released. Five of them will be recaptured later, since they have no means of leaving the area. The search for them will occupy a great deal of police time and manpower, however. That will be to my father's advantage. I have hired the best people – the very best – to get him out of The Hague. A new life – a new identity – is waiting for him a long way from there. This time he will not be found. This time he will have the peace and security he deserves.'

'But . . .'

'The authorities knew nothing of the plot, doctor. You're not part of an operation designed to lure the people organizing the escape into the open. You were part of the escape plan itself. Thanks to Piravani authorizing you to draw on the Borzaghini account, I have been able to pay those people what they demanded. It was a lot – many millions of francs. But it was worth it. I love my father. I cannot let him die in prison. And now . . . he will not.'

Words failed Hammond. He stared at Ingrid and saw his gullibility revealed to him in her mocking smile. Vidor had been working for Gazi all along. And so, in effect, had he.

'There is more I have to tell you, doctor. Listen carefully. It is important you understand. I *am* grateful to you. So is my father. We will trouble you no more. Leave us alone and we will leave you alone. But, naturally, we require some guarantee that you will not supply the authorities with information about how the escape was funded or which UN employees were involved in the plot. That would be . . . inconvenient. So, you should be aware that the recordings Vidor gave you do not contain any reference to your late wife. Nor do the originals. They have been suitably edited. Without that it will be hard for you to disprove any allegations your brother-in-law makes against you. Worse, if your role in the transfer of my father's money out of Switzerland becomes known, it will seem to substantiate those allegations. As will the part you played in engineering the arrest of Branko Todorović, who betrayed my father's trust and deserves to rot in prison. It will look as if you helped my father because the murder of your wife left you in his debt. No one will believe you were tricked into doing it, because no one will believe you could have been so stupid.'

Still Hammond was unable to speak. What was there for him to say, after all, when stupid was exactly what he had been?

'You see, doctor? Your best chance of leading a peaceful and comfortable life is to say nothing to anyone about your dealings with us. Then there will be no case for you to answer. Please give the authorities as much to use against Todorović as you like, though. Tell them you met Zineta when you went to The Hague to watch my father's trial and she persuaded you to help her obtain the tapes in order to punish Todorović for taking her son away from her. She cannot contradict you, can she? And Piravani—'

It was Ingrid's use of Zineta's name – her casual contempt for the woman who had died in Hammond's arms – that finally broke him. He lunged across the compartment, intent in that moment on closing his hands round her throat and tightening them until she was choking for breath and begging for mercy. What he would do then he could not have said. Silencing her was as far as his thoughts would carry him.

And even that was too far. Ingrid was ready for him. He never actually saw her take the spray out of her pocket. Perhaps it had been nestling in her palm all along. A spurt of Mace hit his eyes like a flame. He cried out and bowed his head, then fell back against the bench behind him.

'We're nearly at the top,' said Ingrid, her voice close to his ear, as if she was determined he should hear her through the pain that blinded him. 'I'll be leaving you there. You should find some water if you can, to rinse your eyes. The effects last about half an hour. So, we won't be seeing each other again.'

The train slowed as it approached the summit station. Hammond tried to open his eyes, but they filled with tears and the pain was too much to bear. He closed them again and covered them with his hands. He could neither speak nor think, let alone see.

'Goodbye, doctor,' said Ingrid. 'And thank you again. For everything.'

THIRTY-TWO

Hammond only reached the toilet at the summit station thanks to the reluctant assistance of some other passengers he blundered into as he staggered off the train. He filled a basin with water and bathed his eyes until he could at least bear to open them again. Even then, the visible world was a teary blur, the sunlight outside the station painfully dazzling.

As he soon realized, however, the pain was a merciful distraction from the horror he felt at how he had been manipulated and to what end. Gazi was free. And he had helped to free him. Ingrid had got from him exactly what she had wanted.

She was long gone, of course, whisked away by car, he assumed. He could see a road winding down the hillside just below the station. Vidor and Furgler had probably been waiting for her. Certainly he did not doubt that they had booked out of the Principessa by now, leaving no trail for him to follow. They had finished with him. As Ingrid had said: '*We will trouble you no more.*'

The next train down to Lugano was due to leave in ten minutes. Quite why Hammond did not wait at the station to catch it he could not have explained, even to himself. He walked away along the path through the sparse woodland covering Monte Brè, with no direction or destination in mind. Snow-capped mountains climbed away ahead of him, the wilderness they enveloped offering a kind of refuge, chill and glaring as it was, from the madness and rottenness of humanity.

But such a refuge was illusory, as the ringing of his phone reminded him. His first thought was not to answer, but when he saw who was calling he knew he had to.

'Hello, Svetozar.'

'Do you know if it's true, Edward?' Miljanović's words came in a frantic jumble. 'We hear Gazi has escaped. Armed men stopped the van taking him to the court in The Hague this morning. There was a shoot-out. Two guards were killed.' Ingrid had said nothing about guards being killed, of course. They were details she had not concerned herself with. 'Several prisoners got away, including Gazi. A few have been recaptured. But not Gazi. Are these reports accurate, Edward?'

Hammond could not speak, could not frame a reply. It all felt so distant from him. And yet he knew it was an event he was only too close to, unalterable and undeniable, a black sun squatting in the sky above his head.

'Edward?'

'I'm sure the reports are accurate, Svetozar.'

'But . . . this is terrible.'

'Yes. Terrible is what it is.'

'You don't sound very surprised. Did you . . . know this was going to happen?'

'I should have done.'

'What do you mean?'

'I mean it's my fault, Svetozar.'

'*Your* fault?'

'Yes.'

'How?'

'I'll explain it to you one day. One day soon. As soon as I can. As soon as . . .'

'As soon as what?'

'I'm sorry, Svetozar. I can't speak any more.' Hammond cut the call, switched the phone off and put it back in his pocket. He took a deep breath of the chill air and felt his slowly healing rib twinge. He looked up into the cloudless dome of blue above him. And tears filled his eyes.

For the next few hours Hammond followed the wooded track that led up into the hills above Brè village. The climb was slow and seemingly endless, but he was barely aware of his surroundings, locked as he was in a sterile debate with himself. What was he to do, when so clearly he could do nothing? Gazi was free and he had aided and abetted his escape. Gazi had needed his help no less desperately than when his liver was failing. And he had helped him, unwittingly and unwillingly this time it was true, but no less crucially.

He came to a shelf of land, high above Lake Lugano, where the trees thinned and revealed the cold, shimmering world about him. He sat on a bank and stared down at the white line of a boat's wake, at the dark specks of lorries moving on the lakeside highway, at a gleam of gold that was a weathervane on a village church. A few yards to his left, the ground fell away sheerly in a cascade of cliff and scree. Self-destruction was close at hand, if he wanted it. He gazed into the blue void and was tempted, for the first time in his life, by the ease and immediacy of such an act: a solution of sorts, a resolution at all events.

Gaze was all, in the end, that he did. At some point, he started back down the track, reaching Brè, exhausted by hunger and despair, as the late afternoon began to suck the warmth out of the sun. He sat in the central square, waiting for a bus into Lugano, tasting the chill clarity of the air and wishing he could somehow dissolve into it. Shame was what he felt most keenly: shame that he had done so much harm and so little good. All his arrogance was gone now, gone where his reputation, he was sure, would soon follow. This was the end for him. Or else it was the beginning of a new Edward Hammond. There were no other choices.

*

The bus came. Villagers returning from Lugano clambered down and ambled off to their homes. There were few takers for the journey back. But Hammond was one of them. So was a young woman who, disconcertingly, looked quite like Alice, uncannily so from behind. Hammond watched her texting happily through the journey down into the city and thought of how he would set about explaining to his daughter everything that had happened, not just in the past two weeks, but at the time of her mother's death thirteen years before. The dread of her reaction was a knot in his stomach. And the worst part of his dread was the fear that he would fail to tell her the whole truth. It was the choice Ingrid had left him with. It was how, finally, she had rewarded him for his efforts on her father's behalf.

The receptionist at the Principessa considerately refrained from commenting on Hammond's dishevelled appearance. She informed him that his friends – Signores Furgler and Vidor – had booked out earlier in the day. 'They said you planned to leave tomorrow, sir. Is that correct?' He answered with the vaguest of affirmatives, having, of course, no real plans at all. He went up to his room and tuned the television to CNN. He did not have to wait long for a report on the sensational events that morning in The Hague.

A reporter was in place near the scene of Gazi's daring escape. Behind her, on the other side of a road, was a wooded park, of the kind Hammond recalled travelling through on the tram with Zineta after his visit to ICTY – clumps of trees between curving footpaths and cycleways. But there were no walkers or cyclists in sight this afternoon. A line of police tape had been strung round the visible portion of the park and armed officers were in place to see it was not breached. The line enclosed half the road as well. Various police vehicles were parked inside it, with blue-clad figures scurrying to and fro between them.

'The bringing to justice by a UN court of one of the most notorious perpetrators of ethnic cleansing in the former Yugoslavia went badly awry here in The Hague this morning,' the blonde-haired reporter breathlessly announced. 'An armoured van carrying six defendants from nearby Scheveningen Prison to the International Court building about a kilometre from here was intercepted and stopped by an armed gang who overpowered the guards using CS gas, killed two of them in an exchange of fire and set the prisoners free. The van is still where it came to a halt, a little way down the street behind me.' The camera panned round to focus on the UN-marked van standing at the side of the road about fifty yards away. Its rear doors were open and white-boilersuited figures could be glimpsed inside. 'Five of the prisoners, named by the authorities as Milorad Ivković, Sretko Lubarda, Dušan Melka, Srdjan Nešković and Ninoslav Rajković, fled on foot, with little apparent assistance from the gang. Lubarda and Nešković later gave themselves up and Melka and Rajković were picked up by the police at the central train station just a few hours ago, leaving Ivković, a former commander of Croatian forces in Bosnia, still on the run, along with the sixth prisoner, Dragan Gazi, undoubtedly the most famous, or infamous, of the lot. His escape appears to have been the gang's main objective. Witnesses say he was driven away in a dark SUV-type automobile, although there are also reports he may have boarded a helicopter that touched down briefly next to the van before flying away towards the coast. That's only about two miles from here and there's all kind of speculation about whether he might have transferred to a speedboat or larger craft offshore. Either way, Dragan Gazi is currently a free man. The former leader of the Serb paramilitaries known as the Wolves, who terrorized Bosnia and later Kosovo in the 1990s, was arrested less than a year ago after eight years in hiding. His capture then was hailed as a triumph for the judicial process. That triumph turned sour today on this normally quiet street in this normally quiet Dutch city.'

'So, a major embarrassment for the International Court, Janice,' the anchorman cut in.

'Absolutely, Gavin. Worse than an embarrassment – a disaster, unless Gazi is swiftly recaptured.'

'And what are the chances of that?'

'Hard to say at this stage, Gavin. The gang that carried this out were certainly ruthlessly efficient. Witnesses speak of a short but ferocious fire fight with the guards escorting the van. As we know, two of those guards were killed and one other, we're hearing, was seriously wounded. But there don't appear to have been any casualties on the gang's side, maybe because the guards were partly disabled by the CS gas fired into their cab. Their assailants were obviously well-prepared *and* well-equipped. It was clearly a meticulously planned operation. So, I guess we can assume they have an equally meticulous plan for keeping Gazi out of the UN's clutches now they've freed him. That won't be easy, though. The Dutch and UN authorities will spare no effort in the search for him. We can expect—'

Hammond pressed the off button on the remote and the television blanked out, leaving him with silence and his distorted reflection in the screen. A meticulous plan? Yes, it was certainly that. He knew, because he had been part of it. He pointed an accusing finger at his reflected self and murmured, 'What next, doctor? What treatment would you suggest now?'

He would go back to The Hague. It came to him as a single clear thought in a fog of anguish. He would go to ICTY and tell them everything. Ingrid had painted a grim picture of what would happen to him if he did that, but what would happen to him if he did not seemed certain to his mind to be grimmer still.

There would probably be an early-morning flight from Lugano to Amsterdam, but passing another night at the Principessa was a prospect his raw nerves could not bear. He persuaded the receptionist to check if there was an overnight train he could catch. And there was. He checked out and headed straight for the station.

Amsterdam Centraal station, early on a cold, dank Friday morning. The underpass was a swarm of commuters, students and laden travellers. Hammond bought a paper at the news-stand and stared at the front-page headline. *Gazi ontsnapt*, blared *De Telegraaf*. And Hammond had little doubt what *ontsnapt* meant. There was a photograph of Gazi in military fatigues, dating from his years of terror in Bosnia, and another of him, looking older but no less wily, in his ICTY mugshot. There was a photograph of the bullet-scarred prison van as well, along with pictures of the two guards who had died and a map of The Hague, with a helicopter super-imposed over the North Sea shoreline.

Hammond went up to the platform where the next train to The Hague would leave from and sat down on a bench beside a man reading another paper with Gazi's face on the front page, under the headline *De Wolf is vrij*. Hammond sighed and looked away.

He had had ample time to think during his largely sleepless journey from Lugano. Horror at the situation he found himself in had given way eventually to several bleak but unarguable pieces of logic. Ingrid had said telling the authorities everything he knew would be 'inconvenient', but if inconveniencing her was all he could do, so be it. The effect of such revelations on Alice, not to mention the rest of his family and friends, hinged on the extent of their trust in him. Perhaps it was high time he found out what that was. Doing so involved landing Piravani in a lot of trouble, but that could not be helped and Hammond suspected Marco would actually have urged him on if he could. Then there was Vidor, who might be intending to stay in his UN post, at least for a while, in order to avoid attracting suspicion. That plan was only viable if Hammond kept his mouth shut, of course. Vidor was relatively small fry in the conspiracy to free Gazi, but he might be a source of valuable leads. And bringing him down would give Hammond some satisfaction to set against the exposure of his folly to official scrutiny.

The result of that scrutiny was the big imponderable, by which he knew he should be more worried than he was. Would the authorities believe him? Or would they treat him as a willing and well-rewarded hireling of Gazi's? If the latter, then he was in the process of digging his own grave.

The train rumbled into the station, drowning the announcer's voice just as she reached Den Haag Hollands-Spoor in her recital of where it would stop. Hammond stood up, leaving his newspaper on the bench, and moved towards the slowing carriages.

From Hollands-Spoor station he could have taken a taxi or a tram to ICTY. Instead he decided to walk and, realizing how close he was to Zineta's apartment, found himself choosing, without properly understanding why, a route that passed it.

There was nothing to see, of course, except her name on the card beside her bell. *PEROVIĆ.* Just that, in neatly inscribed capitals. He retreated to the edge of the pavement and looked up at the attic windows. They were closed and uncurtained, reflecting a grey slab of flat Dutch sky. For some reason, he thought of Zineta's rubber plant, and wondered if anyone would water it.

The media were out in force at ICTY, the concourse in front of the building jammed with vans sprouting aerials and spewing tangled snakes of cable, engineers scurrying around while reporters and cameramen gossiped and smiled and slurped cardboard-cupped coffee. They generally looked more gratified than appalled by Gazi's escape.

As he threaded a path between them, Hammond heard one man shout into his mobile: 'They've definitely got Ivković. He made it as far as Rotterdam, apparently. But still no sign of the big fish. Looks like he slipped through the net.'

The security staff were grimmer-faced than Hammond recalled. The man behind the counter announced the courts were closed in a fractious tone that suggested the massed media folk and sundry sensation-seekers had already tried his patience.

'I don't want to sit in on any of the trials,' Hammond explained. 'I—'

'We are closed to the public today, sir.'

'You don't understand. I—'

'We expect normal business to resume next week.'

'I'm here about Dragan Gazi.'

'Obviously his trial will not resume this week.'

'I have information about his escape.'

'You can telephone the communications service if you wish, sir. Their number is—'

'*I have important information.*' Hammond's raised voice succeeded in silencing the man and commanding his attention for the first time. 'Believe me, your bosses will want to hear it.'

THIRTY-THREE

They believed him in the end. But the end was a long time coming. From his arrival at ICTY that Friday morning in late February to his release from custody without charge – though hardly, in the more traditional summations of guilt and innocence, without a stain on his character – was a period of nearly five months.

During those months Hammond was lodged, by the deepest of ironies, in the very same detention unit at Scheveningen Prison as Gazi had been. Giving himself up to the UN rather than the Dutch police had been a smart move, according to his lawyer, though of course it had in no sense been a calculated one on his part. The lawyer was an old schoolfriend, David Ashton, who would not have been equipped to represent him in the Dutch legal system. The cosmopolitan English-speaking world of ICTY was a different matter, however, and though, theoretically, the Dutch authorities might choose to prosecute him on their own account, Ashton thought it highly unlikely. 'My understanding is that they've agreed informally to cut through the jurisdictional issues by letting the OTP decide whether you're basically a witness or a suspect. So, *if* the OTP signs off on your case, you'll be home and dry, old man.'

The OTP was the Office of the Prosecutor for the International Tribunal. After Hammond had made a full statement of his involvement in the Gazi affair, and been questioned about it, and re-questioned, and then re-questioned again, he was consigned to

Scheveningen to await their conclusions. Ashton travelled from London once a week or so to brief him on progress – or the lack of it.

It was from Ashton that he learnt of the significant stages of the investigation. Vidor had never returned to his post at ICTY. It seemed he might have been a better judge of Hammond's likely response to the position Ingrid had put him in than Ingrid herself. One of Hammond's principal objectives was therefore vitiated from the start. Vidor had vanished as effectively as Gazi, leaving no clue to his whereabouts. Ingrid shuttled between Buenos Aires and Madrid, issuing haughty denials of all Hammond's claims and deploying an army of lawyers to fight her corner. It soon became apparent that evidence of her involvement in the escape amounted to little more than Hammond's word against hers. The money trail from Lugano to Liechtenstein via Grand Cayman petered out in a maze of anonymous accounts. That Hammond had authorized the transfer of Gazi's funds was clear. But establishing precisely where and with whom they had ended up was, according to Ashton, like trying to untangle spaghetti. 'And by the time they've finished, old man, it'll be stony cold.'

Investigators were dispatched to Belgrade to question Piravani as soon as he regained consciousness. He was reported to be recovering well and it was not long before a message from him reached Hammond via Ashton. 'Tell the doctor it was my choice to move against Todorović and to give him access to the Gazi account. I don't blame him for any of the consequences and I intend to do everything I can to help the UN track down Gazi. And thank him for getting me such good treatment here, would you? He probably saved my life.' What Piravani failed to mention was that he intended to negotiate immunity from prosecution by ICEFA – for helping Gazi plunder Serbian state funds – as the price of his cooperation. News that he had gone back to Italy to continue his convalescence confirmed he had been successful in this. His next message to Hammond – 'Wish the doctor luck' – had a distinctly valedictory quality to it.

Piravani's hopes of seeing Todorović answer for his crimes at The Hague were in the end frustrated by the Luxembourg authorities, who preferred prosecuting him and his surviving underlings for the murder of Marcel Delmotte. The magistrate in charge of the case travelled to The Hague twice to examine Hammond and assured him Todorović would not be treated leniently. 'He will spend many years in prison, *monsieur*. I can assure you of that.'

The tapes Hammond and Piravani had gone to such lengths to procure were thus rendered irrelevant, of value to ICTY only if and when Gazi was recaptured. The chances of that happening seemed to dwindle by the day. Evidently, Ingrid really had hired the best. Her father had disappeared without a trace. Reported sightings cropped up for a while, but they all proved false and as the case slipped out of the headlines they steadily diminished, then stopped altogether. Ashton suspected this came as a relief to ICTY. It meant their embarrassment over the affair faded from public attention. Security for prisoner transport was tightened and a dedicated band of investigators sustained a worldwide search for Gazi. But their search received little or no publicity. And they probably preferred it that way.

The consensus of opinion at the Scheveningen detention unit was that Gazi had fled to South America. Paraguay was commonly suggested as a bolthole, though for no particular reason other than its reputation as a safe haven for Nazi fugitives in times gone by. Hammond was regarded by the other inmates as some kind of hapless dupe suckered into assisting Gazi to escape, which was, he had to concede, an accurate enough judgement. To his surprise, no one showed him the least hostility. This was, he came to realize, a reflection of how Serbs, Croats and Bosnians who had once been at war with one another, and were accused in many cases of extreme acts of barbarism, contrived to coexist peacefully under one roof in the Netherlands. They were all in the same boat. And rocking it made no sense.

Physically, conditions at the unit were as comfortable as anyone could reasonably expect, if not more so: a cell to oneself, with a shower, toilet, writing desk, computer, radio and TV; communal games rooms, library, kitchen and gymnasium; a $25 telephone card per month and unlimited visiting rights. *Het Oranje Hotel*, it had been dubbed by local residents, and Hammond could certainly recall staying in worse hotels in his youth. But he had been able to book out of those, of course. And there had been no bars at the windows.

Ashton reckoned he could successfully challenge ICTY's right to detain Hammond, on the grounds that it exceeded their remit to investigate war crimes in the former Yugoslavia. But he feared the Dutch authorities would then immediately arrest Hammond to stop him leaving the country before ICTY had concluded their investigation of his case. 'There's a real prison right next door, old man. Trust me. You don't want to go there.'

So Hammond remained where he was, a semi-voluntary detainee, secretly grateful for a place to hide from the world, surrounded by people who had far more to be ashamed of than he had. He learnt to cook such Balkan delicacies as Black George's schnitzel and to speak rudimentary Serbo-Croat. He played chess and gave English lessons to those who asked for them. He also became many inmates' first port of call for medical advice, thereby earning the gratitude of the unit's doctor for reducing his work-load. He read voraciously and kept fit as best he could. He attuned himself to the unit's rhythm of life. He adapted. He adjusted. He settled in.

His gravest concern throughout was how his relatives, friends and colleagues in general – and Alice in particular – would feel about him in the wake of what was by any analysis a spectacular fall from grace. He was glad neither of his parents had lived to see the day St George's Hospital suspended from duty the doctor assorted tabloid newspapers portrayed as either foolish or corrupt or both. There were hints in the press, fuelled by belligerent quotes from Alan Kendall, that he might be something even worse – a man who had traded his surgical skills for his wife's murder.

Alice visited him three times during his detention. The first of those visits was by some way the most harrowing for both of them. She was frightened and confused. She did not believe he had asked Gazi to arrange Kate's murder, but she did not quite disbelieve it either. He told her what Zineta had said about the way Gazi's mind worked and explained how deeply he regretted taking the job in Belgrade that had cost Kate her life. He explained how deeply he regretted many things. But, when she left, he had no idea whether she would ever trust him again.

Her second and third visits demonstrated, painfully and tentatively, that she would. She had talked the situation through with her new boyfriend, Jake, a young man who sounded like a heaven-sent embodiment of good sense. 'He asked me whether I seriously thought you'd have come forward now, when you didn't need to, if you really had done such a horrible thing. I realized you wouldn't have, of course. And I think I realized I'd known that all along. I was just . . . so angry with you, Dad. I still am. But you know what? I'm a little less angry every day.'

The same, alas, could not be said of her uncle. Bill Dowler had reluctantly admitted to Alice that Hammond was almost certainly telling the truth. That did not mean he absolved him of responsibility for Kate's death, however. 'Your mother would still be alive if he hadn't gone chasing a fat fee in Serbia.' There was no denying that. Bill was right. So were the two Scotland Yard detectives who came to interview Hammond as part of their review of the evidence in the case. 'You haven't come out of this too well, have you, doctor?' No. He had not.

But at least he was alive, unlike Zineta, whose brother Goran came to see him and broke down in tears while describing the grief-stricken condition of his elderly father. 'He thought she had made it through the bad times. He thought she would be there to hold his hand when he died. Now . . . he waits for death without her.' An apology was all Hammond had to offer by way of consolation. 'I'm so sorry I couldn't save her, Goran – sorrier than I can say.' And that was absolutely true.

Zineta was survived, of course, by her son. But Patrick Bartol was also Dragan Gazi's son, making Gazi's escape a cause of nagging anxiety in the Bartol household, as Mary Bartol admitted when she paid Hammond a visit. 'Will he come for our boy one day, do you think? Patrick has had so much to cope with these past few months. He watched Zineta die. And now he knows she was his mother, not me. That would be bad enough. That we could . . . manage, I think. But a monster for a father – a monster who is out there somewhere, hiding, waiting, watching, planning – is too much to bear.' Yet bear it they had to, as she was well aware. 'I wondered . . . if you could come to Luxembourg when all this is settled, and . . . speak to Patrick . . . about Zineta . . . and Gazi . . . and . . .'

'I'll come,' Hammond told her. 'I'll do whatever I can.'

'Thank you,' she said. And he realized with a shock that those were the first real thanks he had received from anyone for a very long time.

Some degree of grudging official gratitude for his candour did exist, according to Ashton, and was bound to tell in his favour eventually. A crucial step forward came when his account of what had happened after he and Vidor left Luxembourg was corroborated in an unexpected fashion. A man suspected by the German police of involvement in organized crime around the world was found dead at his apartment in Frankfurt. Bernhard Mittag had been tortured, possibly for the purposes of interrogation, then garrotted. Among his possessions were discovered several false passports, one of them in the name of Hans Furgler. Who had killed Mittag and what information they had extracted from him before he died were matters the German police could shed little light on. But the Hotel Principessa in Lugano held a photocopy of the Furgler passport and there was no doubt Mittag was the same man, raising hopes at ICTY that among his known associates might be found other members of the gang behind Gazi's escape. 'Don't hold your breath, old man,' was Ashton's advice to Hammond. 'But this could be just what's needed to convince the OTP you're actually one of the good guys.'

Ashton was certainly right about the pace of OTP

decision-making. Spring gave way to summer and the only hard evidence of the passage of time was the blossoming of the trees flanking Pompstationsweg, the road that ran past the front of the prison. Not that any of Hammond's fellow inmates seemed seriously to doubt that he would, sooner or later, be on his way.

'You do not belong here, Edward,' said Milorad Ivković after one of their regular chess games, in which Hammond had recorded a rare victory. 'The Prosecutor will admit that in the end.' Ivković had been with Gazi in the armoured van on the day of the escape and had stayed on the run longer than any of the others, although that had still amounted to little more than twenty-four hours. He stood accused of being responsible for multiple murders, rapes, deportations, acts of inhumanity and the wanton destruction and plunder of property. But of that they never spoke. He was a mild-mannered man, with the philosophical air of a retired professor. 'So,' he continued, 'what will you do when you rejoin the outside world?'

'I don't know,' Hammond replied evasively, having in reality given a lot of thought to the matter.

'Well, something will turn up for you, I am sure. At least you will not be a fugitive. I think sometimes I do not envy Dragan. He is free. But he must always fear recapture. Every day. Every hour. And what is freedom worth if you must be looking always over your shoulder?'

What Ivković was fundamentally saying, Hammond decided later, was that he could enjoy the peace of mind that came from knowing when and how he was to answer for what he had done, whereas Gazi, wherever he was hiding, lived with insecurity and anxiety as his constant companions. It was a comforting thought, though not comforting enough to reconcile Hammond to Gazi's evasion of justice. However circumscribed his liberty was, it *was* liberty. And he had no right to it.

Hammond's own liberty was finally restored to him by a low-key exchange of e-mails between Ashton and the OTP. '*It has been concluded that Dr Edward Hammond has made full disclosure of his dealings with Dragan Gazi and that there is no basis for any charges of collusion with Dragan Gazi to be brought against him.*' His days at Scheveningen were over.

He made his farewells and walked out into his future.

THIRTY-FOUR

The last e-mail Hammond sent on his detention-unit computer before leaving Scheveningen was to the chief executive of St George's, resigning from his consultancy. He suspected his resignation would be welcomed by the hospital hierarchy after his lengthy suspension. For him, it was the burning of a last bridge connecting him to his old life, which he could not return to for the simple reason that he was no longer the man who had led that life.

He was not returning to England either. Not yet, at any rate. It was mid-July. Alice and Jake were in Turkey. There was no one waiting for him at home. He had accepted Miljanović's invitation to work at the Voćnjak Clinic on a six-month contract, to begin whenever he was free to start. It was the only job he had been offered, but that was not why he had accepted. There was work to be done in Serbia – genuinely valuable work that he was genuinely qualified for. It would be something to throw himself into. And it would be partial repayment of a debt he felt he owed the many Serbs who had suffered because he had prevented Dragan Gazi dying in 1996.

He had made it clear to Miljanović, however, that he could not start straight away. 'Of course not,' Miljanović had responded. 'You will need a holiday first. On a beach, maybe.' But Hammond was not going on holiday. He was heading for Luxembourg.

*

He stayed for only a few days, spending one of them with Mary and Patrick Bartol. The family had moved into a rented townhouse in Luxembourg City, while they tried to find a buyer for the Forêt Pré house. The memories of bloodshed and death were too raw for them to have remained there and Patrick had had fewer nightmares since their departure. But he was beset nonetheless by the fear, which he was disarmingly willing to articulate, that he might have inherited his biological father's tendency 'to kill people', as he put it with childish bluntness. The fact that Hammond was a doctor meant his assurances to the contrary made a greater impression than anything the Bartols had said. A shadow seemed to lift from the boy's face.

They discussed Zineta that day too. Hammond found himself talking about her as if he had known her for years. 'She was a fine person, Patrick,' he said. 'You should be proud of her.'

Patrick nodded. 'I am.' And Hammond believed him. It was a pride that would grow as the boy grew into a man. A mother he had never known, who had laid down her life to save his, would never be forgotten.

Goran Perović had suggested during his brief visit to Luxembourg that the Bartols should take Patrick to Serbia some day to meet his grandfather. Émile had resisted the idea at first, Mary revealed, but had softened his stance since. 'We've been seeing a counsellor – the authorities insisted on it as part of the unravelling of Delmotte's fraud – and she says it's something we really have to do. In the autumn, probably. During Patrick's half-term.'

So, this was not to be the last Hammond saw of Zineta's son. Among all the endings and beginnings, there were also continuities. And this was one he sensed he might come to treasure.

From Luxembourg Hammond flew to London. It was in no sense a homecoming. He stayed in Wimbledon long enough to work his way through a pile of mail and pack a couple of suitcases. Then he set off for Belgrade.

*

He arrived in the crushing heat of early August. The change of season since his last visit made Belgrade look and feel like a different city. Miljanović met him at the airport and drove him to his new apartment: a spacious and comfortably furnished duplex within easy reach of the clinic.

He would also be supplied with a car, Miljanović explained, and a cleaner who was on the clinic's payroll. 'Everything will be taken care of, Edward. And if it isn't . . . let me know.'

Miljanović took him out to dinner that evening, at Langouste, an elegant and expensive restaurant with a terrace overlooking the confluence of the Sava and the Danube. The sun set slowly over the tower blocks of New Belgrade as they toasted their renewed working relationship with champagne. 'Don't worry,' said Miljanović with a grin. 'The clinic is paying.'

'That's what's worrying me.'

'Why? We are lucky to get you. Even the director understands that. By the way, I should give you this.' Miljanović took a letter out of his pocket and passed it across the table.

It was in Cyrillic Serbian and utterly impenetrable to Hammond, who shrugged helplessly.

'Confirmation from the Ministry of Justice that they have no . . . problems with you working here,' Miljanović explained. 'The director insisted we get it in writing.'

'Well, it's good to have, I suppose.'

'I get the feeling they don't want to reopen their inquiry into the death of ICEFA agent Uželać. Corruption of state officials is an embarrassing subject.'

'What about Gazi? Isn't he an embarrassing subject?'

'Not much of a subject at all, Edward. The average Serb would like to forget all those bloodthirsty old generals you spent time with in The Hague. The Karadžić trial, when it begins, will mean they can't. But Gazi? His escape was big news, of course. But that was nearly six months ago. What is the English saying? Out of sight . . . out of mind.'

'He's not out of my mind.'

'Not yet, perhaps. Give it time. Now you're here, I plan to keep you busy.'

'Good. That's just what I need.'

Miljanović smiled. 'Then you've come to the right place.'

Miljanović did not fail to deliver on his promise where workload was concerned. Hammond was thrown into the midst of numerous complex cases and was astonished by the relief he felt at returning to medicine. It truly was his vocation. Whatever else he did, he should never abandon it. In a hospital, in his reassuring white coat – reassuring to him as well as his patients – he was a force for good, for clarity, for hope, for resolution. It was where he belonged.

He had only been in Belgrade a few weeks when Alice and Jake, who were making their way home from Turkey by train, stopped off to see him. They stayed for four nights. There was ample room for them in the apartment. Hammond spent a Sunday with them on Ada Ciganlija, the cigar-shaped island in the Sava where Belgraders went to swim and sunbathe. They hired bikes and explored the quieter northern shore, where they chanced upon a secluded raft-restaurant and stopped for a lunch that lasted most of the afternoon.

Nothing profound or meaningful was discussed. Gazi was not mentioned. Nor was Kate. The time for that, Hammond sensed, would come later, when he and Jake knew each other better. He was confident such a time would come. There was something open and instantly likeable about the young man and something enduring about the way Alice looked at him. As for the way she looked at Hammond, there was still a measure of caution in it. She loved him because he was her father. In the end, he knew, that would be enough to rebuild their old trust and ease. But they were not quite there yet. It was a work in progress.

*

A month passed. Hammond devoted himself to his caseload at the Voćnjak Clinic. He got to know the staff and they got to know him. He bedded in, to the extent that he began to wonder if he might extend his contract.

Early in October, Mary Bartol e-mailed to say they would definitely be visiting Belgrade during Patrick's half-term at the end of the month. Could Hammond do her the enormous favour of discussing with Goran Perović how best to handle their encounter with his father? Hammond replied that he would be happy to.

That evening, he pondered, not for the first time, nor, he suspected, the last, the question of where Gazi might be hiding. His escape was, in a sense, the easy part. His continued freedom was the truly devilish trick to pull off. South America was the obvious answer, since Ingrid spent much of her time in Buenos Aires. But any contact with her would be risky in the extreme. The mystery hinged, he concluded, on what Gazi wanted from the life beyond Scheveningen he had bought for himself. But to know that Hammond would need to understand Gazi a great deal better than he did – or had any wish to. Finding him was someone else's responsibility. And that was a blessing.

But not all blessings endure. Only a few days later, Hammond was enjoying a lunchtime walk in Topčider Park, admiring the autumn colours, when his mobile rang. He generally received few calls, having guarded the number carefully since acquiring the phone, and was concerned it might herald an emergency at the clinic.

He was met instead by a terse text message from a number he did not recognize. '*Want to know where he is?*'

Ten minutes later, Hammond was still staring at the message. He was sitting on a bench beneath a plane tree, cradling the phone in his hand, torn between chasing the promise of a clue to Gazi's whereabouts – he did not for a moment doubt it was Gazi the texter was referring to – and turning his back on the mystery. But he knew himself well enough to understand the futility of trying to pretend he had never received the message. It was there, on the tiny screen, before him. And even if he erased it, it would still be in his mind. He surrendered.

'*Where who is?*' he texted back, reckoning it was safer to act dumb.

The response was almost instantaneous. He felt as if an unseen creature had suddenly wrapped a tentacle round his leg. '*You know who.*'

Yes. He knew. And the texter knew he knew. '*OK. Where?*'

'*Be at your house in london 1800 tomorrow to find out.*'

'*Why not tell me now?*'

'*Be at your house in london 1800 tomorrow to find out.*'

'*Who r u?*'

'*Be at your house in london 1800 tomorrow to find out.*'

'*How do I know this isnt a hoax?*'

'*Be at your house in london 1800 tomorrow to find out.*'

He tried to break free. '*Cant make it.*'

But the texter did not believe him. '*Be there.*'

'And you will be there, of course,' said Miljanović, nodding at Hammond across the desk in his consulting room at the Voćnjak Clinic later that afternoon. 'You know it. I know it. Your anonymous caller knows it too.'

'I can be back within forty-eight hours, Svetozar,' said Hammond. 'If a trip to London is all it takes to get the information ICTY have been looking for without success for eight months . . .'

'You really believe you're likely to get that information?'

'I don't know. But I have to try.'

'No. You don't. But clearly you're going to.'

'You think I'll be wasting my time?'

'I hope you will be. I fear something . . . much worse.'

'What?'

'A trap of some kind. Which you'll be walking straight into.' Miljanović leant forward and fixed Hammond with his gaze. 'You should forget Gazi, Edward. Let those who are paid for it carry on the search for him. Put him out of your mind.'

'I can't do that.'

Miljanović sighed. 'I know.'

THIRTY-FIVE

The house in Wimbledon felt less like a home every time Hammond returned to it. He arrived in the middle of a grey and windless afternoon to find the whole street locked in autumnal still-ness. Waiting patiently indoors for six o'clock to come was an intolerable prospect. But a walk on the Common and a drink at the Hand in Hand hardly quelled his anxieties. Miljanović's advice to ignore the summons, which was effectively what the message had amounted to, seemed ever sounder as the minutes ticked by.

On his way back from the pub, he met a neighbour heading towards the Common with her dog. They had a brief, fragile conversation, in which the reasons for Hammond's absence from the area for so many months were not once specifically referred to but hovered at the reticent edges of their exchanges about Alice and her new boyfriend and the spectacular colouring of the horse chestnuts.

'By the way, Debbie,' he asked impulsively as they parted, 'you haven't seen anyone hanging around my house recently, have you?'

'No.' She frowned. 'No one.'

The light was failing as six o'clock drew near. Hammond stationed himself in Alice's room on the top floor, which commanded a good view of the street, watching and waiting. He could not fail to see anyone who approached. If he did not like the look of them, he did not have to open the door. It was as simple as that. He had control of the situation. He was in no danger.

Perhaps the texter meant to contact him again by phone. Hammond's mobile was on the windowsill, ready for any such call. But six o'clock came and went. And it did not ring. Nor did he see any pedestrians, apart from Debbie, returning from the Common with her dog. Perhaps Miljanović was to be granted his wish: it was just a wild-goose chase. Five minutes slowly passed. Then ten.

And then the phone rang. Not Hammond's mobile, but the land line. The extension in his bedroom on the floor below was the closest. He raced downstairs towards it.

It had reached the seventh or eighth ring by the time he made it, narrowly beating the answerphone to the jump. 'Hello?'

'Good evening, doctor.'

Hammond knew the voice at once. The delay in his response was due to simple incredulity. 'Vidor?'

'Yes. Didn't you guess the messages were from me?'

'Why would I? You helped Gazi escape.'

'True. But now I'm willing to help get him caught again.'

'Why?'

'What does that matter to you? Maybe I haven't been treated as well as I was promised. Maybe I just don't think the old bastard should get away with it. Maybe lots of things. All you need to know is that I'm willing to give him to you.'

'Didn't they pay you enough?' Hammond asked, not troubling to hide the bitterness in his voice.

'Draw your own conclusions. Do you want to put him back behind bars or not?'

'Of course I do.'

'Good. I need someone to tip off ICTY for me. I can't think of anyone better qualified than you. But I need your guarantee that you won't tell them where the information came from. I don't want Ingrid on my trail.'

'You'd trust me to keep your name out of it?'

'You're a man of your word, Edward. Of course I'd trust you.'

Incredibly, Vidor seemed to be trying to flatter Hammond into compliance. But flattery was hardly necessary. 'All right. I'll do it. Where is he?'

'South America.'

'You are going to be more specific than that, aren't you?'

'Certainly. But only when we meet.'

'Why do we have to meet? Just tell me where Gazi is and I'll do the rest.'

'I have my reasons for preferring to do this face to face. It's the only way you're going to learn more.'

Hammond sighed. 'All right. Where and when?'

'Tomorrow. In Buenos Aires.'

'You're in Buenos Aires?'

'No. But I will be when you arrive. I've booked you on a flight out of Heathrow at nine fifteen tonight that'll get you there at nine thirty in the morning.'

'What makes you think I'm going to travel halfway round the world at your say-so, Stevan?'

'Because you want Gazi out of your life and off your conscience. And that's what I'll give you. But only if you do as I say. You're not going to stop now, Edward. You'd never have left Belgrade if you weren't determined to see this through to the finish. So, you'll be on that plane. I know you will.'

Hammond had promised to phone Miljanović that evening, but when he did it was not with the news his friend had been hoping to hear.

'You're going to Buenos Aires?'

'Yes, Svetozar, I am. I'm close to the answer now. I have to take this last step.'

'How do you know it is the last? Vidor said you'd get the answer in London. Now it's Buenos Aires. Where next – Honolulu?'

'Vidor was involved in setting up the escape, so there's good reason to think he knows where Gazi escaped *to*. He insists on telling me face to face, probably so he can persuade me it wouldn't be in my best interests to tell ICTY he was my informant. Well, I'm willing to be persuaded if that's what it takes to nail Gazi.'

'He lied to you before, didn't he?'

'Yes. But there's no reason for him to be lying now. He'd only be wasting his time as well as mine.'

Miljanović's sigh was audible on the line. 'You generally only find out why a lie is told after the event, Edward. Often long after. You know this. It is a crazy risk to go. But you're going, so . . . all I can do is wish you luck . . . and hope you don't need it.'

Hammond could not have denied that what Miljanović had said was simple common sense. But nor could he have denied that Vidor was a credible source of information concerning Gazi's whereabouts. He had played his part in the conspiracy cynically and capably, but was clearly no zealot for the cause of Greater Serbia. He had done what he had done for money and if, for whatever reason, he had not been paid what he considered his due it seemed somehow characteristic of him to respond in just the way he was now doing.

Besides, the truth was, as Miljanović had intuited – and Vidor, for that matter – that Hammond could not ignore the chance to put Gazi back where he deserved to spend the rest of his life: prison. The burning sense of his own stupidity he had felt while watching the CNN report of Gazi's escape that day in Lugano had faded over the eight months since. But it had not gone away entirely. To be judged, as ICTY's investigators had judged him, a dupe rather than a villain was no kind of commendation. And it was not a judgement he wanted to go on living with.

He slept better than he had expected to on the plane, waking only when the descent began to São Paulo, where there was an hour's stop before the flight continued to Buenos Aires. There he found a message from Vidor waiting for him on his phone when he switched it on after clearing customs. *'Evita's tomb noon.'* Vidor had wasted no words.

He had travelled from a European autumn into a South American spring. The taxi from the airport – where the tourist information booth had supplied him with a city map and the location of Eva Perón's tomb – dropped him near the main entrance to Recoleta Cemetery. Warm sunshine had attracted numerous customers to the pavement tables of the cafés opposite. Hammond had the best part of an hour to spare before his rendezvous and spent most of it sipping coffee and mineral water in circumstances that would have been idyllic – sweet-scented air, gentle thrum of nearby conversations, trees in full green leaf, sunlight falling mellowly on terracotta roofs, a soporific undertow of jet lag – but for the urgency of the occasion.

Even that failed to stop him lapsing into a reverie. He had never been to Buenos Aires before and was surprised by how Parisian the city seemed. He was reminded of a spring fortnight he and Kate had spent in Paris in the first year of their marriage. They had stayed in a small *pension* in Montparnasse, quite close to the cemetery. Their anniversary had fallen halfway through the holiday. It was at a pavement café very like this that Kate had presented him with a gift – a heart-embroidered white cotton handkerchief for their cotton anniversary. He still had it somewhere, stowed away in a drawer. Quite how, within ten years, they had allowed their tender love of those times to disintegrate, he could not in that memory-laden interlude even begin to imagine. 'I'm sorry, Kate,' he heard himself murmur. 'Truly sorry.'

Vidor could not have known how apt his choice of meeting place was. Kate's ghost walked with Hammond along the alleys that criss-crossed Recoleta's walled city of the dead, past grandiose marble mausolea and soaring statues of mourning angels. So many things had gone wrong in the thirteen years since he had lost her – and with her a grievous portion of his own past.

309

It was time – high time – to shore up one right thing against them.

Eva Perón's tomb was a relatively modest memorial by the standards of many of its neighbours, but the cluster of tourists eager to be snapped beside her final resting place made it easy to find. Vidor was not part of the throng, but Hammond was content to wait patiently for him to show himself.

Vidor, however, had other plans. A short, paunchy figure in a crumpled linen suit and floppy-brimmed trilby materialized with eerie stealth at his elbow. 'Dr Hammond?' He had a round, jowly face and dark, twinkling eyes. He looked like a local, though his English was only faintly accented. Hammond would have put his age at sixty or so and guessed that, though well-educated, his occupation was not entirely conventional.

'Yes, I'm Hammond,' he responded cautiously. 'Who are you?'

'Enrique Dobson.' He plucked off his hat, revealing a bald crown, over which greased strands of bottle-black hair had been ineffectually trained. 'My, er, grandfather was English,' he said, apparently feeling his surname required explanation. He extended his free hand in greeting and Hammond found himself shaking it. 'Señor Lazović sent me.'

'Who?'

'He said he had arranged to meet you here.'

'I arranged to meet a man called Vidor.'

'A . . . Serbian gentleman?'

'Yes.'

'Then . . . I believe your Vidor must be my Lazović.' Dobson smiled and cocked his head, lowering his voice confidentially. 'I have never met Señor Lazović, doctor, but the subject of the enquiries I have carried out for him means it is quite possible – very possible – that Lazović is not his real name.'

Any more than Vidor necessarily was, it occurred to Hammond. He did not say as much. Dobson's expression suggested there was no need to. 'What's your line of business, *señor*?' Hammond asked.

'I used to be a journalist. I still am, when anyone is willing to pay

310

me for an article. When they are not, I . . . freelance in other . . . capacities.' As clear as mud, thought Hammond. 'Señor Lazović asked me to meet you here and 1 . . . set out the results of my enquiries. Why don't we move . . . somewhere less crowded? There is a tomb a little way from here I need to show you, doctor.' He gestured vaguely towards the next alley on the right. 'Shall we?'

It was a curved black marble panel, with a weeping Grecian woman draped around one edge, clutching a garland. Inset in the panel was a photograph of a good-looking dark-haired boy, smiling fixedly. The inscription read:

NIKOLA ALEXSANDR GAZI
21 MAYO 1980 – 25 SEPTIEMBRE 1993
PARA SIEMPRE BELLO, PARA SIEMPRE JOVEN

'For ever beautiful, for ever young,' murmured Dobson.

'Touching, I'm sure,' said Hammond. 'But why do I need to see it?'

'Nikola Gazi died in a motorcycle accident, doctor. You probably don't know the details. He was a pillion passenger. The rider of the motorcycle was an eighteen-year-old called Carlos Rueda. His father, Ernesto Rueda, was a former friend of Dragan Gazi. They first met in Chile in 1973. There's evidence they both worked for the DINA, Pinochet's secret police, running torture centres and carrying out assassinations. They moved to Argentina together in 1977 when the DINA was closed down and appear to have provided the same sort of services for the military junta here during *la Guerra Sucia* – the Dirty War, when thousands of so-called enemies of the state disappeared, never to be seen again. After what you would call the Falklands War in 1982 it was obvious the military would have to restore democracy, so Gazi went back to Yugoslavia, leaving his family behind, and Rueda opted for a quieter life as a businessman.

'The twenty-fifth of September 1993 was Carlos Rueda's

eighteenth birthday. The motorcycle was a present from his father. There was an all-day party at the Rueda residence in San Isidro. Carlos tried out his new bike, naturally. Everything was fine. Then, just as it was beginning to get dark, he went for a longer ride on the machine and took Nikola with him. The boy begged to be taken along, apparently. He was not wearing a helmet. Carlos went too fast, also naturally. There was no other vehicle involved in the crash. Carlos simply lost control on a bend. Nikola was thrown headfirst against a wall.' Dobson clapped his hands together. '*Muerto*. It must have been instantaneous.'

'And Carlos?'

'Nothing worse than cuts and bruises. A lucky escape for him. Or so it must have seemed. At the funeral, Nikola's mother, Isabel Nieto-Gazi, made a point of forgiving Carlos for causing her son's death. Dragan Gazi was not there, of course. He was too busy killing Muslims in Bosnia. But, if he had been present, we can be sure he would have forgiven no one. A few weeks after the funeral, Carlos disappeared on his way to college. He has never been seen since.'

'You think . . .'

'Executed on Gazi's orders. That is what everyone thinks. The body would have been secretly disposed of. It was probably dropped from a helicopter into the Río de la Plata – an old Dirty War tactic, as Ernesto Rueda would have known well. The lack of a corpse to bury was part of the punishment for the family. Gazi had struck, as Rueda must have feared he would. Revenge mattered more than friendship. Rueda's wife died of cancer three years later and he returned to Chile – a broken man, as they say.'

'Very interesting. But it's not exactly news to me that Dragan Gazi is a bloodthirsty bastard.'

'Señor Lazović instructed me to tell you the Rueda story. He said it would . . . help you understand.'

'Understand what?'

Dobson shrugged. 'I do not know. But . . . you should hear the rest of what he instructed me to tell you. Perhaps . . . you will understand then.'

THIRTY-SIX

'Gazi married the actress Isabel Nieto a few months after arriving in Buenos Aires in 1977. A whirlwind romance, you could say. Or Gazi's bid for some glamour in his life. There was certainly nothing glamorous about what he and Rueda did for the junta. Their experience in imposing a reign of terror was invaluable. And the work kept them busy for the next five years. As for Gazi's marriage, it didn't work out. Isabel refused to leave Argentina in 1982 and Gazi refused to stay. So, they parted. They're still married, of course. Isabel is a good Catholic and wouldn't contemplate divorce.

'She lives on an *estancia* about a hundred kilometres from the city. She runs it as a hotel as well as a ranch. There's a surprisingly large number of people willing to pay for a taste of gaucho life. She dropped Gazi from her surname after he was indicted for war crimes. I don't think she has any fond feelings for him. Maybe the Rueda business was just too much for her.

'The same doesn't seem to be true of her daughter Ingrid, whose own marriage, to the son of a department-store owner, collapsed, it's said, because of her insistence on standing by her father. She came out of that with quite a lot of money and owns an apartment in one of the city's smartest blocks. It's actually not far from here. Her property holdings don't stop there, though. The most difficult and time-consuming part of the enquiries I've made for Señor Lazović has been finding out how much real estate she owns. I've established that her lawyers have used complicated trust arrangements to make several purchases on her behalf in recent months: a ski-lodge in Patagonia, a beachside apartment at Punta del Este over in Uruguay and a vineyard near Mendoza. None of them came cheap. I don't know why she bought them, of course, but I suspect Señor Lazović suspects they're being set up as places where she can spend time in secret with her father. I doubt ICTY's investigators are aware of these properties. I had to pull a lot of strings to get hold of the information.

'Chile under Pinochet; Argentina under the generals; Serbia under Milošević: Gazi's record as a servant of brutal regimes is hard to beat, I'd say. You'd think it would be impossible to love such a man even if he was your father. He has the blood of thousands of innocent Chileans, Argentinians, Bosnians and Kosovars on his hands. But still Ingrid wants to shield him from justice. What a woman, no? I wish I had a daughter who was half as loyal.'

They had left Recoleta Cemetery and walked north towards the National Museum of Fine Arts as Dobson related what he knew. Vidor – or Lazović – had told him he would meet Hammond at Floralis Genérica, a gigantic steel sculpture of a flower, with petals that opened by day and closed at night. It stood in Plaza Naciones Unidas, on the other side of the road behind the museum.

'I will leave you here, doctor,' said Dobson, pausing breathlessly at the roadside. 'Señor Lazović said you should wait for him alone.'

Hammond squinted ahead through the bright sunlight. No one was loitering by the huge metal flower. 'Do you know why I'm here, Enrique?' he asked, without looking round at his companion.

'I think so. I make all sorts of checks when people hire me. For my own protection, you understand. Your name cropped up in connection with Gazi's escape. I can put two and two together.'

'And make what?' Hammond turned to face him.

He was met by Dobson's broad, well-practised smile. 'Nothing, of course. I got through the bad times here in the seventies and eighties without being "disappeared" or getting strapped to a table

314

on the orders of bastards like Gazi and Rueda and having my *cojones* wired up to a generator. I managed that by adding things up . . . but never shouting about the results.' He offered Hammond his hand. 'I wish you good luck, doctor.'

Hammond watched from the other side of the road as Dobson wandered off in the direction of the museum. Then he turned and headed along the path that led across the lawned plaza to Floralis Genérica. There was still no sign of Vidor. He took a slow turn round the sculpture, lingering in the shade of one of the towering petals as he puzzled over what Vidor had hoped to achieve by sending Dobson to meet him at the cemetery. Hammond needed no convincing that Gazi deserved to spend the rest of his life in prison. Surely his presence in Buenos Aires proved he was willing to play his part in bringing that about. All he needed—

His phone started ringing. He snatched it from his pocket. 'Hello?'

'Good to see you, Edward.' It was Vidor.

'Where are you?' Hammond glanced around, half expecting to see the man skulking behind a bush.

'Turn to your right and look south. See the tall building in the middle distance with the blue ship at the top?'

Hammond turned and looked, as directed. He saw the building at once, decorated with the bright-blue likeness of a sailing ship. 'What about it?' he demanded.

'I'm on the top floor, watching you through binoculars. I'm glad to see you're alone.'

'Is all this cloak-and-dagger stuff really necessary, Stevan?'

'Very. I'm running a lot of risks to meet you.'

'You are going to meet me, then?'

'Of course. This building is the Hotel Goleta. I've booked you a room. Come on over and check in. Then take the elevator down to the parking garage. Sub-level two. I'll be waiting for you.'

The Goleta was a mid-rise mid-market establishment that looked as if it catered mostly for business travellers on an adequate but by

315

no means lavish budget. An escort to his room was not part of the package, so Hammond was free to go straight down to the garage.

As the lift doors opened on to a dimly lit cavern of concrete pillars and parked cars, he asked himself whether he was now running the same risks as Vidor, whatever they were. If the gang responsible for Gazi's escape had somehow got wind of Vidor's intentions, they might both be in grave danger. But it was a danger he knew he had to face. He had come too far to turn back. He had to go on. To the end.

A pair of headlamps flashed from a distant corner of the sparsely occupied garage. He headed towards them. They belonged to a vehicle strategically parked midway between the pools of sallow light cast by widely spaced fluorescent tubes. It was a large hard-top pick-up truck, with grilles over the headlamps and thick layers of mud and dust on the tyres and bodywork. The only glass visible in the windscreen was in the arcs scraped clear by the wipers, through which Vidor gazed out expressionlessly.

He looked thinner than Hammond remembered – unshaven and hollow-eyed, like a man who had been driving himself too hard for too long. He was no longer wearing glasses. And there was a recent scar over his left cheekbone. He signalled with a twitch of his head for Hammond to get in and only then released the door locks.

Hammond climbed into the passenger seat. As he closed the door behind him, Vidor re-engaged the locks. 'You ought to know,' Hammond began, 'that I—'

'Save it,' said Vidor, cutting him off. 'We don't have the time – and I don't have the patience – for you to tell me what you think of me for betraying ICTY and helping free Gazi. Nothing is as you think it is.'

'How is it, then?'

'You'll find out before we part. I promise you that.'

'All I need from you, Stevan, is Gazi's location. I'm not interested in anything else. That includes the workings of your conscience – if you have one.'

'Very well. After listening to Dobson, you can't doubt Ingrid has plans to supply her father with several comfortable hideaways.'

'What of it? Tell me where he is and her plans go up in smoke.'

'Did you wonder why I hired Dobson?'

Hammond had wondered. Researching Gazi's activities in Chile and Argentina several decades back seemed to him entirely beside the point. 'Gazi's a monster, Stevan. OK? Always was. Always will be. I understand that. It's a pity you didn't understand it before taking his money to help spring him from jail.'

'But I did. I understood very well.'

'Then why did you do it?'

'Means to an end, Edward. There was no other way.'

'No other way to get rich quick. Is that what you mean? Is that *it*?'

'No.' Vidor turned to look at him, his face a mask of shadows. 'That's not it at all.'

'Where is he? Just tell me. Then you and I can go our separate ways.'

'You make it sound easy. Tracking him down actually involved a lot of hard work. It also cost several people their lives.'

'What do you mean?'

'They deserved to die. I don't regret what I did.'

The temperature in the car seemed suddenly to have plunged about ten degrees. 'Hold on. Did you . . . kill Furgler?'

'You mean Mittag? Yes, I did. He would have told his bosses who was after Gazi if I'd let him live. I had no alternative.'

'And there were . . . others?'

'There were.'

'You . . . killed them all?'

'As many as I needed to.'

'They said Furgler – Mittag – was tortured before he died.'

'He had information I needed. He didn't give it up easily.'

Until a few moments before, Hammond had supposed Vidor was motivated by a grudge at being underpaid or in some other way cheated by the gang responsible for Gazi's escape. Now the chilling realization was creeping over him that this was about something else – something else altogether. 'Are you going to tell me where Gazi is?'

'Yes. But there are a few other things I have to tell you first. You see, I've been looking for him for a long time. Nine years in all.'

'*What?*'

'It was only after Gazi went into hiding in 2000 and the whole Milošević regime collapsed that anyone was willing to tell me the truth about how my brother Marinko died and why, later, the rest of my family was slaughtered. I learnt Gazi was to blame. He gave the orders. First Marinko was executed. Then my sister, my other brothers and my parents were taken out. They'd got together to celebrate my father's seventieth birthday. Gazi's men broke into the apartment and shot them all. I wasn't there, of course. I never was. I was the one who got away and planned to stay away. But I couldn't stay away after that. I could forget my country, but not my family.'

'If you hate Gazi so much, why—'

'It'll be clear to you soon enough. Just listen. I resolved to hunt him down and kill him. But no one knew where he was – no one who'd talk, anyway. That's why I went to work for the UN. Because I thought they'd give me the resources I needed to find him. But it was the Montenegrin police who arrested him in the end, so I never had the chance to get at him before he was safely locked up at Scheveningen. Well, you've been there. You know the kind of place it is. *Het Oranje Hotel* gets it right. It's more of a hotel than a prison. Nothing for sure like Goli Otok, the labour camp where my father spent a few years as his punishment for being overheard questioning Tito's infallibility in front of his students. He was a teacher who thought teaching involved speaking freely. What a fool he was. A fool I loved, of course. A fool Gazi murdered on his seventieth birthday.

'ICTY works on the principle that depriving mass murderers of their liberty for the rest of their lives is a just and adequate penalty. First Scheveningen, then some soft Scandinavian prison where they can write their memoirs and enjoy a more comfortable old age than any of the lonely women back in Bosnia and Kosovo they casually widowed. It's not enough, by a long way. That's why I took the bribe I was offered to help plan Gazi's escape. Not for the money, but for the chance his renewed freedom would give me to finish the job I started nine years ago: to hunt him, to corner him and to make him pay what *I* judged would be an adequate penalty for his crimes. The gang behind his escape did more than just free him, you see. They also arranged safe havens where he could stay free. That meant there was a trail I could follow, starting with Mittag, that would lead me eventually to where he was hiding. I found him four days ago, in Panama.' Vidor paused then, as if savouring the memory.

'Is that where he is now?' Hammond ventured.

'No. Not now. I . . . removed him.'

'You mean you killed him?'

'I didn't say that.'

'Whether you did or not, you've made it obvious you don't mean him to be handed back to ICTY. So, why bring me here?' It was the question that had to be asked. What was Vidor planning – and where did Hammond figure in that plan? He had been lured to Buenos Aires for a reason. And he needed to know what it was.

'This isn't just about Gazi, Edward. It's also about you and me.'

'What do you mean?'

'Why do you suppose he had my brother killed and the rest of my family wiped out?'

'I've no idea.'

'Marinko fought with the Wolves in Bosnia, you know. He was loyal to the cause of Greater Serbia. He was loyal to Gazi. Then, one day during the post-Dayton truce, he hanged himself. At least, so my parents were told. But my sister Tanja never believed it. She always was a terrier. She convinced my brothers there was something highly suspicious about his death. They started asking questions. And they went on asking them. Until Gazi decided the questions had to stop. There's something you need to understand about Marinko, you see. He was one pure kind of guy. He didn't smoke. He hardly drank. He wasn't into drugs or prostitutes. Gazi knew that. And he'd have got his blood group from his medical records, of course. But still he went to the trouble of persuading him to be tested for hepatitis and HIV. He needed to be sure.'

'Sure of what?'

'My parents weren't told Marinko was dead until three days after he supposedly hanged himself. The excuse was that there were problems identifying him. But Tanja learnt from staff at the hospital where he was taken that his CO in the Wolves had said he had no recorded next of kin. That was bullshit. He'd have recorded next-of-kin details when he went on active service. And nobody seemed to know who'd found him. He lived alone in New Belgrade. If he was going to kill himself, he'd have done a quick, efficient job of it, with a bullet. The soldier's way. Hanging? Forget it. But hanging doesn't involve blood loss, of course, or damage to internal organs, as long as the victim's not actually brain dead when he's cut down. And apparently Marinko wasn't. Get the picture?'

Integrity of internal organs; screening for infective agents; no next of kin to consult: a picture was indeed forming in Hammond's mind. And a terrible one it was.

'I changed my name to Vidor so no one would connect me with Marinko and guess what I was up to. My father used to talk about King Vidor as an example of what you could accomplish if you got out of Eastern Europe: you could wind up directing Audrey Hepburn for a living, with a home in the Hollywood hills. Lazović is an alias as well. The name I was born with was Zarić: Stevan Zarić. My brother was Marinko Zarić. Mean anything to you?'

'I don't think so,' Hammond replied hoarsely.

'No? Well, maybe Miljanović never gave you the donor's name. Or maybe you forgot it because it didn't seem important. Maybe you always try to forget about the donor in these cases. But the fact is, *Doctor* Hammond, it was my brother Marinko's liver you put in Gazi thirteen years ago.'

Hammond heard the click of the revolver being cocked an instant before he saw the pale light fall on its snubbed barrel. It was pointing straight at him.

'Get out of the truck,' Vidor said quietly.

THIRTY-SEVEN

'I knew nothing about any of this,' said Hammond. He stood trembling in the half-light of the garage, struggling to find the right words to persuade Vidor that he should not kill him. 'You must believe me, Stevan. I would never have turned a blind eye to the murder of an organ donor. It violates every medical ethic I've ever worked by.'

Vidor walked slowly round the bonnet of the truck, keeping the gun trained on Hammond. When they were only a few feet apart, he stopped. His face was in shadow, as it had been inside the car. There was no way to read his expression. 'What are the ethics of giving a mass murderer who's terminally ill another couple of decades to go on killing?' he asked, as if genuinely curious about what the answer might be.

'I didn't know he was a mass murderer then.'

'No? Maybe you thought he was in line for the Nobel Peace Prize. Come on, Edward. Admit it. You didn't want to know what Gazi had done in Bosnia – or where the donor had come from. You just wanted the money.'

'The fee was attractive, of course. I don't deny it. But—'

'How much did Gazi pay you?'

'Does it matter?'

'I'd like you to tell me.'

It occurred to Hammond that he might already know. A lie at

this stage could be fatal. 'Two hundred and fifty thousand pounds.'

'And Miljanović? How much did he get?'

'I don't know. That was between him and Gazi.'

'But less than you?'

'Yes. Less than me.'

'So that makes you the person primarily responsible for the operation.'

'I suppose so, yes.'

'Yet you knew nothing about how Gazi's new liver had been obtained.'

'I had no reason to enquire into the matter. A surgeon always tries to avoid contact with a donor's family to guard against any suggestion of coercion.'

'But Marinko's family didn't know he *was* a donor.'

'There must have been collusion somewhere along the line. That's clear. Probably at the first hospital your brother was admitted to. The Voćnjak Clinic would only have been told there was a patient on life support who might be suitable for a liver transplant.'

'Meaning you're not to blame?'

'For your brother's death? No. I'm not. And I don't believe you really think I am either.'

'What about for saving Gazi's life?'

'I'm a doctor, Stevan. I tend the sick.'

'Especially the ones who pay well.'

'If I'd known as much about Gazi then as I know now, I'd have refused to treat him. But someone else would have taken my place. It wouldn't have changed anything. Surely you—'

There was a squeal of rubber on concrete from the direction of the access ramp. Headlamp beams slid round the bays as a vehicle descended into the garage. 'Get behind the truck,' Vidor snapped. 'Quickly.'

Hammond turned and walked unsteadily to the rear of the truck. There was clearance of about six feet between it and the wall. As he stepped into the space, he felt the hard prod of the gun in his back.

'Don't try to attract any attention, Edward,' Vidor rasped in his ear. 'It would be a big mistake.'

A large dark saloon car came to a halt most of the width of the garage away from them. The engine died. A man got out and slammed the door. While the echo of that was still rumbling around them, a second door slammed. A woman had also got out. There was a beep from a key-remote. Then she and the man made their way over to the lift, chatting in Spanish as they went. They never even glanced towards Hammond and Vidor.

The lift arrived. The doors opened and closed. The voices were cut off. They were alone again.

'Open the tailgate,' said Vidor quietly.

Hammond wanted to ask why, but did not dare. He found the handle, turned it and pulled the door up. It rose under its own power until it was level with the roof, then stopped.

'The lower half as well. There are bolts either side.'

Vidor stepped back a pace to give Hammond room for manoeuvre. He slipped the bolts and lowered the gate. The rear of the truck was now fully open. The interior was crammed with boxes and what looked like piles of fabric.

'There's a lamp bracketed to the roof on the right-hand side. Switch it on.'

Hammond saw the projecting lamp. He fumbled around it until he found the switch and pressed it. The interior of the truck was suddenly brightly lit. The piles of fabric were actually vividly patterned rugs of various shapes and sizes, lying on a waist-level shelf, with cardboard boxes and wooden crates crammed in below.

'For customs purposes, I'm a carpet dealer. There are a lot of borders between here and Panama.'

'You drove all the way?' Hammond asked, glancing round at Vidor, who had taken care to stand just clear of the glare of the lamp.

'It was the only option, considering my cargo. Though none of the policemen I met were much interested in what I was carrying

323

once I'd pressed a wad of US dollars into their sweaty hands. But you'll be interested, Edward. You'll be very interested. There's a sliding tray at floor level. Pull it out.'

Hammond looked down and saw the crates and boxes were resting on a tray just clear of the floor of the truck. He found a handle and, beneath it, a lock release. Then he slid the tray out on its rollers.

The largest of the crates was fully six feet long: a solid rectangular timber box, the lid fastened with three thick leather straps.

'Open it,' said Vidor.

'What's inside?'

'Open it and find out.'

A strange, cloying dread rose in Hammond as he unbuckled the straps. A widely spaced line of holes had been drilled in the wood, so small he only noticed them as he stretched under the shelf to release the last strap. He stood up then and turned towards Vidor. 'What is this?' he asked.

Vidor raised the gun at arm's length. '*Open it.*'

'All right.' Hammond signalled with open palms that he would not resist. 'All right.' He turned back, stooped over the box and heaved the lid off. As he did so, Vidor laughed.

A man lay inside the box, dressed in a T-shirt, long underpants and socks. He was also wearing some grotesque kind of nappy, from which rose a stench of excrement and stale urine. His mouth was gagged and his hands were tied behind his back. His ankles were tied with the same length of rope, stretched taut so that he could not straighten his legs. He had dark brown wiry hair and a beard and a waxily smooth face that looked at odds with his wizened neck and sinewy limbs. An uncomprehending instant passed before Hammond realized who he was looking at. Then, in the fearful yet defiant gaze of Dragan Gazi's icy blue eyes, he knew – and was known.

'Some expensive nips and tucks from a cosmetic surgeon, a very unmilitary beard and a bottle of hair dye don't improve him, do they?' said Vidor.

Hammond propped the lid against the side of the box and stepped back. Gazi followed his every move with his eyes. 'What in God's name are you doing, Stevan?' he asked, looking round at Vidor.

'Gazi would like to know that too, I'm sure. Every time I close the box, he wonders if I'll ever open it again. And every time I do, he wonders if I'm going to kill him.'

'And are you?'

'Eventually. When the time comes. But there are things to be done first. Here.' Vidor removed something from his denim jacket and tossed it to Hammond: a small digital camera. 'Take his photograph, please. Take several. So it's clear how he's being held.'

'Is this really necessary?'

'Yes. I took some in Panama before we left. But I think we need some more, showing him in his box. Please. Go ahead.'

Hammond made no effort to vary the angle or range of the pictures. He took six in all and they were more or less identical, with the date and time recorded in one corner of the frame. Then Vidor called a halt.

'That'll do. Now put the camera in your pocket.'

'I don't want the pictures, Stevan. They're yours.'

'But I can't show them to anyone and you can. In fact, I hope very much you will. To one person in particular. Will you do that for me? As a favour.'

'Who?'

'Ingrid. She must be in no doubt I've taken her father. I want you to tell her what I've done. The pictures will prove it's true. She'll have to believe it.' Vidor lowered the gun. 'I'm not going to kill you, Edward. I might have, if you'd ignored my message and stayed in Belgrade. Then I might have come for you. As it is, I need you to do this for me. And I think I have the right to ask it of you. Can you honestly disagree?'

Hammond could not. But even so he was revolted by what Vidor had done to Gazi – more so than if he had simply put a bullet through the wretched man's head.

'Think what you're doing, Stevan. Torturing Gazi pulls you down to his level. Let me call the police and have him—'

'I'm the police here, Edward. I'm the law for the rest of Gazi's life, however long or short that is. And I'm not torturing him. I'm punishing him, along with his daughter. I have a message for Ingrid. It's this. She's never going to know her father's fate – when he dies, how he dies, where he dies. She's never going to have his body to bury in a fancy tomb in Recoleta Cemetery. I'm going to do to him what he did to Carlos Rueda. I'm going to "disappear" him.'

'There has to be—'

'A better way? No. This is what Gazi deserves. No prison cell. No grave. No memorial. Just . . . extinction. Go to the authorities if you want and tell them everything you know. I don't mind. I'm a fugitive for good now. It doesn't really matter how many people come after me. But speak to Ingrid first. Make her understand. There'll be no contented old age for Dragan Gazi. She's lost him. For ever.'

Silence fell. Hammond could not find it in him to prolong his appeal to Vidor's nobler instincts. He had little doubt that Gazi would suffer cruelly before he died. It was an affront to his soft-bred Western European liberal principles. But those principles had done less than nothing for all the many thousands of Gazi's victims spread over two continents and three decades. Perhaps the time had truly come for him to reap as he had sown.

'Ingrid's apartment is at Avenida Cornualles two six one,' said Vidor softly. 'It's not far from here. Contact her as soon as you like.'

Still Hammond did not speak. But his silence conveyed its own meaning. It acknowledged that he would see Ingrid and deliver Vidor's message. It acknowledged that he could not refuse to.

A few minutes later, he watched the truck drive up the ramp leading to the higher level of the garage, then heard it power up the next ramp beyond that to the street. Vidor was gone. And Gazi with him. They had not ceased to exist. Yet Hammond felt certain he would never see either of them again.

326

*

Avenida Cornualles 261 was a handsome Beaux-Arts apartment block no more than a ten-minute walk from Recoleta Cemetery, where Nikola Gazi was buried, but his father never would be. The smartly uniformed porter on duty in the gilt-and-marble foyer advised Hammond that '*la Señora Hurtado-Gazi*' was in residence, but currently out. Hammond declined to leave a message.

He walked a little way down the road to one of three benches set round a small lawn in the shade of a gum tree. There he sat for the better part of an hour, monitoring arrivals and departures at the apartment block, while birds whose songs and plumage he did not recognize hopped and fluttered in the trees and the low hedge behind the bench.

He knew he would have to report what had happened in the garage of the Hotel Goleta. He could not condone the actions Vidor had chosen to take. Yet he could not condemn them either. Gazi's ruthlessness had finally met its match.

As for Ingrid, her response to the news Hammond had for her was hard to predict. He was taking a risk in contacting her. Yet, strangely, he had no misgivings. It was not that he wanted to pay her back for blackmailing and double-crossing him. It was simply that his agreement to treat Gazi thirteen years before had left him with a debt he could never hope to clear. It was in his power to reduce it, though, by instalments and degrees, by undertakings given and carried through. The dead could not be brought back to life. The living could not all receive their dues. The world, he knew, more certainly than he ever had before, was an imperfect place. But there were no other worlds to choose from. This was the only one.

He saw Ingrid pass by him in a taxi, oblivious to his presence, and was able to catch up with her before she entered the apartment block. The porter was hurrying out to assist her with an armful of designer-label carrier bags when he reached her. She was wearing white rather than her trademark black. Perhaps, he thought, white *was* her trademark in Buenos Aires. The excess of jewellery was the

327

same, though, and the gardenia perfume, of course. He would remember her by that if nothing else.

'Ingrid,' he said.

She turned, frowning in irritation, her eyes concealed behind dark glasses, her scarlet-lipped mouth compressed. Then she realized who he was. And her irritation changed, first to bafflement, then to anger. 'What are you doing here?' she snapped.

'I need to talk to you. About your father.'

'There's nothing you can say that I want to hear.'

Hammond nodded. 'You're right. You don't want to hear it. But I'm afraid you're going to have to.'

AUTHOR'S NOTE

I am very grateful to Professor Roger Williams for giving me many valuable insights into the career of a liver surgeon and for making our discussions on the subject so enjoyable.

I am also grateful to the authors of the following works, which helped me understand the nature and consequences of the Balkan conflicts of the 1990s: *They Would Never Hurt a Fly* by Slavenka Drakulić; *Madness Visible* by Janine di Giovanni; *With Their Backs to the World* by Åsne Seierstad; *Like Eating a Stone* by Wojciech Tochman; *The Ministry of Pain* by Dubravka Ugrešić.

Robert Goddard was born in Hampshire and read history at Cambridge. His first novel, *Past Caring*, was an instant bestseller. Since then his books have captivated readers worldwide with their edge-of-the-seat pace and their labyrinthine plotting. His first Harry Barnett novel, *Into the Blue*, was winner of the first WHSmith Thumping Good Read Award and was dramatized for TV, starring John Thaw.